NECROMANCER ABBEY

ADRIENNE BLAKE

NECROMANCER ABBEY
Souls and Shadows, Book 3

CITY OWL PRESS
www.cityowlpress.com

Cover Design by MiblArt. All stock photos licensed appropriately.

Edited by Tee Tate.

For information on subsidiary rights, please contact the publisher at info@cityowlpress.com.

Print Edition ISBN: 978-1-64898-109-8

Digital Edition ISBN: 978-1-64898-108-1

Printed in the United States of America

To James who quietly puts up with my crazy.

Chapter One

CATHERINE MORLAND

WHEN I WAS SEVEN YEARS OLD, I SWORE I SAW A SPECTER RISE FROM her grave. My childish heart was arrested as the woman in white ascended, untouched by the soil that once held her. Her pale, alabaster skin, though probably once beautiful, bore the lackluster pallor of death. She hovered above her resting place, her stockinged feet barely scraping the sod beneath while her burial shift fluttered gently with the night breeze.

Her haunting black gaze fixed on me. For a moment, the apparition paused, as if unsure of my purpose beside her grave. But then she smiled, and seeming to forget me, she floated on by, hell-bent on heading to who knows where and to what purpose. She was soon lost in the fog that shrouded us.

The sun returned. I began to breathe again and then fell into a dead faint. At least, that's how I remembered it.

"Are you daydreaming again about your imaginary ghost friend?" I opened my eyes. My older brother, Jimmy, stared down at me as I lay on the grass.

I pushed myself up onto my elbows, frowning. "It's not a daydream if it happened, twit."

"So you say."

I picked up my Kindle and forced myself up. It had been lovely lying on the grass soaking up the sun, and if Jimmy hadn't ruined the moment, I could have sunbathed for hours. I pushed past him and headed for my favorite tree. With his leg in a cast, there was no way he could bug me high in its limbs.

"No fair," he groaned as I hoisted myself up on the lower branch and began to climb. I had scaled this one so often as a child I could do it blindfolded now.

"Blah, blah, blah." My favorite spot in the tree branched out about ten feet above the ground. The branch was strong enough to support me, even now that I was twenty, and had a convenient cross branch I could rest my other leg on, making a sort of seat. I nestled into the trunk, planning to make an afternoon of it with my Kindle. I had a gothic novel to read, full of spirits, abbeys, boogeymen, and ghouls. My favorite.

"Don't fall asleep up there," Jimmy grumbled, wrinkling his nose in frustration. "You'll be sorry if you do. These cast things really hurt." He tapped on his own for good measure and then hobbled off.

Why was he making such a song and dance of it? After all, his cast was coming off today. Thank goodness for that. He'd done nothing but moan since he'd broken it playing ice hockey a few days ago. Dad, who was a skilled magical healer, had reset it with the *Os Emantur Ligna* incantation but insisted he wear the cast anyway to ensure the adhesion set. Jimmy looked none too impressed when the cast went on, but Dad's word was law, and he knew better than to meddle with it. So what if he missed a couple of games? Better that than break the damned thing again.

As Jimmy passed the stone wall by the graveyard, I spotted a Prius on the other side of it, circling round toward our drive. The car belonged to our neighbor, Matthew Allen. I heard he'd found himself a wife at last, and curious to get a look at her, I climbed back down out of the tree.

Jimmy waved at them. I suppose he was as curious as me because cast or no cast, he picked up his pace to greet them. They must have noticed, because the Prius slowed, and the driver window slid down.

"Still wearing that thing?"

Matthew Allen was a thin man, with forever dirty fingernails and an unkempt ginger beard that made me want to grab a pair of scissors. He was rumored to be worth a small fortune, though I never saw him spend a penny of it. He had a large property separated from ours by the graveyard.

Mom was thankful for that, because his own ran wild, and the weeds would have spilled into our garden were it not for the enchantments laid by the cleric that managed the cemetery. It wasn't that Matt didn't look after his place—no, he was what Mom called a tree hugger and lived off what he grew on the land. He said manicured lawns were pointless adornments. Personally, I thought they were pretty.

Jimmy glanced down at his cast and grinned. "Not for much longer. It's coming off later today after Dad gets home." He bent lower, trying to get a better look at the woman in the passenger seat. As he did so, I caught up and bowed my head to do the same.

"Hello," I said.

Seeing where our attention lay, Matt turned to acknowledge the woman by his side.

"Well now, I'd like you both to meet the woman who captured my heart. This is Sylvia, my new bride. Sylvia, this is Jimmy and Catherine Morland, two of our neighbors."

Sylvia leaned across her husband to get a better look at us outside his window. Unlike her husband, she had a ruddy complexion, and the seat belt strained to contain her. She was dressed from head to toe in black velvet and held her wand expectantly in her left hand.

"Hello," she said, sweetly enough, but then words failed her, and she waited for us to continue the conversation.

"Hi," I said. "Nice to meet you." I ran out of things to say myself.

"I was thinking about popping over in a bit," Matt said. "To introduce Sylvia to your mom and dad. Do you think they'd mind? I would like them to meet each other as soon as possible."

"Not at all." I forced a smile and kept my tone light. "I think they would love you to. Jimmy and I are just going in, so we can tell them you're coming if you like. What time were you thinking of?"

"About four? Before dinner?"

"Yeah, I'm sure it'll be all right. I'll ask them to call you if it's not."

"Perfect. See you then."

The Prius rolled off, the gravel drive making more noise than the car.

"That's not the kind of woman I imagined he'd marry," Jimmy remarked.

"Oh? Howzat?"

"I figured he'd bring home a beanpole tree hugger like himself. She looks as if she could snap him in two."

"Opposites attract, maybe," I suggested. "As long as she makes him happy."

A wicked grin creased the corners of my brother's mouth. "And maybe she has a handsome son who can carry you away. You're always complaining there are no decent wizards around here to whisk you off your feet."

"I do not!" I said, though I had to confess the thought had its charm. "Some of us have other things to think about besides the opposite sex. Anyway, you go and tell Mom they're coming over. I want to finish my book."

Jimmy nodded and limped back to the house.

I had been too young to remember Matt's first wife, who, according to Mom, had run off to explore her *spirituality*, whatever that was supposed to mean. Whatever his troubles, he had always been nice to us, sharing some of his produce and regularly preparing a basket of something delicious for us at Halloween.

Jimmy had just reached the bottom of the lane when a black Ford truck pulled up close to him. The driver wound down his window and beckoned my brother over. I could just about see the man's face. He was about our age, maybe a few years older than me, with brown hair. He looked all right. Not what I would call a looker but passable. I was too far away to hear what was said, but after leaning into the window, Jimmy straightened up and pointed toward the Allen house. The young man nodded, turned back into the road and drove off. I quickly forgot all about him.

The wall to the cemetery was low, and I had long legs, so I cleared it with ease. It was no coincidence I'd been dreaming about my first encounter with that ghost. She had made her appearance on my seventh birthday. After that initial meeting, whatever sensation had drawn me to that grave died, like it hadn't happened at all. For years after that, I'd felt nothing at all, and like Jimmy thought, I'd begun to convince myself it had been nothing more than a fanciful dream of my seven-year-old self.

Then, just before my fourteenth birthday, I'd felt a strange sensation in my tummy, like a knot, calling me back to the cemetery, and to that grave. When I'd told Mom about it, she'd freaked out and grounded me for a month. Mad, she'd been. Like I'd told her I'd planned to murder someone or something. I'd never seen her go so berserk.

"I'm not gonna have a daughter of mine..." Mom caught herself in time.

"What?"

"Nothing. Stay in your room."

It was the first time she'd ever locked me in anywhere. Perhaps I should have been scared, but I had been too focused on this strange new feeling inside me. It grew stronger by the minute, and although I was locked up, it was all I could do to stop myself from shimmying down the drainpipe outside my bedroom and answering the call. Mom would have skinned me alive if I'd tried it—so I fought the urge and stayed inside.

When she finally let me out, I wanted answers and stood in the doorway with my hands on my hips. "What's going on?"

Mom checked me over, hair, teeth, limbs, and arms, like I was a prize goat. "Nothing. Don't ask me about it again." I knew her well enough to know the subject was closed.

Now another seven years had passed, and here I was again. I was feeling that same drawing sensation in my gut. This time, I shared that I felt it with no one. Mom had been looking at me funny lately, almost like she was half expecting something, but I'd kept my mouth shut and pretended nothing was happening. I didn't want to be locked up again.

It wasn't a bad feeling, quite the reverse. It was hard to describe, something like a calling, a calling that filled my entire soul with raw energy, and I welcomed it and wanted to nurture it. Back then, Mom had made it sound like it was something bad, something to be ashamed of, but I knew she was wrong. To me, it felt like the most natural thing in the world, and I wanted to see what would happen if I gave in to it.

Jimmy went inside, and I headed straight for the one grave, hidden behind the abandoned church, lying beneath the shade of the drooping branches of an ancient Yew tree. This little stretch was on unconsecrated ground. The final resting place for the damned and undesirable.

No one could see me here. Between the church and the tree, I was hidden from sight. The feeling, whatever it was, had been quietly calling to me for days, but now that I was here, the pulsing quickened, and a strange pull around my navel radiated throughout my entire body, like a thousand tingles that intensified the closer I stepped to the grave. I knelt before the stone of my great-great-great-and-then-some-grandmother and namesake and read the marking for the thousandth time.

Here lies Catherine Morland,
Hanged 1693.
May God forgive her.

Above the text, the stonemason had carved a circle of butterflies, which Dad had explained represented eternal life and resurrection, and had been etched secretly a few years after her death. I remember Mom scowling at me when he'd told me all this, but her disapproval had only made me more curious, so I'd looked her up. Although we lived in Misty Cedars, Pennsylvania, she'd been put to death around the time of the infamous Salem witch trials.

I put my hand out to the weathered stone. It felt rough to touch. The energy was most intense here, but I wasn't afraid. If I had to choose one word to describe it, I'd have called it harmony. I closed my eyes to let the sensation run through me. Don't ask me how, but I knew I wasn't in danger. If anything, I felt more alive than ever.

Now wasn't the moment. I knew this instinctively. It was no coincidence the first time had happened on my birthday, I was sure of it, but if it felt this good now, how great would it be in two days when I turned twenty-one?

"What are you doing?"

At the sound of Jimmy's voice, I let go of the stone. I hadn't heard him approach, yet he was right behind me, at the footstone of the grave. I noticed the cast was off his leg. It was the first time I'd seen him smiling in days.

"You know you're not supposed to be here," Jimmy said.

"We're not kids anymore, Jimmy. They can't tell us what we can and can't do. Don't be such a jellyfish." I pushed myself up and brushed the sod off my jeans. "What do you want?"

"Nothing. I just wanted to show you my leg."

"How does it feel?"

"Good as new," Jimmy said, patting his thigh. "At least it does now that stupid cast is off."

I nodded. "Um, you won't tell them, I mean, where you found me?"

He chuckled but didn't answer. "Come on. The Allens will be over in a bit, but Mom wants to know all about her now. She asked me, but I don't know what to tell her, so she told me to come and get you."

I laughed. "Boys." I followed him back to the house.

Although we amused ourselves by talking silly nothings on the way, my focus remained at the grave and how those tingling sensations faded the farther I walked away from it. That had to mean something, right?

Chapter Two

WEDNESDAY'S CHILD

Given the right ingredients, Mom could conjure up the most amazing meals, and today was no exception. I imagined she'd been fussing over her stove ever since Jimmy had warned her that Matt and his new wife were coming to visit. Even before I walked through the door, my senses were attacked by the delicious aroma of butterscotch and spices. *Wow*! Mom was pulling out all the stops. She clearly wanted Sylvia Allen to like her.

I was not disappointed by the stack of goodies she'd conjured since hearing the news. Even now, she stood over a fresh batch of shortbread cookies. Her apron was covered in flour as she waved her hands in the air, weaving intricate patches of colored icing on the tops. Mom was an earth witch who prided herself on never using a wand and only exercising silent incantations. She had no desire to learn new magic or ley line magic and had a deep dislike of the unknown. She was fond of saying if she couldn't stick it in a pot and pop a label on it, she didn't want it in her house.

She looked up as I walked in. "Hello! Isn't it exciting? What's she like then? What did you think of her? Is she one of us?"

By that I knew she meant earth witch. I waited for Mom to catch a breath before answering. "She seemed nice enough, but I only saw her for a minute. She didn't say much, just hello, ya know?"

"What does she look like? Is she pretty?"

"Slow down!" I helped myself to a sugarcoated pecan puff. It imploded in my mouth the second I chomped on it. No one could make puffs like Mom. "She had a nice face. I'd say she was a little bit younger than you, maybe. I think you'll get along."

"But is she, you know, an earth witch?"

"How should I know? I only saw her for a second." Hmmm. She *had* been holding a wand, but I thought it prudent to skip mentioning this.

Mom opened her mouth to say something, but our attentions were both drawn to the stomping and squealing overhead. Not that I batted an eyelash. Being one of ten kids—six home-grown, four adopted—constant screaming and shouting was part of my normal day.

"I've banished them upstairs while I work on these cookies. Your dad is cleaning them up and keeping them quiet-ish."

Quiet-ish, in our house, meant under 7.5 on the Richter scale. Not that I was complaining. I was used to it.

Jimmy sauntered in from another room. He sat down at the table in front of the cookies but didn't take one. He stretched his leg and elevated it, testing it out. "Did your ghost friend turn up?"

I could have slapped him. Mom immediately stopped what she was doing and glared at me. "Please don't tell me we're back to that again? Cat!"

"Does it matter? I mean, I'm twenty-one. I don't see what the big deal is."

"*Nearly* twenty-one, Cat. You're not there yet. Well? Did you see something?"

I knew what Mom wanted me to say. That the old feelings had died inside me and she had nothing to worry about. Not that I thought that there ever had been anything to worry about. I figured Gaia wouldn't bless me with a gift I shouldn't possess, but clearly Mom thought otherwise. I shook my head. "No." When she wasn't looking, I shot Jimmy a foul look. He pretended not to notice. *Snitch.*

Mom narrowed her eyes, as if she didn't believe me. "I keep telling you all, nothing good comes from meddling with the dead. That's dark magic, that is, and we haven't had a dark witch in this family for generations. We don't need one now."

"I didn't meddle. I saw a ghost, *one* time, and that's all. I don't see why you're making such a big deal of it, really. It's not like I'm doing anything wrong."

Before Mom could answer, we all heard the gate slam outside. She whipped off her apron and hid it inside the pantry. The noise escalated upstairs, followed by what sounded like a herd of elephants on the stairs. Dad appeared first, then a swarm of younger siblings.

"These look good," Dad said. Like me, he selected a pecan puff and popped one in his mouth. As the others reached to do the same, Mom swatted away their hands.

"Wait. You can have some soon enough. Don't mess with my display."

With a swish of her hand and a silent incantation, all the flour was out of her hair and off her clothes, which twisted into a pretty updo. She wasn't bad looking for a witch of her age, which was good for me because I was told I looked just like her. Mom had black hair, now graying a little at the temples, hazel eyes with long lashes, and pretty lips that were forever smiling. She wore a long, blue bay dress she'd picked up at the beach and liked wearing around the house. Dad looked casual enough in jeans and a loose shirt. He was a handsome man, but the years had turned his hair completely white, and there were worry lines around the edges of his eyes. I sometimes wondered if the last kids we'd adopted were two kids too many for him. Still, he never complained, his philosophy being, *if it made my Jane happy...*

When the Allens knocked at the door, Mom dashed to answer it, and Dad sneaked in another puff behind her back. He saw me watching and winked at me. I grinned back.

"Well, hello and welcome." Mom stood back, holding the door wide enough for them to pass. She looked a little flustered, but I knew she was delighted to let the newlyweds come inside.

Matt ushered his bride before him. Now that Sylvia was out of the car, the marked differences between the couple were even more evident. Matt's gray, loose-fitting shirt did nothing to mask the painful thinness of his gangly arms, legs, and shoulders. For a rich warlock, he sure didn't look like he had much to live on. In contrast, Sylvia looked like she'd never missed a meal in her life, but she carried her extra pounds well, and though ruddy, she had a very pretty face with twinkling eyes that suggested much mischief. Her long black hair showed no signs of graying but was scooped up under a black beret. She wore a long black dress with dark-green collar, typical of the more traditional of our kind, and cuffs that swept down to the floor, covering her neatly polished, and surprisingly tiny, sandaled feet. Thankfully, there was no sign of her magic wand, which might have caused Mom to pop a vein. I wondered if Matt had warned her about that.

"Thank you." Matt stepped over the threshold and wiped his dusty Crocs on the mat. "Let me introduce you to my lovely new wife, Sylvia. Darling, this is Ricky and Jane Morland, Jimmy and Catherine you met earlier, and these are all their lovely children." He swept his arm around the room. My brothers and sisters were too excited to stand still, and introductions at this point would have been nigh impossible.

"I'm so happy to meet you. My, my, you have so many children." Rather than being overwhelmed, Sylvia looked delighted by their numbers, though more than once she had to dodge out the way of a wild young sibling of mine darting about her feet.

"We were blessed with ten." Dad covered his irony by scooping one of the ten up into his arms. He tossed him over his shoulder, and as soon as I realized he'd grabbed our youngest, Joe, my baby brother climbed down and ran off again and into another room.

"I'm afraid Gaia hasn't favored me with that blessing yet." There was no bitterness in her tone. *So much for introducing me to a potential boyfriend*, I thought. Sylvia's attention fixed on the cookie tower, and after a moment, she smiled up at Mom. "Did you conjure these yourself? They look delicious."

"I did, thank you for noticing."

Mom pulled out another chair for Matt, and he slid in beside his wife. "I was just going to put the kettle on to brew something nice. Would you like some? It's my own recipe, made with loose-leaf black tea, blended with sweet apples, cinnamon, and spices. I add a touch of vanilla for smoothness."

"That sounds amazing. I'd love some."

Mom puttered about by the sink, pouring cold water into her cast-iron kettle. She set it on the stove and lit the burner, and then began fussing about with her favorite pewter-colored mugs. She never used any kind of magic to make tea—never. She said it never tasted right, no matter how good the spell. Amy, my youngest sister, insisted on getting under her feet so Mom shooed her away from the stove and out of the kitchen. It was quieter now all my siblings had run off elsewhere to play.

"How long have you lived here?" Sylvia's gaze swept our rustic kitchen, adorned with garlands of dry flowers and herbs, and with shelves stacked with Mom's pots and pans and old cookbooks. Thick oak beams supported the ceiling, which over the years had been etched to show the names and dates of some of the people who lived here.

Dad scraped a chair across the floor and took a seat adjacent to them. "My family settled here back in the seventeenth century, and there's been a Morland in this house ever since."

"Indeed?" Sylvia looked impressed. While the kettle boiled, she helped herself to a plain butterscotch cookie. Her eyes rolled with delight. "Mmmm, Matt darling, you need to try one of these. They're simply divine."

Matt reached over and politely did as he was told. He nibbled the cookie carefully and nodded his approval. "You're a lucky man, Ricky."

Mom beamed. "What about you, Sylvia dear? Where are you from?"

Sylvia smiled, her hand hovering over the cookies as she debated what flavor to tackle next. "My people live in New York City now, although I'm proud to say I can trace my line back to Salem. We still have friends and family there."

"Do you go back there much?" Mom put a hot mug down in front of her, and Sylvia breathed in deeply.

"Smells divine. Not as often as I should."

"I imagine New York to be a very exciting place," I said, taking a seat at the table and helping myself to an iced sugar cookie. Mom glanced at me but didn't stop me. Sitting so close, I caught the distinct scent of pumpkin spice and vanilla.

Sylvia sipped her tea and turned to focus on me. "Have you never been? I'm surprised, seeing how you live so close."

"I've never been out of town. I'd like to one day. When I'm of age."

"How old are you?"

I didn't mind her asking. "Twenty-one. On Friday as a matter of fact."

Sylvia's gaze turned upward as she thought. "That means you were born on a Wednesday."

I nodded. "Yes, yes, I believe I was."

"Wednesday's child is full of woe." Sylvia said this more to herself than to me.

"I never did like that rhyme."

Sylvia's thoughts returned to earth. "Why's that?"

"Well, you know, I'd rather have the fair of face option."

"Well, you got that, didn't you? Anyway, I never take the woe thing literally. It just means you'll be challenged and will have difficulties to overcome. This isn't always a bad thing, Catherine. Challenges build character."

I liked that she knew my name already. And I liked her. Maybe it was because she'd seen something of the world, but I wanted to know more about her. I could have asked her lots of things on that first encounter, but I suspected Mom wouldn't have approved, so instead I helped myself to one more pecan puff and sipped a little of my tea.

"So how did you two both meet?" Mom asked, anxious to get into the conversation.

While the elders talked, my thoughts turned inward, and I tried to imagine a magical life in New York. I'd heard the pixies in Central Park were smarter than the ones here in Pennsylvania, and the gargoyles on the churches a lot more menacing than the sleeping ones here in our village church. I hoped one day I would get to see them. If Mom would ever let me leave this village.

When I came down from the clouds, Matt was asking Dad whether he had any ginseng he could spare, and Mom had got up to boil some more water for the tea. Sylvia, however, was staring at me. I didn't think she meant to be impolite—she just looked curious. Shy, I turned away, pretending to be interested in another cookie, although I'd really had enough.

"You can see them, can't you?" My hand froze in midair before it reached the cookie.

"Excuse me?"

Dad and Matt leered at me curiously, then shrugged and continued with their conversation.

"The ghosts. They rise for you, don't they?"

My mouth dropped open, because although I heard her, Sylvia's lips hadn't moved at all. Her eyes were twinkling as she stared at me over her cup. No one had heard her speak but me. Her voice was inside my head.

"I thought so." Sylvia put her cup down and ran her finger around the rim. "Don't be afraid, little one. We can talk later."

My mother returned to the table and poured fresh water into the pot. Sylvia smiled as if nothing had happened. She sat a little forward, delighted at the second offering, but I knew I couldn't sip another drop.

Nothing like that had ever happened to me before, and I was shocked at the ease with which she'd done it. I didn't know whether to feel delighted or afraid, but one thing was for sure—I was intrigued. I didn't leave the table for the remainder of their visit, but as much as I wanted her to, Sylvia didn't speak to me that way again. I was disappointed, but what could I do? It wasn't as if I could answer in kind.

At last, Matt stood up and stretched his thin arms.

"What, are you leaving already?" Mom couldn't have looked more disappointed.

"Yes, I think we should." Matt stood behind his wife to help with her chair. "It's been a long day for us both, and we could use an early night. I hope you don't mind. Ricky, why don't you pop over in the morning and I'll give you some of that ginseng you wanted?"

I tried not to smile and reveal my thoughts. They were newlyweds after all.

Sylvia turned to me. It was the first time she'd looked at me since doing *the thing*. "I'd love that, Jane. I'm new to the village. Perhaps you and Catherine could show me around?"

Mom sighed. "You know I would really like that, but I clean over at old Edith's in the morning. I help a few of our elderly neighbors a couple of times a week. It wouldn't be fair to cancel on such short notice, but maybe Catherine could come over. You have nothing going on, do you, Cat?"

I shook my head, delighted at the opportunity to visit Sylvia on my own. "No, not that I can think of. We should all be done with breakfast by then."

"Well, that's settled. Would nine o'clock be too early?"

"Not at all, I'll see you then."

Matt and Sylvia made ready to leave, but quick as a flash, Mom pulled a flat box out of a drawer, and with a wave of her hand, it twisted into an assembled box. She filled it full of cookies and handed them to Sylvia. "Please. Take these with you, with my compliments. It was lovely meeting you. We're so happy you've come to our little village."

"As am I." When no one was looking, Sylvia winked at me. "See you in the morning."

I nodded.

"Good-bye," Mom said.

"Bye." Dad closed the door behind them and went off in search of the kids, who were conspicuous by their silence.

I sat down, anxious to hear the inevitable after-visit autopsy. If that meant being buried under a swarm of cookie-eating monsters, then so be it.

While my parents swapped notes, and my brothers and sisters devoured the remains of the cookie tower, I pondered whether to tell Mom about what had just happened. Every lesson and fable grilled into us since childhood screamed to me that I should, and that this was exactly the sort of thing Mom would want to know. But another voice inside me told me I should keep my mouth shut about it.

What if Mom forbade me from going anywhere near Sylvia? If I told her she had microwaved her thoughts into my head, Mom would probably go mental. She would say this was dark magic, conjured by a dark witch. But if she stopped me, how would I ever learn how to do that myself? No, I couldn't and wouldn't miss this opportunity. So, while my parents went back and forth on the color of Sylvia's dress and how happy Matt was looking, I resolved not to breathe a word about any of it to either of them. Something strange and magical had just happened to me. Somehow Sylvia had known I could connect with the dead. I couldn't wait for tomorrow when I'd have Sylvia all to myself and could ask her all about it. There would be no sleep for me tonight, that was for sure. But I had something new to learn about myself, and that was a whole lot more important than an undisturbed forty winks. I could hardly wait to hear what Sylvia had to say.

Chapter Three

THE RED SQUIRREL

"I don't know where Mouse is, and what's more, I don't want to know." I covered my face with my hands and stifled a scream.

My kid brother Joe looked up at me with accusing eyes as if I'd hidden his frog someplace on purpose, just to spite him. Honestly, I would have sworn everyone was being especially obtuse this morning. It was like they knew I wanted to get away.

On the upside, Mom had got up super early, and if I had been behaving suspiciously at all, she'd been in too much of a hurry to notice. Dad, as always, got up at dawn and had long since gone to work.

He had tied a couple of ginseng roots together and had left them for me to find on the kitchen table. I shot an anxious glance at the clock. It was nearly nine. To my utter relief, I saw a quick jerk under a tea towel, and a moment later, Mouse hopped out from underneath it, and Joe scooped his pet frog into his pocket.

"Thank goodness for that," I said, pushing my annoying little brother toward the door. "Now scoot or you'll be late for class."

I grabbed the ginseng and closed the door right behind him. Unlike nonmagical school, class didn't start until nine thirty, but it was a fair hike across the village, and if Joe and the others didn't get a move on, they'd all be late. I could still see my brother Jimmy, right at the end of the lane, herding the others like sheep. He looked back and waved Joe on to hurry to catch up with them. I left him to it, my mind now on other matters entirely.

My path led me past the cemetery and beyond the notorious grave. The pulsing in me quickened the closer I got, and at one point became so strong, I almost forgot why I was going by it at all. The idea that I might soon learn what this all meant filled me with excitement, and it was that thought alone that urged me beyond the stone and over to Matt's house.

At one time, the Allen house had probably been the most prestigious in the village. The all-red stone exterior had corner gables and decorative cornices over the bay windows. There were signs of rot in some of the frames, and Virginia creeper covered most of the brickwork.

At the corner of the house, wood smoke oozed from the biggest chimney I had ever seen. The house itself was partly surrounded by a black iron gate, but the gate, like the house, had seen better days. Sections were hanging on their hinges, and some panels were entirely missing. Some would call the place derelict, but to my eyes, it was the most beautiful home I knew.

I passed Matt bent over an elevated plot of land, spade in hand, and from the sweat on him, I imagined he'd been at whatever he was doing for a while. The shovel handle looked almost as wide as he did. There was a muddy pile of freshly harvested potatoes by his side. All this could have been achieved by a simple magic spell, but as he was fond of saying, farming was his favorite exercise.

"Oh good, you remembered!" He pointed to the ginseng in my hand.

I held it aloft and shook it. Like I would forget! "Yup, where do you want it?"

"Sylvia's in the kitchen. Take it to her, would you?"

I nodded.

"Hey, take some of these potatoes to your mom before you go back. We have plenty."

"Sure, will do."

I dodged a couple of roaming hens and went in through the open oak door. The kitchen was in the back of the house, and I wandered into the familiar front room with its threadbare but cozy damask sofa, Indian rugs, and ornate, marble fireplace tall enough for me to stand in. There was a fire burning there now, and a cauldron filled with something green and intensely aromatic. I caught the whiff of mint, basil, and ginger, and wondered whether the brew was for eats or a spell.

"Come on in, Catherine. I'm in the kitchen."

As far as I could tell, I hadn't made a sound, but perhaps Sylvia had heard me talking to Matt in the garden. I'd have been surprised since the kitchen was all the way in the back.

"There you are!" Today, Sylvia wore a deep-purple dress with black lace at the cuffs that draped Tudor-style down to the hem. Her wavy hair was loose today and tumbled down her back and over her shoulders. Flecks of white peppered the tips, and with her hair down, she appeared much younger than she had yesterday. "I'm so glad you could come, little one. I'm sure there is much you would like to ask me. But first, some tea. Do you like mint? It's my favorite."

"Sure, yes, please," I said. I noticed Mom's cookie box on her kitchen counter. It was sitting beside a row of small black pots, none of which were labeled. I suspected they were herbs and wondered how she knew one from another, since they were all identical. I had never seen them here before, so I guessed they were Sylvia's.

There was a large stone pestle by the sink, like Mom's, and more dusty tomes along the shelves than anyone could read in a lifetime.

Sylvia smiled as I perused them. "They're mostly ley line texts. Of course, I practice earth magic—what good witch doesn't—but my passion has always been the higher arts."

"My mother doesn't approve of ley line magic."

"That's not unusual." Sylvia picked up a volume at random, wet her finger, and opened the book. The leaves were loose and the binding a little delicate. It had clearly seen a lot of use. "This is my personal favorite. I've had it since I was your age. You can have a look if you like."

What I really wanted was to ask her about last night, and how she'd zapped her thoughts into my head, and what my strange impulses meant, but I didn't want to appear rude. I took the tome carefully and opened it. The pages opened naturally to an inked drawing of an ancient dwelling with an old man crouched low, his right palm touching a small cluster of stones close to the earth. There were unfamiliar runes under the picture and some text in a very old language I struggled to make out.

. . .

Cîgendlic âlecgan dôð belîðan

I guessed from the images it had something to do with the dead, but beyond that, its meaning escaped me. Below the heading were more words written in the same obsolete language, but I had no clue what they meant.

"Beautiful, isn't it?" Sylvia looked over my shoulder and smiled at me as I glanced up at her. "It's Pagan—very old English. It says *Calling to the Dead.*" Her eyes misted over with delight. "I believe this goes back to the beginning of the beginning of all things magical. It's the first book I ever owned on magic, and it's how I fell in love with the art. Let me show you something."

Sylvia rose and opened the box of Mom's cookies sitting on the counter. She offered me one.

Confused, I reached in and took a piece of shortbread. "Err, thanks." I was about to nibble at it when she shook her head.

"No, wait. Just hold it for now."

She turned back to the shelves, her fingers wavering before her as she perused the volumes. This time she selected a smaller book, and after flicking through the pages, she put it down in front of me at an open page. Looking down, I saw that this was also written in a language I didn't understand.

"Don't worry. This volume has slightly less advanced magic, and anyone can use it. Put your palm on the page."

Excited to see what Sylvia had in mind, I did as I was told. I sensed nothing at first, and then I felt a slight tickle, nothing as intense as what I'd felt at the grave of my ancestor, but it was like a faint echo if it. "Should I close my eyes?"

"No need. Now, think of a squirrel. There are plenty in the garden outside."

"A squirrel?"

"Yes. Concentrate hard. And keep your hand flat on the page. You don't need to breathe a word."

I felt a little daft, sitting in Matt's kitchen, imagining a random squirrel. I probably didn't need to, but I held my breath. I was about to exhale when I heard a scuffle, and a moment later, a red squirrel appeared at the open window, hopping about from foot to foot, as if unsure why it was there.

"Offer her the cookie." Once again, Sylvia's voice was inside my head, just as it'd been last night. "There's no need to speak. Talk to her like I'm talking to you."

Excited, I offered the squirrel the cookie in the palm of my hand. *Come on, sweetie. I promise I won't hurt you.*

Glancing up, I saw Sylvia smiling, as if she could hear my thoughts. The squirrel hopped down onto the counter, wavered for a while, and leapt across to the kitchen table. It darted cautiously from left to right, and then it must have sensed it was safe because it stepped up to my hand and climbed onto my fingers. I watched in awe as the squirrel nibbled at the end of the cookie, paused, and settled in, sitting down in the crook of my hand. It chewed for a moment or two, and when the cookie was small enough, it vaulted back onto the table, carrying the shortbread with her.

My heart danced as I felt the squirrel's gratitude, and I almost cried before it bounced away again, taking her prize with her.

"That was amazing!" I sat straighter in my seat and stared at the books in awe. "Do you have any more like these? Maybe one I can understand and borrow? Like this one?"

Sylvia shook her head sadly. "As much as I disagree with your mother's opinion, I must respect her wishes. We both know she wouldn't want you to keep such books in your house."

I slumped in my seat. She was right of course. Mom would never approve, but I so wanted to learn it all. Sylvia had handed me something precious, and now that I'd had a taste of it, I yearned for more. But what could I do? As she said, Mom wouldn't stand for it.

"But I want to learn." I blushed at the whine in my voice. "I have all these feelings inside me, and all I want to do is understand them. I can't help it if Mom doesn't get it, but whatever it is, I don't think it's as bad as she makes it out to be. The small squirrel didn't seem to think so."

"You are right." Sylvia twirled her wrist, and two fresh mugs of peppermint tea appeared before us.

With a little reluctance, I politely closed the smaller book and took a sip of the tea, which was just at the right temperature. My head seemed to clear, and my emotions calmed a bit.

"You will soon be of age and when you are, you would be perfectly entitled to find out more of who you are and what your powers are."

I nodded. She was quite right. At twenty-one, I would be considered mature and free to make all my own choices.

"But you are also wrong," she continued.

"What about?"

"Your mother. She understands better than you think."

I very much doubted that but didn't want to sound too childish about it. More than anything I wanted Sylvia to like me, and adults didn't pout and throw hissy fits. "Maybe. So what can I do?"

Sylvia smiled and took a long draft of her own tea. "Your dad is a doctor, I understand?"

"Yes."

"He has the same aversion to ley line magic as your mother?"

"Maybe not as much, but he knows how she feels about it. It's a shame, really. Ley line doctors make a ton of money. All Dad can do with earth magic is set a few bones and apply a few herbal remedies. He works all the hours under the sun, and I feel sorry for him sometimes."

"And you. Any desire to follow in your father's footsteps?"

I laughed. "Me, do medicine? No, not really. Jimmy plans to, but it's never really appealed to me."

"So, what do you plan to do with your life?"

"To be honest, I have no idea. I hear the grass looks a lot greener on the other side of the fence, but since I never get to look over the fence, I have no idea what that means. I would like to be a good witch. Well, the best witch I could possibly be. I don't think I'll ever learn what that is sitting here, doing the same thing, day in and day out."

"I agree. What you need is the chance to broaden your horizons."

"And how do you propose I do that?" I asked.

"You should spend more time with people like yourself."

"People who can get inside my head like you did?"

Sylvia chuckled and cupped her mug in her hands. "Just so." The smile left her face, and her gaze turned serious. "There is a power in you. I felt it the moment we met. I know what you're feeling. I, too, experienced something similar when I was your age. You just need to learn how to channel it."

I opened my mouth to interrupt her, but she raised her hand to stop me. "So many questions. It's understandable, I know, but not everything can be answered at once. Do you trust me?"

I nodded. Sylvia was little more than a stranger, but for some reason, I did.

"Good. How would you like to come work for me? I have a small agency in New York, kind of a magical boutique, but it's more than just a store. More of a place for our kind to network, like a sort of chamber of commerce. I take paid interns from time to time and have a lovely apartment overlooking Greenwich Village. We could spend the summer there, if you like, and you will get a chance to meet people like you, who will help you understand your potential. What do you think?"

The excitement grew in me with every word. Me, go to New York City? Was she crazy? Of course, I would love that! The word yes sprang to my lips even before she finished. I was sure Mom wouldn't mind. After all, she might not know Sylvia too well, but Matt was a dear old friend who would never put me in harm's way.

"Are you serious? Can we go tomorrow? What does an intern do? Would you really let me live with you?"

Sylvia laughed at my volley of questions. "First things first. You might be of age, but you should still ask your parents' permission, or at least for their input. I plan on living here for a long time, and the last thing I want is to alienate my new friends on my first day. A little diplomacy might go a long way."

"I'm sure they'll say yes! I mean—I wouldn't say too much about the ley line thing, some extra money would be a good thing, and hey, I have to get a job sometime, don't I? When can I tell them? Can I tell them straightaway? When would we go? I'd go tomorrow if I could!"

"Tomorrow might be a bit soon for my poor husband. After all, he just got me here."

I slumped in my seat. Now that the seed was sown, I wanted to go. "When then?"

"My business pretty much runs itself these days, and I can do most of my work from this kitchen if I have to. But there is a social meeting I must attend in a couple of weeks. That would give you time to prepare and would give your parents a chance to get used to the idea. I suggest you talk to them tonight—calmly—and if everyone is agreeable, we can all meet for dinner to discuss the particulars. But Catherine..."

"Call me Cat, please."

"Cat—if they're dead set against the idea, I won't be able to take you. As I said, I'm new here, and I don't want to upset my neighbors. You understand, I hope?"

I nodded, albeit reluctantly. I knew Dad would be all for it, but I had a sneaking suspicion Mom wouldn't be so easy to persuade. She knew me all too well. I would have to introduce the topic very carefully, concealing my excitement, or she'd be on me like a flock of hungry crows.

Sylvia rose from the table, picked up the big book and the little book, and took her mug to the sink. I wanted to read more, but she was right. Mom would have a fit if I brought either of them into the house. But even worse, she'd be disappointed in me, and that was the last thing I wanted.

"Will you be taking that little book to New York with you?"

Sylvia shook her head. "I don't think so."

I frowned.

"I have a much better idea." She slid the tomes back into their places on the shelf. "When we get to New York, we'll find you one of your own. One that speaks to you, as my books whisper to me."

My frown disappeared. "They whisper to you?" My tone was almost reverent.

"Of course. The language of magic is unimportant. True magic has its own language, and it's not English, or Dutch, or German, or Latin. You will learn this soon enough, along with many other wonderful things."

I nodded and stared at her bookshelf, unable to even conceive how fantastic such a thing could be. I took a sip of my tea, and ignoring Mom's probable objections for the moment, I began to dream of a life in New York.

Chapter Four

THE STRANGER

Mom thrust another lunch box into a backpack, her jaw set hard as she fought against the words I suspected were in her heart. I'd told her about Sylvia's proposal for New York. Anyone would think I'd slapped her in the face then, and her mood didn't seem much improved now, even though today was my birthday. She zipped up the bag, and with an annoyed flick of her wrist, the bag drifted out of the kitchen and into the hall, landing on its proper hook, next to all the other stuffed bags.

In contrast, as I'd half suspected he would, Dad had been delighted. As Mom shooed the last of the kids out of the kitchen screaming "Happy birthday, Cat!" as they had been doing all morning, Dad bounced in and kissed me on the top of my head.

"How's my birthday girl then?" He wrapped his arms around me and slipped a package covered in pink tissue paper with a silver bow into my hands.

"Thanks, Dad." I grinned and began unraveling it. I knew he wasn't going into work today. He'd never missed any of our birthdays and had promised to take me out to lunch. Which meant him, Mom, all the kids, half my friends from the village, and anyone else he could rope into a surprise party would be showing up. Not that I was complaining. The only difficulty was pretending to be surprised when everyone turned up at The Goblin King Diner, our favorite local restaurant.

Inside the paper was a small, oblong box. I opened it, and to my delight I withdrew a silver necklace with a half-moon pendant. A small arrow hung from the top of the moon and swiveled freely.

"It's a compass," Dad said. "So, you'll always be able to find your way home."

My cheeks burned with pleasure, and I kissed him. "Is it magic?"

Dad shook his head. "Nope. Just a little something pretty."

"Thank you so much. I love it! Will you help me put it on?" I opened the clasp and offered it to him, thankful as much for the chance to dodge Mom's gaze. Dad took it gladly and expertly secured it to my neck.

Mom's scowl faltered for a moment, and a faint smile tweaked the corners of her lips. "I'm glad you like it. How are you feeling today?"

I didn't need an interpreter to tell me what she referred to. The feelings inside me had been growing stronger every day. I hadn't breathed a word about it to anyone, yet somehow Mom knew. I guessed she didn't need any special kind of magic to get inside my head. I didn't want to lie to her, but I knew the truth would hurt her too. I chose avoidance and misdirection.

"Pretty excited. I've always wanted to go to New York, and I'm counting the days." I left the kitchen in search of a mirror to inspect my new treasure. It was enchanting, and I held the pendant aloft, watching the arrow settle on north.

Yet it wasn't the north that tugged at my heartstrings. From the window by the mirror, I could see the church, and though the calling was always weakest in the morning, I felt an odd desire to go out now. Yet something was different this morning. I couldn't exactly put my finger on what it was, but I wanted to be outside.

I knew Mom was watching me, so I pretended to be fascinated by my necklace.

"I think I might go for a walk," I said. "Get a bit of air."

"Put on a coat. It's a little chilly out there this morning." Mom picked the necklace package up from the table and tossed the wrapping in the trash. She stuffed the velvet-covered black box in a drawer.

"What time's lunch?"

Dad was pouring himself some coffee, and he slid into a chair at the kitchen table before answering. "Be back by noon."

"Okay." I nodded and grabbed my black poncho from a hanger by the front door. "I won't be long." I pulled the poncho over my head. It almost completely covered my light-gray sweater and nestled just below the waist of my jeans. I slipped my buds from my pockets and popped them in each ear.

I didn't have to look back to know Mom was watching me. At twenty-one, I was too old to lock in my room, but I knew she'd put me there if she could. I closed the door softly behind me and braced against the exceptionally cool morning. When I turned around, I found myself staring at clusters of balloons and ribbons and HAPPY 21ST BIRTHDAY banners, which surrounded the house and could be seen for miles around. I chuckled and, looking back, saw Mom and Dad waving from the front window. I shook my head, pretending to be exasperated, but really, I was secretly pleased.

For a little while, I entertained myself with crunching the fallen maple leaves under my feet. I had several friends in the village I could call on, but I was pretty sure I'd be seeing them later. Right now, I wanted to be alone with my thoughts while the Spell Sisters crooned in my ears.

I might have meandered a little, but what the hey, I knew where I was headed. How could I not? It was like my twenty-one years on this earth all led to this day. But what was I going to do tonight? Wander out on my own and dance around an unconsecrated grave? Dance naked in the moonlight and call on the spirits of the undead to rise again? Yeah, right, Mom was definitely going to let that happen. I'd been wondering what I was going to do when the time came for days. And now here I was, and I still had no clue.

The thought occurred to me that Sylvia might be able to help. I had a feeling she'd be home—the word was she liked to work first thing, but I was sure she wouldn't mind in the circumstances. This was a unique occasion, and it wasn't as if there was anyone else I could turn to for help. On the other hand, I owed her a lot already. I didn't want her to think of me as a nuisance.

I'd just picked up the pace to head that way when something caught my attention in the graveyard. Curious, I removed my earbuds and popped them in my pocket.

Having lived in this village my entire life, I knew all the names on the headstones by heart. On the far side of the church, just after old Mrs. Truckett's stone, was a blackberry bush. I often relieved it of its fruit this time of year, but it looked like for once, someone was there ahead of me.

A young man, maybe six feet tall, or perhaps a little taller, was harvesting berries into a half-full, oversize ceramic colander. He wore a brown tweed jacket, jeans, and I noticed a pentacle tattooed on the backs of each wrist. A hawthorn wand was casually sticking out of his back pocket. He didn't appear to notice me at all.

"Ahem."

He looked round at the sound of my cough.

"Oh, hello." He smiled and turned back to the bush to continue picking berries. He had a nice, if unremarkable face, and I had this strange feeling I'd seen him before, though right now I couldn't place him. "I'm guessing you're Catherine. Sylvia said you'd be popping by. Be a sweetheart and help me pick these berries."

"Excuse me?"

"I've eaten most of what I've picked, and she really wants to bake a pie."

Growing on church property, this bush belonged to the church, so he was technically stealing. Not that that had stopped my family picking berries here for years. It irritated me somewhat that he should be brazenly stealing the berries that I usually stole each season.

I felt a little stupid, just standing there, so I did as he suggested and started to help him pick. Not that that made me feel any better.

"You know my name, but who are you?"

"Oh." The young man shoved the colander under one arm and offered me his right hand. "Henry. Henry Tilney. Nice to meet you."

His hand was stained purple with berry juice, but I shook it anyway.

So, there I was, picking berries in a graveyard with a complete stranger who knew my name. I wondered if the day could get any weirder.

"Do I know you?" I dumped a handful of berries into his colander.

"No, we haven't met exactly, but I saw you when I asked your brother for directions the other day."

The penny dropped. He was the driver of the black Ford truck I'd seen. "How did you know Jimmy was my brother?"

"Sylvia's orbuculum. I was helping her unpack it when I saw a vision of you and your brother in it. I asked her who it was, since I'd just run into him, and she told me who you were and that I might as well get to know you since we'd be spending a lot of time together soon enough."

I stopped picking berries. This guy *really* liked to talk. I wondered if he always talked too fast and too quickly when he was nervous. I knew I sometimes did. And what was with the orbuculum? "You were spying on me in her crystal ball?"

"No, of course not. Your image popped up when I handled it. It wasn't like I'd asked it to."

"Really?"

"Sure. You're going to New York, aren't you? It probably made the connection."

Yes, but what had that to do with him? "She only just invited me."

"Well then." Henry carried on picking berries as if this were all perfectly natural. Yet I couldn't have been more confused.

"When did you say you saw us?"

"The day she arrived."

"But she didn't invite me to New York until after that. It just sort of came to her—it wasn't planned."

Henry shrugged. "Divination is a wonderful gift. I wish I had it. Not many do." He looked inside the colander and gave it a little shake. "Well, I think that's enough, don't you?"

"Sure, if you want to make ten pies."

He chuckled. "If you say so. I've never baked a pie in my life. I guess we should get going then. You *were* heading over to the house, right?"

Confused, I nodded. I wasn't sure I liked this divination thing. It put me at a clear disadvantage. "Yes, yes, I was."

He grinned, popped a berry into his mouth for good measure and began walking around the church. I fell into step beside him.

"What else do you know about me?" I asked.

"Not a lot. That's pretty much it, really. I suspect I'll soon know a lot more, seeing as I'm going to be your mentor."

"My what?"

"Your mentor. I think that's why she sent me out here to run into you. So we could get to know each other, informally like. It's going to be my job to show you the ropes in New York, as much as I can. At least when she's back here. Plus, we'll be taking care of her shop."

My head was popping with a flurry of emotions, but like a kid on her first day of school, I couldn't think of a single thing to say.

"This is all assuming we get along, of course," he added. "If you don't like me, I'm sure she'll find you someone else."

I didn't answer him. We'd just scaled the cemetery wall and were passing my ancestor's grave. I felt the familiar tug in my belly button and paused.

Henry was a few steps ahead before he turned to see what I was about. "Is that the grave?"

I nodded. "You sure know a hell of a lot about me."

"You'll be fine as long as you don't touch the headstone."

My attention went to the somewhat innocuous-looking stone with its simple inscription. I closed my eyes, and my mind went back fourteen years, to my seventh birthday. For the first time in forever, I remembered kneeling before the stone and running my fingers across the chiseled words. A moment later, the ground pulsed beneath me, and afraid, I stumbled back a few feet, wondering what on earth I had done. I watched in bewildered awe as the apparition rose from the ground. I remembered not being afraid—just spellbound. I'd forgotten about touching the stone that day.

"Really, is that all?"

"Sure. You're the boss of the dead after all, not the other way around."

"I don't understand," I said.

Henry tilted his head to one side as he studied me. "Hasn't anybody told you?"

"Told me what?"

A grin teased the corners of his mouth. "Why, that you're a necromancer of course."

If I'd been holding those berries, I'd have dropped them everywhere.

Chapter Five

THE CRYSTALS

"A NECROMANCER?" DUMB SURPRISE MUST HAVE REGISTERED ON MY FACE.

"You know what a necromancer is, don't you?"

"Well, no, I mean, yes, of course I've heard of them. I just don't know what they do."

Henry turned back toward the house, and eager to learn more, I fell into step beside him. "Are you pulling my leg? You're a witch. You were born into a magical family. How do you not know any of this stuff?"

When he put it that way, I did feel a bit stupid. What would he think of us if I told him about Mom's fear of higher magic? I didn't want to chance it, so I kept silent.

As usual, we found Matt working in the yard. He nodded when he saw us approach and didn't appear the least surprised to see us together. He jerked his head toward the house. "She's in the kitchen."

We found her sitting at the kitchen table with an assortment of crystals lying about before her. A pot of apples popped and bubbled on the stove, filling the room with the most delicious scent. Behind Sylvia on the counter, two sheets of pastry were aligning themselves inside a pie dish. After the edges self-crimped, they floated through the air and glided into the heated range. The oven door closed quietly on them both.

When Sylvia saw us, she grinned. "Ah, my valiant soldiers have returned from the brambles, bearing the fruit of the fairies. Pop the colander in the sink for a quick wash while the pie crusts prebake, would you?"

Henry did as instructed, and Sylvia pointed to a seat across from her, motioning for me to join her. "Would your mom appreciate some of those, do you think?"

"Maybe. We've collected quite a few already. Mom and I use them to make syrups and healing teas for Dad's practice." I didn't mention that she usually kept a bowl in the living room as the berries were said to attract wealth and affluence. Not that we ever saw any of that.

"Well, maybe she would appreciate a pie. I will give her one when they're done."

"Thank you." It wouldn't last a day—the kids were big fans of pies.

Henry joined us at the table.

"Now look at these." Sylvia opened her hands to draw my attention to the crystals on the table in front of her. "What do you think?"

I closed my eyes and focused on the crystals. As an earth witch, they all called to me on different levels, but I sensed nothing but harmony and good sensations. "You have a very nice collection."

"I would like you to select one of them. Whichever calls to you the most."

I opened my eyes in surprise and caught Henry studying me with some curiosity. I wondered if he was looking at me with more than just professional interest. His attention turned to the stones when he saw me watching him.

Sylvia was smiling. "Well, it is your birthday after all. Go on. Pick one."

"Are you serious?"

"Of course. Go ahead. Choose one."

I looked at the crystals. They were all so lovely. The range of colors was staggering, from soft grays, reds, aquas, and blacks. Some were shiny and smooth, others rough and porous. Initially my eye fell on a shiny black crystal. It was perfectly oval, and far prettier than any of the others. I reached to examine it, but before I touched it, I felt a strange burning in the palm of my hand, and I hesitated. I pulled back and looked at some of the others.

This time a second stone called to me. It was a rough, blue stone of many shades, and when I focused on it, I experienced a sense of inner peace and tranquility. It wasn't half as pretty as the first one, yet somehow, I knew that was the one for me. I picked the small stone up and turned it over in my hand. "This is azurite, I believe."

Sylvia nodded. She took it from me. "Are you sure this is the crystal you want?" She picked up the black one I'd considered first and held it in her other hand, offering them both to me at the same time. "Your first choice is the prettier, I think. This is obsidian. It's very powerful."

I examined it again. The crystal certainly was lovely, but I'd never experienced that burning sensation before, and I didn't like it. The way Sylvia was looking at me made me wonder if she guessed as much. My mind was made up. "I think I like the blue one more."

Sylvia smiled. "As you wish." She returned the obsidian stone to its place on the table and closed her fingers around the azurite. She closed her eyes, and though she said nothing, her lips moved silently.

I felt concern and glanced at Henry, who smiled reassuringly, as if this were a perfectly normal thing. It wasn't like I hadn't seen crystal magic performed before, but I hated not knowing what it all meant.

Sylvia opened her eyes and her fingers, and staring down, I saw she had set the crystal in a small silver ring, which she offered to me.

"Are you sure?" I hesitated to take it. Set like this, I sensed its value and wondered if it was right to accept it at all. "I can't imagine what something like this must be worth. I can't possibly accept it."

"It isn't a question of whether you can accept the ring. It's whether the ring will accept you. Anyway, now it's true value can only be revealed to you, and no one else." Gently, Sylvia took my left hand and placed the ring on my middle finger. I was not surprised when it fit perfectly. Once again, a sense of inner peace overwhelmed me. "There. Very pretty." Sylvia smiled, admiring her work.

"Thank you." A question had been eating at me since the moment I'd got here, and I thought now might be as good a time as any to ask. I wasn't quite sure how to phrase it, so I just blurted it out. "Henry seems to think I'm a necromancer. Is he right? And if he is, what exactly does that mean?"

I thought she might laugh at me, since I sounded ignorant even to my own ears. But instead of laughing as I thought she might, Sylvia pondered for a moment and then tried to explain it to me.

"Quite simply, necromancers are able to communicate with the dead.

Once you have full command of your powers, you can summon them at will."

My cheeks burned, not with embarrassment, but with mounting dread. This didn't sound like a good thing to me. "Why would anyone want to do that? The dead are at peace. Why would anyone want to disturb them?"

"There are as many answers to that as there are questions in the universe. What you must understand is that necromancy is a rare and uncommon gift, not a curse. It opens the door to a wealth of knowledge unknown to most of the living. Because of that, many of our kind fear it, but it's not the gift itself that's evil, but the necromancer's use of it. Remember that, Catherine, in the challenges to come."

I didn't like the sound of *challenges.* "What if I don't want to be one? Can I choose to ignore it?"

The familiar smile left Sylvia's lips. "All gifts, left untouched, shrivel and die inside their owner. They're a part of who you are. It's never wise to deny them. When they die, a small part of you will die with them."

I didn't like the sound of that, either.

Sylvia's kindly smile returned. "Don't worry about it for now. It's a lot to take in, I know, but in the coming weeks, you will learn more about yourself than you ever thought possible. Believe me, it's not all bad! Henry will be there to support you, as will I, don't forget that. But today is not the day to worry about it. It's your birthday! You have come of age, have you not? We should be celebrating that now, and nothing else."

Henry had been studying me all this time. He looked relieved, now that Sylvia had explained things to me, and his expression was friendly enough. I was a little sorry I'd been annoyed with him earlier. He was here to help me after all. His gaze wandered to my throat. "That's a pretty necklace."

My reached up to touch it. "Yes. My parents gave it to me this morning."

"It's very unusual," Henry said. "Is it magical?"

"They didn't say."

Sylvia began putting the unwanted crystals away into a small wooden box, and as she did so, the range door opened, and two perfectly cooked pie shells floated up to the counter to cool down. The last stone she put away was the obsidian. Part of me wondered what would have happened if I'd chosen that one. It appeared I was not to find out.

Sylvia took the box to the sink and placed it on the sill before washing her hands. "Catherine's parents are strict earth witches. They're not likely to offer her anything to encourage this side of her, now, are they?"

Henry's brow furrowed. "Is that so? It seems a waste of talent to me."

"Does it?" I almost snapped at him. My annoyance with Henry returned, and for some reason, I wanted to defend my parents. "They're entitled to what they believe, the same as the next person, don't you think? Earth magic is a gentle art, and the price of magic no more than a few herbs and flowers. Higher magic demands a much higher price. Mom has always made it clear she doesn't want us dabbling in things we don't understand, in case what we have to pay is more than we can afford. Is there anything wrong with that? I'm sure all she wants to do is protect us. Well, me."

Henry shook his head. "I suppose not. But that's not what *you* think, is it? Otherwise, why would you want to go to New York? If you believe what your mom believes, then you'd be better off staying here, wouldn't you?"

Since I'd never been to New York, I really had no idea how to answer him. One thing was for certain. I really did want to go. "I guess there's only one way to find out, isn't there?"

Sylvia ran the tap over the blackberries and pulled any stems left on them. Once they were cleaned, she added the berries to the cooked apples and blended the two fruits together. She then filled the cooked pie cases with the filling. Once done, strips of pastry rose in the air and intertwined to form a lattice pattern over the top of both pies. Sylvia removed an egg wash from the fridge, coating both finished pies before putting them back in the oven for their final bake.

"There. All done." She rinsed her hands in the sink and dried them on a tea towel. When she sat down with us again, her attention returned to the ring. "In time, the azurite stone will help you channel your power over the spirit world. It's not especially powerful, but it will enhance your connection with the dead and will help you comprehend the needs of the unliving mind. In time, you will understand it better, but for now, you know all you need to today."

I ran my fingers over the ring, which still felt unfamiliar on my skin. I hoped I hadn't said anything to offend her and make her change her mind about New York. Before I could ask, we heard a door open somewhere in the house, and then Matt walked into the kitchen.

"So how's the birthday girl? Did Sylvia give you your present?"

I grinned and held my hand aloft so Matt could examine the ring. He took my fingers in his own. "Very nice." The newlyweds exchanged a meaningful look, which I pretended not to notice.

When he let go, I pushed my chair away from the table and stood up. "Anyway, I guess I'd best be off. I promised Dad I'd be back by noon. He's taking me out for a surprise birthday party." I rolled my eyes, hoping to come off as a sophisticated adult, yet I'd never sounded so childish.

Henry also stood up. "Would you like me to walk you home?"

I laughed and glanced over my shoulder as if the house were there, right behind me. "It's okay. I think I can manage it. I have a compass."

Henry lowered his head, and I wondered if I'd said the wrong thing. But then I noticed his shoulders were shaking a little. Was he laughing at me, or did I amuse him? It was hard to say.

Sylvia came up from the table and gave me a warm hug. "It was lovely seeing you. Tell your mom I'll bring over a pie later, will you? And we can fix a date for your internship after your party. I'm sure now we have your parents' consent you'll be eager to set a date."

I smiled at Sylvia, then Matt, and nodded. "Yes. Yes, I am. And thank you for the ring. Both of you." I held out my hand to Henry. "It was nice meeting you, Henry. I hope we'll see each other again very soon." He accepted mine and shook it heartily.

"I don't doubt it. Happy birthday, Catherine." His final expression was more amusement than offense. I supposed that was something. I didn't want to start my relationship with my mentor on the wrong foot. It also occurred to me that I liked how he said my name. In fact, there was a lot I liked about him. But right now, I was feeling a different kind of pull on me. It was my birthday after all, and I needed to get home. It seemed the compass at my neck was working perfectly fine after all.

I waved good-bye to my new friends, turned, and headed back to our little cottage. My mind raced with thoughts of rings, necklaces, and necromancy, but for now, I had to put all these things aside. Now was the time for birthday cake, banners, and balloons. It wasn't going to be easy, that much I knew.

It had turned colder outside. I hunched my neck into my shoulders, and pulling my poncho close, I lowered my head and headed home. As I passed old Catherine's grave, I felt the familiar calling. This time, however, I understood what it meant and felt good knowing that nothing would ever happen unless I wanted it to, which right now, I did not. I gave the spot little more than a sideways glance and hastened my steps to get to my party.

Chapter Six

THE VOICES

I WASN'T QUITE SURE HOW MOM WOULD REACT IF SHE SAW THE RING, especially since we hadn't known Sylvia for very long, and though crystal rings were perfectly normal for earth witches to wear, I didn't want her making a fuss. The last thing I wanted on my birthday was an atmosphere, so I slipped it off my finger before I got home and hid it in my pocket. I told myself it wasn't lying exactly, but that didn't stop me from feeling a little guilty. It seemed the older I got, the more I had to hide from her. I wondered if it would always be like that from now on.

It was so quiet, the balloons and banners were all I could hear, flapping in the wind. I knew they were all inside—Mom, Dad, the whole tribe, crouching low and pretending to have forgotten all about me. They did this every year, and I wasn't so old yet that it didn't give me pleasure. Playing my part, I let the smile slip from my face as I opened the front door. All was silent.

"Hello, is anyone home?" I heard a faint giggle followed by a *shush!* though I pretended not to hear it.

I wandered into the kitchen. That was empty too, so I opened the fridge door and helped myself to a seltzer. As I pulled the ring tab, I heard another chuckle but pretended not to hear that either and made for the living room. I knew they'd be in there. After all, it was the only room with objects for them to hide behind since they wouldn't use concealment charms—that required ley line knowledge. I knew they were all crouched behind the sofa.

"Ah well, I guess everyone forgot about my birthday." I put my soda down on the coffee table and was about to flop into the chair when everyone started shouting at once.

"Surprise!"

"Happy birthday!"

"Ha-ha, fooled you."

"Neener, neener, neener!"

Instead of sitting, I put my hand to my chest and gasped, feigning shock as one by one my siblings revealed themselves. "Oh my, you gave me such a fright! Where did you all come from?"

"We were hiding!" Little Joe giggled with delight and ran at me, hugging my legs. "You didn't know we were there!" He looked so happy, gazing up at me. I couldn't remember being that small or that innocent.

Mom and Dad smiled gratefully. They knew I'd sussed them out but were happy I'd played along for the younger ones.

"No, Joe, you got me good." I peeled him off my legs.

Dad started herding everyone over to the door. "Come on, get your coats. We have to be at the restaurant in twenty minutes. Chop, chop, look lively."

With a wave of his hand, nine coats of different colors hovered in the air, from smallest to largest, waiting for nine sets of arms to claim them. Only Jimmy's coat was missing from the lineup, since he had just started medical school and had left two days ago. While all the little arms and legs were flying about, Mom took me to one side.

"I was looking out for you from the kitchen. Where did you get to? I couldn't see you from the window."

I knew what she was thinking. "I popped in to see Matt and Sylvia. And no, I didn't go *there*."

My right hand was stuck in my pocket, and I toyed with the silver band hidden inside. Perhaps I should show Mom the ring, to reassure her I hadn't visited the old grave. I was just thinking this when Dad began herding everyone through the front door. I broke away from her intelligent gaze under the pretext of grabbing my bag and joining the others. Without a backward glance, I followed everyone out into the street. The door pulsed purple as Mom closed up behind us with a silent spell. Two by two, with Dad leading at the front and Mom and me bringing up the rear, we marched along the four streets leading to Main Street, the home of our favorite eatery, the Goblin King Diner. The route led us around the side of the church, inevitably passing my ancestor's grave.

I felt the familiar tug in my navel, only this time the impulse was stronger than ever before. I tried to ignore the feeling, ever conscious of my mom's watchful gaze. Only there was something else this time, something new. Was that—voices? The cacophony grew louder, like many people shouting, and the noise only became more deafening the nearer I got to the grave. This had never happened before, and afraid, I tried to shut my mind to it, but the voices intensified, almost screaming, demanding I hear them. A million emotions crowded my mind, a wailing cocktail of joy, confusion, and despair.

I wanted the voices to stop. It was too much, and my own thoughts were being drowned out by the screams and laughter of so many dead. Something inside me snapped, and the world around me began to spin, and suddenly I was falling. A set of arms caught me, stopping me from sinking to the pavement, but I remembered nothing else, and the world turned black.

More voices, only gentler this time. The hushed tones of frightened children and the gentle hands of someone carrying me. I was moving. I didn't know where I was going. I felt safe. Then I blacked out again.

When I woke, I could hear two men talking. The first I couldn't quite place. The second was Dad. There were other voices still, only much fainter than before.

"She just fainted. I'm sure she'll be fine now."

"Jane isn't so sure." That was Dad. "I've asked her to mix up a tonic to help her sleep."

"If you think that's best, but I assure you, all she needs is a little time."

"What do you know about it?" There was a note of suspicion I had never heard my father use before.

I opened my eyes. I was on the sofa in the living room. Dad and Henry Tilney were chatting over by the window. I groaned when I shifted, and they both stopped talking and turned to examine at me. "What happened? Why aren't we at the diner? Why am I back home?"

Dad came over and crouched in front of me. "You fainted. Are you feeling better now?"

"I guess." Henry was staring at me. His habitual amused expression was gone for the moment. "What's he doing here?"

"He carried you home." There was no gratitude in Dad's voice. In fact, he sounded unusually hostile. I wondered what he thought Henry was guilty of. Did he think this was somehow Henry's fault? And this explanation, though perfectly rational, left me more confused than ever.

"Why?"

Henry crossed the room and sat on the end of the sofa. "I happened to be passing and saw you fall. Right place, right time I guess."

"I'm going to see if that tonic is ready." Dad straightened up and left. He smiled kindly at me but turned his back on Henry.

What on earth is going on?

I pushed up onto an elbow. Other than a faint whispering going on in my head, I was almost myself again. I wanted them to stop. Still, I lowered my own voice so no one but Henry could hear me. "There were voices. So many of them. And they were screaming. I don't understand. I thought you said if I didn't touch the headstone everything would be okay?"

I don't know if he took his cue from my tone, but Henry lowered his voice to match mine. "Why aren't you wearing the ring Sylvia gave you? The crystal is supposed to protect you. If you don't wear it, this will get worse as the day goes on. A new door has opened in the spirit world. They can get a bit excited."

I felt foolish. I didn't want to explain about Mom. I wanted to put it on now to see if it quieted the demons in my head, but I still didn't want Mom to see it. "For the love of Gaia, why didn't anyone tell me? We could have avoided all this!"

"We thought you knew!" Henry furrowed his brow, perplexed. "I thought that that was why you'd avoided the cemetery on the way to her house. I'm sorry, we should have spelled it out clearly, no pun."

"Well, I didn't."

"Come on, where is it? Put it on."

Henry took my hand in his, and I felt yet another sensation that had nothing to do with what had happened. I suddenly noticed his eyes were a beautiful shade of blue. Funny, I hadn't thought him at all handsome at first, yet now...my heart went bumpity-bump. To cover my feelings, I let go and pushed myself up into a sitting position, then slipped the ring from my pocket and put it on. The voices ceased at once.

At that moment, Dad came back into the room, carrying a mug of something in his hand. "What's that?"

For a second, I was confused. He sounded almost angry and was quite literally glaring at Henry. And then I realized he was probably thinking Henry had just proposed to me. I held the ring aloft so Dad could see it more clearly. "Oh, um, it's a crystal ring. *Sylvia* gave it to me for my birthday. Nice, isn't it? I was going to show you all in the diner, but then..." I let my head flop to one side and let my tongue out, imitating fainting.

Dad stared at me, as if making his mind up about something, and his expression softened.

"That was nice of her."

I guessed Henry sensed he was out of the firing line for now, and like a shrewd tactician, he took his chance to escape. "Well, I should leave you to take your medicine. Take care of yourself."

"Thank you." There were things I should ask him, but my head ached, and I was in enough trouble as it was. I told myself I'd be seeing him again soon enough, and any questions would either keep till then or I could call him later.

"Thank you for bringing my Cat home." Dad offered Henry his hand, and Henry accepted and shook it.

"No problem." Henry nodded at me and walked out of the room.

Odd, I didn't want him to go, but I could hardly ask him to stay. Dad bent down and handed me my tonic. It was some kind of herbal tea, and I circled my fingers around the mug, comforted by its warmth. I stared at the door Henry had just exited. There was so much I needed to know. I took a sip of my tea, and though I felt better almost at once, I knew Mom would join us soon and I'd be assaulted by more questions. There was only one thing I could do to avoid them.

"Do you mind if I take this up to my room? I'm much better, but I think I ought to lie down for a bit. Do you think that's a good idea?"

"Very sensible." Dad took the mug from me as I stood up. My timing was perfect, because Mom came in just at that moment.

"I'm going to my room." I took back the mug and trotted over to the stairs. "I'm sorry about the party, but if you don't mind, I just want to lie down. I'll be fine on my own. Go to the diner. Don't disappoint the kids. Tell them I'm fine and enjoy the meal."

"Are you sure? I can stay here with you if you like."

I smiled at Mom. She really was worried, but I wanted to be alone. "No, please, I'm fine. You all have a good time."

Before she could think of a reason to stay back with me, I began to make my way upstairs. As I closed the door, I heard them whispering below. I knew they were concerned about me, but then so was I. This thing, this power, whatever it was, was inside me. I needed to get a handle on it, and I was never going to get any answers hiding at home.

I waited until I heard them all leave, and instead of going to bed, I pottered across to the window and snuggled in the recess with my tea. My room had a good view of the cemetery. I pulled a throw blanket over my legs and stared out at it for a while, then thoughtfully down at the ring on my finger. I was grateful for Sylvia's gift, but I needed to do better than just mask the voices in my head. I had to understand them and to control them. I wanted to go to New York to learn what I could from Sylvia and Henry, and the sooner I got there the better.

Chapter Seven

NEW YORK

I didn't see Henry Tilney again until I got to New York, and I had to say, it wasn't a moment too soon. This was a good thing, because since the day I'd fainted, my nights had been tormented by dark thoughts of the dead rising in various states of decay from their graves.

I hadn't dared take off the ring, not since he'd suggested I put it back on. I was a little curious. There were plenty buried in New York, sometimes in places you wouldn't expect, but I had no desire to faint again, especially now I was so far from family. Or to hear these dreadful, spooky voices, all clamoring for my attention.

Not that life was bad for me now, not at all. I hadn't really known what to expect from this internship. This first week, we'd gone from one meeting to another until it all became quite a blur. Sylvia had shaken a lot of hands and introduced me to a lot of magical people, none of whom I could recall, though it opened my eyes to the variety of races that lived side by side in the sprawling city. I'd never even seen a goblin in our quaint little village. Or an ogre, or a troll, or any of the dozens of different species that seemed ubiquitous here. It was marvelous. Although I wasn't learning much new magic, I was certainly seeing it. Almost everyone back home had some magic, but I was amazed at how the magic community blended in so seamlessly with the nonmagical people, or numpies as we liked to call them. They could be standing side by side, but the numpy New Yorkers were so busy with their hectic lives that a wizard war could be running under their very noses, and they'd never see a thing. We were invisible to them, like a blind spot they could never see into. Their oblivion was both amazing and baffling, yet oddly, as the days wore on, I realized this worked both ways. We were as indifferent to them as they were ignorant of us, yet somehow, we existed in blissful harmony. It really was something to behold.

Sylvia had the most amazing apartment. It was in a prime location in Greenwich village, close to all the best cafes, bars, and restaurants. The magical community was most intense here, taking full advantage of the artistic traditions of the area. No one looked twice at druids decked out in ceremonial robes, and even fae could sometimes flaunt their wings in public without fear of shocking any onlookers, and often did.

Sylvia's big thing was networking, and to that end I'd been to so many swanky restaurants and shaken so many hands it was amazing my wand arm hadn't fallen off. I'd met all manner of people sitting in shadowy booths. Sylvia didn't care—green hands, pink claws, or purple tentacles, it didn't matter a jot. She would wave to them all, and they would gleefully wave back, happy to see her.

It wasn't all work either, or at least, it didn't always feel like it. Since this was my first time in the Magical Apple, Sylvia had wasted no time showing me the sights. Getting around was easy with the New York Magic Cabs Service, *Taking You For A Ride Since 1929*. For a dollar and ninety-nine cents, the goblin-green-colored taxis would take you anywhere you needed to be in less than five minutes, guaranteed. Not a problem for cabs that were as comfortable sharing subway and train lines as the streets. The first time a cabbie had shot underground, I'd almost wet myself when we barely dodged an oncoming subway car, yet the driver had taken it all in his stride, and Sylvia hadn't even looked up from her cell phone. I had so much to learn, and I was loving it. In a few days, we had toured the entire city, taking in Times Square, the Statue of Liberty, Chinatown, and the Empire State Building. She'd steered clear of The New York Public Library, probably because it was known to be haunted, and she felt I should avoid the dead at all costs, at least for now, even though I was wearing my ring.

Everywhere Sylvia went, she knew people. In each location, little packages were always being exchanged, words were whispered, tips were given and taken. It became clear to me very quickly I was under the tutelage of a master. And yes, I loved every second of it.

This afternoon, we were at her boutique in Greenwich Village—*Casting Trouble*. I was standing at a table in the back, dressed in a black T-shirt with the shop name on the front in bold silver letters and the rest of my clothes protected by a new black apron. Sylvia had me measuring liquified toad tongues into small vials. The stench was appalling, but apparently the brew was quite efficacious for the treatment of arthritis and gout. I took her word for it. There were lots of such fascinating things in the jars and containers all over the place. Tiny eyeballs in round pots, oozy black pills that looked like licorice, reams of lamb's wool, and so many things adorned the walls and shelves. And there were kittens everywhere, not cats, but kittens. According to Sylvia, they were there to guard her stock. I had no idea how these little balls of fluff could act as a deterrent, but I took her word for it. Most of the time, they just slept and purred. They were quite docile, all things considered.

Everything was orderly back here, and though nothing was labeled, Sylvia knew exactly what everything was and how everything worked.

"So once you're familiar with our inventory and how we sell it, Henry will show you how to make it. He should be here shortly." Sylvia nudged my hand gently just before I spilled the nasty brown ooze on the table instead of into the vial. "Careful, dear. Honor the poor toad's sacrifice. Don't let any go to waste."

"Sorry." I held my hand steady, not wanting to disappoint her. "Um. What time is Henry getting here?" The truth was, I'd been looking forward to his arrival, but I didn't want anyone to know quite how much.

My attempt to sound casual was an epic fail because a knowing smile teased the corner of her lips. "Not long. And no, I'm not reading your thoughts, dear. I won't do that again unless you want me to. It's just not polite."

"Thank you. You were going to show me how to do that at some point?"

"First things first. We'll get to that one day." Sylvia dragged an enormous mortar and pestle across the table and began pulverizing something that looked like fingernails. "And it's a good thing too. Matt wants me home as soon as possible, poor dear."

I bet he does!

I hadn't spoken a word, but Sylvia still laughed. "Now, now. I don't need to get inside your head to know what *you're* thinking."

I thought about the small apartment over the shop Sylvia kept a block or so away. There were two bedrooms, to be sure, but I wasn't sure Mom would like the sound of me being all alone with a man I hardly knew. Come to think of it, I wasn't that keen on the idea myself. "Where does he stay when he's here?"

"Oh, his family have their own place up on the East Side. He generally stays with them when he's in town. They have an abbey on Northanger and Fifth, very swanky. Just a subway ride away."

"An abbey? In Manhattan?"

"Yes, it's a wonderful place. The family fell in love with the building in England and brought it over stone by stone. I'm sure he'll show it to you at some point if you ask."

I couldn't even begin to imagine what it must be like. Most of the places I'd seen in the city were so tiny you couldn't swing a kitten in them, so the thought of an entire abbey was mind-boggling. "Well, I definitely can't wait to see that."

"Now don't you worry. In any case, I have another intern coming to join me next week. Isabella Thorpe. She'll be staying with you in the apartment."

"Oh? I didn't know you had more than one."

"Well, you know, I like to do favors. Your brother asked me to take her on, actually."

Surprised, I pushed the cork into the bottle and added this last one inside a box of twenty I'd already filled. "My brother?"

Sylvia picked up the unlabeled box and walked off to store it on a shelf. "Shoo, Shoo!" The kitten who had been draped across the shelf idly stretched on its front paws, then wandered off to another part of the shelf, and immediately fell back to sleep. "Yes. She's the sister of one of his college friends, and apparently, she's the same age as you. I don't normally train two interns at once, but between you and me, I think it was your mom's idea. She didn't like the thought of you being up here all alone, and well, I can't say I blame her."

I smiled to myself. That sounded like Mom. I wondered what Isabella was like and whether we'd get along. I made a mental note to call Jimmy to ask him about her when I had a spare five minutes. Was she was pretty? The thought brought Henry to mind.

"How did you and Henry get together?"

Sylvia popped several bunches of dried herbs toward me, along with a box of what looked like purple glass test tubes. "Add a sprig of this black cohosh, two drops of primrose oil, and add a couple of leaves of this sage. Crush the sage first." Sylvia pointed to each bunch in turn. "His dad thought about investing in my little venture here, but in the end, I don't think it was grand enough for him. After his dad lost interest, Henry just kind of stuck around. He's a unique young man."

"He is?"

"I think so." Sylvia watched closely as I crushed some sage into the other herbs. She inspected my work and nodded her approval. "Very good. Now spoon all that into the glass tubes and cork 'em."

"What's this one for?"

"It helps fertility. I've had a lot of interns here. We go through some basics, like we're doing now, but eventually we start homing in on the intern's specific talents."

"What was Henry's?"

"Henry's gifts are more spiritual in nature. He'll soon be ordained as a magical cleric."

I stopped what I was doing, totally taken aback. "That's the last thing I would have thought."

"You don't like the idea?"

"No, it's not that." I continued what I was doing. "I dunno. It's just not what I imagined him doing, that's all."

Sylvia laughed. "Not glamorous enough for you young ones, I suppose. Anyway, you can ask him all about it yourself when he gets here. Finish this all off and I'll treat you both to lunch."

Just at that time, the shop bell signaled the arrival of a new customer up front. For all her size, Sylvia moved like a ballet dancer, as if she were walking on her tiptoes, to see to them, and I continued with my task. Her news had surprised me. I couldn't help thinking of old Father Collins back home, the village priest. He wasn't the most exciting person I knew, and his magic was old-fashioned, so maybe that's why I took such a grim view of the profession, but who knew? Perhaps the younger ones did more exciting stuff.

I was just thinking about Isabella and what she'd be like when the bell rang again. This time, Henry appeared. A huge grin spread across his face when he saw me. Did that mean he was pleased to see me? I wished Sylvia had taught me how to read minds. He seemed different this time, taller somehow, and he wore a black leather jacket over a shirt and sweater. I thought he appeared far too sophisticated and sexy for a cleric. His mischievous baby blues fixed on me at once.

"So how goes the new recruit? New York seems to suit you. You look very, um, perky." His grin widened when he said this, and I wondered if he were thinking something else entirely. Was he teasing me?

"Hello," I said. "I like it. I like it a lot. Everyone has been very friendly."

"I bet they have, and why wouldn't they be? There's a lot for them to like."

My cheeks burned, and instead of answering him, I focused on pounding those herbs into dust.

"So you're not missing home at all?" He sat on the edge of the table and watched me work. "You might want to go a little easy on that sage. What did it ever do to you?"

I hadn't realized I'd been so aggressive and eased off with the pestle. "Thanks. And no, not really. It's only been a week. Jimmy's coming to visit me soon when he gets some time off his studies."

"He'll enjoy himself. You must make sure you show him all the fun spots. I've heard you've seen quite a bit of the town already."

"Some of it."

Sylvia bustled into the back, and I was glad not to be on my own with him anymore. For some reason, he made me feel really uncomfortable, and my cheeks burned whenever that twinkle came into his eyes.

"How are you doing with those herbs?" Sylvia pulled the half-full box of tubes toward her and examined the contents. "Never mind, you can finish these later. I'm starved. What say we all go over to the Laughing Dragon, my treat. I'm in the mood for some good Japanese food, and they have the best sushi in the village, and that's quite an achievement."

Henry nodded and slid off the end of the table. I tidied up my work, wandered over to the sink, and washed my hands in Sylvia's very pungent lavender soap. I rinsed as much as I could and then returned my black apron to a peg beside the sink.

"All ready then?" Sylvia held the door open for us both.

I followed her into the store, passing the displays of herbs, candies, and gifts, and slipped by Henry, who held the front door open for me. Sylvia joined us, and after locking the door using a sparkly wave of her hand, the three of us headed over to her favorite restaurant.

The Laughing Dragon was a few blocks away, and close enough to walk to. While we sauntered, Sylvia and Henry chatted about this and that, everything and nothing, and I found myself more than a little content with my new life in the Magical Apple. Since arriving in New York, the truth was I hadn't a moment to spare for my dead ancestors, or the alleged power inside me, or even what the future had in store for me. My life was everything pleasant, and as we walked along the busy sidewalk, I ignored the brisk chill in the air and how the season would soon be turning to something much colder and far less agreeable.

Chapter Eight

THE LAUGHING DRAGON

We were greeted at the Laughing Dragon by the shortest Japanese man I had ever seen. Though having not seen many in my lifetime, that wasn't saying a lot. When he saw Sylvia, his grin widened, and he approached her with open arms. She bent forward a little to embrace him, and they brushed each other's cheeks the way I'd seen Europeans kiss.

"Ah, Miss Sylvia. So good to see you. I hear you're married now? My heart is broken. I thought you'd marry me! What will I do now?"

Sylvia, as always, relished in the attention. "Why, Lester, you old goat. You should have made me an offer."

"I would, but my wife might have something to say about that." Lester glanced over Sylvia's shoulder to where Henry and I were quietly watching. "And Henry, is this your new woman? I may have to take her from you. She is beautiful, yes."

He took my hand in his and gave it a cordial squeeze, flashing a set of the most perfect teeth I had ever seen, though they looked odd in his heavily wrinkled face. It was hard to tell how old he really was. "Nice to meet you," I said.

Sylvia stepped in to prevent any misunderstanding. "Lester, meet Catherine, my new intern."

"Please, call me Cat." I wondered how often Henry came here with other women. I smiled, hoping Lester couldn't read minds too.

"Come, I'll find you the best seat in the house." Lester linked my arm through his, and after doing the same with Sylvia, he led us all into the restaurant. I glanced over my shoulder and saw Henry right behind us, watching with amusement.

There was a sushi bar in the back, but Lester led us through a heavy black curtain to a much larger room. There were six teppanyaki tables set up in a hexagon, all filled with diners. In the middle of them all was a fire-breathing dragon. It was the first dragon I had ever seen, and I instinctively stopped in my tracks and drew back. The dragon had gleaming black scales and intelligent yellow eyes that fixed me with a curious stare.

Lester must have felt his arm pull because he glanced back to see why I'd stopped. He smiled. "Don't worry. She's friendly enough. She's the cook." Even as he spoke, a burst of flames left the dragon's mouth, lighting up the table and cooking a round of shrimp instantly. As soon as they were cooked, the diners moved in with their chopsticks.

Partially reassured, I continued to our table, which, considering it was supposed to be the best in the house, looked just like all the others in the circle. I wondered if he said that to all his customers.

"This is wonderful, thank you," Sylvia said, taking the seat Lester had pulled out for her.

Perhaps taking his cue from Lester, Henry did the same for me, and I cautiously sat down, waiting to see what the dragon would light up next.

"My pleasure. Let me just get you some menus." And Lester was off.

A moment later, Lester returned and handed out the menus.

"Has anyone ever been burned?" I cast my eyes around the restaurant. All the other diners appeared happy enough, most of them wielding chopsticks like pros. I looked down at mine with some trepidation. They were still wrapped in their little white packet. I'd never eaten with chopsticks in my life.

"Not since a silly accident during prohibition, but they weren't supposed to have any alcohol at the table," Lester explained. "It was as much the bootlegger's fault as the dragon's."

Lester was here during prohibition? Just how old is he?

"The special tonight is filet mignon and shrimp combo. For my friends, I give dessert for free."

Sylvia opened her menu and smiled warmly. "You're very kind, Lester, thank you. Can we order some drinks?"

"I get you your favorite hot tea. On the house."

"Thank you again," she said,

Henry playfully shielded his lips with his menu and leaned into me. "Sylvia brings a lot of business into this restaurant. He's very grateful."

I turned a little too quickly, not realizing how close his face was to mine. Our eyes locked for an instant, though Henry didn't appear to mind at all. He was smiling at me. "Oh, I see." I was suddenly very interested in my own menu. Though in truth, with my heart all a-flutter, I couldn't think straight or read a word on it.

"It's the first rule of business." Sylvia closed her menu and watched as the dragon breathed the tiniest puff of flames to light a little girl's birthday cake at the next table. "You scratch my back and all that. Networking is so important, my dear. We each have a limited set of skills, but friends can do favors. Remember that."

I nodded. I tried to see what Henry was doing out of the corner of my eye. I didn't want to look directly at him in case he caught me out again. Or maybe I did. I was so confused. "Um, now that you're here, what's next?"

"Excuse me?" He lowered his menu.

"In my training? Is there some kind of plan we follow? Or do we just wing it?" I didn't want to remind either of them I came from a long line of earth witches, and bottling herbs wasn't exactly tasking my brain. Sylvia especially had been so generous, and I didn't want to appear ungrateful. Yet I was here to learn, not sight-see, and I was hungry for more.

Instead of answering, Henry looked over at Sylvia. He didn't say a word, but she nodded. I wondered if they were speaking through telepathy or just knew each other so well that each already knew what the other was thinking.

"Now that Henry's in town, perhaps we can kick things up a notch, to make sure you're comfortable with everything before I leave. If not, there's still time for you to come home with me. How does that sound?"

I nodded, glad we'd be moving forward. I hope it involved a spell book and telepathy and who knew what else they might be willing to teach me.

A waitress came over, and placed small pots of tea in front of us. Sylvia and Henry both opted for the special. Never having eaten at a Japanese steakhouse before, I played it safe and ordered the same. The waitress took our orders and left.

The dragon scuttled from table to table, emitting small bursts of fire when needed, cooking the food that appeared magically on the tables. Every now and then, she would entertain the diners with an elaborate show of onions, arranged in the shape of a volcano, which she would light on each table, all at once. Tiny dragons of various colors would fly out through the center of the volcanoes and then disappear in a puff of smoke. Excited, the younger diners clapped and cheered, a few small ones cried, and Henry and Sylvia watched, mesmerized, though I was sure they'd both seen the show dozens of times before.

As we settled in, I noticed Lester usher in a new diner, all on his own. He appeared to be about my age and was quite good-looking, enough so to draw the eyes of all the ladies in the room. He ignored all of them and focused for a moment on the menu Lester handed him. He had sandy-blond hair, full lips, and a very straight nose. His eyes, which were currently downcast, were almond-shaped and looked intelligent. He certainly cut a striking figure, but there was something about him that wasn't quite right and put me off. The way he sat, maybe, casually lounging as if he were deigning to grace the restaurant with his exalted presence. It was hard to say. All the same, he wasn't exactly hard on the eyes.

After seating his new customer, Lester returned to our table. "There is a guest at table four who would like to meet you." He pointed to a table to my right, where a group of wizards were finishing their meal. I recognized them by their auras, though to an untrained eye, they looked like regular businessmen.

Sylvia smiled. "Ah yes, John Gates. I'd been hoping to run into him for some time. Excuse me, all. I'll be back in a tick."

Henry and I smiled at her as she took off and wandered over to where the group were sitting. They all seemed happy to see each other, and when Lester brought Sylvia a spare chair, I guessed she might be there for some time.

I stared across to where the newcomer had just lowered his menu and was talking to his waitress. After a while, she nodded and took his menu away. His gaze fell instantly on mine, and embarrassed, I turned away. Some universal power made me look again, only to find him still staring at me. I pretended to be interested in the dragon, though she'd resumed regular cooking and was not entertaining the diners like before.

Henry leaned into me again, smiling as always. "You should try the tea. It's very refreshing."

I nodded as Henry kindly poured me a cup. Grateful for the distraction, I took a small sip. It had a flowery taste I wasn't familiar with. "This is nice. What is it?"

"Jasmine. Do you like it?"

"Very much so."

"I'm guessing this is your first time in a Japanese steakhouse?"

I nodded again. "I've never used chopsticks before either. Is it hard? I'm frightened I'm going to look like an idiot. Maybe I should ask for a knife and fork."

"You can if you want to." Henry ripped his little packet and separated his chopsticks. "But you'll be fine with practice." He waited patiently, and I realized he wanted me to do the same.

Nervous, I opened my own and pulled them apart, as he had done. "Okay."

Henry held his in his right hand. "You're right-handed, so hold them like this."

I watched as he held one stick only in his right hand and balanced it on his ring finger. I did the same.

He then took the second chopstick, which he let rest on his middle finger. I tried to copy him, but my control was poor, and the sticks were all over the place.

"No, your grip is a little tight. Hold them like this, see? Keep the bottom stick more stable."

I focused hard but couldn't quite get it. Henry covered my hand with his, and I kept my eyes lowered, hoping he sensed nothing of what I felt when he touched me. What in Gaia's name was wrong with me? I wasn't a little girl anymore. I was an adult, or at least I was supposed to be. *Deep breaths, Cat. Ignore the warmth of his hand.*

"Let your top fingers do all the work. Lift it up and down, like so." He gave a small demonstration, his own sticks moving with ease and confidence, none of which I felt. "Now, see if you can pick up your napkin."

I furrowed my brow and concentrated. It wasn't easy, but Henry was patient, and when I looked at him for guidance, he gently corrected my position. After I while, I managed to get a reasonable, if not perfect, hold on the napkin and held it aloft.

"Excellent. The rest is just practice. Have a try with your dinner, but we'll ask for a knife and fork for you just in case."

I smiled gratefully, knowing I was going to need them. Straightening up, I noticed the lone diner still gazing my way.

"That man over there, do you know him?" I barely glanced at him as I spoke, not wanting to appear too obvious.

Henry cared less and looked straight over. "No, can't say I do."

"Why do you think he keeps staring at me?"

Henry chuckled at that. "I imagine he likes what he sees."

My cheeks burned, and I wished I'd never mentioned it.

There was a shuffle and scrape of chairs to our right. Sylvia and one of the men were standing. They both seemed mighty pleased with themselves, so I imagined the meeting had gone well. She kissed him in her preferred European style and then rejoined us at our table. She sat back down in her chair, and Henry poured her a fresh cup of tea.

"Thank you, dear. Well, well, that was fortunate. I've been after that man for weeks. He wants me to go back with him in a few days to help with his magical realty company in Virginia. The people with him are investors, and they're flying south after that. Henry, I know it's a little sooner than we planned, but I need you to take charge of things up here. Would you mind?"

"Not at all." Henry sat back and took a sip of his tea. I studied him, but he showed no signs of annoyance.

"What's magical realty?" I asked.

"When there's no more room in the city, it's a way of maximizing the living space. It's very big in New York now. You can triple the living area and make a fortune. I want to get in on it now, before everyone else does and the market is saturated."

I must have looked confused because Sylvia added, "You'll understand when Henry takes you to see the Abbey."

Henry's eyes widened with curiosity.

"I was telling Cat about your home the other day. She said she'd like to see it one day, and I said you probably wouldn't mind showing it to her."

Henry nodded. "Sure, if we get a chance."

"Good, well, that's all settled then. I should be back in time to greet Isabella. You don't mind, do you, Cat? Only I've wanted a chance to move into real estate for some time, and I'd hate to miss out."

I shook my head. "I don't mind if Henry doesn't. Or Matt."

"Well then, that's settled. I'm sure I can trust you both not to blow up the shop."

As she said this, the food materialized on our table, signaling the show was about to begin. I sat back in my chair, not wanting to be grilled alive by the fire, however pleasant the dragon seemed to be.

For the moment, the young man across the way was obscured from view. Relieved, I put my chopsticks down in front of me and took a sip of my delicious tea. The scent of soy sauce, rice, and sizzling steak filled the air, teasing my senses and whetting my appetite. I had a feeling this was going to be an awesome week, and for the first time since arriving in the restaurant, I relaxed a little and began to enjoy the show.

Chapter Nine

ISABELLA

I'd slept with my apartment window open. Along with fresh air, I woke to the sound of sirens and the bustle of the street below. The sirens didn't alarm me. Their drone had been almost constant since I'd arrived in the city, and most of the time, I was able to block the sound out.

I could hear Sylvia bustling about in the next room, preparing for her journey. She had called Matt last night, and impatient to see his bride, he had insisted she didn't wait so she could get home all the earlier. Sylvia agreed on the spot and booked her flight right away.

I glanced at the clock. Six thirty. *Oh Gaia!* My alarm wasn't set to go off for another hour, and I turned over and hugged my refreshingly cold pillow. I'd just closed my eyes again when there was a gentle knock on my bedroom door.

"Ugh." Whatever else came out of my mouth wasn't English.

Another, slightly more urgent, knock. "Are you decent?"

"Sure." I straightened my pajama top and pushed myself up on my elbow. "Come in."

The door opened, and Sylvia slipped into my room. She was fully dressed and had a coat draped over her arm. "Sorry to wake you, but there's a car waiting, and I need to get going. I've left you some money in an envelope on my desk for food and living expenses, and you have my number if you need anything else. Don't hesitate to call me. No matter what it is. Oh my, I think that's everything, but if there's anything else, I'll call and let you know. Do you have everything you need?"

"I think so." I pushed myself out of bed and slipped some pants over my pajama bottoms in case she wanted me to help with her bags.

"No need to get up, dear. I'm all set, really. I just wanted to be sure you had what you needed. I'll call you later, okay?"

"Sure." I peered out of my window and down to the street. A goblin-green Magic Cab had somehow managed to park in the ridiculously small space between two limousines. The driver in his green livery was standing on the pavement, leaning against his cab. He stared up in my direction and seemed impatient to be off. I gave him two thumbs-ups to confirm Sylvia was on her way down. He gave me a wry grin in return.

"Oh, and there's a little something else on the desk as well. I hope you like it."

"What is it?"

She winked at me. "You'll see. Don't mess with it until you speak to Henry. Well then, I best be off. The meter's running. Oh, I almost forgot. Henry's sister is coming into town today, so I'm leaving the shop closed. He said he'd pick you up later, around five for dinner. Try not to blow up my apartment before then! Oh, and don't worry about the kittens. They can more than take care of themselves. Toodle-oo." Sylvia kissed my cheeks in her signature way and then left in a hurry.

The moment the door to the apartment closed, I felt cast adrift. I was all alone, in a strange apartment in New York. It wasn't a bad sensation, but a little unsettling. I stepped back to the window and looked down, curious to see how the driver would maneuver out of that tiny space. In a little more than a minute, Sylvia was on the street with him. The driver took her small case and opened the door for her, and once she was settled inside, he deposited the case in the trunk. A moment later, he was in the cab, which crunched up like an accordion, and they were off.

Curious to see what Sylvia had left for me, I strolled out of my bedroom and over to her desk, which was by the window in the living room. The envelope full of cash was sitting on a large book. A thrill of excitement rushed through me as I realized at once what this book must be. I thumbed through the notes, pleasantly surprised at how much money she had left me, but put that aside for now and picked up the book. It looked old and was heavily bound in a faded gray leather. There was an elder tree embossed on the front.

Almost reverently, I opened it. The book was titled *The Magical Art of Necromancy*. I strolled over to the couch and sat cross-legged, settling in and fascinated. Slowly, I thumbed through the pages. It was chock-full of rhymes and recipes and incantations, none of which made any sense to me, although at least I understood the actual words.

Be still dear heart,
Thy time hast past,
Eternal slumber calls to thee,
But if thy rest
Be not in peace,
Then rise again and Blessed Be.

The tome was filled with many similar chants and invocations, and I wondered which I would get to use and on what occasion. I was conscious of Sylvia's warning and took care not to read anything out loud, and in any case, half the ingredients needed to invoke some of the spells were unknown to me, or at least inaccessible, like eye of newt or bat claws. I was sure I wouldn't find too many of those in the kitchen, labeled or not. I suspected most could be purchased in Sylvia's shop, but I wasn't about to go looking for them, and even if I did, I'd have a hard time finding them without Sylvia's help. I wondered if that was why she kept things unlabeled. Safer that way.

I was so absorbed I lost all track of time, so I was startled when the doorbell chimed. I wasn't expecting anybody. It had to be Henry. I snapped the book shut and stowed it under a cushion. I still had my pajama top on but was decent enough for my mentor, although he had come much earlier than Sylvia had anticipated.

I flung the door to the apartment open but stopped dead in my tracks when I saw my visitor wasn't Henry at all, but a woman. A very beautiful woman, with curly blond hair and laughing blue eyes.

"Oh."

"Oh, hello." The woman looked around me, evidently expecting someone else. "Isn't Sylvia home?"

I grabbed the door and pulled it in a little closer. My gaze fell to the bag at her feet.

"Um, no, not at this moment. Can I help you?"

"I certainly hope so. I'm Isabella. She should be expecting me. You must be Catherine."

"Oh," I said, taken aback. I scratched my ear. "I didn't think you were supposed to be here until next week?"

"Oh, well, that's most unfortunate because I'm here now. Are you sure she thought it was next week? I'm pretty sure her email said today. Is she going to be long? I've come quite a way."

"Possibly." Remembering my manners, I opened the door a little wider. "Um, come on in. I'm sure this can be easily straightened out. I'll call Sylvia now and let her know you got here early." *A week early.*

Isabella picked up her bag and stepped inside. She began looking around, her smile not leaving her face, so I guessed she was pleased with what she saw, just as I had been when I first got here. After all, it was a nice room, with bright furnishings and a great view of the village. She waited patiently over by the window while I dashed in my bedroom in search of my cell phone.

Sylvia picked up on the second ring.

"Um. Hi, sorry to bother you," I said.

"Is everything okay?"

"Yup, yup, everything's fine. Only Isabella just showed up, and I'm not quite sure what you want me to do with her. I thought you said she wouldn't be coming until next week?"

I wandered to my bedroom door and looked into the shared living area. Isabella had just sat down on the sofa and pulled my tome out from under the cushion. I opened my mouth to say something, but she showed no interest in it and put it on the table by the sofa. She saw me watching her and smiled sweetly.

"Oh, really, I was sure it wasn't until next week," Sylvia said. "Never mind. Put her in my room for now, and I'll call her later. I'm sort of in the middle of something, but I'm sure it's okay. I guess I'd better call Henry and let him know we have his other lady."

"Or I can tell him," I said, trying to be helpful.

"Yes, that's very kind of you. Have him call me later, will you? My, my, it never rains but it pours. He'll think I'm going out of my mind. Look, I must go. Talk soon."

The call ended, and I dropped my phone on the bed. I strolled back into the living room, and Isabella looked up at me expectantly.

"Sorry about that," I said. "I just wanted to let Sylvia know you were here. She says she'll call you later. She's in the middle of something now."

"Of course."

"Sylvia said to put you in her room for now. I think you'll be sharing with me when she gets back."

Isabella bent down and picked up her bag, and then waited for me to show her the way. I opened the door to Sylvia's room and swept up some laundry draped on the bed. "We share a bathroom." I pointed to a door between the two rooms. "The rest is what you see."

Isabella untied her belt and removed her coat. As she did so, her two midsize silvery wings stretched out, as if delighted to be free.

"You're fae?" As soon as I blurted the words, I feared she might think I was being rude, but her easy smile never left her face.

I had never seen anything so beautiful before. I wanted to reach out and touch a wing, but didn't want to scare her and appear like some freak.

"I am. And you're a necromancer. I must say you're not a bit like what I expected. Nice to meet you." She held out her hand for me to shake, and I took it, thankfully.

"What did you expect?" I laughed.

"Someone wrinkly and spooky."

We both laughed. "Well then."

She looked at me expectantly, and for a second, I wondered what she was thinking, and then the penny dropped. "Oh, right. I'll leave you to settle in."

"Thank you."

Isabella closed her bedroom door, and I sauntered over to the sofa to recover my magic book and the envelope of cash. I took them both to my room and stashed them inside my bedside table. For a few blissful minutes, the apartment had been all mine, but now I would have to get used to sharing it again, this time with a total stranger. I had never met a fae before, so I had no idea what to expect nor knew what she was here to learn. Perhaps she had an unusual gift too?

I dropped onto the unmade bed and stared up at the ceiling. Isabella was certainly pretty. I wondered what Henry would make of her and whether he would like her more than me. She was easy on the eyes with the kind of fun-time look men often preferred. Not that I thought myself unattractive, far from it, but still the self-doubt demons came and messed with me.

After a few minutes of tormenting myself, there was a light knock on my door. I'd left it ajar, and Isabella peered around the corner. "I hope I'm not disturbing you, but do you have any plans for today? It's my first time in New York, and I thought it might be fun if we went out. What do you think? I'll buy you a coffee. And a donut?"

"I need to shower first, but if you can wait fifteen minutes, sure."

"Great. Let me know when you're ready, then."

As soon as she was gone, I kicked up off the bed again and made a beeline for the shower. If I were honest with myself, I was quite excited by the idea of spending a little time in New York with another girl.

When I was scrubbed, brushed, and decked out in jeans and a thick sweater, I joined her in the main living area.

Isabella was back in her coat and sat patiently on the sofa. She smiled as I approached. "All ready, then?"

"Yes. All set."

Isabella nodded and grabbed her bag. "Awesome. Let's go have some fun."

I led her out into the hall, and with a flick of my wrist, the apartment was secured. I wondered what fae typically did for fun. I had a feeling I was about to find out.

Chapter Ten

ALAKAZAM AND HAM

WHEN WE HIT STREET LEVEL, I TURNED RIGHT. IT WAS THE DIRECTION Sylvia and I always went, at least, in the short time since I'd arrived in Greenwich Village, so I continued on autopilot. It took us to the best restaurants, the closest subway, and the coolest events. For some reason, Isabella went confidently left, and I halted, thinking she would realize I had gone the other way and would follow my lead. She did turn, but she held her ground and waited for me on the sidewalk.

"Um, do you mind if we go this way? There's a place I saw on the way in, and I wanted to try it." Isabella crooked a finger over her shoulder.

"Oh?" I wondered what had tickled her, but I thought, what the hey. Maybe she'd found someplace cool? I was game to try new things. "Okay. What was it?"

"Just a quaint little deli place. It smelled delicious as I walked past, and I thought we could check it out."

I nodded. "Sure."

"I'm hoping my brother might still be there. He popped in as we were passing and said he'd get something while I took care of things. He may have gone back to his rooms, but it hasn't been that long."

"Your brother?"

"Yes. Sorry, didn't I mention him? John's studying here with your Jimmy, and he met me at the station this morning. He wanted to make sure I found the apartment okay. I said he should come right up with me, but he didn't want to intrude."

"No, I don't think you did." I removed a strand of hair from my face and tucked it behind my ear, though it was a losing battle against the brisk wind. I didn't know what to feel about this new development. I felt wrong-footed and apprehensive. If she had merely wanted to meet with her brother, she could have done that without dragging me along. But maybe she had just forgotten to mention him, and I really wanted us to be friends. "It doesn't matter though. What's he like?"

"John? He's the best brother in the world. I'm sure you're going to like him. If he's not there, you'll hook up with him sooner or later, I'm sure."

I remembered Sylvia had mentioned he was one of Jimmy's college friends. "What subject? What's his major?"

"You know, I don't think he's quite sure. He went there to be a doctor, but I don't think he likes it as much as he thought he would. I suppose he's figuring out what he wants to do." Her smile returned, brighter than ever. "He'll get there. He always lands on his feet, does my brother."

Alakazam and Ham was a small deli, set back in the street in a smallish alcove. There were a couple of bistro tables set outside, though they were presently unoccupied, probably because of the bite to the air. It had a weathered shiplap frontage, and a foldable A-frame signboard listed the specials as *Mama G's famous pastrami on rye, Nevermore Cannolis,* and *All-You-Can-Chug Lattes.* The windows were filled with all sorts of dried mushrooms, many of which I recognized, though some I did not, waxed cheeses, and dried meats. Isabella had been right—the aroma wafting out from the store would be enough to stop any traveler in their tracks, myself included.

As I took a moment to admire the outside, several satisfied customers left the deli and a few more brushed past me on their way in. The place was packed with customers, and Isabella held the door and ushered me inside.

It was a small shop, with seating toward the back, a counter chock-full of goodies, and two servers taking orders. The menu was listed in full on a chalkboard behind the counter, and I examined it carefully as I decided what to have for breakfast.

"Looks like we missed him." Isabella half shrugged and joined me examining the board. "Oh well. It was just an idea."

I was half glad. I'd only just met Isabella and wanted to know all about her, not that her brother would have stopped me from doing that, but it might have slowed things down a bit.

The customer ahead of us accepted a brown paper package and a steaming cup of something hot, and we took our place at the front of the counter. A rather tall satyr stood behind it. I knew what he was by his aura —his horns were hidden under a cap, and he wore a net over his goatee beard. His eyes lit up as we stepped forward, and he ran his tongue over his lips. This was another first meeting for me, and I was instantly on my guard as I'd heard satyrs could be tricky when roused or excited. This one looked to be both. His name tag read Gavin.

"Well, well, two young beauties in my store, I wonder what they're hoping for?"

Gavin winked as he spoke, and Isabella and I exchanged glances. Rhyming satyrs were said to be the worst.

"I'd like a medium hot latte and an egg bagel please." I returned his suggestive leer with a polite smile and rummaged in my bag for a few bucks.

Isabella laid her hand on mine. "Put that away. This is my treat."

"Are you sure?"

"Yup, no problem. This one's on me."

Gavin turned his attention to Isabella.

"There's nothing like a handsome fae to stir the loins and make my day."

"I'll definitely stir your loins if you're not careful, you hotbed of naughtiness," Isabella said. "In a steaming cauldron with sharp copper tongs." Gavin winced, and Isabella looked over his head at the menu. "I'll take a bacon on rye with lettuce and tomato and a hot apple cider. Oh, and one of these." She picked out a blueberry muffin from a basket on the counter and tossed it playfully in the air. I admired her sass and wished I was half as confident.

Unperturbed, Gavin grinned and set about fixing our order. He turned around to prepare my bagel, and his shirt had *Lickable* emblazoned on the back. I watched his companion behind the counter, a second satyr whose name tag read Earl. His shirt read *Tart*. The two servers had similar coloring, and it occurred to me they might be brothers. They shared a suggestive glance and wink, and I cringed a bit on the inside. Isabella, however, seemed to take all this in stride.

We collected and paid for our orders and wandered over to a spare table at the back of the store. Even with my back turned, I sensed Gavin and Earl check us out and wondered how bad it would get if we gave them an inch and flirted back.

Isabella took a seat with her back to the deli, so I sat across from her, facing the shop front. The food on our trays smelled heavenly. One thing was for sure, these satyr boys knew how to cook.

"I'm sorry we missed your brother."

Isabella smiled as she arranged her plate the way she wanted it and discarded her tray to the left of us. "Oh, it doesn't matter. It's not like I won't see him again soon. Anyway, enough about him, I want to hear all about yours."

"Jimmy?" Surprised, I covered my mouth and swallowed my first bite of bagel. It sure lived up to expectations, and the eggs were so creamy and light. Isabella had picked a winner, and I wondered if Sylvia had eaten here before. Most likely, since it was so close to her apartment. "I thought you knew him? Didn't he tell Sylvia about you?"

Isabella blew on her hot cider and sighed. "No, not really. John knew he knew Sylvia and asked him to put in a good word for me. I never actually met him."

"So your brother and mine share some classes?"

"I think so. Or at least they did. Who knows what John's up to nowadays? He's such a social butterfly. More likely they met at some party on campus. That's more his style. Do you think it would be all right if I take my coat off in here? My wings are feeling a bit cramped."

I glanced over Isabella's shoulder at the table behind us. A pair of succubi had just sat down, and their leathery wings, though folded down, were out in plain view. "I think it's okay. No one's said anything about them, and nobody seems to mind what anyone does around here."

Isabella followed my gaze and saw the succubi wings on full display. "Good point." She slipped out of her coat and stretched her silvery wings as far as they would go. "Much better. It's a new coat, and the wing pockets are a little tight."

I was here to learn more about my necromancy powers, and I wondered what Isabella's special skill was. Did she even have one? I was considering whether it would be polite to ask when the little bell over the door jingled and a new customer walked in. He was incredibly handsome, and every female head in the house turned as he walked through the door. I recognized him at once as the man from The Laughing Dragon last night.

I must have been staring, and Isabella shifted to see what I was looking at. "Ah, it's John. He came back for us."

"That's your brother?"

Isabella nodded and waved him over to our table. She shuffled over to the wall so he could sit with us.

John wore a very expensive-looking leather jacket, which I noticed he kept on. I wondered if his wings were anything near as glorious as his sister's and how large they would be, since his shoulders were like an ox's.

"I was hoping I'd catch you." John helped himself to a swig of his sister's cider. I noticed she didn't object, and I got the feeling he was used to getting his own way. He looked at me with the kind of confidence that commanded admiration. He sure was hot, but he knew it, and in a way that protected me from his charms.

"Not using chopsticks today, then?"

"No, thank Gaia." I laughed, oddly pleased he'd remembered me. "I'm afraid I'll always be more comfortable with a knife and fork."

"I wish I'd known who you were yesterday. I would have introduced myself, then."

Isabella stepped in. "Oh, this is Catherine, Jimmy's sister."

"Yes, I think I've figured that out." He smiled, and I felt his eyes all over me, weighing me up. He clearly knew his powers, and it was also apparent he liked using them to unsettle people. Or maybe just women. Who knew?

I looked over his attire. He was exceptionally well-dressed for a student. All I ever saw Jimmy in were jeans and sweaters. I wondered if he always took such care over his appearance, or whether he'd made a special effort for his sister.

"So what plans do you ladies have for today?" John's eyes twinkled as he smiled at me. "Are you getting up to anything fun?"

I shook my head. "We haven't really had a chance to make any plans."

"Well then, since you're both new to the Magic Apple, how about we play tourist and go on one of those magical bus tours? My treat! How does that sound?"

Isabella clapped her hands. "That would be great. Yes, I would love that. I've always wanted to see the Secret Merlin monument in Times Square."

"Is that on the tour?" I asked. It was like a Mecca for all witches and wizards. As a kid, I'd been bottle-fed on stories connected to the ancient stone, and how if you put your hand on it, Merlin himself would speak to you. I bit my lip. I really wanted to see this.

"What do you say, Catherine?" John's mischievous gaze was piercing, and I half wondered if he could read my mind. "Are you up for it?"

"Please, call me Cat." I looked at my phone. Sylvia had said Henry would come for me at five, and we'd gotten off to a late start. Still, there were a few hours between now and then, and I did want to see the sights—the monument especially. And I didn't want to come across as a party pooper on my first day with them.

"How long do they take? The tours? I need to be back at the apartment by five at the latest."

"Hot date?" Isabella winked at me. John smirked.

"Henry is picking me up for dinner. Oh, and I was supposed to call him to tell him you were here."

"Come on." Isabella put all her trash on the tray and stood up, ready to leave. "You can text him on the bus, can't you?"

"Yes, I suppose so." I did the same with my cup and plate and made my way to the trash can. I wouldn't want to miss Henry but was sure I had plenty of time.

As soon as Isabella had her coat on, John ushered us both back through the store. Gavin and Earl were busy serving customers, but Gavin looked over the dwarf in front of him and waved us good-bye.

"You're going now is such a rot, but come back soon for something hot."

I chuckled and shook my head. I really would have to return here sometime. The satyrs were a hoot. Maybe with Sylvia. And a bucket of saltpeter.

Chapter Eleven

THE MAGIC TOUR BUS

THE DAY HAD WARMED UP A LITTLE, AND THE SKY WAS NICE AND CLEAR. We walked along the busy sidewalk to one of the many Magic Tour bus stops in the city. John and Isabella liked to talk a lot, and since I liked to listen, this suited me just fine.

There was a goblin-green-colored Magic Tour bus waiting at the stop. We climbed aboard, and Isabella made straight for the upper deck.

"Won't it be cold up there?" I asked.

"Ha, are you a witch or what?" Isabella plowed ahead and took a seat at the very front of the bus.

I felt embarrassed and didn't want to admit I didn't know ley line magic and hadn't thought to bring any potions with me. Luckily, I didn't have to.

"Never mind, I'll take care of us."

I sat next to her at the front, and John sat on the seat beside us. As soon as we were settled, Isabella put her hands together as if in prayer. "*H¯æte.*"

A gentle heat enveloped my body. Even the tips of my fingers, which generally felt the cold the most, suddenly tingled and were toasty. "Thank you. I'm going to have to learn that one."

Isabella grinned. "You're very welcome." As if to prove the point, she took off her coat and spread her wings.

The conductor was a goblin. I would have guessed him to be quite young, though it was hard to say because his acorn hat and woolen scarf covered most of his face and head. In contrast, his feet were bare, and I wondered how cold his toes got working on the bus. He meandered down the aisle heading straight for us, since we were the only passengers on the top deck. Without so much as an upward glance, he turned his ticket machine and reeled off three individual tickets. "Thirty dollars each, and a buck for a guide."

"Thirty dollars?" John rolled his eyes. "That's a bit steep, isn't it?"

"I don't make the fares. I just sell the tickets. If you're too cheap to pay, get off my bus."

I knew goblins were brusque at the best of times, and this one seemed especially snarky. I wondered what on earth had induced him to take this job, since he clearly wasn't a people person.

"Three tickets and three guides then." John pulled out his wallet and rolled off some notes.

The goblin's eyes lit up at the sight of the money, which he quickly stashed in his very deep pockets. He pulled out three guides, colored to match the bus, and handed them to John.

"Will there be a commentary?" Even Isabella's most charming grin didn't crack a smile on the miserable creature's face.

"Wait and see."

"How long before we leave?" I glanced at my phone. Time seemed to be passing faster than usual.

"When I have a few more passengers. This bus doesn't run on air, you know." And then he was off.

As soon as he was out of sight, Isabella chuckled. "I wonder what climbed under his hat!"

"If I know anything about goblins, he's probably their employee of the month," John said. "The ones I've met have been a lot worse."

I could only half smile because I kept thinking about the time. I was sure Henry would be upset if I was late. Would he even wait for me? While John and Isabella perused their guides, I slid my phone out of my pocket. I pulled up Henry's number, but when it rang through, I got his busy phone.

"Dang." I started to send him a text. After all, I had promised Sylvia I'd let him know about Isabella. I was halfway through composing it when my phone died. "Huh?"

"What's up?" John asked.

"My phone. It just turned itself off."

"Try turning it back on then," Isabella suggested.

I was already doing just that. I waited a moment for the screen to light up. "Nothing."

"Maybe the battery's dead?"

"Shouldn't be. It was fully charged this morning, and it usually lasts all day."

John lowered his eyes, and I wondered what he was thinking. I tried the power button again, but it just wouldn't work.

"You can use my phone if you like." Isabella held her phone out to me, but I shook my head.

"No use, unless you know Henry's number. I never memorized it."

"Look, stop worrying. We'll be back in plenty of time," John said. "These buses run several tours a day—it'll be fine."

I wasn't so sure. "Sorry, John, I'll pay you, of course." Thirty bucks was a lot of cash for me, but Sylvia had left me a generous sum, and I didn't want to take the chance and miss Henry. I stood up, determined to get off the bus. At that moment, the engine roared, and the bus rolled forward, knocking me into my seat.

"I guess more people came on downstairs."

Isabella reminded me of my baby brother Joe, her excitement was so raw and unfettered. John didn't seem interested in the tour at all. However, he seemed thrilled that I'd missed a chance to get off. It seemed important to him that I remain with the party. I could tell from the appraising way he kept glancing at me that he liked me. Boys had looked at me that way before. Was that all it was? He fancied me? I remembered, though, that he was fae, and that their kind were never to be trusted. Even if they were hotter than Hades.

An image of the goblin appeared before us, floating in the air like a holographic balloon. The image remained in place, about a foot over our heads and high enough for the whole deck to see him if need be. His acorn cap was still on his head, but he'd pulled the scarf down, revealing a set of very tiny and sharp pointy teeth.

"Hello and welcome to the New York Magic Bus Tour. My name is Grogwold, and I'll be your tour guide on this journey. As always, safety first. Wands cannot be used on any part of the bus. May I also remind you the tour company is not liable for lost children who turn invisible while the bus is moving. Keep small children away from the tour guide at all times. He gets hungry." Grogwold sniffed and wiped his nose.

"Our first stop will be the famous House of Magic, New York's first and oldest magical supply shop. They have an awesome display of wands confiscated during the Salem trials, though these are not available for purchase. Chippings of charred firewood from the same period can be bought for a reasonable price, which I'm told are efficacious in salving potions. The shop's quite a way on the other side of Central Park, so for now, sit back, and enjoy the ride."

I already spent enough time in a magic shop, so I was more than delighted to give this one a miss—at least for today. Neither Isabella nor John seemed to mind. However, I couldn't really get out of the other places they wanted to see, like the druid circle hidden in the basement of the Rockefeller Center and Tinkerbell's Shadow over the main entrance to Macy's. To be honest, I was glad I didn't, because they were awesome. Each time the bus didn't shoot off but waited for us to climb back on board. Still, since there were so few of us, we made good progress, and I began to think we'd make it back to the apartment in time after all.

We'd been out for a good couple of hours when, at last, the bus rolled into Times Square. Grogwold's image hovered over us again.

"Get off at the next stop for the Secret Merlin Monument. Witch lore suggests it was stolen from the Cornish shores by the last of the true Celtic druids a few years after the voyage of Columbus. However, goblin lore tells a somewhat different tale. We believe the stone to be the center obsidian stone taken from Stonehenge, known locally as the Necromancer's Stone, given as fair payment to the Goblin King for services rendered during the Fantastic Wars of 1322. It was later brought to the Americas in the bowels of the Santa Maria and hidden near the first Goblin Bank in New Holland, close to the area you now know as Wall Street. Through witchcraft and trickery"—at this point, I got the distinct impression Grogwold's gaze was directed at me—"the enchantments protecting it were breached, and the stone relaid in its current position in

Times Square. Now anyone can see it, except humans of course, if they invoke the proper spell—see page three of the tour guide for instructions and a coupon for a free tour valid for six months."

His image *popped* into nonexistence as the bus rolled to a stop.

As soon as Isabella secured her wings inside her coat, we left the empty top deck and jumped out through the lower center doors. In Times Square, the buzz and activity of New York intensified threefold. Everyone and everything was moving so quickly, and for a second, I just stood on the sidewalk, taking it all in.

"This is incredible." I stared up at the tall buildings, the advertising boards, the shops, the street vendors, the traffic, all of it, trying to capture the moment in my memory. "And it's just how I imagined it would be."

Isabella stood beside me with her mouth open. She seemed as impressed as I did. "I've never been anywhere so exciting."

I glanced back at our bus and wondered at the awe of magic. Our bus was an ostentatious goblin green. And though we were surrounded by hundreds, if not thousands of New Yorkers and tourists, none of the numpies appeared to see it. Somehow, they always seemed to be looking the other way. I loved magic.

Isabella watched me as I pulled out my phone again.

"Just checking to see if it was the bus," I explained. "But it's still dead."

She nodded and cocked her head to one side in sympathy.

Still, time was pressing. While the others gawped, I opened my tour guide in search of the clues that would lead us to the Necromancer's Stone. I turned to page three. Most of the page covered the various attractions, but at the bottom of the page was a small rhyme.

I am a number,
First under the sun,
Before all and after none
What am I?

That was easy, I thought. The number one.

I am everything.
All eyes are on me.
But I am empty.
What am I?

I am base. I seem nothing,
I am the very bottom of the top.
Everything depends on me.
What am I?

I had no idea what the second and third rhymes meant. Dad was more into puzzle stuff than I was. I found myself wishing he was here. I noticed the others had moved a few feet away and were still taking in the sights. "What do you think this means?" I asked. I read all three rhymes out loud, told them the answer to the first one, and then asked for their help on the second and third.

Isabella looked as confused as I was. John smiled. He opened his own copy and read the words for himself. "It's funny, but I'm pretty sure I read something about this a few minutes ago." He turned the cover over and stared at page three. "Yes, the answer is on the page, look." John pointed to an article about the history of One Times Square a few paragraphs above the rhyme.

I scoured it quickly and read what was evidently the most critical section out loud. "Although it is one of the most iconic buildings and lucrative advertising spots in the whole world, One Times Square, also known as the Times Tower, remains notoriously empty. Although the ground floor is let, all the upper floors are unoccupied. The public at large attribute this to the cost of renovations, although we believe there are mystical powers at force preventing the building being used for any nonmagical purpose..."

"Oh," Isabella said. "I see. But what about the third part of the rhyme? The bit about the bottom and the top?"

"I don't know," I confessed. "Let's head over there and see if we can work it out."

We edged our way through the crowds, and I watched as the endless fleet of Magic Cabs weaved their way through the sea of yellow ones, all working in complete harmony. Magical beings were a little less obvious here than in the more artsy Greenwich Village, yet here they were, merrily mixing with everyone else. I spotted dwarves on newspaper stands, gremlins selling gold watches for a buck to unwitting tourists, fauns and satyrs selling discounted tickets to Broadway shows, and succubi selling something far less savory in the shadows. Each one was perfectly disguised. You would have to be magical yourself to recognize them, yet they were there, going about their business, happily earning a living.

John was the first to reach One Times Square. There was a Walgreens on the ground level, and I craned my neck up at the 363-foot-high skyscraper—so it said in the tour guide—and wondered at the magnificent advertising above. At the moment they were showcasing Sony, Pepsi, and Hocus—the latter, I had recently learned, was a very trendy outlet for magical clothing. What did nonmagical people see when they looked at that sign?

I read the last part of the rhyme again.

I am base. I seem nothing,
I am the very bottom of the top.
Everything depends on me.
What am I?

"Hmm. Something at the bottom that everything depends on?" I scoured the ground near the base of the building but could see nothing. Looking up, I noticed a couple of elves talking animatedly over at the corner of the building. I wondered if they had been on the bus with us, which was possible since most of the other passengers had remained on the warmer lower deck. Odds were they were working on the same puzzle as us, and elves were notoriously clever, if not the friendliest of creatures.

Isabella and John followed me. The elves were chuckling, and one of them kept touching the wall. As we drew closer, they saw us coming. They frowned, and then, sticking their noses in the air, they moved off. They were clearly not the most sociable of elves, but I wasn't offended—I knew their ways.

They had been standing in front of a large stone at the corner of the building. It wasn't hidden at all but was there in plain sight for anyone to see, if they knew what they were looking for. Carved in the center were runes depicting all the elements: earth, wind, fire, and water. And at its heart was a rune I had never seen before. It appeared to be two wings rising upward, with a circle in the middle, possibly a head. I was no expert, but I was pretty sure this was the necromancer rune. The cornerstone probably looked like regular brick to humans.

"This must be it!" Excited, I put my hand to the wall, just as I'd seen the elves doing a few seconds before. On the eve of my birthday, a thousand voices had entered my head. Since wearing Sylvia's ring, those voices had been silent, but now they were back, and this time louder than before. Everything inside me arrested, the world went black, and I felt my body falling. John's strong arms caught me, and the last thing I recalled before the world went black was the look of surprise on his face. After that, I knew nothing more.

Chapter Twelve

A NICE CUP OF TEA

When I opened my eyes, John was holding me close in his powerful arms. My head hurt like Hades, and it took a moment for me to remember where I was. I wondered what time it was. Fearful of missing Henry, I pushed away. My head swam, and John grabbed hold of me again.

"Not so fast, Cat. You've given us one scare already. Don't be in such a hurry to do it again."

Isabella, who was right there next to him, gently squeezed my upper arm. "What happened? You put your hand on the stone and fainted."

I tried to sit up. I was on the sidewalk, and people were hovering about us, cameras out in case something exciting was going down. Isabella started pushing them back. "Go on now, there's nothing to see here. She fainted, that's all. Just give her room."

The crowd began to disperse, evidently disappointed it was nothing more dramatic than that.

I remembered now. The voices. All the screaming and the laughing, pounding inside my head, all at once. I twiddled the ring on my finger, wondering why it hadn't worked this time. John and Isabella were waiting for an explanation, but I didn't want to tell them what I'd felt. Heck, I still didn't understand it myself. How I wished Henry were with me now. He would know what to make of it.

I pulled my phone from my pocket. It was still dead. "Can we just get back on the bus? I think I'd like to return to the apartment."

John and Isabella exchanged glances.

"I think you should get a drink or something first. Some hot tea maybe? We don't want you passing out on the bus." Before I could answer him, John led me along the sidewalk. Too feeble to object, I followed along, and since I knew it to be the precise remedy my dad would have prescribed, I went without objecting.

The first cafe we came to was nonmagical, but that was okay. I didn't need any special potion or brew. With both pairs of wings safely tucked inside their jackets, no one would have suspected either Isabella or John of being fae, and since witches looked pretty much like everyone else, we all fit right in.

John pulled out a chair for me and we sat down and waited for the waiter to come over. A middle-aged woman with hair colored too dark for her face came to take our order. She held an order pad in her hand and wore a fake smile on her lips. From her slumped and fed-up posture, I gathered she was having a bad day.

"What can I get ya?"

"Just three hot teas," John said.

"Coming right up," she said flatly, and wandered off.

Isabella shifted her seat so she sat a little closer to me. "So what happened? One minute you were fine, and then *poof!* Down you went like a sack of potatoes, white as a ghost. Does that happen to you a lot?"

I shook my head. "It's nothing to worry about. Low blood sugar, I suppose. I'll be fine after I've had a cup of tea." The truth was, I *was* fine. Maybe a little shaken up, but the voices were silent now. Like at my ancestor's grave, the dead had called to me. But this time, there were so many of them, not just the occupants of a small village cemetery, but thousands upon thousands of voices. This time, it stopped when my hand left the stone, and I was thankful for that at least, or they might have driven me mad. I wished I could tell Isabella and John, but my heart told me not to, and I decided to listen to it.

The grumpy waitress returned with our teas. She placed them in front of us and then headed straight over to the next table. Going by her new broad grin, I suspected she anticipated bigger tips from those customers. I took a sip from my cup, but it was too hot, so I put it down.

John was busy texting someone, and when he finished, he stared directly at me. "I was sending a message to your brother." He peered sideways at Isabella. The two shared a knowing glance, and I wondered what it meant. They obviously knew something I didn't.

I felt a sudden sense of panic. What if Jimmy told my parents about what just happened, and they told me to come home? I would die if that happened. "Why? What for?" I tried not to sound suspicious.

"Well, I didn't tell him you almost fainted in the middle of Times Square, though maybe I should have, but he did ask me to let him know if we ever hooked up. Now seemed as good a time as any."

"Don't tell him about the fainting thing. He'll tell Mom and Dad, and that would be bad."

John grinned, confirming my suspicions that he'd considered it. "Fine, I won't."

I had had enough. This had been a bad idea all round, and I wanted to be off. "What time is it now?" I took a sip of my tea; it was still too hot, but I was anxious to get moving.

"Three thirty. Bags of time still."

Hmm. I wondered. The bus wouldn't necessarily get going when we were on it, and it might have more stops to make before returning to where we picked it up. I had a bad feeling.

"Maybe we should order a sandwich or something. I don't know about you guys, but I'm getting rather hungry." John turned, looking for the waitress.

Was he doing this to annoy me? He knew I was pressed for time. "Um, look, if you do, would you mind getting it to go? I really want to get back."

"Oh, stop worrying." John caught the waitress's eye, and she weaved her way through the tables and waited for his order. "I've never known such a worrywart. It'll be fine, I promise. Can I see a menu please?"

The waitress nodded and went off to find one.

Frustrated, I downed my tea as fast as I could. It was still piping hot, but I had had enough. Was he delaying me on purpose? What did it matter to John if I met up with Henry or not? I decided I'd better get going before I lost it and alienated my new friends.

I wiped my lips on my napkin and pulled enough notes from my purse to pay for everyone's tea. I dropped them on the table and stood up, ready to head back. "Look, sorry, I gotta go. Henry's my mentor, and it would be rude to be late. You guys stay here, finish your tea, and catch up with me back at the apartment."

Isabella looked up at me, surprised. "What are you gonna do?"

"I'm going to catch a cab. I need to have a shower anyway before he gets there. I feel all grungy." I didn't mention I wanted some alone time. I'd had enough company for one day. "The secret thought you need to open the apartment door is banana peel. I'll see you back there." I turned to John. "It was really nice meeting you, John. I'm sure we'll meet up again soon."

At that moment, the waitress returned with the menu. John looked up at her and shook his head. "Never mind, it looks like we're leaving after all."

The waitress's scowl said it all, and after snatching up our money, she wandered off in a huff. So much for the big tip I left her.

"If you feel that strongly, then I guess we'd better go too."

"You really don't have to," I said. "I'm a big girl. I can find my way back on my own."

I didn't wait any longer. I made straight for the roadside, knowing they would try to stop me if I hesitated. I was vaguely aware of the scraping tables behind me as the two hurried along to catch up.

Isabella was the first to reach me, and she cast me a furtive glance, clearly afraid they'd upset me. "Is everything okay?"

"Fine, I feel a lot better. I just want to get back. You guys hop on the bus. I'll meet you back at the apartment. Go on, have fun. There's still so much to see."

The second I flagged a taxi, a goblin-green Magic Cab pulled right up beside me. Before either of them could argue, I jumped right in, deliberately not sliding across the seat so they couldn't follow me into it. I closed the door and opened the window. "Please, have fun. I'll feel bad if you let me ruin your day, but I think it's best I go home and lie down a bit. I'll be all right, I promise."

Isabella smiled sympathetically, but John looked positively annoyed. Not that I cared right now. Good-looking or not, he ignored me once too often, and in any case, who did he think he was? I smiled one last time and pressed the button to close the window. The driver took the hint immediately and drove straight off, as I imagined the pair of them standing on the pavement, wondering if I was mad. And perhaps I was.

"Where to?"

My driver was a high elf. I couldn't see his face, but there was no mistaking the pointed ears that poked above his head, indicating his rank among his own kind—and beautiful green eyes looking back at me in the rearview mirror. It seemed rather a lowbrow profession for one of his kind, but I didn't dare pry. Elves were proud creatures at best, and an inquiry might offend him. In any case, I had enough worries of my own.

"Greenwich Village and Grove. What time is it?"

The driver glanced at his dash. "A little after five."

"What?" My heart raced in panic. Surely he was wrong. "Are you sure?"

The elf raised his eyebrows but checked again. "Pretty much."

Had Isabella and John lied to me? And why would they do that? They knew I wanted to get back to meet Henry, and I was late already. I checked my phone, and my heart jumped when I saw the power had returned. I pulled up Henry's number and tapped impatiently as I waited for Henry to pick up.

"How long before we get there?" I asked the driver.

"How fast do you need me to be?"

"Yesterday."

I almost dropped my phone as the cab zoomed forward, forcing me back into my seat. Luckily for me, I managed to hold on to it as I heard Henry's voice on the other end of the line.

"Oh, Henry, I'm so glad that's you. Look, I'm so sorry, but I went out with Isabella and her brother, and we lost all track of time. I'll be home in a few though. Isabella got here a week early, and we all went sight-seeing on the spur of the moment. I'm sorry. Somehow time got away from me, but I'm on my way now."

Henry was quiet. "You didn't get any of my texts?"

"No, sorry. My phone was dead. I had no power all afternoon."

"But you have power now?"

I hated the incredulity in his voice. "Yes, sorry, I'm not sure what's going on with my phone, but it's been acting up all day. Anyway, I'm almost home. I should be there in five minutes."

He was quiet again. "Don't rush on my account. I came over early to pick you up, that's why I was texting you. My sister's flight was delayed, and I'm on my way to the airport now to get her. You might as well stay with Isabella and her brother, and I'll call you later after we've had something to eat."

My heart sank. He didn't sound like himself. "I'm so sorry." And I meant it.

"Don't worry. Just have fun. If I don't call you tonight, I'll see you at the shop tomorrow. We can talk then. Look, traffic is heavy. I have to focus. Bye for now." He hung up.

He didn't sound annoyed. More flat. Maybe he was tired. Or maybe his day wasn't going to plan. Heck, I could relate to that, but he didn't sound himself, and that made me feel bad. I slumped in my seat, feeling sorry for myself. All I'd wanted to do was spend time with Henry, and thanks to John and Isabella, that wasn't going to happen. And though my rational brain knew it wasn't their fault, that they hadn't done this on purpose, a voice inside me told me there was something I wasn't seeing here. But I was sick of hearing voices in my head, so I tried to shut them down and focused on the landmarks as the streets of New York zipped by me at the speed of light. And I tried not to think of Henry. But that was asking a too much of myself, as I thought about him all the time.

"You can slow down now. It's okay, I'm not in a hurry anymore."

The driver nodded, and I pulled up Henry's texts. There were seven of them all told, his tone changing slowly from excited to exasperated. What was it with people arriving early or not leaving when they said they would? Freakin' inconveniences, the lot of 'em.

Chapter Thirteen

SERIOUS MAGIC

Isabella had arrived home quite late in the evening. There was a gentle rap on my bedroom door, but I ignored it and pretended to be asleep. It was just as well, as it was soon clear she had brought her annoying brother with her—I could hear the two of them in the apartment, whispering and giggling among themselves. I guessed it was in the nature of fae to be mischievous, but whatever they were up to, I couldn't join them in their merrymaking. I was still mad at John for making me miss Henry. So I kept my door resolutely shut, even after the front door closed and I knew John had left at last.

Come morning, I felt tons better. I could never hold a bad mood for very long, and I also knew that in a little while I would be at the shop, and that Henry would be there working with me for the best part of the day.

I showered quickly and stared at Isabella's door as I munched on my breakfast cereal. Time was passing, and as far as I could tell, she hadn't showered yet. If she wasn't careful, she'd be late on her first day. I slid back my chair, and with my bowl in hand, I knocked on her bedroom door.

"Isabella, are you up?"

Nothing. I knocked a little louder. "Isabella?"

"Go away." Her voice sounded muffled, liked she'd pulled a comforter or pillow over her head. Maybe she had.

"I have cereal. Do you want some?"

Nothing.

Satisfied I had done my duty by her, I wandered over to the kitchen, downed the last dregs of my cereal, then put the bowl in the sink, and filled it with water. It was still a little early, but I wanted to see Henry so bad, and I had a feeling if Isabella ever got her lazy butt out of bed, she might want me to wait for her and make me late again. I went into the bathroom, brushed my teeth, and was pulling on my poncho by the front door when the door to her bedroom opened. Her tiny nightgown had just enough fabric to be decent, and her beautiful wings hung heavily behind her as she dragged herself over to the bathroom. She waved at me on her way. "You go ahead. I'm not much of a morning person."

"I can see that." I grinned and held on to the open front door, wondering if I really ought to wait.

"Really. Go on. I'll be right behind you. See you at the shop. I know where it is."

She closed the bathroom door behind her, and then I heard a deep groan, followed by the sound of running water from the shower. Satisfied she knew what she had to do, I headed off to work.

The weather was pretty much as it had been the day before. The wind was perhaps a little milder, but not much, yet I didn't care. All I knew was I was a few minutes away from seeing Henry, and that was all that mattered to me.

I was delighted to see the lights were already on in the shop, which meant he'd opened early. I bit my lip, knowing that these days women, even witches, were supposed to be cool about their relationships with guys, but my heart trumped my head, and heck, I liked how he made me feel. It was all I could do to stop myself from running in the store, and I was glad I didn't, because Henry wasn't alone. There was a very petite young woman at his side, petting a tuxedo kitten. This itself was odd because the little things generally detested being petted. Her aura said witch, but her face told me something else. The likeness was too startling—that *had* to be Henry's sister.

They both looked up as I approached. Henry smiled, though his smile was not as bright as I remembered it, and I wondered if he were mad at me after all. I checked my excitement and smiled at his sister.

"You must be Eleanor," I said as I reached them. I offered my hand, and after putting the kitten down, she shook it warmly. "You look just like your brother. I'm Cat, how do you do?"

Eleanor grinned. Her eyes were set deep like Henry's, both shy and mischievous at the same time. I liked her at once. "Slightly better-looking, I hope. Pleased to meet you. Hank's told me all about you."

It took a second for me to realize she meant Henry. I never really cared for the name Hank. Anyway, I was itching to know what he'd said about me but thought it best not to ask. My concern must have registered on my face because Eleanor took pity on me and smiled. "Don't worry. It was all good stuff, I promise." Then she looked over my shoulder, at the door. "I thought the new girl was starting today?"

"Oh, she's right behind me. She'll be here any second now." *At least I hoped she would.*

"Late night?" Henry eyed me with something like amused suspicion, but there was more to it than that. A little disappointment, maybe?

"Her brother came back with her, and they were chatting for quite a bit. You remember that guy in the Laughing Dragon restaurant who kept looking at me? That's her brother, John. They're both fae."

Henry raised an eyebrow but said nothing.

Eleanor straightened her scarf and pulled her bag firmly over her shoulder. "Well, I'd better be off. I just wanted to come in and take a look at the place before meeting up with Dad for lunch. I've heard so much about it after all, but this is the first time I've actually had a look inside. Maybe when you're all done, we could get together for dinner or something. What do you think?"

I realized she was asking me. "I would like that very much."

"I can't tonight," Henry said, "but tomorrow, sure, if you're free, Cat?"

I would have said yes to any day of the week to be honest, but I pondered for a second and then nodded. "Sure, I think so." *Happy dance.*

"Well then, I'll see you soon."

"Yep, off you go." Henry grinned. "Some of us have work to do." He kissed his sister on the cheek and led her over to the front door.

I could see how much he loved her. They reminded me of Jimmy and me, and were maybe even closer than that. Perhaps they didn't have eight other siblings to contend with. She left the shop, and he closed the door, causing the bell to ring. He looked up and down the street, perhaps expecting to see Isabella, who I hoped was hoofing it. Would she have stopped for coffee?

"Is it just you and Eleanor, then?" I asked when Henry returned.

"Nope. She's the youngest, but we have an older brother, Freddy."

I smiled at the thought of there being another Mr. Tilney at home. "Oh, is he cute?"

A shadow crossed Henry's face. "My brother is quite the ladies' man. I'd steer clear of him if I were you. He throws women out with the bathwater."

"Duly noted," I said. I didn't really know how to steer clear of someone I'd never met, but Henry was making a point, so I let it slide.

Henry tinkered with some glasses, and I wondered what lesson he had in store for me today. I sincerely hoped we'd be moving on from potions work. And there was something else on my mind. Something I wanted to bring up before Isabella got in.

"About yesterday. Something happened, and I wanted to ask you about it."

Henry stared intently at a small blue bottle. "You know, sometimes I wish Sylvia would use labels just like everyone else. Yes? What is it?"

"I think I mentioned we went on the tour bus. When we got to Times Square, I put my hand on The Necromancer's Stone and passed out. That was why I was late. The ring didn't save me." I twisted it nervously on my finger. "There were so many voices..."

Henry put down the blue bottle and stared at me. "Are you nuts? You put your hand on the stone? Why would you go and do a daft thing like that?"

I shook my head. "I didn't realize—I didn't think."

Henry's expression softened. "I don't suppose it was your fault. I guess you'd never heard about the stone either. Your parents kept you woefully in the dark. Look, there are lots of artifacts and objects that can channel your power. The one in Times Square is arguably the most powerful, and I'd urge you not to mess with it again. You're not ready for it and might not be for years."

"How could I ever be ready for *that*?" I asked. "It almost killed me."

"In time, you will learn how to control the voices, but it takes a lot of magic and control, and we haven't begun to scrape the surface of all that. I can see the first thing I'm going to have to teach you is how to recognize them when you come across them. Otherwise, you'll be in serious trouble."

At that moment, the bell dinged, and Isabella strolled in. I lowered my eyes, and I think Henry sensed I didn't want to discuss this in front of her. "We can talk about this some more later," was all he said.

Isabella looked nothing like the sorry heap I'd left at the apartment. Her hair shone brilliantly, and she removed her coat slowly and provocatively, stretching out her magnificent wings, which almost filled the shop. Her gaze fixed on Henry, demanding the admiration I guessed she always got when she turned on her full fae charms.

She held a beautifully manicured hand out to Henry, like a queen reaching out to her subject. She was fantastic, and I was jealous as Hades. "Hi, I'm Isabella, lovely to meet you. I'm so pleased to be here."

Henry took her hand and shook it robustly. "Nice to meet you." He looked up at the clock, just as the minute hand clicked forward onto 9:10 a.m.—she was *late*.

"I'm sorry. I didn't mean to be late on my first day." Isabella smiled coquettishly, clearly expecting to be forgiven.

Henry didn't comment, but though his smile remained fixed, his silence spoke volumes. This tactic wrong-footed her a little, and she withdrew her hand cautiously and tucked her wings behind her back.

"I have a few things I need to attend to this morning, but Cat can show you where everything is, like the little girls' room, can't you, Cat?"

"Sure."

"Do you have any questions before we get started?" Henry asked.

"Um, what happens if I accidentally set something on fire?"

Henry raised an amused eyebrow. "Does that happen a lot?"

Isabella shook her head.

"Good, but if it does, use the fire extinguishers on the walls." He pointed to one a few feet from where we stood. "There are a lot of volatile substances in these jars. If you used the wrong spell, you might blow us all up." Henry picked up the blue bottles and handed one to Isabella. "You'll be mixing some love potion antidotes later today while I work on some other stuff with Cat here. I'll show you a few to get you started, and if anyone comes into the shop, I'll see to them up front."

His gaze went up and down Isabella's silk shirt and pencil skirt. "It can get a bit grungy back here mixing potions and messing with raw ingredients. I suggest you come in something a little more practical tomorrow. Do you have any jeans and a plain old T-shirt? If not, I'm sure one can be found for you. And use an apron when you're mixing things in the back. Cat can find you one of those as well."

"I'm sure I have something suitable, but if you have something you want me to wear now, I'd be happy to change."

The bell at the front of the shop rang, signaling our first customer of the day. "Cat, see if you can find her a store shirt from the box. I'll be back in a minute."

"Sure."

Henry skipped off, and after sharing a quick smile with Isabella, I led her to a cardboard box full of shirts like the one I was wearing myself and pulled out one in her size. Like mine, it had *Casting Trouble* emblazoned on the front in elegant silver lettering. "There's a room you can change in out the back, and you'll find an apron hanging on the back of the door."

"Thanks."

As Isabella went off to get changed, I smiled. It looked like Henry was impervious to Isabella's many charms after all, and more than a little relieved, I allowed myself a tiny victory dance on the inside. Call me daft, if you like, but I couldn't help myself.

Isabella returned a moment later, but not even a T-shirt and shoddy apron could diminish her beauty. She winked at me and nodded to the front of the store where Henry was still chatting to a customer. "Is he always so formal?"

I never thought of him that way but didn't want to appear confrontational. "He's very nice. You'll get used to him."

"Oh, like that is it?" Isabella's knowing smile was irritating. "Well, I don't know if you noticed, but my brother likes you lots. I do hope you're not going to disappoint him and make goo-goo eyes at another dude."

"Goo-goo eyes?" Henry couldn't have picked a less timely moment to return. "Is that a term?"

Mortified, I could only hope Henry had missed the first part of the conversation. However much he'd heard, I certainly couldn't look him in the eye now.

Indifferent to all of it, Henry picked up a package containing what I instantly recognized as licorice root and a potato peeler. Isabella looked confused, wondering where he was going with this. I had a pretty good idea, having seen Mom make antidotes for love potions hundreds of times for our magic school.

"Right, let's get you started on these antidotes. I want you to slice the root as thinly as possible, like so." Henry carefully cut five long shreds down the full shaft of the root and tied them with a small red string. "Then pop them into one of these blue bottles and pour ten drops of this licorice root extract over the top. Ten drops mind you, not a drop more or less, or our customers will lose all their hair. When you're done, pop in a little cork like this, and then line them up, twelve in each box. You try."

Isabella took the root from Henry, but her hand shook as she tried to peel it, resulting in tiny shards rather than the long strips Henry had made when he'd done it. She looked up anxiously.

"Keep practicing. You'll get the hang of it. Do you have any questions?"

Isabella shook her head. "It's fiddly, but I can do this. Don't you worry."

I admired her confidence as she knitted her brow and went at the roots with a vengeance. Her next cut produced a much longer shred.

Henry watched her for a few seconds; then, seemingly happy with her progress, he smiled in my direction. "You'd better come up front with me."

"I thought you preferred us minions hidden in the back?"

"I do, but we don't want to be disturbed for this."

I thought there was less chance of that in the back, but intrigued, I followed him through the door that led to the shop. Henry made straight for the front door and locked it. Two kittens instantly appeared and set to watching the door.

"There. We won't be long, but the last thing I need is customers waltzing in while we practice this magic. Sylvia wouldn't mind us closing for a few minutes—she's pretty good about that sort of thing."

"Right, I see," I said, wishing I did.

He not only closed the door but also pulled down a black shade so no one could see through the glass. He then turned off all the lights. There was enough light to see by, but it was significantly darker. "Just a precaution."

I held my breath. At last, we were going to do some serious magic.

Henry came and joined me behind the counter. I knew he was just doing his job, and I was doing what Sylvia had employed me to do, yet I felt a tiny thrill knowing that I was going to have him all to myself, albeit in a very small way and only for a little while. I tried not to let my pleasure show on my face as he came close, though I felt suddenly warm and was very conscious of my breathing being shallow. I prayed to Gaia Henry wouldn't notice any change in me.

We were in an oasis of boxes and jars. Their contents seemed to shift in the shadows, though nothing moved when I looked closely. I wasn't afraid —this was the world I lived in, and there was little here I hadn't glimpsed in my own village and sometimes in my own home.

Henry pulled out a purple box from under the counter, and when he removed the lid, it was full of a vibrant, gold-colored powder that shimmered in the darkness. It wasn't anything I'd seen before.

"What's that?" I asked.

"Egyptian pixie dust. It's very old, very rare and very powerful. It costs an absolute fortune, but Sylvia told me I could use some of it on you, but we mustn't go mad."

I peered closer into the box, wondering what was so special about it. "What does it do?"

Henry pulled out his hawthorn wand and hesitated over the box. "It has many uses. But before we do this, I need your consent."

I wasn't expecting him to ask that. "What for?"

"You want to know how to read minds. One of the things this does is stimulate the part of your brain that's receptive to mind reading. We can then practice on each other, but it's invasive, and I want to be quite sure you're up for in before we begin."

I caught my breath and put my hand down flat on the counter for some discreet support. Just moments ago I'd been thinking thoughts about him, thoughts no innocent young apprentice should probably be thinking. At the same time, this was one of the things I most wanted to learn. I didn't know what to say.

"Err, yeah, sure, I'm up for it I guess."

Henry cocked his head to one side. "The only thoughts a person can read are the focused ones. You have to think them in sentence thought. Otherwise, it's like pea-soup in there—a big ugly mess. Oh, and I should probably mention, once we open the door, the change is permanent. You will always be able to do this, whether you like it or not. Do you still want to do it?"

I nodded. "If it's gonna happen sooner or later anyway, might as well be sooner. Oh, should I take off this ring? Will it interfere with the magic?"

"No, not at all. You can leave it on. Very well." He smiled and then waved his wand. A gray mist surrounded us.

"Do you give your consent for us to experiment with Egyptian pixie dust?" he asked again.

I giggled, imagining us in a church about to get married, me in my white wedding dress, and the minister waiting for my answer. Henry cocked his head sideways and frowned.

"Umm, yes, yes, I do."

As soon as I gave my consent, the mist evaporated. I looked at him with wide eyes, a little bewildered.

"Sorry, but I take that sort of thing very seriously."

I understood, though I was still grinning.

"When the powder is in the air, I want you to breathe it in deeply through your nose. Keep your eyes closed and don't open them until I tell you to. Remember, you only have to do it the once; after that, you'll never have to use the stuff again. Are you ready? Because you can still change your mind if you're not sure."

I nodded, both nervous and eager to get on with the lesson at the same time.

"Good, this will be quick. If you hesitate, the powder will be wasted."

"I understand."

"Good. Remember—eyes closed. On the count of three. One—two—three." Henry drew a small S pattern with his wand over the box, and a tiny amount of the dust, maybe less than half a teaspoonful floated up into the air. It hovered like a small cloud in front of me, and though my heart was racing, I stepped right in, closed my eyes, and took a deep breath.

I felt a tickling in my nostrils and then a series of small explosions that reminded me of pop rocks going off in my head. The sensation wasn't frightening, just weird.

"Don't open your mouth or open your eyes yet. I'm going to massage your temples. Don't worry, it won't hurt. Are you ready?"

"Mmm-hmm," I replied, afraid to move my head or open my mouth.

A moment later, I felt his hands on either side of my face. Ever so gently, he began rubbing my temples, making small circles with his thumb. He was so close to me I could smell his breath, which smelled pleasantly of mint. I was in danger of shaking, but I kept a hold of myself.

"Just think this. What's your favorite flower?" His voice was unusual. It was definitely Henry's, but clearer than normal, his diction more perfect.

Hmmm. A flower. I remembered the field of bluebells near to our house. We'd skip through them on our way home from school and put them in our hair. I liked bluebells.

"You're thinking bluebells, right?"

"Yes."

"Open your eyes."

I did as he told me.

"I'm thinking daisy." Only Henry's lips didn't move. I could hear him as loud as if he were speaking, but it had all been in my head. He still cupped my head in his hands, but he was no longer massaging me. His gaze was fixed on mine, and he was smiling. I suddenly realized my eyes had been glued to his lips, and embarrassed, I pulled away, in case he read more in my head than I wanted him to.

"Wow, that's incredible."

Henry turned and carefully put the lid on the powder and restored it to its place behind the counter. "Telepathy is a fairly rare gift," he explained in his usual voice. "It's not uncommon in necromancers, though some don't learn how to do it until they're much older. The powder just helps things along. It wouldn't work at all if you didn't have the gift to begin with."

"But you have it, and Sylvia does. How rare can it be?"

"Trust me, it's rare. That's why she was so interested in you. And me when she first met me. I joked the other day that she collects us like dolls."

"So now I'll be able to read minds?"

"Yes, but not so fast. We must respect the privacy of everyone else. After all, you wouldn't like some stranger poking about in your head, would you?"

I picked up a jar and pretended to be interested in its contents, though I couldn't have been less so. I just couldn't risk looking at him. "I suppose. So why show me? What's the point if we can't use it?"

"The most important thing about the gift is that it not only allows you to read minds, but it also helps you block people from reading yours. We'll work on that some other time. But eventually, you won't need a ring to block the voices in your head, no matter where they come from. You'll have more control, and trust me, you'll be a lot happier with your gift than you are now."

"I'll believe that when I see it."

He smiled. "Well, for the rest of the day, I want you to help Isabella and resist the urge to read my mind. I'll sense it at once if you do. And don't try it on Isabella. She's fae, and it doesn't work on them. You'd be wasting your time."

Pity, I thought.

Henry grinned, and I wondered if he'd just read my thoughts.

"Hey, can I tell when someone is reading my mind? Like, are you doing it right now? How can I know for sure?"

"You can kinda feel it when they do. But they can't read anything in there other than what you tell them, like a regular conversation. The problem, as you've already discovered for yourself, comes when they all start talking at once."

That was a relief, at least.

"Are you two up to no good?" Henry and I turned to see Isabella watching us. She was grinning and motioning over to the locked front door, where the blind was still down. "Do you want me to leave you alone?"

Henry strolled out from behind the counter and pulled up the blind. The kittens left their post and retreated into the shadows. "No, we're done for now. How are you getting on with those roots?"

"Better, but I'd like you to come and have a look at what I've done before I do any more, just in case I'm making a complete hash of it."

"Sure."

As Henry unlocked the door, a werewolf waltzed in. I'd have known what she was, even if she'd hidden her aura, because it had been a full moon last night, and her coat hadn't quite retracted. I suspected that was why she was here in the shop.

Henry indicated with a subtle nod that we should go through to the back again. As we retreated, I looked back over my shoulder. Hairy as she was, the lady werewolf was a hottie, and I wondered if Henry would flirt with her.

"Is Sylvia not here? Damn it. I suppose you'll have to do. I demand you provide me with wolfsbane repellant spray. I am sick to death of being followed everywhere by horny werewolves." Her voice was so deep it made my spine vibrate. But I laughed inwardly and left him to it.

While Henry took care of her, I joined Isabella in the back. She had made pretty good progress on the antidote, and her small bottles were all stacked and ready for inspection. I picked one up and sniffed it.

"These look perfect to me," I said, after checking a few more bottles.

Isabella smiled, and picking up the potato peeler, she began slicing up the next root. When she was done, I took over tying the shards with the red string, adding the ten drops of extract to each bottle. I had made this stuff so often I could do it in my sleep, and that was a good thing because I had a lot on my mind right now. And though I should have been thinking about the lesson and all Henry had told me about the dos and don'ts of telepathy, in all truth I wasn't thinking about that stuff at all. All I could think about were his hands on my head as he'd caressed me, and those gentle lips and eyes, which just a few minutes ago were so close to mine. I knew now I was falling for him, and there was no magic on earth that could stop it. And that was fine by me. I was ready to fall under his spell and prayed to Gaia he would reciprocate. I wanted him to so badly.

Chapter Fourteen

THE MAGIC BANANA

THE FOLLOWING DAY, JIMMY SENT ME A TEXT SAYING HE WAS IN TOWN and asking what time they let me off for lunch so he could pick me up.

Henry was sitting at the table with Isabella, watching as she put wolfsbane leaves into the distiller to extract their oils. Yesterday's werewolf customer had wiped out most of our stock. I hoped it was keeping her unwanted suitors at bay until the current lunar cycle was done with.

"Sorry to interrupt, but my brother asked me if I can meet him for lunch. What time would be okay with you?"

Henry slid off his chair and came over to where he had me fulfilling our shipment orders for the day. Compared to this, potions seemed positively exciting. Brown wrapping paper, tape, string, address label, write the shipment details by hand into the big orders book. My brain had gone walkies hours ago.

"You know, I didn't even know there was such a place as"—I examined the header on the invoice—"Vale do Javari. Now I do. Oh. Is this an error? This confusion oil is expensive, isn't it? It says zero due."

"This shipment is a gift in thanks for certain herbs and seeds Sylvia receives from that region that she can't get somewhere else."

"But confusion oil?"

"Apparently they brush it on the barks of trees to confuse parrot poachers. It just needs a solid invocation spell, and it's good to go. I couldn't approve more. You know, if your brother's in town, why not invite him to join us for dinner tonight? Four is a good number."

"That's a nice thought," I said. "You don't mind?"

Henry picked up one of the heavier boxes to move to the docking area at the back of the store. "Sure, why not?"

Across the room, Isabella sat up a little straighter. "Oh, you're all going out for dinner? Can I come?"

"Sure, the more the merrier," Henry said.

I was glad he'd looked away just then because I didn't want him to see me frown. I saw plenty of Isabella as it was. Not only that, I didn't like that she'd practically invited herself. Not to mention her inevitable next question.

"Can I invite my brother, John, too?"

Henry paused midstride. "Sure." I noticed he didn't sound quite so convivial this time. Perhaps he was regretting his "the more the merrier" comment. Oblivious, Isabella grinned and got back to her work.

I typed Henry's proposal for dinner instead of lunch into my phone and Jimmy quickly replied with a "yes," and I suggested he meet me at the apartment at five. He agreed.

"All set."

Henry nodded, and I slipped my phone back into my pocket and carried on labeling.

"I'm looking forward to meeting your brother," Isabella said. "John's told me all about him. I hear he's quite a whiz in class. Not to mention something of a looker, but how could he not be, being your brother?"

I should have been flattered by the compliment, but I wasn't. I felt manipulated. I wondered if Henry felt the same too.

"He can hold his own, I guess." I peeled the final label from the backing paper and attached it to the last box. I carried the boxes out to the docking area and stacked them on top of a similar pile. "There. That's done. What's next?"

The shutter was up at the back, and Henry was looking down the back alley, waiting for the UPS man to arrive at the shop. There were several kittens sitting on the tops of boxes, looking out. I wondered why they didn't make a run for it, but I'd never seen a single one try to leave the store.

"It's nearly lunch time. Why don't you break off now?" He spun round quickly, not realizing how close I had been behind him, and almost knocked me off my feet. Luckily, he reached out and caught me. His face was inches from mine.

My gaze went from his lips to his eyes, which were locked on mine. Delighted, I saw what I wanted to see there, a mirror of my own feelings. I relaxed in his embrace and held my breath, realizing he was about to kiss me.

"Did I hear someone say lunch?" Isabella was right behind us, tucking her wings inside her jacket. "I'm starving. Can I go first?"

Henry let me go, and the moment was lost.

I could have killed her.

Thank Gaia I'd showered already because Isabella was taking forever. I wouldn't mind, but Jimmy was due any moment, and I needed to pee, bad.

"Have you fallen down the toilet or something?" I yelled through the door. "I need to use the thingy."

"Can't you use a bucket or something?" she yelled back.

"No, I can't!"

"Just a minute."

I shook my head and plopped down on the sofa, reaching for my magic book. I flipped through it every chance I got, surprised at how much I understood. There was a section on mind reading, which included the trick Henry had used with the Egyptian pixie dust. Earlier I'd caught Isabella reading it when I came out of the bathroom. I wasn't surprised—Henry had said she should get one of her own. Isabella had been flicking idly through the pages, shaking her head, but then shrugged and tossed the book onto the sofa.

"All reads like gobbledygook to me," she'd said. And then she ran off. Not that I cared. In fact, I was secretly pleased Isabella hardly understand a word of it. It merely reinforced what Sylvia had said about this book being well and truly mine. If Isabella wanted a book like it, she'd have to find one of her own.

Bang on five o'clock, the doorbell rang. Excited for the evening to start, I put my book aside and jumped up to answer it. But it wasn't just Jimmy standing in the hall. John was with him. I was accustomed to giving Jimmy a hard squeeze, but not wanting to give John any ideas, I tempered my enthusiasm and settled for a smile.

"Well, are you going to let us in?" Jimmy asked, grinning back and sharing an amused glance with John. I hoped he didn't think there was something developing between me and Isabella's brother, and bothered by this, I dropped my own smile and opened the door wide for them to pass inside.

"Isabella's finishing up. She shouldn't be much longer." At least I hoped she wouldn't be.

I stood awkwardly, clasping my hands in front. I didn't like the way John was looking me up and down, like a piece of meat under appraisal. Before I could stop him, he planted an uninvited kiss on my cheek. "Good to see you're feeling better."

In turn, Jimmy shot me a worried glance. "You were sick?"

"Nothing special. Just a blip." I narrowed my eyes at John. By Gaia, the man had promised not to say anything, yet he had broken his word the first chance he'd got. If he was trying to win me over, he was certainly going about it the wrong way. "Have you heard from Mom and Dad? I keep meaning to phone them."

Jimmy shook his head. "No, I guess I'm just as bad as you. I should call them soon and let them know I'm alive."

I took out my phone and thumbed into my contacts list. Moments later, I heard the ringing tone, and a familiar voice answered.

"Hey, Dad, it's me. I'm here with Jimmy, and we're about to go out to dinner with friends. We just thought we should let you know we're doing fine and everything's okay. How are you and Mom keeping? And the horde? Good, good. No, the job's great. They're teaching me stuff, so it's interesting. Miss you, though. We'll visit you soon enough. I'll call again, and so will Jimmy. Take care!" I smiled at Jimmy. "Done."

At that moment, the door to the bathroom opened, and Isabella stepped out. She wasn't wearing makeup as far as I could tell, but her skin looked vibrant. Her eyes were brilliant, and her wings, unrestrained, stretched to their full, glorious length before they magically disappeared inside her custom-made shirt. Her jeans fit her perfectly, two long legs disappearing into a pair of slightly heeled leather boots. I could hardly be surprised by my brother's admiration when I could barely conceal my own. I would have closed Jimmy's jaw with the crook of my finger if I could have done so without embarrassing him.

"Umm, Jimmy, this is my roomie, Isabella. And this goof is my brother, Jimmy."

Jimmy crossed the room and shook her hand with more vigor than necessary.

"I've heard so much about you," Isabella said, gazing up at him with those gorgeous eyes of hers. I could only imagine the effect this must be having on him. Funny how John had similar eyes, but they didn't quite have the same effect on me.

"All good, I hope." Jimmy shot a playful glance at me, but I shrugged. The truth was I'd barely talked about him at all, but I had a feeling neither of them cared about actual details right now. They looked far too pleased with each other.

I heard a cough behind me. I turned to see John was grinning. "Well, perhaps we should get going if we don't want to be late."

I couldn't have agreed more and grabbed my poncho off the hook by the door.

Jimmy stood aside, gallantly allowing Isabella to leave ahead of him, though his eyes dropped to her backside as she passed, and I shook my head in mock disapproval, even though I found the whole thing funny just the same. Was I just as drippy with Henry? Once everyone was out, I cast the lock up spell behind us.

A few minutes later, we were on the street, and no sooner did John raise his arm than a Magic Cab pulled up by his side. The window slid down, and a dwarf troll driver stuck his head and elbow out of the car.

"Where to?" The troll's voice was low and booming, but a lot more pleasant than I expected. Maybe city trolls were less aggressive than their mountain cousins. At least I hoped this one would be.

The poor thing could barely fit into the driver's seat. Though a fraction of the size of his mountain brethren, his still rather ominous bulk filled the entire front of the cab. His neck was so bent forward, I wondered how he could bear to be hunched up like that all day.

"Where are we going again?" Jimmy asked.

"The Magic Banana," I replied.

"Hop in," the troll said politely.

"Will we all fit in the back?" I asked dubiously.

"Sure you will."

Somehow, we all managed to bundle into the rear seat, and the cab pulled slowly off.

I was squeezed in between Jimmy and John, and though I was pretty sure there was enough space for John to put his arm somewhere else, he found it convenient to drape it over my shoulder. His fae cologne smelled of wood smoke. It was pleasant, if a little heavy for my taste.

"So how are you liking New York?"

I turned to answer my brother, only to find the question was not for me.

"Loving it!" Isabella tucked a lock of loose hair behind her ear and shifted so her back was against the taxi door and she could see Jimmy better. "Not that I've seen much, since Henry keeps us busy, but I like what I've seen so far. I really want to go ley line watching from the top of the Empire State Building, but I haven't had a chance yet."

"I wouldn't mind checking that out myself. Perhaps we could do it together?" Jimmy suggested.

"I would love that."

John shared a wicked grin with me. If he had been Henry, I might have enjoyed the gesture, but I disliked being intimate with John and didn't want to give him ideas. I turned my head and pretended to be interested in the view outside. There wasn't much traffic about, but the driver was going awfully slow.

"I thought Magic Cabs were famous for being superfast?" I whispered.

"I don't think this one got the memo." John grinned.

Still, we had plenty of time, so I wasn't worried about being late—just anxious to get out for other reasons. The third time John's fingers strummed on my neck, I was ready to bite his wings off. Enraged, I was about to punch him in the unmentionables, but lucky for him, at that exact moment, the driver pulled up to the curb and all our attentions went to the front of the cab.

"Seven fifty," the driver said. I reached into my purse to get the fare, but Jimmy was way ahead of me.

"This one's on me," Jimmy said. "You can pay for the one back if you like."

"Fair deal," I said. I also noticed that though John had his hand on his wallet, he'd been rather slow to pull it out. Isabella hadn't made any show of paying at all.

"Thanks, mate," John said. He opened the door and shuffled out. I was next, and the others followed us out curb side. Jimmy paid the troll through the window. The tip was fair, nothing out of this world, but the troll couldn't have been happier. He tapped his forehead politely and drove off.

"I didn't know trolls could drive," Isabella said.

"I wasn't aware they could actually talk," John added less charitably.

"I thought he was very nice." After making that comment, I made for the double doors that led into the Magic Banana, anything to put some distance between me and John. From what I gathered, the restaurant was famous for being able to conjure up whatever you ordered right at your table, no matter how exotic or bizarre. I looked forward to seeing how it worked. It was also very low-key, affordable to everyone, no matter their budget, and the decor was pretty rustic. The tables were rough oak, the lighting dim, and there were monkey nuts all over the floor. There were barrels of the things all over the dining area, and I helped myself to a handful as we stood in line behind two other groups.

The hostess was about to serve us when suddenly Henry appeared at my side. He smiled, and the hostess acknowledged him with a nod. "They're with our party. Come on in. We got here early and ordered drinks for everyone. I hope you don't mind?"

My heart jumped to see him, and although he was behind me, I knew my brother would be grinning.

John stepped forward to shake Henry's hand, and though their greeting was cordial, it wasn't exactly warm.

"Have you been waiting awhile?" I asked.

"Just a few minutes. Not long."

We all followed Henry into the restaurant. The place was buzzing, diners were chatting animatedly, and every now and then, people in strange outfits would appear with food and then disappear with *pops* and a whiff of smoke. Fascinated, I wondered what they were about.

"We're just over here." Henry shuffled into a corner booth where his sister, Eleanor, was sipping a smoking purple cocktail. There were similar glasses full of the same purple liquid in the center of the table. Beside her was an older man, who looked like Henry but with silver hair and a goatee, and sat so rigidly I thought he might have been in the army. That had to be their dad. "Let me introduce you to Pops. Dad, these are the girls I told you about. This one's Cat."

I smiled in his direction. He nodded back. "Forgive me if I don't get up, but my children insisted I sit in this corner. And please, call me Frederick."

"Nice to meet you, um, Frederick. Or is it Freddy?"

"Actually, call me the General. Freddy's what we call my eldest boy, and you don't want to go mixing us up."

"And this one's Isabella." Henry motioned to Isabella, who smiled her sweetest, but with little effect on the older man. Like Henry, he seemed immune to charm in general. "This crazy goof is Cat's brother, Jimmy, and this is Isabella's brother, John."

The men exchanged polite hellos.

"Last but not least, this is my sister, Eleanor."

Eleanor smiled warmly at Jimmy, John, and Isabella. Introductions being over, everyone squeezed into the corner booth, and I noticed Jimmy slid in immediately after Isabella. John and Henry both waited for me to slide in, and I was delighted when Henry beat John to the punch and moved in next to me.

"So how does this work?" I asked, eagerly looking around the restaurant and watching as strange individuals kept appearing and disappearing from nowhere. As I spoke, a rather ordinary-looking waiter joined us briefly, leaving us with a bunch of menus before scooting off again. I was secretly disappointed he wasn't as exotic as some of the others.

"It's rather cool really." Henry passed me the first menu, which I passed on until everyone had one. He then placed one of the purply drinks in front of me, and I took a sip. It tasted like champagne and Concord grapes, and the smoke tickled my nose. I liked it a lot. "The restaurant has locations all over the world. You can pick whatever you fancy, and cooks teleport from their restaurants with the food you requested."

"That's pretty amazing," I said.

"Ooh, this is going to be fun," Isabella said.

Jimmy nodded, unable to take his eyes off her.

The General picked up his knife and fork and began to polish them with his napkin. "My son tells me your father is a doctor?"

I realized he was talking to me. "Yes, and my brother wants to follow in his footsteps," I added. Jimmy glanced our way, only half listening before turning his attention back to Isabella. I sighed, hoping he wasn't going to moon about like that all night.

"You don't?" the General continued.

"I'm not sure. Maybe. I haven't decided yet. I'm learning—other things —at the moment."

"Well, you should. It's an excellent profession. Very lucrative, I understand."

"Yeah, I guess it can be," I replied.

"I'd like Henry to settle down into a profession one day, instead of moping about in a magic store like a crazed kid in a toy shop. His late mother would turn in her grave if she had any notion of his gallivanting about."

I had no idea Henry's mother was dead. I squeezed his hand beneath the table. Henry merely smiled and shook his head, and I got the impression they both visited this subject a lot. He gently let me go.

Eleanor must have been thinking on the same lines. "Now, now, Pops, play nicely, or we'll send you home without any supper."

The General grunted and turned his attention to John. "I hear you're also training to be a doctor."

John sat up as straight as the General and puffed out his chest. "Yes, sir. If all goes well."

If he can find five minutes to study, I thought.

"Excellent. Have a word with my son here, when you can—maybe you can knock some sense into that brain of his? If you ask me, he should have followed me into the Wizard World Inquisition, like his brother did. That would have straightened him out."

"If you say so, Pops." Henry's smile was indulgent.

I didn't want to mention I was glad Henry hadn't, and not just because I would never have met him if he had. The Inquisition was established to ensure our world coexisted peacefully with nonmagical beings, but I'd never heard good things about anyone who joined. Maybe the General and his son were the exception.

Thankfully, the waiter returned, killing that conversation before it took off. "Good evening, and welcome to the Magic Banana. My name is Austen, and I'll be your server for tonight. Do you all know how the restaurant works?"

"Yes, I believe so," Henry answered for all of us.

"Very good. I see you're all enjoying our signature magical refilling cocktails, but can I tempt you with something else perhaps?"

Henry looked around the table, but we all shook our heads.

"I'm happy with this purple stuff." I took a sip just to show I was.

"So have you all ordered?" Austen asked.

Odd question, I thought. I grabbed my menu, which up until now I hadn't even looked at.

Inside was a colorful picture map of the world. I stared at it, completely confused.

Henry opened his mouth to explain it to me, but I was already tapping a spot on the map. I'd chosen India. A beautiful girl in a sari, no taller than six inches, appeared on the surface. She offered up a bowl full of something very orange and meaty. As she held her bowl up to me, I breathed in the wonderful spices and wondered how the room wasn't a muddle of aromas, since we were all choosing something unique, yet the only scent I was aware of was the one coming from her bowl. I loved magic. Especially *gourmet* magic like this.

Still, I wasn't quite in the mood for garam masala, so I shook my head. The girl smiled and disappeared. Glancing around the table, I saw everyone else making similar choices, being tempted by tiny people all around the world.

The second time I tapped on England, half expecting someone to pop up with a plate of fish and chips, but instead, a rather hot-looking six-inch young man, wearing a chef's coat and a puffy white hat that made me think of the Pillsbury doughboy, offered me a tantalizing bowl of beef and scalloped potatoes.

"Oh, what's that?" I said aloud, intensely interested.

"Lancashire hot pot with carrots and peas," the man said in a British accent.

Intrigued, as much by him as the dish, I nodded, and with a quick puff, he disappeared, and my menu went blank.

"Ha, that was fun," I said.

I noticed everyone was handing their menus back to Austen, so I did the same.

"What did you order?" John asked.

"Something very English, I think. How about you?"

"Something from Iceland. I was in the mood for fish."

For a moment, we all discussed our individual orders, each of us intrigued by the novelty of the menu and wondering what everyone had gone for.

"I suppose you have some very exclusive restaurants back home," the General said. "You probably find these urban tourist traps quite vulgar."

I gulped down my purple cocktail and licked my lips. No one in their right mind would call the feeding holes back home *exclusive*, but I didn't want the General to think we were *that* poor.

"They're certainly not as high concept as some of these New York restaurants, but they're nice enough in their own way."

"I'm sure you're being very modest." Although he was talking to me, the General's focus was on Henry. Henry smiled but looked away and started a discussion with Eleanor. I got the feeling he understood his dad all too well, which was more than I could say. I felt like the General was trying to unearth some truth about me. I didn't know how much he knew about my background, and I felt uncomfortable going into it any more than I already had.

There was an audible *pop*, followed by a beautiful Turkish woman in a belly dancing outfit standing beside Eleanor. She carried a plate of adana kebab, served with pita bread and a red onion salad. It looked both delicious and healthy at the same time. The server placed the dish in front of Eleanor, bowed slightly, and after another *pop*, she was gone.

Over the next few minutes, there were several *pops* as one by one our meals arrived. My Lancashire hot pot was the last to arrive, but I didn't mind. It was fascinating to see all the food coming from around the world.

There were lots of *thank yous*, and *this looks delicious*. My cute little English chef was even cuter at full size. After placing my meal in front of me, he unfolded my napkin and laid it across my lap. Then he smiled and popped away.

There was little talking as we tucked into our amazing dinners. I drained the last of my cocktail and watched with wonder as it magically refilled itself. The cocktail left me feeling warm and fuzzy, and I found myself very relaxed and more talkative than usual. Not that I was alone. The Magic Banana's signature drink soon loosened all tongues, and the conversations began to flow thick and fast as everyone finished their dinners. Only the General seemed unaffected. A lifetime of toasts in the wardroom had given him immunity, no doubt.

The only thing that bothered me was John. Though I didn't mind talking to everyone, it was clear he wanted to monopolize my conversation, with his *what did I think of this* and *what did I think of that*, but each time I returned his volleys with a lob, opening the conversation back up to the general table and refusing to be boxed in by him. I was baffled by his determination, when I was so clearly uninterested and when any fool could see how much I preferred talking to Henry. At least I thought so.

"So, John, do you have any idea what you will do after you graduate?" the General asked. "Do you have a particular field in mind? It seems all the money's in nonmagical patients—I could never understand why, but there it is."

John pushed away his empty plate and puffed out his chest. "I have several options I'm considering, but I'm not ready to make a final decision just yet. There's still plenty of time before I have to specialize."

Glad of the opportunity to get away from John, I leaned into Henry and whispered in his ear. "Little girls' room."

"Oh, right." Henry slid out of the booth so I could get out.

As I stood up, my napkin dropped to the floor. A slip of folded paper fell from it, and Henry picked up both and handed them to me. Without thinking, I opened it up. Written inside was the English chef's phone number and a message: *WhatsApp me!*

Henry looked down at the note and grinned. I laughed and slipped the note inside my pocket.

"Hold on, I think I'll come with you," Eleanor said.

There was a momentary shuffle, and after locating where the restrooms were, she and I headed in that general direction. For a horrible second, I thought Isabella might come along too, but she and Jimmy quickly turned back to each other and were soon lost in their own private conversation.

The ladies' restroom at the Magic Banana was quite small, with two stalls and a double sink area. I was just drying my hands when Eleanor came to wash hers.

"I take it you're not enamored of the handsome young fae then?"

I smiled. "Is it that obvious?"

She grinned and rinsed off her hands. "He's certainly persistent. But I think you'll break my brother's heart if you give in to him."

I flushed and watched my cheeks blaze red in the mirror. "Oh, I most certainly wouldn't want that." She'd taken me completely by surprise. I mean, I'd hoped that Henry perhaps liked me as much as I liked him, but aside from some moody looks that were hard to read, he'd never actually indicated by word or deed that he had any feelings for me. Well, except perhaps that moment when I thought he might kiss me, but sometimes I wondered if I'd been wrong about that too. Yet here was Eleanor practically saying that Henry Tilney did have such feelings. I tried to act nonchalant, although the joy in my heart made me want to scream out loud.

"Hasn't he said anything to you yet? Poor Hank can be a little socially awkward. Sometimes my dear brother needs a good kick in the right direction."

I shook my head. "He hasn't had much of a chance. Isabella is always there in the day, and her brother sniffs around me like a love-sick dog when she's not. Whenever I try to get away, Isabella manages to invite herself along. Frankly, I'm surprised one of them isn't here in the restroom with us now."

Eleanor laughed and then looked thoughtful. "How would you like to come and spend a few days with us up at the Abbey? I'm sure Dad won't mind, and I'm pretty sure my brother would like it too."

Delighted beyond imagination, I bit my lip to stop from gushing like an idiot. What an amazing opportunity! At last, I'd be able to find out if Henry was truly interested in me, away from the watchful eyes of the terrible fae duo. Plus, I'd get a chance to see what Henry was like in his natural habitat. I wondered, was he as wonderful on his own turf as he appeared to be at Sylvia's shop, or would he have any annoying habits like leaving the top off the toothpaste and stuff like that?

"Sure, I would absolutely love that. You sure no one will mind?" By which I meant the General. I didn't want him getting mad or something.

"No, of course they won't. Well then, that's settled." Eleanor dried her hands under the automatic dryer. "I'll make sure Henry's free and will text you after dinner."

"Great!" I opened the door and let her leave ahead of me. As we returned to the table, I felt elated. I hadn't imagined an opportunity like this would come so soon, and I couldn't be happier it had.

As we approached, Henry stood up, allowing me to slip back into my seat. I took a sip of my lovely cocktail and settled into my chair, hoping he'd be pleased about this as I was.

"I can never understand why women always go to the bathroom in pairs." John chuckled, and we all laughed with him.

After all, nothing could spoil my evening now, not even John and his patronizing drivel. He could have said almost anything at that point, and I'd have laughed along. The only thing that mattered was the weekend ahead of me and what would happen if an opportune moment presented itself. As the talk turned to pudding, and my thoughts focused on apple crumble and custard, which would complement the Lancashire hot pot perfectly, I secretly dreamed of being alone with Henry. Of walking and talking to Henry. And if Gaia willed it, of being kissed by him. After all, a girl could hope, couldn't she?

Chapter Fifteen

YOUNG LOVE

I'D HAD A THOROUGHLY GOOD EVENING, EVEN THOUGH IT HAD PROVED A bit more expensive than I'd been led to believe. I didn't have to wait long to get the green light on the proposed trip—my phone dinged in the Magic Cab home, and Eleanor confirmed we were on.

"What are you grinning about?" John asked as he stared at my phone.

"Oh, just stuff."

He scowled. Fae were never ugly, but his black mood diminished the beauty of his face, and I saw the cunning and spite clearly behind the long lashes of his eyes. At last John was getting the hint that his attentions were unwanted.

As for Jimmy and Isabella, they might as well have been in a different cab for all the conversation we got from them. The occasional slurp told me they were kissing, an activity that had started the moment we'd left the restaurant. I'd made sure I was sitting at an angle to give them both privacy, and so I didn't have to watch them have at it. John, on the other hand, was staring right at them, and I was sure this view did nothing to help his mood.

"You know, it's rude to stare."

John glared at me but said nothing.

When we jumped out of the cab, Jimmy and Isabella ran straight into the apartment building, but I held back. It was bad enough sharing the cab with them. I certainly didn't want to listen to them snogging in the elevator.

Since no one else was offering, I paid the driver and watched as she sped off. From his stiff gait, I could tell John's expectations were low, but he hung back all the same.

"I guess somebody's happy." He cocked his head toward the building, but he wasn't smiling.

"They both seem very into each other." It felt an obvious thing to say—they had left us in no doubt about that.

"You and Henry seemed thick as thieves over dinner."

"Yes, yes, I suppose." I wanted to say that I liked him a hell of a lot but didn't feel the need to stick the knife in any deeper than I already had.

"Well then, I think I'll be off. You don't mind if I don't see you up to your apartment?"

I glanced at the revolving doors, which were about ten feet away, and grinned. "I think I'll be able to manage from here. Are you going to catch a cab home?"

John stared up at the cloudless sky. The stars were hidden in the glow of city lights. "No. I think I'll walk. I'll see you soon." I wondered if he could afford a cab and considered offering his fare, but then thought that might offend him. He certainly dressed well. But I was beginning to think that was all a show.

This time, there was no friendly kiss on the cheek or hug good-bye. He bent his head down thoughtfully and sloped off. I felt a little sorry for him, but not much. I had never led him on or encouraged him in any way and was relieved the message had finally got through. A brisk chill around my neck reminded me how cold it was, so I turned and went inside.

When I let myself into the apartment, Jimmy and Isabella were in full smooch on the sofa. They were so lost in themselves they didn't acknowledge my arrival, or ask after John, so I wondered if they'd even heard me come in. Not in the mood to play gooseberry, I slipped into my room, changed into my jimjams, and crawled on the bed. I amused myself for a few minutes looking at some pictures I'd taken over dinner. Somehow, I'd accidentally on purpose snapped Henry in almost every shot.

As I snuggled into my pillows, I stared at his face. I adored his face.

And in a few days, I would have him almost to myself. No Isabella or John. Just us and his family. I wanted so desperately for them all to love me. I thought about the General. That he was ambitious for his children was clear enough, and what father wouldn't be? I wondered what he thought about me. Did he think I was good enough for his younger son? I did not come from a rich and powerful family, that was for sure, and we certainly didn't live in anything as grand sounding as an abbey. I supposed he knew why I was here and what my particular skills were. I wanted him to think I was a hard worker, diligent at my studies, and worthy of the time Henry was spending on me.

I slipped out of bed and opened my bedroom door. Jimmy and Isabella were snuggled down on the couch, talking softly to themselves. Her long, beautiful wings were out and were wrapped about my brother in a cozy embrace. I thought of butterflies in love.

"Excuse me." I didn't expect an answer as I tiptoed softly over to the couch to pick up my magic book. For a second, I caught Jimmy's eye. He looked so happy, ensnared in her wings. I smiled and crept back to my room and carefully closed the door.

As soon as I was facedown on my bed, I opened the book. If the General admired diligence, then I would not disappoint him. I had come to New York to explore my magic, and that was exactly what I intended to do. No one would think of me as a slacker. I turned page after page, reading spells to heal the sick, spells to make you happy, spells to make you beautiful. All these things were commonplace enough, but I was looking for something very particular, something that would make an impression.

Tired, I rolled over onto my back and stared at the ceiling. It was late after all, and we'd had quite a night. The poor General. I'd had no idea he was a widower—Henry hadn't mentioned anything, but then again, why would he? It wasn't like we were a couple or anything—at least, not yet. I wondered how she'd died. The General didn't seem that old, so his wife probably wasn't either. Maybe that was why he was so interested in the medical profession. He was probably devastated at losing his wife so young—who wouldn't be? He probably missed her like crazy.

Hmmm. Love. Thinking about the two lovebirds outside made me think of Henry. I pictured him kissing me, just as they were kissing. I rolled over on my comforter, and with these pleasant thoughts in my mind, I soon fell asleep.

Chapter Sixteen

TOTALLY WICKED

OUT OF SIGHT WAS NOT OUT OF MIND. HENRY HAD MENTIONED SYLVIA and he emailed daily, and the next day I received an email of my own.

Hola! Henry tells me you're making excellent progress and that his sister invited you to the Abbey for a few days. I think this is an excellent idea, but don't neglect your studies. Use the opportunity to practice if you can. I'll be back before you go to keep an eye on Isabella. I'll see you on your return. Most of all, have fun. Toodle-oo. S.

Good. I felt better about going knowing I had the boss's blessing. I closed my laptop and left the bedroom. Isabella was up uncharacteristically early and was sitting crossed-legged on the sofa, chomping on a piece of toast. Her wings hung loosely behind her over the back of the couch.

She looked up as I approached, her happy smile telling me she was pleased with last night's developments.

"Well?" I plopped down beside her and stole a piece of toast from her plate. "Someone had a good time last night by all accounts."

Isabella leaned affectionately into me. "I did. Oh, I hope you don't mind, but you have to admit, your brother is gorgeous. I couldn't say no to him."

"I can see how you would think so."

She laughed. "Well, he's your brother, so I suppose you don't look at him the same way as I do. But trust me, he's a hottie. I should try to snap him up before he graduates and everyone else chases after him. After all, once he becomes a fully fledged doctor, there'll be women chasing him day and night, and he probably wouldn't give me a backward glance then."

I swallowed a large chunk of heavily buttered toast. "I wouldn't get ahead of yourself. After all, you only just met him last night." I didn't like my own tone, and fearful of offending Isabella, I pushed myself up off the sofa and went to make a coffee. "Sylvia's coming back, did you hear?"

"Yup, I got an email from her this morning. Pity. I was getting comfortable in there." She motioned over to her bedroom. "I suppose I'll have to move my stuff in with you. You'd better not snore."

"And you'd better not fart," I countered. Her eyes widened in shock as if she'd been scandalized, but then the corners of her lips curled upward in amusement.

Perhaps I should have told her about my invite to the Abbey, but I was jealous of my time alone with Henry and his family and afraid she might find a way to wheedle an invite of her own. In all honesty, I thought it a certainty she would try. Still, she would have to be told sooner or later—sooner really, if I didn't want Henry to accidentally blurt something out. I pondered how I might phrase it delicately.

Before we'd gone out last night, Isabella had been working on a good luck potion Henry had asked her to master. The stuffed bottle containing half the potion mix was sitting on the ledge over the sink, but there was a mass of congealed seaweed coating pretty much every inch of counter space, which she hadn't bothered to clean up. Irritated, I worked around it, determined not to do the job for her, though a part of me wanted to wipe it all up.

"I hope you're working on a cleaning spell."

Isabella barely looked around. "Oh, yeah, in a bit. Don't worry about it."

As the coffee chugged, I glanced at the time. It was still super early, but I supposed I ought to be thinking about getting ready for work.

"Do you want to use the bathroom first or should I?" I asked.

"Oh, you go ahead. I've already showered. Jimmy's coming over in a bit, and we're going out for the day."

I turned around, surprised. "You're not working today?"

Isabella shook her head. "Nah. I'll text Henry in a bit and tell him I have a headache. I'm sure he won't mind."

"Doesn't Jimmy have a class?"

Isabella shrugged and put her plate down on the side table. "He never said."

I thought about Jimmy's exams, which I knew would be coming up soon. Still, it was just one day. My brother was a hard worker, and it wasn't like he made a habit of skipping classes. I poured a lot of milk into my mug to cool down the freshly brewed coffee.

Without another word, I took my coffee into the bathroom with me and set the mug down on the sink. I sat on the toilet, not quite ready to jump in the shower but needing to be alone. I couldn't help wondering about that potion mix. I was pretty sure it had been full before we went out last night, but now there was less than half left. It couldn't have evaporated.

A nagging voice in the back of my head told me she'd used the other half on Jimmy. He would never have known if she had. It wasn't like he had to drink the stuff or anything. With that type of potion, you simply had to pop the cork and whisper an incantation to find the desired target. And there had been plenty of whispered words between them last night.

The *good luck* potion I knew Henry favored had almost the same ingredients as a Cupid's Arrow love potion, so it wouldn't be too difficult for Isabella to tweak it to get what she wanted. Then again, maybe she'd accidentally mixed the ingredients up a bit—potions weren't exactly her strong suit.

Hmmm. Perhaps it wasn't an *actual* love potion, but the idea of Isabella using magic to manipulate my brother's feelings was bad enough. The funny thing was, she probably didn't even need to use it. No one would say Isabella was short on charm. Half the guys that met her in the shop seemed ready to fall in love with her. She might of just spilled it or something. I wouldn't put it past her—tidiness was not her strong suit.

I chugged down the dregs of my coffee, and feeling a little more alert, I turned on the shower. As soon as the water was warm enough, I stripped off and stepped in. One good thing about Isabella playing truant was that I'd have Henry all to myself today. And though I was above mixing a good luck potion to make him desire me, I was not beyond upping my level of personal grooming and slapping on my favorite lippy. Thinking of Henry made me forget about Isabella and her shenanigans, and I began to smile. Today was going to be a good day—I could feel it in my bones. As I applied the conditioner onto my newly shampooed hair, I closed my eyes and with renewed dreams of kissing Henry, I began to sing: *"Sleigh bells and love spells, music and wands..."*

Henry was serving an older witch when I arrived at work, so I acknowledged him with a wave and headed straight to the back room where I intended to start assembling the day's orders. Fully expecting to be alone, my heart skipped a beat when a young man stepped right in front of me, barring my path and looking down at me from a great height. He must have been six feet three at least and positively oozed charm and sex appeal.

"Whoa there, lady. Customers aren't allowed in the back. Not unless they're willing to pay a toll for the privilege."

There was a self-assured twinkle in his eye, and his gaze roved freely over my body, head to toe. Cheeky brute. I correctly guessed several things at once. This guy was used to getting his own way, he was typically very successful with the ladies, and since the family resemblance was unmistakable, this had to be the infamous brother, Freddy Tilney.

"I'm not a customer. I work here." I slipped around him and retrieved my apron from the hook on the back of the door. Judging by his grin, Freddy knew this already and was just messing with me. His look softened as he switched to adorable boy mode, but I remembered being warned about him and resolved not to allow myself to be swayed by his charm. "You must be Freddy. I've heard a lot about you."

The bad boy grin didn't falter for a second. "Totally wicked, I'm sure."

"That about sums it up."

Freddy sat down at one of the tables. He picked up a bar of coal tar soap, sniffed it, and pretended to examine it closely, but I knew he was really studying me. It crossed my mind that he was nothing at all like his brother, Henry. Even if I hadn't been warned about him, there was something unsettling about this man that told me to be on my guard and not be fooled by his easy banter.

"I'm guessing you're Catherine." He looked behind me as if expecting someone to materialize at my shoulder. "Where's the other one?"

"Isabella?"

"Yes. I've heard a lot about her *too*."

I didn't like the *too* part of that provocative sentence but thought it wiser to ignore it. "She isn't coming in today."

"Pity. I came specially to see her." Freddy pursed his lips. "Henry says you're coming to the house for a bit of a party this weekend, and I find myself at rather a loose end. I thought I might invite your friend to join us for some fun. Do you think she'd come if I asked?"

I shook my head. "I think she's already made social plans for this weekend. Maybe some other time?"

"Yeah, perhaps." Freddy put down the bar of soap, and the pungent smell lingered in the air. I thought he might be waiting for Henry to join us, but instead he got up and made to leave. I heard a faint hiss behind me and turned to see a tabby kitten had arched its back and was as rigid as a broomstick.

Freddy grimaced at the kitten but didn't comment on its obvious dislike for him.

I bit my lip to hide my grin. "Not a cat person, then?"

"No, not my favorite mammals."

I wondered if he were allergic to them. Or if they were to him.

"Well, it was lovely meeting you, Catherine, but the day's getting away from me. I may or may not see you this weekend, we'll see. Anyway, it was a pleasure. Bye for now."

I watched as Freddy made his exit through the store. Henry was still working with the older witch, and the two brothers merely nodded as the elder passed through on his way out. It seemed Freddy really *had* come to check out Isabella and, having been thwarted, saw no need to overstay his welcome. As soon as the bell over the door jingled and Freddy was gone, I returned to the table and picked up the list of daily orders. So that was the older Tilney brother. Well, well, well. I had no doubt now he was every bit as wicked as his brother had suggested he could be. At least the kitten seemed to think so. And my feminine intuition was screaming he could be a hell of a lot more. Much, much more.

Henry shot a look in my direction, and I could tell he was curious about what we'd been talking about. I smiled mischievously and left him to it. A minute or so later, the bell over the door signaled the customer had finally left, and then Henry dashed into the back.

"No Isabella?"

"Sick. Didn't she send you a text?"

"Maybe. I haven't had a chance to look. There was a run on hoof oil. So you met Freddy?"

I nodded, and to conceal my smile, I pretended to be interested in a pile of parsley bundles laid out neatly on the table. I picked out one whose leaves were turning black and tossed it into the trash bin beside the table.

Henry stood stiffly beside me, checking the messages on his phone, but I could tell he expected me to say more. Perhaps it was bad of me, but I loved his uncertainty—and perhaps, jealousy?

"Did he say he was coming home this weekend or not?"

I shook my head. "He wasn't sure. You know, he looks a lot like you. Taller though."

Henry looked at me askew, and I suspected he would have loved to read my mind right now. I knew he wouldn't, not without my permission, but he was probably dying to just the same.

"So what did he say?"

I pulled some of the parsley leaves and began crushing them in the large stone mortar. "He didn't say a lot. He was more interested in Isabella than anything. What did you tell him about her?"

It was Henry's turn to look coy. "Not much."

I couldn't hide my smile this time and focused on crushing the leaves. "Well then. Now we both know as much as each other."

Seeing he was getting nowhere, Henry changed tack. "I was thinking I should go back to the apartment with you on Friday. We can take share a Magic Cab if you like. My sister keeps the truck when I'm in town, so I usually ride the subway, but it'll be easier to take a cab with your bags."

"Oh, right, yeah, seems sensible. I don't have a lot of gear, but the book is kinda heavy." Distracted by the conversation, I lost my grip on the pestle, and it shot out of my hand and onto the floor. We both reached for it, but he got there first, and I almost banged my head into his on the way back up.

"Ugh, sorry." Sometimes I could be such a klutz.

Henry put the pestle down flat on the table as the bell heralded a new customer. "Well, I better get back to it. Let me know if you need anything."

"Sure." I watched him disappear into the shop, a little annoyed that he hadn't kissed me. I really hoped he would try to, and soon.

Chapter Seventeen

THE WARLOCK BACHELOR

ISABELLA SAT IN MY BEDROOM, STARING IDLY AT HER REFLECTION IN THE mirror, lost in thought. I decided now was as good a time as ever. "We'll be gone for a few days, at least until Henry or Sylvia tell me I have to come back to work."

"What? Oh yeah, right."

Earlier I'd read an interesting spell on levitation and had been toying with Sylvia's Rubik's cube ever since, though without much luck. I was on my back as it floated two feet over my head. Getting it up there was one thing, but rotating it to solve the puzzle was giving me trouble, and it kept bobbing up and down. Plus, it wasn't the only thing above me. Lacy hosiery was caught up in the chandelier, and tubes of lipstick and hairbrushes were floating in the air. I tried hard to focus on the puzzle, but Isabella's tone was so uncharacteristically nonchalant that my concentration wavered, and the cube fell and smacked me square on the forehead.

Isabella didn't even notice. She continued to stare into the mirror.

I swung my legs off the bed. "Is everything okay? You sound a bit funny."

"Oh yeah, I suppose."

"Jimmy coming over later?" There was no reason to suppose he wouldn't be. My brother couldn't seem to leave her alone now—there was a new notification from him on her phone every few minutes.

"Err, no, not tonight. I, uhm, well, I have an old friend coming into town, so I put him off. I'll see Jimmy tomorrow I think."

"Oh, right."

Isabella swung round, picked up the Rubik's cube, and fiddled with it. "You doing anything fun with Henry tonight?"

I shook my head. "Not that I know of. I was thinking of just having a quiet night in. We've been eating out quite a bit lately, and I need to watch my funds."

"I hear ya. Well, I had thought about bringing my friend back, but since you'll be in, I'll make myself scarce—give you a bit of room. You're probably tired of seeing my face night after night."

Hungry, I pushed myself up off the bed and sauntered over to the door. "Don't be silly. I'm gonna fix myself a PB and J. You want one?"

Isabella shook her head and stood up. "No thanks, I'll be eating out. In fact, I'd better get a move on. Clock's ticking."

I had to admit, I wasn't sad to have a little me time. There were some complex spells I wanted to practice, and though Isabella and I both regularly practiced magic, I felt self-conscious over some of the trickier stuff. Henry had tasked me to practice a calling spell, somewhat like the magic I had used on the red squirrel. Since we were in an apartment building, I thought I would try it on a starling: they were common enough in New York.

So while Isabella strolled into the bathroom to dip her wings in cold cream, I grabbed a loaf and some jars from the refrigerator and set about making my dinner. I would save some of my bread to offer to the bird.

Ten minutes later, Isabella emerged from the bathroom, and I caught my breath.

"Holy Gaia! You look stunning! This must be some friend."

A wry smile twisted her glossed-up lips. "You could say that." She removed her coat from the back of the door, and before I could ask any more questions, she pulled it on and turned, her hand already on the handle, ready to go. "Ciao, bella." Then she blew me a cute kiss and was gone, leaving only the whiff of her captivating perfume behind.

If she wasn't seeing Jimmy tonight, I wondered who she was seeing, dressed as a goddess like that. More importantly, my tummy was gurgling, so I focused on my dinner and forgot all about her.

It was the perfect night. Snuggled cross-legged under Sylvia's oversize throw, I ate a whole plateful of PB and Js and read this new summoning spell most carefully. When I had summoned the squirrel at the Allen's house, all I had to do was put my hand on Sylvia's spell book and think of a squirrel. My text made no mention of putting my hand anywhere. The incantation looked very unfamiliar, and everything felt—well—just different.

There was nothing for it. I would have to trust that Henry wouldn't lead me astray and that this was the correct spell.

I'd had no idea how the magic worked, and suspected that in some part, Sylvia had helped me when I was with her. This was confirmed when I first spoke the words written in the book:

"Hrînan ðēon me."

At first, I heard nothing, but then I could hear a chaotic whoosh of air as a ton of birds flocked to the window of my apartment, their tiny wings beating frantically as they reached the glass.

"Shoot." I stopped concentrating, and the birds flew away. Thank Gaia I hadn't opened the window, or I'd have been cleaning up bird poop for the rest of the evening.

Still, there had been some success, even if on a larger scale than I'd desired. I shouldn't have been surprised—I'd had the same problem with the Necromancer's Stone in Times Square. I read the text again, but there was nothing in the words to focus the energy on an individual subject. I flipped through the pages of my book, looking for something smaller that could help me, but found nothing...at least, nothing I could practice without considerable risk to myself or the apartment.

After about an hour, I gave it up as a bad job and decided I would ask Henry about it in the morning. That was the sensible thing to do. My father would approve.

Since I was all caught up on all my other studies, I put my book aside and settled down in front of the television and watched the season finale of

The Warlock Bachelor. I went through a whole box of Kleenex as Dexter and Julienne broke their disguise enchantments, proving you couldn't deny true love. Somehow it always found a way. Still sobbing tears of joy, I scrambled off the couch and hit the sack sometime around midnight, thoroughly exhausted.

In the middle of the night, I woke with a start. The walls in the apartment were thin, leaving me in no doubt what was going on in the next room. It seemed Isabella had hooked up with Jimmy after all. The two of them were going at it like stoats. I picked up my phone. *Oh Gaia, three a.m.?*

I flopped back on my pillow and tried to get back to sleep, but it was hopeless. The giggles and thumping were just too loud—they were having way too good of a time bonking next door. I thought about Henry and wondered if we would ever get that far? *Praise the day.* I was too tired to cherish such thoughts for very long.

I thought about banging on the wall. Indeed, my fist was literally in the air, and then I thought of Jimmy and how he wouldn't thank me for interrupting him. Whatever he was doing. Tired beyond belief, I whispered *"Rîm scêap,"* mimicking the counting sheep spell Mom had taught us all as kids—only she'd used a sparkling powder. A burst of green light exploded over my head, and around a hundred or so tiny green sheep were skipping through a meadow. After counting at least thirteen little furries dancing in the air, my eyelids grew heavy, and I was out like a light. Thank Gaia.! I didn't want to stay awake through that.

Chapter Eighteen

GOOD LUCK POTION

"I THINK IT'S TIME YOU CONSIDERED BUYING A GOOD WAND." HENRY was sipping a brew of something thick and licoricey that could probably have resurfaced a road. It looked like total ick to me, but since I didn't have to drink it, I didn't have to like it. It smelled better than it looked. "This sounds like a focusing issue, and though you don't need a wand, it'll help get you started."

"Yes, you're probably right." I knew Mom would have a fit if she could hear me, but I was a big girl now, and I was here to learn all I could. If that meant I needed a new wand, then a new wand I should have.

Ironically enough, that was the one magical item Sylvia didn't stock. You needed a special license to sell wands, not to mention the increase she would need in security and insurance. "Where's the best place to get a good one—on a budget?"

Henry, who had been taking a wee break after restocking Sylvia's supply of holly berries ahead of the solstice, put down his mug and scratched his chin. "There's a few places I can think of. Nicholas and Greer's is the best, but I can barely afford the bags in that place. Duck Bills is dirt cheap, but the wands are a bit dicey and tend to fail after a couple of years. One minute you're casting a watering spell, and the next second there's a tsunami in Peru. Do not go. You should try Midas Banks. Never mind the name, her stuff is reasonably priced, and she won't rip you off. It's the closest."

"Just how many wands shops are there in the city?"

"A fair few. There's a lot of demand, so why wouldn't there be?"

I couldn't argue with his logic and closed up my book. Our break was over. It was time to get back to work. "Well, I just hope they're not too expensive, even the cheap ones." I stashed my book inside my bag and stowed it under the table. My favorite kitten, a pretty little ginger I called Hex, although none of them had actually been given names, came and sat beside it. When Henry wasn't looking, I tickled her under her chin—she was the only one who let me.

"They can run from a few hundred dollars to thousands."

My heart sank. I'd just sent some of my wages home to Mom, and my funds were getting low. "What if I didn't get a wand? Is there any other way to focus the magic?"

Henry, who was heading to the front of the store, stopped in his tracks and slapped his forehead. "Gaia, am I an idiot or what?"

I stared at him, my brow knitted in confusion.

He pointed to my hand. "The ring. You have a perfectly good focusing object right there."

I toyed with the azurite ring on my finger. "Instead of a wand?"

"Sure. It can work just as well as a wand, possibly even better if you learn to use it right. We can talk about it later, okay?"

"Sure."

Funny. I hadn't thought about the ring in forever. It was funny how quickly you could become so forgetful of something around your fingers, no matter how unfamiliar or heavy it had seemed at first. Yet I had. On the upside, this at least wouldn't cost me a dime, and that made me a happy bunny indeed.

I was reaching for some empty recyclable glass vials when my phone vibrated in my pocket. I pulled it out and saw a missed call from Jimmy. I grimaced. I really, really didn't want to talk about what I'd heard last night. All of that was between him and Isabella, not me, and though I couldn't be certain that was what he wanted, I didn't want to take the chance that it might be.

All tied up. Call later.

I shot off the quick text and put my phone back inside my pocket, and then pulled the vials toward me and said, "*Âðierran.*" In a flash, they were all freshly sanitized and ready for reuse. My phone buzzed again. Sighing, I whipped it out. *Might as well get this over with.*

"Hey, Jimmy, what's up? I can't talk long. I'm at work."

"Hey, you, I was trying to reach Isabella, but she's not answering her phone. Is she with you?" His tone was anxious.

Young love. Like I can talk. "No. Maybe she's in the shower. From what I heard, it was quite a night."

"Oh, right. Made a bit of a night of it, did she? She said she was meeting up with an old friend."

I caught my breath and switched my phone to the other ear. "Wait. What? You weren't with her last night?"

"Me, no. She told me she had plans. I guess she got home kinda late."

Son of a banshee. My heart sank. What on earth was I supposed to say now? I had to think. Maybe I'd got it wrong. I'd been half-asleep last night, after all. "I, um, I suspect she's lying in. She was—err—off sick yesterday, and I assumed she was pulling the same stunt today. I'd try her again. If you don't hear from her, call me later when I get home. I'm sure she's just in recovery mode."

"Yeah. You're probably right." The phone went dead, and I stared at the wall. Could I have been wrong? Now that Jimmy was gone, I had time to think more clearly. There was no way I'd misheard the party in the room next to mine. *No. Freakin'. Way.*

I dialed Isabella's number, but it went straight into her voice mail. "Hi—it's me. Call me when you get a moment. Bye."

I stared at the vials, trying to think but my mind was a total blank. I strolled into the main store where Henry was atop a ladder, rotating some of the stock on the top shelf. He glanced down, and seeing me hanging about, he slid down the side of the ladder like a boss.

"How are you doing with those vials?"

"All done." I stared at my feet.

Henry must have noticed something was up because the next thing I knew, his hand was on my shoulder. "Is something the matter?"

"Did Isabella call in today? I confess, I didn't bother checking to see she was all right this morning, but it's not like her to say nothing at all."

He shook his head. "Not a thing. I texted her earlier, but she didn't text back. I just assumed her head was still bad."

I really wanted to tell him what I'd heard last night, but Henry was Isabella's boss, or was good as, and I didn't want to get her into any trouble. "Yeah, most likely. Anyway, what do you want me to do with those vials now they're all cleaned up?"

"As soon as they're dry, fill them up with Isabella's good luck potion. The last batch she made for me was pretty good. Just filter them and pop a cork in."

"Sure."

I must have sounded flat because Henry crooked his finger under my chin and tilted my head up. "Are you sure you're okay?" His gaze searched mine, and I stared at my hands, afraid I might give something away.

"Yeah, just tired. I had to spell myself to sleep last night." I'm not sure he bought my excuse, but he let me go.

"If she doesn't check in soon, maybe you should head out early tonight and check on her."

"You sure you wouldn't mind?"

He grinned. "I think so. Help me through the lunch rush and then head on home. I can hold the fort here. It's not like I haven't done it before."

"Thank you. I'll come in bright and early tomorrow to make up the time."

"There's no need. You've earned it, really. I was telling Sylvia last night what a hard worker you are. I'm sure she wouldn't mind."

I blushed and returned to the back of the store. The jar of good luck potion Isabella had made was sitting by the sink. I collected it and sat at the worktable. As I began filtering the liquid into the vials, I thought about Isabella. She was a big girl, I supposed. She and Jimmy had hardly been an item for long, and it was her business what she did or didn't do with her own body. That said, I couldn't help thinking about what it would do to my brother when he found out, as he inevitably would. I knew Jimmy. He had fallen for her and fallen hard. I didn't even want to think of what this would do to him.

I spilled a little of the potion on the table. "Shoot. Money down the toilet." I wiped up the mess with an old rag and shook these thoughts from my head. I had a hundred or so vials to fill before lunch and needed to concentrate. My brother's love life would have to wait for the time being. I slipped the spout of the filter inside one of the vials and focused on the task at hand.

Chapter Nineteen

TRUE LOVE

I HADN'T EVEN GOT MY PONCHO OFF WHEN I HEARD SYLVIA'S SLIGHTLY raised voice coming from her bedroom.

"Well, whatever was wrong with you, you seem perfectly fine now. I'm sure you'll be right as rain for work tomorrow."

Isabella replied, but I didn't quite catch what she said.

"Never mind, I'll make the bed myself. Just pick your clothes up off the floor, and I'll see to the rest myself. There's a dear."

The door opened, and Isabella emerged, her wings drooping in a sulk, though she rolled her eyes when she saw me. She was still in her flimsy night dress, and I wondered if she'd been in it all day—though a wicked thought in my head told me she might have just put it back on. Had Sylvia walked in on her *in flagrante delicto*? That would have been something to see.

"Hey, Cat. I didn't hear you come in. Raining, huh?"

I hung my poncho up and tucked my wet hair behind my ears. "You could say that." Rain didn't cover it. It was coming down violently out there, and I hadn't thought to take my umbrella with me. "I guess I'll be staying in tonight."

Sylvia popped out behind her. I'd hung my poncho over her gray velvet cloak on the hook behind the door, but she was dressed quite formally in her elegant silver dress and shimmering scarf, and didn't look like she'd been home long enough to settle in. I now noticed her travel bag, sitting unpacked beside the sofa. Her tight lips and harangued expression told me she wasn't best pleased with how things were in the apartment. I shot a glance across to the kitchen. Apart from several mugs and cereal bowls, it didn't appear too bad. There were also two wineglasses. Jimmy didn't drink wine.

"Well, hello, dear. My, my, don't you look like a drowned rabbit. I guess I just missed it." She checked her watch. "You're home a little early. Is there anything wrong at the store?"

I shook my head. "No, nothing at all. Henry sent me to check on Isabella."

"Ah, right. I'll unpack and then boil some water so we can all have some tea."

I had to confess I felt less than delighted as Isabella took her stuff into my room. Well, I'd come to think of it as mine, even if it wasn't.

"It's okay. I'll put the kettle on." I went straight to the kitchen and poured some water into the empty kettle, mesmerized by the hollow sound as the water gushed in. Anything was better than thinking about Isabella and who she'd been with last night, though part of me was dying to know. If it hadn't been Jimmy, then who was it? If Sylvia hadn't been home, I'd have had it out with her. After all, we were guests in this apartment, and it could have been *anyone*, and *anything* could have happened. It didn't sit well with me that I'd been asleep with a total stranger in the next room. All right, maybe Isabella was there, but did I really know her? The more I thought about it, the more I wound myself up.

"Thank you, dear. I'll be done in a jiffy." Sylvia closed her bedroom door.

All alone again, I set to clearing the dishes. I could have used magic, but I didn't want to join Isabella in the bedroom just yet and was grateful for the distraction. I'd cleared some drawers out for her earlier and figured she could work the rest out for herself. She usually did.

I was drying the glasses when Isabella emerged from our room. She shimmied straight over to me and leaned close to whisper. "You'll never guess!"

"What? That you're not sick and have been fooling around with some dude in Sylvia's bedroom all afternoon?"

Isabella pulled back. "Wow. How did you guess that?"

"It's a bit obvious after what when on last night."

She blushed pink. "Oh. You heard that?"

I rolled my eyes. "Like I had a choice?"

Isabella grinned and grabbed hold of my arm. "Oh, Cat. He was so amazing! I never thought a man like that would even look at me twice, let alone—well—you know. I think this time it's true love."

I thought about what she'd said about meeting up with an old friend and decided to be charitable. "Well, just promise me this. Whatever you do, let my brother down gently, okay? He's a good guy. He deserves that at least."

To be fair to Isabella, she had the grace to color a little more. "I will, I promise. I mean, I like your brother a lot. He's sweet, but Freddy Tilney's in another class entirely. The man's just so dashing and rich, and before long, I couldn't say no to him. He's clearly used to getting whatever he wants."

I turned to face her, leaving a mug suspended in midair.

"Wait! What? You're telling me you're seeing Freddy Tilney?"

"Sure, why not? He said you'd met him. Isn't he just gorgeous?"

My brain sprinted to catch up. "But I thought you said this was an old friend? Someone you'd known for a long time."

Isabella squished her face up and tried to look all cute and playful. It didn't work on me. "Did I say that? Oh well, maybe it came out wrong. Oh, don't look at me like that, Cat. It's love. True love. I couldn't help myself, really, I couldn't." She sighed, as if remembering a delicious moment.

The kettle whistled, and I used the excuse to turn and finish putting tea into the infuser. I was irritated by the idea she thought everything was outside her control. What, she had no will of her own? If I knew anything about Isabella, I knew *that* was a load of toad poop.

"Just remember what I said, will you? Break it to Jimmy gently. He likes you a lot."

Isabella stood with her back to the counter, her wings folded gently around her hips. "I will. Eventually. Just not yet."

I felt a flash of rage, but I swallowed my bile. It took all my self-control not to shout at her. "Why not? The sooner the better. Would you rather I spoke to him?"

She shook her head. "No, no. I'll do it. Give me a day or so, please. I *really* do like him. Give me a day or so to think."

I clunked her mug down on the counter, furious. "Don't leave him dangling too long. If you haven't told him by the time I get back from the Abbey, then I will."

Out of the corner of my eye, I saw Isabella cast me a sly, mischievous look. I had half a mind to call Jimmy up then and there but wanted to give her the chance to do the right thing. I guessed a few days wouldn't hurt. Jimmy was unlikely to die of a broken heart in so short a time. At least I hoped he wouldn't.

So this was true love, then? If my own encounter with Freddy Tilney had been anything to go by, then I very much doubted it, but perhaps I was being unkind. I knew too little about fae to understand the depth of their true feelings, and no one who looked at Isabella could question her beauty. She was entitled to true love as much as the next person, but one comment still stuck in my craw and made me doubt her sincerity. "Dashing and *rich*." Those were her exact words. Was that her true motive after all? No one who knew us would believe we were rich, but Jimmy was a med student with prospects. And everyone seemed to be supposing we came from money. To be fair, I had done nothing at all to dispel this notion, but then why should I?

"This is awesome tea," Isabella said. She peered at me over her mug, and I knew what she was thinking. She wanted us to be friends again and for this conversation to be over. Come to think of it, so did I.

"Glad you like it. How about we order Chinese tonight? There's not a lot in, and I don't fancy going out in this rain."

Sylvia chose that moment to emerge from her room. She had changed into a more casual black dress with fringe tassels, and her hair was loosely tied up on her head. She looked pretty tired, but less grumpy than when I first saw her. "That's an excellent notion. I'm buying, and you girls can tell me how you're doing over dinner." She took the offered mug of tea from my hand and snuggled down on the edge of the sofa, curling her feet up under her.

Isabella shook her head. "Sorry, I'd love to, but I can't. I told Freddy I'd go out with him later. In fact, he's probably on his way over right now."

Sylvia's reply was indifferent. I got the impression she had yet to warm to our fae friend. "Oh, if you must. Another time, perhaps. All the more for me and Cat," she added cheerily.

Isabella clasped her mug and took it through to our bedroom. I thought she was being a little bit rude. After all, by all accounts, the two had never met, and Sylvia was doing her a huge favor giving her not only a job but also providing her with bed and board. Still, who was I to argue? All I knew was if it had been me, I'd have canceled with Freddy and met him some other time. But Isabella was Isabella. Maybe, if I were lucky, she would stay gone the whole night and I would have the bed all to myself. If only.

"Well now, how are you progressing through that magic book I got for you? It's much easier, isn't it, having a book all your own?"

I sat down on the smaller love seat opposite her and cradled my hot tea in both hands. "Yes, it really is. Thank you for finding it for me."

Pleased, Sylvia waved her hand dismissively. "Don't mention it. Is everything else going okay?"

"Yes, yes, I think so. I enjoy working at the shop, and I've met all sorts of wonderful people. Henry has me practice a new spell from the book every day, but I'm struggling a little with focus work."

"Oh, well, that can be tricky. Lots of people struggle with that at first." Sylvia's smile did little to reassure me I wasn't letting her down. I had so hoped to ace at everything, and I didn't want her to think I wasn't trying my hardest.

"I am working on it, and Henry said we could spend some time on it while I'm at the Abbey."

Sylvia's kind smile didn't falter. "I'm sure you will. Just don't let it be all about work. Sometimes it's good to have a little fun, you know. Take a leaf out of Isabella's book. She seems to have no trouble at all having a good time."

"I will, I promise. So how was your trip? Did you get what you wanted?"

"Not quite, but I made a solid beginning and made a lot of new contacts. These things take time. It will all come together when it needs to, I'm sure."

Sylvia yawned and closed her eyes for a moment. I wondered if she needed a nap, but she opened them quickly enough when Isabella came out of the bedroom, dressed in a pink shirt with peekaboo cutouts on the shoulders and discreet slits in the back for her wings. Her beautiful hair tumbled loosely over her shoulders, and her skin looked naturally vibrant. Unlike me, she had the sense to carry a clear plastic umbrella. She had no time for small talk but made straight for the door and pulled on her coat.

"Freddy not coming up?" I kept my tone as upbeat as I could.

"No, I said I'd meet him in the lobby. You ladies have a lovely night, and I'll see you later. I'm not sure what he has in mind, so don't wait up."

"Okay."

As soon as the door closed behind her, with a swish of her hand, Sylvia magically opened a drawer in the table by the sofa, and a takeaway menu bearing the Laughing Dragon emblem levitated her way.

"Japanese, did you say?"

"Yes, please."

Sylvia quickly scanned the paper and tapped her lips thoughtfully. "I'm in the mood for sushi." She closed the paper up and held it out to me. "Can you summon this?"

I nodded. *"For-ðyldian hêore."* We both watched as the menu hovered in the air and drifted across the room to where I was sitting. It landed neatly in my hand.

"You had no trouble with that," Sylvia remarked.

"No, because it's not alive. And if I'd lost my focus for one second, it would have fallen." I rubbed my forehead, remembering the Rubik's cube. "You should have seen me trying to summon a starling yesterday. I thought the entire flock was going to come through the window!"

Sylvia smiled. "It's a ley line thing. Nothing that Henry can't fix. Do you know what you want?

I quickly checked out the menu. "Tempura, please."

"Splendid." Sylvia summoned the menu back, and with another swish of her hand, the menu glowed brightly, and the face of a harried Chinese woman appeared in the air. "Two California rolls, two tempura rolls, two miso soups, and, um, add on a bowl of rice for me."

"Delivery or pick up?"

"Delivery."

"Cash or charge?"

"Charge, please."

"Forty minutes. Bye." The image popped, and the woman was gone.

"They're always so busy, but I never order anywhere else." Sylvia plumped up a couple of cushions and settled into her seat. "There, now, we're all set. Why don't you make another cup of your excellent tea, and then we can have a proper catch-up?"

I got up grinning, pleased to have some time to spend with Sylvia before heading off to the Abbey. There was so much to tell her, so much I had seen and learned. Even so, there were some things I couldn't share, not yet. I hoped she wouldn't guess at my feelings regarding Henry. As my employer, I was afraid she wouldn't like it. Not that anything had happened as such, but still.

"Well. What exactly do you want to know?" I refilled the kettle, and after rinsing both our old mugs, I went back to the sofa.

"Well, for a start, what do you think of Isabella?"

Ugh. I'd kind of hoped to dodge that question. I was still angry with Isabella for messing about with my brother's feelings, but I didn't want her fired for it. "She's great. We practice our spells together after work. She helps me with ley line spells, and I help her with potions." That was true enough, and I thought it a reasonable answer. I sighed, remembering Isabella's heat spell, which I was only now beginning to master.

"Well, don't worry. She has an advantage; fae children have magical blood and are born with certain basic skills."

"I still wish I was as good as her at it."

"But you are adept at earth magic. It is your calling, and that's an entirely different type of magic—it's potentially far more powerful, and it's something fae have difficulty getting to grips with. Putting you together was an excellent idea, I thought."

I nodded. That was true, as far as it went.

Sylvia stretched out a sleepy yawn before fixing her intelligent eyes on mine. "What in Gaia's name is she thinking, dallying with Henry's brother?"

Wow. I had no idea that she knew exactly who Freddy was. Had she heard us from the bedroom? If not, Sylvia was better informed than I would have guessed. Indeed, it wouldn't surprise me if somehow, she knew everything that had happened since she left. "I've no idea. I only just learned she was seeing him a few minutes ago."

"Silly girl. That man goes through women like Kleenex. It'll all end in tears, you mark my words."

I couldn't have agreed more. The only question was, whose tears were most likely to fall?

Ding! The food arrived, filling the room with wonderful food smells. And it was delivered by a handsome young man who offered Sylvia a bow and smiled at us before vanishing...more's the pity.

Chapter Twenty

HOME SWEET HOME

SYLVIA HELD THE DOOR AJAR AS BLEARY-EYED ISABELLA DRAGGED herself from the bedroom. Her hair was not as glossy as usual, and she looked like she'd had quite a night. Not that I felt any pity for her. After all, she'd stumbled in around two in the morning and had flopped unceremoniously on the bed, waking me up with all her noise and fussing.

"Come on, sweetie, don't be tardy. There's a lot to do at the shop today."

Judging by the twinkle in Sylvia's eye, I suspected she rather enjoyed inflicting a little torture on Isabella in her current state.

I shared a knowing grin with Sylvia and closed up my own bag, which was all packed and ready for my trip to the Abbey. *Hah! No work for me today!* "Morning, Isabella. How's the head?"

Isabella grunted an inaudible response and stepped into the hall. I assumed that meant she'd had a good time.

"Well, hello, inside!" Henry appeared, knocking on the open door, his handsome smile fixed on his face as he surveyed the action within. His gaze met mine. "Hey, you! Are you all set? I have a cab waiting downstairs."

"Yup, just about." I got up, fighting the impulse to run out of the apartment, desperate to keep my cool. I pulled on my poncho and went to grab the bag, but Henry beat me to it.

"I'll take that. Is this everything?"

I had packed just the one bag, which hadn't been too heavy until I'd shoved the magic book inside. Henry threw it over his shoulder like it was nothing at all and went to join Isabella, who was waiting in the hall, surveying the carpet.

With a wave of her hand, Sylvia had everything locked up. We all bundled inside the elevator, and Henry hit the down button. I totally ignored the meaningful looks Isabella kept shooting me and tried not to feel too smug about having these few days off.

Once we were all through the revolving doors that led to the sidewalk, Sylvia gave Henry and me one of her European kisses. "You guys have fun, and Henry, don't work Cat too hard. I want you both back fit and able to work in the shop, okay?"

"I promise I'll be gentle," Henry said.

Even Isabella managed a faint grin at that. "Don't stay away too long," she said. "It won't be much fun without you."

I kissed Isabella on the cheek. She really did look sorry to see me go. There was an unusual sadness in her eyes, and I wondered if she'd had as much fun last night as I'd assumed she'd had. I gave her a gentle squeeze. "I'll see you soon."

Isabella nodded, and from her weak smile, I knew I was right. Something was up. Since I had to go, I decided to text her later when I got to the Abbey.

"Come on, the meter's running." Henry had opened the cab door and was waiting for me to jump inside.

"Sorry, I gotta run. I'll text you later." I turned and bundled ungraciously into the back of the cab. Henry squeezed in beside me, and once the door was closed, we were off!

Wally the troll was our driver again. He'd picked us up a few times now, and I remembered his name from the medallion inside the cab.

It felt surreal, just me and Henry, like we were off for some strange dirty weekend, only sadly without the dirt—though I lived in hope. "This feels weird, don't you think?"

Henry turned to look at me. "What does?"

"This. Not having Isabella squeezing in beside us, with John in tow."

"Ha-ha, yes, it does feel weird, doesn't it? Nice weird, not creepy weird." I would have liked him to carry on in that vein, but Henry's phone buzzed. He pulled it from his pocket and stared at the screen. "It's Sylvia. She's probably being nosy. Hold on."

While Henry texted a response, I turned to look out of the window. We were heading uptown toward the Upper East Side. I kept smiling, excited to be here at last, free of distractions and interruptions. I breathed in deeply, relishing the hope and anticipation, wanting to bottle this moment forever.

When I turned back, Wally was watching me via the rearview mirror. I noticed he had some new, pink furry dice hanging there. I didn't think I'd seen them before.

"Are they new?" I pointed to them.

Wally raised a chubby finger and gave them a little push. "Yes. They're a present."

He was crunched up in the front of the cab, all four hundred pounds of him, and was driving much slower than the flow of traffic, totally oblivious to the mayhem he was causing in his wake. Not surprisingly, NYC's impatient drivers were somewhat vocal about this.

"Get the hell off the road, you big moron!"

"Ain't you got some place to be, ya loser!"

Yet despite the honks and shrieks from other city drivers, Wally's pleasant smile remained fixed on his face, like he had all the time in the world to get where he was going. For once, I didn't mind either.

"Do you have any kids, Wally?"

Wally's eyes softened. He spoke very slowly and thoughtfully. "Not yet. But I just met the perfect troll-lady on Trollmatch dot com so maybe one day if she likes me enough."

"What's she like?"

His grin widened. "Bigger than I am. She got more strands of hair than most lady trolls. I don't know how I got so lucky, but to me, she's perfect."

Although his head remained down, Henry chuckled at the response. He took a deep breath and stowed his phone away. "You think she's the one then, Wally?"

Wally's skin tone darkened, and I realized he was blushing. "Maybe. I just hope I don't scare her off like the others."

I couldn't imagine how. "She'd be lucky to have you. I think you're wonderful."

Wally's blush deepened. "Thank you. You are very nice lady. Your boyfriend very lucky."

While talking, his focus had been a little off the road, and another Magic Cab driver swerved to miss him, almost crashing into the center island, and was forced to take to the air. "Wally, you complete m—"

Wally put his hand out of the window and waved, though he didn't slow down. "Sorry."

"Um, Henry's not my boyfriend. We, err, we just work together." *Awkward.*

"Aww, that a shame. He ought to whisk you up quick, pretty girl like you, before some other wizard does."

"You think so?" Henry had a wicked glint in his eye.

"Sure. I would. If she were bigger."

I couldn't help but laugh and was secretly pleased Wally talked about me that way. Maybe Henry would take the hint and do something about it. Or maybe I should do something about it myself. I sat back in my seat and pondered my options. I supposed straddling him and sticking my tongue down his throat before lots of wild witchy sex was taking it a bit far. I grinned inwardly at my own silliness.

"What are you thinking?" Henry asked.

"Oh, um, nothing much. You?"

"Same."

I smiled again, wishing I had the guts to show how I really felt.

Henry turned in his seat. Something outside had caught his eye, and by the way he shifted forward, I suspected we were close to the Abbey. He saw me looking at him. "We're almost there."

I strained to look ahead but saw nothing remotely abbeyish. "Where?"

Henry pointed ahead of the cab, but I had no idea what he was pointing at.

"All I see is a cemetery in between all those big buildings."

"Yup, that's it. Home sweet home. Wally, you can drop us over there, by those iron gates, just before that tree."

Wally raised a large hand to acknowledge he'd heard and then turned the car into the curb.

Surprise didn't cover it. I was expecting something grandiose, like the National Cathedral or some such, not a run-down old cemetery in the middle of the most expensive part of town. The tombstones looked seventeenth century. Many were cracked or broken. The grass was unkempt, and weeds had overgrown the stone pathways meandering between the graves. Witch hazel ran wild around the perimeter, and a weeping willow hung forlorn, its branches unmoving, as if it, too, were dead. Heck, there was even a low fog clinging to the ground. Just perfect!

"Lovely." I hoped my fake smile masked my disappointment. I had this strange overwhelming desire to suddenly be someplace else. Anywhere but here. "Maybe we should drive on. I think I'd like to go back to the apartment, now."

Henry must have had some idea of what I was thinking because his mouth contorted into a knowing smirk. I suspected nothing was quite as it seemed.

I reached into my pocket to get some money for Wally, but Henry rested his hand on mine and shook his head. "My treat."

Ever so reluctantly, I climbed out of the Magic Cab and stood by the front window. "Thanks, Wally. See you again soon. Good luck with your lady friend."

"Thank you. Her name is Ethel. I tell her you say hello."

Henry passed him a twenty and waived the change, which I thought was generous of him. I guessed he liked Wally too. "That's okay, keep it. Buy your girlfriend some flowers, Wally."

"Oh yeah, she like flowers. Very tasty. Good idea. Thank you, pretty man."

Henry joined me on the curb, and when Wally drove off, he opened the creaky iron gate that led into the cemetery. I looked around, but there wasn't even a church or any kind of structure. I really, really didn't want to go in there. It was the middle of the day, but it had the creepiness of a graveyard at midnight. Shivering from something other than the cold, I shook my head, clearly missing something. "Are you kidding me? You know I'm a magnet for the dead. Is this some kind of a test?"

"Test? No. This is where I live."

"In a graveyard? Give me five minutes, and if I don't faint outright, I'll be surrounded by specters who shout inside my head and try to drive me insane. No, thank you."

Henry took my hand and held it up to my face. "Look—you're wearing your ring. As long as you have this on, no harm will come to you here, I promise."

I pulled my hand back and shook my head. "Well, excuse me for freaking out, but why do I feel like the world's about to end?"

Henry took my hand again, only this time not to remind me of the ring, but to reassure me. "Do you trust me?"

I bit my lip and decided silence was the better part of valor, so I just nodded. This time I let him keep hold of my hand. I liked him holding it.

"You've nothing to worry about, Cat. It's a little bit of magic to scare off the masses. You must understand. My family is very private, and Dad especially doesn't want anyone snooping about the place. Before we had the enchantments, people used to be very rude, sticking their nose in our windows, wondering if they could visit and wander about inside. Finally, we'd had enough of it all, and now the railings are enchanted to make you want to turn and get as far away as you can."

He wasn't wrong about that. "I don't suppose you thought about buying a padlock for the gate or something?"

Henry laughed. "Come. Once we step inside, you'll feel differently, believe me."

If it were anyone but Henry, I'd have run a mile. "Okay, but if one ghost comes after me, I'll hex you myself or brew you a potion that gives you boils or something."

He laughed. "Don't worry, they won't." He gave my hand a light squeeze, and though I'd rather have gouged my own eyes out, I let him lead me through the gates.

It was as if I'd walked through a cool shower on a hot day and come through dry on the other side. As soon as we were inside the cemetery, the unsettling feeling vanished, and I no longer felt so anxious.

Henry turned to check my reaction. "How do you feel now?"

"Better. I'll let you off this time."

"Glad to hear it."

"Don't get too cocky. We're still in a creepy graveyard, and didn't someone mention something about an abbey? Don't call me picky, but where exactly do you live? All I see are graves and headstones. I was expecting something a bit more, I dunno, Fifth Avenue?"

As I spoke, the branches of the creepy willow tree swished gently, and Henry's sister Eleanor stepped out from behind them. To my horror, I thought she was dead. She wore a simple white dress and walked barefooted, looking totally transparent, like a ghost. For a ghastly second, I thought of my ancestor, and I covered my ring with my hand, seeking its protection.

Henry pulled me closer and squeezed my hand even tighter. "Don't worry, it's just another illusion. I assure you my sister is alive and well and as annoying as ever."

As he spoke, Eleanor stepped forward, disturbing the mist, and I realized she was her full-bodied self again.

"Hi, Cat! I'm glad you've finally made it. I was beginning to think I'd got the day wrong. Hey, Hank. Can I carry something in for either of you?"

My own bag was kind of heavy on account of my magic book, but Henry had carried it down from the apartment, and I could manage well enough from here. "I'm good, thanks."

"Well then, we'd better get inside."

Eleanor turned to lead the way and, still a little anxious, I held back. The two of them chatted merrily enough, and not wanting to be left alone in this creepy place, I followed along. Eleanor led us back to the willow, which raised its branches like a great curtain that we quickly passed through.

There was a gentle *whoosh* as the branch fell softly behind us, and I gasped at what I saw next. The graveyard was still there behind us, but the gloominess had lifted, and the sun shone down on the resting place of the dead, bringing the kind of peacefulness that raised the heart on a cheery summer day.

More importantly, before me, just beyond the trunk of the willow tree was the entrance to the Tilneys' abbey. It was modestly sized, but more magnificent than I could possibly imagine. The entire building was carved from a black material like obsidian. I imagined hooded monks walking through the cloisters on their way to daily prayer or singing songs of praise.

The dark, polished stone could have been grim and terrifying, like the stronghold of an evil witch queen from an old fable. Yet nature had been allowed a home in its nooks and crannies. Virginia creeper scaled the walls, and there were birds' nests in the arches of the cloisters. Beyond these was the entry into the main home, and two great green doors lay open in welcome.

I couldn't hide my smile. Now that we were beyond their defenses, I was sure my visit was going to be simply amazing, and I couldn't wait to see what was waiting for me on the other side of those doors. With a lighter heart than when I'd left Wally's Magic Cab, I hoisted my bag up high on my shoulder and gladly followed the others inside.

Chapter Twenty-One

THE LABYRINTH

THE SAME BLACK WALLS GREETED US ALL ON THE INSIDE. THE TILNEYS had softened the darkness with natural fabrics and earthy-colored furniture. There were friendly pictures of the family everywhere I looked. In the main living room, tall, arched windows allowed in plenty of natural light, and there was a crackling red fire burning in the grate, spreading a cheery warmth throughout the room. It was charming, and I anticipated pleasant evenings, snuggled under one of the many throws, gazing into the flames and listening to their many stories.

"Excuse me, gotta run—call of nature."

As Henry dashed off, Eleanor waited patiently as I took my surroundings all in. "When you're ready, I'll show you to your room."

"Oh, right. Sorry, I'm ready," I said.

"Don't be sorry. It's a very unique place. I'd be more surprised if you weren't curious about it. Follow me."

Eleanor wandered toward a corner of the room, and confused, I hesitated, not seeing a door or hallway there. I thought maybe I'd misunderstood her. But then she turned and disappeared. I followed behind, wondering where she'd got to.

When I got to the corner, I found her waiting for me. "It's confusing, I know. The stone walls create something of an illusion, hiding the halls, and it's easy to get lost in here. Hank jokes we should give visitors breadcrumbs or petals, so they can find their way back. We're used to it, of course, and so will you be soon, I promise."

He wasn't wrong. "It's like a labyrinth," I remarked, thinking of Ariadne, Theseus, and a ball of twine.

"Totally. Wait till we get to the stairs. From the outside, it looks like there's just the two levels, but you'll soon see there's a whole lot more."

"How many are there?" I asked.

"You know, I'm not totally sure. Dad keeps changing it all the time. He just bought one of those magical realty packages and keeps adding and taking away floors without telling anyone—it's very confusing."

I could see how it would be. The hall seemed an endless row of stone, the cold wall illuminated by soft lighting and decorated with more pictures. If these were all relatives, there were a hell of a lot of them.

"Are these all family portraits?"

Eleanor stopped and turned to look at a bunch of them with me.

"Yes, mostly. Mom came from a very large family, and a lot of them are her cousins and nephews and such. She liked having them all around her. I've tried taking some down, but it upsets Dad, so I don't bother anymore."

"He misses her that much?"

Eleanor raised a puzzled eyebrow and glanced at me. "Perhaps. Come on. Let's get you settled in."

I wondered what she'd meant by that, but her tone didn't invite further conversation. She turned a corner, then another, and then we started to climb a winding staircase.

"You're not wrong about these corridors. I think I'm lost already. I'd better make sure my phone's charged, or you might lose me forever." I only half laughed at my own joke.

"I wouldn't rely on it," Eleanor said. "Between the thick stones and the enchantments in place, no signal can get through. If you need to make a call or send a text, you'll need to sit on the stone of Elliot Finn, the old blacksmith, just to the right of the cemetery gates. It's the only place I've ever gotten a signal."

"Ugh. That's not fun. You don't have an old-fashioned landline?"

"No, sorry. We're used to it. Anyway, here we are. Your room's next to mine, so you can knock if you need anything."

That was reassuring at least.

Eleanor opened one of the four black doors in the hall and stood aside to let me in. Like the room downstairs, the guest room was nicely furnished, only this one had a purple flame, making it look dreamy and relaxing.

"Very nice," I said.

"You'll find the bathroom in the corner hidden behind the bed. Lunch will be at noon sharp. I wouldn't be late. Dad gets mad if he has to wait for food. I hope you like chicken."

I nodded. "I presume the General is home, then?"

"Yes. He spends most of his time in his study. He only comes out if he has to, which is as little as possible."

"How about Freddy? Is he home too?"

"Only when it suits him. Which is hardly ever."

My thoughts returned to Isabella and how she and Freddy were doing. Pleasant as she was, I barely knew Eleanor and didn't think I knew her well enough to ask about him. Maybe over the course of my stay that might change.

"Anyway, settle yourself in and come down when you're ready. I have some errands to run, so I'll see you in a bit."

"Thank you."

As the door closed behind her, I dropped my bag down on the end of the bed and rubbed my shoulder. When I had a free moment, I resolved to look up a spell to lighten the load, because that magic book sure was hefty and had probably left a groove on my skin.

As Eleanor had said, I found the bathroom just beyond the bed, concealed by another optical illusion in the back wall. Just as well—another ten seconds and I would have peed myself. As I walked in, a line of purple candles ignited. There were pots of herbs and spices by the sink, typical for most magical houses. I picked up one and, removing the lid, sniffed the contents. I recognized lavender and vanilla at once and smiled. Vanilla was my favorite scent.

After answering the call of nature, I had to feel along the wall to find my way back to the bedroom. *This could get old fast.* There was a large window looking over toward the willow. Just beyond it, the skyscrapers of New York were indistinct outlines, almost as if I were imagining them in the shapes of the clouds. Yet I knew there were real enough. It was bizarre, standing in this calm oasis in one of the busiest cities in the world.

I wondered if Henry was waiting for me downstairs, and whether his room was on the same corridor as mine. I had no idea how many rooms there were. The Abbey was deceptively grander than its modest exterior had led me to believe. A person could get horribly lost in here. And Eleanor had said the General was fiddling with a realty package, so there could be even more floors and hallways and rooms coming into being right now. How the rich lived! Mom and Dad would certainly have appreciated having a few extra rooms. I wondered who was sleeping in mine.

Lunch was at noon, and since we'd made no plans, I decided to relax for a bit. If they missed me, they could come find me. That would be a hell of a lot easier than going out in search of them. After checking my phone, which, as Eleanor had warned me, had zero signal, I kicked off my shoes and flopped down on the purple comforter on my bed. It sure was comfy. I stretched my arms, snow-angel style, and sank into the yielding mattress.

The scent in the room and the crackling purple fire were so relaxing. *I could sure get used to this.* Apparently faster than I could have imagined, because the second I closed my eyes, I forgot all about Henry, Eleanor, the General, and indeed pretty much everything else, because I fell into a deep, untroubled sleep. The kind most people only dream of.

I woke with a start. *Shoot, what time is it?* I must have been holding my phone when I fell asleep because it was by my hand. I snatched it up and groaned when I saw the time. *Noon!*

I jumped off the bed and ran into the bathroom, having to sidestep only a couple of times as I searched for the entrance. *For Gaia's sake, can't these idiots install some regular doors?* There was no time to change—they would have to take me as they found me. I quickly ran a brush through my hair, cursing that I'd never mastered Mom's magic spell for a hair fix—any time I'd tried it, I ended up with a cross between a beehive and an angry octopus. With a little more difficulty, I found my way out into the corridor.

Turn right. I'm sure it's right. The winding stairs had been behind us—at least I thought they were. I ran my hand along the wall to avoid missing a turn, but though I found a set of stairs, they wound upward, not down. Perhaps there was another set farther along the corridor? I traced my way back and walked a little farther. At last, to my relief, I found another set of stairs, but they led to a corridor much longer than I recalled, and none of the portraits on the wall looked familiar. I would swear their disapproving eyes followed me as I hurried past them.

The next turn led to another set of winding stairs that climbed a little. There was nothing for it; up I went, cursing the lack of phone signal in this house when a single call would have alerted Henry to my predicament. It crossed my mind to try to communicate telepathically, but he might think that was rude, and in any case, how many more wrong turns could I possibly make? Considering my lack of control, I'd probably climb in the General's head, and how would I explain that? *I'm terribly sorry, sir. I was looking for your handsome son, whom I should very much like to marry someday.* Um, no.

I had reached a dead end with only one door. To the side of it was a small table, and on the table was a clear vase containing a single lily. It was the only door I'd seen with any kind of marker. I decided to see if anyone was in there now, and I knocked. There was no response. This time, I tried the handle, and the door opened.

This room was much larger but similar to mine, with a huge bed and the same soft purple lighting. Though the curtains had been drawn, the fire was unlit, and the grate so clean I thought it probably hadn't been lit for some time. There was a large dresser with an ornate mirror, surrounded by dozens of children's photographs. I suspected this was Henry's mother's room, and judging by how polished everything was, someone was taking very good care of it. Although I was conscious of the time, my curiosity got the better of me, and I wandered inside, hoping to find a picture of her face, as so far, she hadn't been pointed out to me.

Over by the window, I spotted a wedding photograph. The groom looked just like Henry, only he wore a mustache, and though he was smiling, there was a hardness to his face that was nothing like Henry's. This had to be the General when he was a young man. The woman beside him was dressed in a wedding dress of traditional metallic gray. It was a classic A-line gown, with a sweeping train fringed with silver lace that brought snowflakes to mind. The long sheer sleeves had a similar pattern, but the most beautiful thing of all was the bride herself. She looked just like Eleanor, only her figure was frailer, and her eyes a deep blue gray like the sea before a storm. Henry had inherited her smile.

I instinctively wanted to know more about her. One of the drawers was partially open, and looking down, I glimpsed a pendant necklace. Thinking it might contain another photo, I reached inside and lightly touched it.

"Excuse me? What are you doing?"

My heart skipped a beat, and I turned. Henry was standing in the doorway, and he wasn't smiling now.

"I, um, I'm sorry. I got lost with all the corridors and such." I closed the drawer gently behind me.

"And you thought you'd find your way back by snooping through my mother's things?"

"Snooping? No! I don't know quite how I got here, but I saw the picture of your mom and was curious about her, that's all. She's very pretty, and I wondered if there were more photos. And you guys need some serious signposts in this place. A person could die trying to find a way their way downstairs."

Henry's suspicious frown eased a little. Even he had to know this wasn't the easiest place in the world to get around. "Come on. I'd better get you downstairs. Dad's chomping at the bit, waiting for his lunch. He gets really testy if we don't eat on the dot."

"So I heard."

Relieved to be out of the room and to at least have a reliable guide, I followed him back down the hall.

"How long has it been since your mom passed away?"

"Eight...no, nine years now."

"You were so young. Do you remember much about her?"

Henry cast his gaze thoughtfully downward. "She used to sing to us. At least I think she did. I try to remember the song, and it's always there, on the tip of my tongue, but when I think I remember it, it goes."

"Does Eleanor remember? Or Freddy?"

He shook his head. "None of us can. I've asked Dad about it, but he just gets angry and won't talk about it. It's so annoying."

"I'm sorry I looked in her drawer. It seems dumb now, but I didn't think."

"Don't worry about it. We all do stupid things from time to time."

Henry's easy smile was back, and the awkward moment forgotten. We were back in the dining room in no time at all, and it seemed so easy to find with him beside me. Getting lost seemed so foolish in retrospect.

The dining room was fairly formal. I half expected liveried servants, but there were none to be seen, just a grumpy-looking General sitting with his arms crossed at the head of a longish table, and Eleanor beside him, smiling as we approached.

Henry led me to the seat facing Eleanor and pulled out a chair for me. "Panic over. The halls turned her around a bit, but I found her."

I was grateful he didn't say where.

"You didn't end up in a dungeon, did you?" Eleanor smiled as she pulled a napkin down onto her lap.

"Not this time." I grinned. "But I'm pretty sure I heard screaming."

"That would be the last guest who was late for lunch." The General smiled. However, there was more than a hint of innuendo in his glare, and no humor.

"I'll remember that. But really, how do you keep it all straight in your heads? I was lost two feet from my own bedroom."

"After a while you get used to the portraits. That's why I keep them up."

As the General explained this, a series of bowls began slowly circulating in the air. I reached for the bread bowl and selected a small brown bap, then waited for some chicken salad to rotate my way. As the dishes passed, I took a sip of the white wine someone had poured for me and thought about home. Family meals there were always so chaotic, and I found I quite enjoyed the change. When everyone had filled their plate, the dishes settled in the center of the table, floating again only when someone wanted a refill.

"I could get used to this."

"Oh? You don't eat lunch in Pennsylvania?"

I wondered if the General was always this sarcastic. I noted how Eleanor and Henry were trying their best not to smile. Deadpan humor was an art. They were *terrible* at it.

"No, I mean sitting down to a civilized meal without having a zillion brothers and sisters screaming the house down."

"Don't you miss them at all?" Eleanor asked.

"Sometimes. Mostly I miss the quiet times at night when the kids were in bed. Mom, Dad, Jimmy, and I would sit around the fire, and sometimes Dad would tell us stories. Come to think of it, it's been a while since we did that."

"I'm sure your father has much to occupy his time. A necromancer's time is never his own."

"Oh, Dad isn't a necromancer."

The General appeared confused. "Still, your mother then?"

"Nope, nope. It's just me, I'm afraid, or so they tell me. It seems it skipped a generation or two. I'm the first in a while. None of my brothers and sisters have the gift. Not yet, anyway. That's why I'm so bad at it. Mom and Dad were hoping I'd grow out of it. They're afraid of anything that isn't earth magic."

The General looked genuinely surprised. "Afraid? What utter nonsense. Necromancers are very powerful. When we learned Henry had the power, we did everything we could to nurture his talent. Not that it's done us much good. I've never known a young man so unambitious for himself. *Magical cleric.*" He sneered as he said this last part.

"We've discussed this, Dad." Henry scooped some chicken salad onto his second roll. "The dead don't interest me. We should be more concerned with the living."

"That's ridiculous. Catherine, I hope while you're with Henry, you'll set him straight. You might be a latecomer to the craft, but surely you must appreciate the power you yield? You can talk to the dead, you can divine the future, and you can reveal all the secrets of the past. Why my son chooses to turn his back on these gifts is a mystery to me. It brings greatness to any wizarding family that embraces it. I'm surprised at your family, really I am."

I twiddled with the cup in front of me. "I'm told necromancers can do all that, but between you and me, I can barely shift this teacup."

The General fixed a puzzled stare on me.

"Cat is being modest," Henry intervened. "The potion work I've seen her do in the shop is phenomenal, but she's just getting her feet wet in ley line work. As yet, she doesn't know her own strength, but she will, given time."

The General shook his head. "Well, I don't understand it. How can anyone have all these latent talents and not revel in it?"

"Well, that's a mystery you won't solve over a chicken salad and a glass of wine. Let's enjoy our lunch, shall we?" Eleanor shot her brother and father meaningful glares.

I took a bite of my bap, which smelled of roasted chicken, warm celery, and mayonnaise. "This is delicious; who made it?" I looked around the table.

"I did, thank you." Eleanor smiled at me and winked at Henry. I suspected they both wanted to change the subject. I could help them with that.

"It's a pity Freddy wasn't able to join us. I know he thought about it. I think my friend Isabella would have liked to see the Abbey if she could." I didn't mention that I would rather she didn't, but that was another story.

Eleanor put down her knife and looked puzzled. "Oh, why would she be interested?"

"They've been seeing each other. I thought she liked my brother Jimmy, but your brother clicked his fingers, and she came a-running. She likes him a lot."

Her habitual smile left her face, and she stared at Henry, then her father.

The General put his bap down and took a sip of wine. "Then I suggest you tell your friend to unlike him, and as quickly as possible. My eldest son has a long-standing engagement with Miss Rosemary Westbrooke, the Magic Runes heiress. Unfortunately, my son likes to have his cake and eat it too. Your friend would be best advised to stay well away from him, or she'll wake up one morning thrown out with the bathwater."

"I thought that was all over," Henry said. "With Rosemary?"

"Well, it's back on again. Freddy's no fool. He's not going to walk away from an alliance with a powerful witch family over a trifle, and he certainly won't throw it all away over your silly little fae friend. I'm sorry to sound callous, but that's the way it is." The General pushed his plate away and threw his napkin on it. "Now, if you'll excuse me, I have some writing to do. I've just started the Necromancer Scrolls, Volume III, which takes the history up to the Elder Wars. A fascinating period, full of blood and thunder."

And then he left us.

"If you'll excuse me, I'm off too. Playing gooseberry isn't my thing." Eleanor pushed her chair back but held on to her glass of wine, which she took with her.

"You're an idiot," Henry said.

"But you love me."

I stared at the sea of plates still sitting on the table. "Can I help clear up?"

"No, you're fine. I'll just magic it all away in a bit. You two have fun."

As soon as she was gone, I turned to Henry. "Why didn't you tell me about your brother? Isabella is going to be so upset when she finds out he's engaged."

"Maybe not as much as you think."

"What makes you say that?"

"She knows already. I had a text from him earlier this morning. Sad to say, but Freddy isn't famous for his discretion. And from what I learned, as soon as she found out, she started texting your brother. When one door closes, and all that."

"Are you kidding me?"

Henry shook his head. I'll show you the text if you insist, but fair warning, there's stuff in it that made me blush."

"No, it's okay, I believe you. Poor Isabella."

Henry laughed. "I'd say poor Jimmy. Anyway, enough about them. I promised to teach you some focusing stuff while you were here. If you've had all you want to eat, shall we make a start?"

"Sure, yes, I'd like to."

"Right then. We'll get your magic book and go sit outside. It's turning out to be a beautiful day out there. Let's go and make the most of it."

"You're going to risk letting me loose in those corridors again?"

"Good point. I'll go with you. Lead the way."

We both rose from the table, left the dining room, and headed for the stairs. It was time to concentrate on my training, but I couldn't help thinking about Isabella, and though I knew I should text her to see how she was doing, I found myself even more worried about my brother.

Isabella might be a creature of the world, but Jimmy was not. It wasn't my place to meddle with his love life, but if someone didn't put him on his guard, he could be in for a whole lot of pain. As his sister, I wasn't about to let that happen. I needed my phone, and I needed to find the grave of the blacksmith, so I could send Jimmy a message and put him on his guard. The sooner the better.

Still, first things first. I was about to head out into a cemetery, a cemetery full of the restless dead and their never-ending whispering babble. Perhaps I was finally going to understand what it meant to be a necromancer, or at least get some idea of what all this fuss was about. Half afraid and half excited, I kept close to Henry, knowing secretly that it wasn't the dead that excited me, but the living.

Chapter Twenty-Two

STRANGE SENSATIONS

HENRY LED US CLOSE TO THE OLD WILLOW AND STOPPED A FEW FEET short, avoiding the shade of the tree. He was right—it was a nice day, but cold, so I'd come out in two sweaters, some extra thick wooly socks, and some mittens Mom had knitted, and of course, my usual poncho. Without them, I'd have been shivering. Even so, it wasn't enough.

I put my hands together in prayer, and Henry took a cautious step back. "Oh, come on, I'm not that bad!" I gave him my best squinty eye. "*H¯æte.*"

A shimmering ring of light circled overhead, bringing with it a blanket of heat. *Not too shabby,* I thought. I'd finally mastered Isabella's heat spell.

Henry pursed his lips, impressed. "Hmm. Ley line magic. I didn't teach you that."

"I guess you don't know everything, then." I cheekily winked back.

"I guess not." He drew a square in the air. "*Wegan innierfe!*" Two seats and a small table materialized from nowhere. He sat down at one of the chairs.

I placed the heavy tome on the table. "Well, if we were going to do this sitting down, why not practice inside?"

"What, and risk having you blow up the Abbey? Not a chance!"

As I sat down next to him, I cocked my head to one side, smiling. He had a point. Come to think of it, he also had the most beautiful eyes. Not for the first time, I found myself gazing into them, wondering how they could be so gentle, so clever, so cheeky, yet so thoughtful at the same time. I got all that from a single twinkle, and then I died a little on the inside when I realized he was staring right back at me.

His mouth was set firm, all business and no fun. "Do you think you're ready now?"

Oh Gaia. He must think I'm a total lemon. "Um, yeah, good to go." *Worse and worse. Now I'm talking like a buffoon.*

To my astonishment, in a complete shift of mood, Henry moved the book aside and took hold of both my hands. His eye contact never broke with mine as he pulled off each mitten and laid them carefully on the table. My heart pounded, and I could hardly breathe, wondering where this was going and praying for more than I dared imagine.

"Close your eyes."

I did as he told me. It crossed my mind someone might be watching from the Abbey, but I didn't care. If this was going to be the moment I'd been hoping for, then so be it. If Henry was going to be brave enough to kiss me in front of his family, I wouldn't object. I sat a little more forward, not exactly pouting but making myself available if he wanted to kiss me.

The flesh on my skin tingled as he ran his fingers between my thumb and forefingers. It was so delightful, so sensual, and my whole body came alive at his touch. I wanted to open my eyes so badly, but afraid to break the moment, I kept them closed.

"Are your thoughts focused on what I'm doing to you?"

"*Ahem*. Err, yes, yes, they are."

"Tell me about your breathing."

"My wha—?"

"Your breathing. Where is it focused?"

I cleared my throat, trying to ignore the sublime sensations running through me and focusing on what he'd asked. "I, um, well, I feel it mostly in my chest. My, err, heart."

"Concentrate on that."

I nodded.

"Don't open your eyes."

"I won't."

To my disappointment, Henry let go of my hands, but then his touch resumed on the back of them, where he continued to draw two gentle lines along my arms toward my elbows.

"And now?"

"Now I'm focused on your fingers again." I didn't mention about the electricity coursing through me.

He sighed and stopped. "No, don't think about my hand. Think about your breathing."

The corner of my mouth twisted a little. The impatient edge to his tone told me this wasn't what I wanted it to be. *Oh well.* So where was he going, then? Still, I remained determined to enjoy myself.

Henry took in a deep breath of his own. I wondered if he was studying my face. What was he thinking? Surely he must have some inkling of what I was feeling, and how difficult yet sublimely wonderful this was for me? I so badly wanted to read his mind now. He pulled away, and already I felt the loss of his touch. "Now, I want you to remember how you were breathing. How it felt. Try to keep that sensation. Do you think you can do that for me?"

The experience was still fresh enough, and though my breathing wasn't quite so deep now as when his hands had been on me, that sweet sensation was still there, lingering. I nodded, afraid that talking might make me forget it.

"Okay, now, did you learn the levitation spell I asked you to?"

I nodded again, recalling the painful smack as the Rubik's cube had bounced off my head in Isabella's bedroom. I tried not to giggle. At last, I had an inkling of where this was going.

"I want you to raise your magic book off the table and hold it in the air for twenty seconds. Only, when you say the incantation, I want you to keep your focus on your breathing, as you did just now, and not on the spell or on the book. And don't open your eyes until I tell you to."

"Yes, boss."

Still, I pulled myself together, knowing that as every second passed, the memory of how I felt when he touched me weakened. I remembered where he'd positioned the book and pictured it sitting there on the table.

"*Scierpan ûpweardes*."

It was hard, not being able to open my eyes. After all, how could I tell if the spell was working if I couldn't see anything around me? But I did as Henry instructed and tried to control the ley line power as I called upon it by managing my breathing. A rush of pure magic shot through my body, simulating the sensations I'd just experienced. I was surprised and a bit alarmed by how good it felt.

"You can open your eyes now."

More than a little curious, I did as Henry commanded. To my astonishment, the tome had risen a few feet above the tabletop and was happily hovering in midair.

"Wow!" The second I spoke, the book came crashing down and landed with a great thump on the table top. "Dang."

Henry opened his mouth to say something, but determined to get this right, I sat up straight, bit my lips, and tried again.

"*Scierpan ûpweardes.*"

The book wobbled and then slowly began to rise in the air. Unfortunately, so did my mittens, which, due to their relative lightness, would soon be in orbit if I didn't break the spell. My concentration broke, and everything came crashing back down on the table.

Henry leaned over and picked up one of the mittens that had fallen to the ground.

"Shoot, I thought I had it," I said.

"You did. You're doing great. Just keep at it."

I shook my head. "Some all-powerful necromancer I am. I can't even levitate a silly book."

Henry took my hand, and this time he pressed it affectionately. "Don't be hard on yourself. Most necromancers are trained from the day they are born to control their powers, but you just came to it. It's not your fault your parents tried to shield you. You have it all inside you, and you did it a moment ago, so I know you can do it. You just have to believe in yourself."

"If you say so, Yoda." I was more interested in his hand. How wicked was I?

"I do. Now try again." He squeezed me a little more and then let go. His touch rekindled some of the magic he'd stirred up before.

I closed my eyes and inhaled. My first thought was to empty my mind of any doubts, which would only serve to hinder me. When I reached a place of peace, I called out to the closest ley line and summoned its power.

Something was different this time. I knew I could do it—after all, hadn't I just done it? Knowing that brought with it calmness, and this time, when the magic entered me, I could feel it radiate through every inch of my body. Rather than say the spell to expel it as fast as I could as I did before, I held on to the sensation for a moment, wanting to enjoy this feeling for as long as possible. With every second that passed, the store of power in me grew more intense, until at last, afraid the magic might overwhelm me, I had to let go.

"*Scierpan ûpweardes.*"

I knew I had done it. My eyes were still closed, but I knew. And when I opened them, there was the tome, hovering a few feet off the table surface —no mittens—just the book. And Henry was smiling.

I stood up, and delighted by my own accomplishment, I made the book turn a circle in the air, and then another, before bringing it back down to the table, where it landed gently in the exact spot it had left. Giddy with my success, I would have danced around the graveyard if I wasn't afraid of what Henry would think of me.

"Well done, you," Henry said. "How do you feel?"

"Amazing."

"Good. Because the next part of the lesson is going to be a lot harder."

I sat back down and braced myself. "Oh."

"Yes. You're a necromancer, not just an earth or ley line witch. It's time to commune with the dead."

A new bolt of adrenaline swept through me, and I put my hand to my lips. At last, we were getting down to it. This was why I was here after all. I twirled the ring on my finger, and with a heart swelling with excitement, I waited to hear what he had to say.

A door closed to my right, and glancing up, I watched as Eleanor crossed the lawn to join us. She had changed into jeans and a leather jacket, and looked quite stylish, even with the wooly bobble hat on her head and matching scarf.

"Hey, you two, I'm popping out to run some errands for Dad." She stopped by Henry, and I noticed a secret exchange between them, but had no clue what it meant. “He wants you to pop in for a minute, when you have a chance.”

“Did he say why?” Henry asked.

“Nope. You’ll have to ask him yourself. See ya later.” And then to me, “Have fun!”

“See you,” I said.

Once she was gone, Henry stood up, stretched, and glanced over toward the Abbey. “I suppose I’d better go see what he wants. You don’t mind, do you?”

I shook my head. “I’m not going anywhere. I’ll just practice my awesome skills until you come back.”

Henry grinned. “You do that.” And then he left.

But I had other things in mind now besides practicing my levitation skills. This might be the only time Henry would be away, and I had to find the grave Isabella had mentioned so I could contact Jimmy. I waited until Henry was safely back inside the Abbey and then headed for the willow. I hoped if I passed under it, I’d be able to get back to the Abbey afterward, or at least hoped Henry would have the good sense to come and find me if I got stuck on the other side. It occurred to me I should wait for him to return, but I really wanted to talk to Jimmy and this would only take a moment or two.

A slight chill caressed my cheeks as I passed under the tree. I looked back over my shoulder, and sure enough, the Abbey had disappeared into nonexistence. Ahead, a sea of headstones surrounded me. I hadn’t given them much thought when we’d arrived, but alone as I was now, they appeared more sinister, and my skin began to tingle. I had a strange feeling I was being watched, and my gut told me it was not by the living.

I shuddered, dreading to think what would happen if the ring failed to protect me here, as it had failed before in Times Square. Then again, I had been unprepared in Times Square. This time, I was aware and ready to invoke the ring’s power to protect myself. Cold, and suddenly determined to get this over with, I pulled my poncho close about me and started scanning the names on the stones.

What grave was it she said? Finn something or other? I recalled she’d said it was over by the cemetery gates, so I focused my search in that general direction.

One stone caught my attention. A clean pot of unseasonably fresh lilies had been placed before it, standing out from the neighboring chipped and mud-splattered bowls containing wilted or dead flora, if any at all. On this stone, the black granite still presented as shiny as the day the mason engraved it, standing superior among the tired, almost-illegible graves surrounding it. I veered toward it, curious to see who was buried there.

I was not surprised by the name on the grave, though was a little taken aback by the inscription beneath it.

Beneath this little plot of earth
lie the remains of Eleanor (Nell) Tilney,
née Drummond.
Born Dec 3, 1965 - Died June 18, 2012

Wife and mother of Frederick, Henry,
and Eleanor Tilney.
Gaia will atone.

Gaia will atone. I stared at the last sentence for a few moments, wondering exactly what it was supposed to mean. Atone. Atone for what? What on earth could their mother have done that required everlasting atonement? Or had something been done to her? And the inscription seemed so cold and unfeeling. No beloved wife or mother. No dearly departed. Nothing. Whatever had happened, it had piqued my interest to such a degree that I decided to ask Henry about it when he came back. Now though, I had more pressing business to attend to.

The protection of my heat spell had worn off. Rather than cast another, I pulled my poncho close and walked a little faster, ignoring the foggy vapor of my own breathing and quickly scanning one stone after another, in search of the precious graveyard hotspot.

At last I found it. This headstone read:

Elliot Finn,
Blacksmith
Died 1692.
Reunited at last with Esther,
his beloved wife.

Sweet. No mystery here. Phone in hand, I turned it on and checked for a signal. Nothing. I held it up slightly over my face and began to circle the grave to connect with the outside world. Whenever I moved closer to the stone, I'd get a single bar, but I had to get even closer to it to get a second, and it would quickly fade in and out. In the end, I had to stand right in front of the stone, conscious I was probably standing over poor Elliot's head and wishing I could be anywhere else but this close to the dead. I'd seen what happened in movies. It never ended well for the hero.

I punched in Jimmy's contact and prayed. "Come on, Jimmy, pick up."

The phone called twice, and then he answered.

"Hi, Jimmy. It's me. Cat."

For a second, my brother was silent, and I wondered if I'd lost the signal. There were three bars on the display, which should be enough. I put it back to my ear.

"Oh, Cat. It's you. How are you doing?"

I'd never heard my brother so downbeat. "I'm fine. I was just calling to see how you were."

Another pause. I double-checked the phone, but the line hadn't dropped.

"I saw Isabella this morning," Jimmy said. I waited for him to go on. His tone told me everything I needed to know, but I wanted to hear it from him. It was his heart, after all—his news. "It's all over between us. We're done."

"What happened?" My brother had a big heart to trample, and I ached to be with him, wishing I could comfort him.

"She sent me a text clearly meant for someone else. After she sent it, she must have realized and came to find me, but it was too late. I didn't think she was like that. I knew she was fae, but I thought she was different. I thought I could trust her."

"Jimmy, I'm so sorry."

He was quiet for a moment, and then, good-natured soul that he was, he turned the conversation back to me. "What's the Abbey like?"

I returned in the direction of the Abbey, although I couldn't see it, keeping half an eye on that signal, just in case I lost it. "It's wonderful. Very gothic—like my favorite books. Everyone is being very kind. The General's a bit odd, but maybe he'll grow on me. Eleanor is lovely, and Henry is helping me with my spells. You'll have to see it for yourself, 'cos it's hidden in the middle of the city like Brigadoon. You'll love it."

"I'm sure I will. How long are you there for?"

"I dunno, it's been left open ended. I'll text you when I know for sure."

"Sounds good. Look, I'd better get back to my books. I have an exam coming up."

I knew this was an excuse to get off the phone, but I understood. "Sure. I love you, Jimmy."

"Me too." The call ended.

"Who do you love?"

Coming out of nowhere, Henry's voice startled me so much, I jumped back in surprise. My buttocks scrapped against the top of the blacksmith's headstone, but though I felt a slight dizziness, the power of the ring, or perhaps the enchantments surrounding the cemetery, saved me from the onslaught I'd felt at Times Square. My palm flattened against my chest as I recovered from the shock, but that was all.

"Sorry, I didn't mean to make you jump." Henry held two steaming mugs in front of him, and the distinct aroma of hot chocolate invaded my senses. He held one out to me.

"Thank you," I said, taking the mug. "I thought I'd check in on Jimmy. You don't mind? I was worrying about him, so I wanted to clear my mind so I could concentrate on your lessons."

Henry's smile softened into a look of concern. "Is he all right?"

I gave a negative grunt in reply. "No, but he will be. It'll just take time." There was a dollop of melting cream on top of the chocolate, and I licked it with the tip of my tongue. The chocolate was still too hot to chug, so I cupped the mug to warm both hands and began walking slowly back toward the willow. Henry followed in silence and paused with me when I stopped at his mother's grave. Now we were here, I hesitated, wondering how to phrase my question without causing offense.

"Can I ask what happened? To your mother?"

Henry lowered his gaze, and a sadness diminished his natural smile. "They never told me at the time. All we knew was she had passed, and that was enough to take in as it was. I saw the death certificate much later. That said heart failure." His gaze wandered upward toward the sky, as he languished in some distant memory.

I regretted bringing this up. Deciding to put my own morbid curiosity on hold, I took a sip of my chocolate. "This is good," I said, tipping the mug ever so slightly toward him.

His attention returned to me. "I'm glad you like it. Shall we get on?"

"Yes, please."

Henry led the way back to the willow, and I followed. I was still curious about the inscription on the stone, but it didn't seem like the right time to ask about it right now. And we had some work to do. Work that could require communing with the dead. Perhaps, with a little patience, I might soon be able to glean some answers, without upsetting Henry at all. With that notion in mind, I marched to the willow tree, determined to learn as much as I could, so I could unravel some of her history by myself later.

Chapter Twenty-Three

THE PATRIOTS FAN

WE DID NOT PASS UNDER THE WILLOW, BUT INSTEAD, HENRY TOOK A path around it. Of course. Only then did I realize there were no graves beyond the willow, just the Abbey itself.

Henry's pace remained determined, and it was soon clear to me he had a particular parley in mind. I confess, I was more than a little intrigued and walked quickly behind him, anxious to see where this was going.

"You may have overheard me tell my father I have no interest in disturbing the dead."

"Yes, I think so," I agreed. "I remember something about it anyway."

The style of the stones behind the willow were a lot more modern, and the inscriptions more easily read. Henry stopped by a newish grave marked by a marble weeping angel. The figure had fallen to her knees, her arms shielding her face as she clung to a book on a pedestal. "It grieves Dad to no end, but it's something I feel strongly about. The dead have passed over and should be left there in peace. As necromancers, we have the power to summon them, but merely having a power is no justification for using it willy-nilly. At least I think so anyway."

I shifted my weight from one leg to the other as I pondered this, and then I followed Henry's lead and leaned forward to place my mug at the side of the grave. "So? If that's the case, what's the point of us and all this training?"

"Sometimes, the dead will reach out to us. I have no objection to them communicating with the living for their own purposes. I simply object to disturbing their peace for our own personal gain. You hear about these grave robbers, waking up Great-Uncle Pete just so someone can get their hands on his coin collection. It's despicable."

"I suppose so." To be honest, I hadn't really thought of it in those terms before. Personal gain wasn't what I was about, or at least I didn't think so.

"All I'm saying, really, is each of us has a duty to examine our own motives before we go diving in. If they want to talk to the living, well, so be it." Henry rested his hand gently on the back of the bent over angel and petted the stone affectionately. "Take my friend George, here. We first became acquainted two years ago, after an unfortunate accident at a rival shop brought him to this place a little earlier than he would have liked."

I looked around Henry to read the inscription on the stone.

George Udolpho
Born 1999 - Died 2019
His bright future came too soon
And explosively.
We will always miss you, George
Don't come back.

I covered my mouth as I tried not to laugh at that last comment. "Oh my Gaia poor George. What was that about?"

"Not everyone is as adept with a spell pot as you are. Seriously, Cat, sometimes you don't give yourself enough credit. Anyway, poor George here wasn't paying attention and threw the wrong ingredients into someone else's cauldron. Luckily, he was the only one working that day, but he got to meet Gaia much sooner than anyone expected."

"Poor thing."

"Yup. He was only just twenty. His passing over was troubled, and shortly after he was buried here, he made his presence known."

"Oh? How did he do that?" I asked. "Did he rattle a few chains? Spook a few tourists?"

Henry laughed. "No. I found him hovering outside my bedroom window the night of the Super Bowl. He's a huge Patriots fan and died a few weeks before the game. He didn't want to miss it."

"He crossed over from the dead to watch a football game?"

"Hey, love is love. I don't judge. Anyway, George isn't quite ready to say good-bye to the Magic Apple, so every now and then, he pops up to say hello. As you can probably guess by the inscription, he has no desire to go home. He's an odd one, but I don't think he'll mind a pretty girl summoning him to say hello."

I blushed, pretending not to be pleased he'd called me pretty, but I was delighted just the same. These immature thoughts were super embarrassing, but I couldn't help how I felt. "So you want me to summon George here?"

"Yup, exactly."

"Should I go grab my spell book?" I pointed over my shoulder, back to the willow, but Henry shook his head.

"No need. I can tell you the incantation. You just need to focus like you did before, and all will be well. And don't worry, I'm right here should anything go wrong. Okay?"

I sucked in a ball of cold air and squared my shoulders. I had to confess I was excited. And not the least bit afraid because, as Henry had pointed out, he'd be right there.

"So what do I do?"

Henry moved to stand behind me. "In a minute, I want you to channel all your emotions into that ring and put your palm out across the grave. Then, when you feel you have enough power stored, say these words. *Stincan ûðe wægn swogen.*"

That was a mouthful. I raised my eyebrows and looked at him sideways.

"*Stincan ûðe wægn swogen*," he repeated. "Say it now before you draw on the ley line to get the hang of the words."

"*Stincan udh waggon snogen.*"

"*Ûðe*. Purse your lips, like this." Henry puckered up, and I couldn't stop from giggling. He cocked his head to one side, trying to appear stern, but I knew he was laughing too. "Come on, you can do it."

"Maybe if you're Welsh. *Ûðe wægn*." It sounded silly to me, but Henry nodded, so I guessed I'd done it all right. "What does it mean?"

"Arise from the dead, sort of. Ready to give it a go?" he asked.

I stood alongside the actual grave and closed my eyes. Henry hadn't said I needed to, but I knew it would help me concentrate and just went with it. As before, the power of the ley lines entered my body, and as before, I waited, letting the pressure build inside me until I could sense something like a ball of magic, desperate for release. I held out my palm over the raised earth, and when I felt the moment was right, I spoke the incantation and opened my eyes.

"Stincan ûðe wægn swogen."

At first, I saw nothing, but then a mist of silver light emanated from my ring and slowly circled the grave. It was heavy, like a malignant fog. The mist dropped low to the ground as it caressed the hallowed sod, as if sensing what lay beneath it. As soon as it had gone full circle, the earth under my feet trembled and the branches of the willow whooshed behind me, moved by an invisible force.

The mist I'd created was sucked into the earth, and when it reappeared a moment later, it took on the ghostly shape of a young man. He was about Henry's height, but his frame was more delicate, and his silvery hair was stuck to his face, like a bad case of bed hair. His football shirt had the number twelve emblazoned on it, and I imagined Tom Brady's name on the reverse. I was glad he had all his limbs. At least his ghost showed no signs of his having suffered what must have been a fairly violent death.

George took one look at me and wrinkled his brow in puzzlement. When he saw Henry, his whole face lit up in a happy beam. He drifted over toward him. He raised his hand as if to high-five him, and then, like he suddenly remembered he was dead, he dropped it lamely to his side. "Tonight's not a game night, is it? I didn't think I'd be seeing you again until next week." There was a slight mystical echo to his voice. Though dead as he was, I could hear the trace of a New York accent.

He sounded younger than I would have expected. Henry had said he was twenty, but I double-checked the dates on the stone to make sure there was no mistake.

"No, there's no game tonight," Henry said. "I just wanted to introduce you to my friend, Cat Morland. She's staying with me for a while, and I thought you might like to meet her."

He turned to me and smiled. I was sure his dull eyes would have twinkled if they could, but he broke into a big smile, revealing a large gap between his molars. "Is she one of your trainees?" he asked Henry.

Henry nodded. "Yes, she is."

George looked impressed, eyeing me up and down in a way I suspect he wouldn't have dared if he were living. "Wow, you have the best job. There were hardly ever any women at our place, and never such good-looking ones."

I smiled at the compliment, knowing he intended no offense.

George closed his eyes, and his spirit began to drift back toward the grave. His shape became less defined, fading by degrees until at last, he was nothing more than the mist out of which he came. The mist circled the grave like a cat looking for a comfortable spot to rest in, and then with a small puff, it thumped against the ground, and all trace of George was gone.

"Wow, that was awesome," I said. "But why did he go so quickly?"

Henry took a step back from the stone, ready to return to the willow. "Your magic wasn't especially strong. Next time try spindling a little more, so he can stay for a longer time. You did real good, Cat. I'm proud of you. How do *you* feel?"

"Brilliant, as it goes. Should I have another go? I can try to pull a little more this time."

Henry shook his head. "No, not today. George isn't quite ready to cross over just yet, and I knew he wouldn't mind a short summoning, but I wouldn't push him too far. Let's give it a day or so, and then maybe we can try again." He picked up both our mugs and began walking back toward the willow, so I fell into step beside him.

"What do you want me to practice on in the meantime?" I asked. The truth was, I felt like I was on a roll and wanted to do it again. Heck, I'd have woken every darned soul in the cemetery if Henry would allow it.

"There are several different versions of this spell in your book. Learn them. Learn the incantations. And practice spindling more magic. The more you can hold inside you, the more competent you will become."

I liked the sound of that.

"That should keep you busy until dinnertime, anyway."

"Okay, I promise. I'll study. What are we going to do tonight?" I didn't want to sound too eager but was hoping for a little alone time with Henry, preferably without magic books or incantations.

"Not sure yet. Unfortunately, I have to go out with Dad before dinner. Just for a few hours. That's why he asked to see me."

My disappointment must have registered on my face because he added, "I'll make it up to you later, I promise." We had just reached the willow tree, and Henry gallantly pulled back the branches to allow me to pass under them.

"Anything fun?" I asked, trying to sound upbeat about it, though I felt more hollow than anything.

"Just a little family business. Nothing for you to worry about. I don't think we'll be gone very long."

That was something, at least. "Is Eleanor going with you?"

Henry shook his head. "Nope, 'fraid not, but I think she has plans of her own. You think you'll be able to survive in a big bad abbey, all on your lonesome?"

I laughed. "I'll do my best. Just be sure to leave plenty of breadcrumbs so I can find my way around in there." I nodded in the general direction of the Abbey.

"I will," he said.

As the branches fell behind us, I paused and turned to face him. Here, under the protection of the willow tree, we were quite alone. I ached for him to kiss me, and I stood still, my gaze fixed on his face, leaving him in no doubt of my intentions and offering him the perfect opportunity to make a move.

Henry came close and looked like at last, he might take the hint and finally go for it. He stood before me, staring back into my eyes, his own dancing with hope and desire. This was the moment things would start for us, I was sure of it.

Henry shifted the mugs in his hand out of the way, but the move was so clumsy he almost dropped them, and the remnants of my hot chocolate dribbled out and stained his coat. "Shit," he cried, his tone a mixture of frustration and apology.

"Never mind, I know a good spell for that. I'll take care of it when we get inside. Give me those mugs."

Henry shook his head, and with a wave of his hand, the stain vanished. Still, he handed the mugs to me, and I placed them on the ground by my feet. "Now do what you were just about to do."

Henry's smile returned, and he stepped forward and caressed my cheek. I tilted my head up and held my breath as he bent slightly and brought his lips to mine. The taste of chocolate still lingered on his lips. His kiss was gently probing, and I found myself pushing up to his body, wanting more.

"Good Lord, the things that go on under this poor ol' willow tree." Eleanor had come back and was smiling at us. She brushed past, continuing toward the Abbey. "Oh, don't let me stop you."

But the mood was broken. Henry cleared his throat and said, "We'll continue this later, when I get back from my trip with Dad."

I nodded, sorry for the interruption yet delighted we were finally getting somewhere. It wasn't magic that made me feel so delighted as I went to collect my magic book. Although maybe it was. The best kind of magic. I picked up the heavy tome and followed Eleanor inside. Henry came behind with the empty mugs.

We'll continue this later. Thinking about this made me smile, and I wished it was later already. Later couldn't come soon enough.

Chapter Twenty-Four

A NEW SECRET

After one last stolen kiss in the hallway, Henry made his excuses and left to get ready for his trip. He promised he'd be back before dinner, and I consoled myself with thinking the sooner he left, the sooner he'd get back.

I'd found my room with relative ease, floating along almost on autopilot. As soon as the bedroom door closed, I dropped the book on the bed and flopped down right beside it. There would be no studying now, not for a bit anyway. I was too busy reliving that wonderful kiss out there under the willow. I closed my eyes and ran my fingers over my lips, my skin tingling with the thrill of the memory. I'd waited so long for this moment to come, and now that it had, the wait had been so worth it.

After a little while, I heard a few doors closing downstairs, and I pushed off the bed and strolled over to the window. Sure enough, there was Henry, buttoning his coat and watching the Abbey door. I opened my window to wave good-bye. A rush of cold air enveloped me.

Henry looked up, and seeing me there, he smiled and blew me a kiss.

"You off then?" I said. I was being Captain Obvious, but I didn't care. Any excuse to talk worked for me.

"Yes. Dinner is about six. We should be back by then, you know Dad." Henry laughed, and I smiled along with him.

The front door slammed, and the General marched on by him, leaving his son to catch up. I only saw his dad's face once, but judging by the scowl planted there, he was not in a good mood.

Not that I cared. My gaze returned swiftly to Henry, who I watched diligently until he was lost under the branches of the willow tree. I wondered if he'd be thinking of our kiss as he passed through it. I could think of little else.

I was about to close the window when the door opened again, and this time, Eleanor came through it. I thought she might be going with them, her steps were rapid as if she was hurrying to catch up, but when she reached the willow tree, she stopped.

I also thought she might have forgotten something and was about to call down and offer my services when the branches swayed, and a young man appeared. He was much taller than she was, with a thick mop of curly brown hair and the murky brown aura of a werewolf. He was good-looking, too, in a rugged, Chris Evans kind of way.

The two embraced immediately and kissed. Eleanor hadn't mentioned a boyfriend, but since she hadn't known me for very long, I was not surprised by this. Her dating a werewolf was something else. That was ballsy, and I wasn't sure I'd be up to taking the same risk. Werewolves were nothing if not unpredictable.

After a moment, the two pulled apart, and he spoke, his voice a deep rumble. "Thank Gaia, you know I almost ran straight into your dad."

Eleanor glanced over at the willow, as if she expected her father to reappear at any time. "He didn't see you, did he?"

"I don't think so. If he had, I have a feeling we'd know about it. He'd be running after me with a stick and a spray bottle of Febreze."

"Yes, you're right. Anyway, we don't have long. You'd better come inside before we freeze to death. I swear it's getting colder by the second."

The werewolf nodded, and the couple hurried back toward the Abbey. Realizing they would see me, I stepped back—just as Eleanor began to look up. My heart thumped against my chest. Had the curtain moved, betraying me? Had she seen me? She would know this was my room. I hadn't meant to spy on her, but I felt awkward all the same.

The door closed below, and all went quiet.

I knew I was as free as I'd been before, but not knowing where Eleanor and her friend were hanging out, I suddenly felt like a prisoner in my room. After all, I certainly didn't want to disturb them. It was clear from that brief encounter outside that their time together was limited. And like she'd said herself, who ever wanted to play gooseberry? Also, I didn't want to hear growling and snarling and yowling, depending on what might be happening. I'd never be able to look Eleanor in the eye again.

Nope, for the next few hours, I would have to be happy with my memories of Henry kissing me and my magic book. I flopped belly down on my bed and pulled the book close to me. True, I really didn't feel like studying right now, but on the other hand, I didn't want to disappoint Henry, after promising him I would.

I flipped the pages, searching for the chapter I had seen on Necromancy and summoning the spirits of the dead.

I studied with interest the pages on so-called black magic. There were graphic images of reanimated flesh, howling ghouls, and— "Oh, yuck!" Hag-like witches simpered over the torn bodies of the recent dead as they tried to glean their secrets. One image had an old woman doing unspeakable things to a corpse, and even though all things gothic fascinated me, I knew I would quit being a necromancer at once rather than subject myself to that.

The images left me with a better understanding of my parents. No wonder Mom had such a fear of necromancy—it was rarely depicted in a favorable light. However, I wasn't here to mull over grotesque images of the old and recent dead. I had been tasked with learning some spells, so I flipped the pages more quickly, seeking the relevant passages to help with just that.

A little while later, I heard doors closing downstairs and then hurried footsteps across the gravel path. I didn't get up. I'd been caught at the window already and didn't want to be accused of snooping.

I'd been reading for over an hour, and my head was crammed full of spells and incantations, so much so I thought I would burst, or more likely fall asleep forever and never wake up again. My brain was so numb now I seriously doubted I'd be able to remember a single spell if Henry asked me.

Mmm, Henry. I glanced at my phone to check the time. It was five thirty. He would be home soon. As I pushed myself up off the bed, there was a knock at the door. I straightened my clothes and went to open it.

Eleanor stood in the hallway. Her cheeks were a little flushed, but other than that, there were no signs she'd had company a few minutes ago. She looked beyond me, as if checking to see if I was alone when she must have known I had to be. "Can I come in?"

I stood aside to let her pass.

My book was still open on the disheveled bed. She sat down and glanced at the open page before closing it. "You must excuse me," Eleanor said. "Unlike my brother, I wasn't blessed with the gift, and I find the images disturb me."

"No problem. They disturb the hell out of me too!" I walked over to the window, and turning, I leaned against the sill. I had a hunch about what she wanted to talk about but thought it best to keep quiet and let her lead. I didn't have to wait too long.

"Victor and I have been together for a few years now. Pop doesn't approve of his kind, so we've been meeting in secret. It didn't matter at first—after all, it was just a bit of a fling when it started, but well, it's much more serious now, and neither of us are sure what to do next."

"Why don't you just tell him? Times are changing. People are much more accepting of that kind of thing now than they used to be."

Eleanor's laugh was humorless. "You've met Pop, right? He'll never accept him as a werewolf—they have little magic and are frowned upon by a lot of our kind, especially the older magicians."

I frowned, hating to hear what she was saying but knowing it to be true.

Eleanor furrowed her pretty brow and studied her well-manicured nails. "The only chance we have is if Victor makes it big. He's been speculating a lot of late. He's very good at guessing the market, unless it's a full moon, of course, and then he's careful not to trade, but he's slowly making quite a fortune for himself. And if there's two things Pop loves above all else, it's fame and money. If Victor's ship comes in, we might have a chance."

"Or you could run away together. It's not like you need his approval."

"We've talked about it, and it might come to that. Anyway, we'll see."

She sighed as she pushed herself off the bed. "Well, I suppose I'd better leave you to it. They'll be home soon, and judging from what I saw earlier, you'll be eager to look your best."

I chuckled, a little embarrassed but also pleased. "Sorry about that, it just happened, I never even expected it."

"Ha, you didn't? Well, I did."

Eleanor smiled, and I raised my hand to tidy my hair. I had been lolling about on the bed for a while after all. "Yes, you're right. I ought to freshen up."

"I suspect my brother will adore you either way."

We laughed together this time.

"Don't worry about your dad finding out about Victor. My lips are zipped. Or Henry, either. Omertà. Nada. Sisters before misters. Pinky promise swear."

"Ha, I know you won't," she said.

A strange smell made my nostrils tingle. What was it? Where was it coming from? I leaned closer to Eleanor, sniffing the air between us.

"What's wrong?" she asked, frowning.

"Uh, you might want to consider changing your clothes and taking a shower. Victor's scent is lovely, but he's all over you. I think your dad might notice. Henry certainly will."

"Oh. My. GOODNESS." She turned and sprinted out. I heard her cry, "Thank you!" before her footsteps faded.

Anything for you, dear future sister-in-law, I thought, and I cracked up laughing.

As I closed the bedroom door behind her, I thought about her friendship with Victor and was a little sad for them both. Henry and I were lucky. I could see no reason at all why the General would oppose our relationship, and I imagined Henry couldn't either. Poor Eleanor. I wandered into the bathroom and turned on the shower faucet. I didn't have much time, but I still wanted to look my best. I would make dinner if I hurried.

I stripped off quickly and languished for a moment under the hot jets. As I closed my eyes, I forgot all about Eleanor and thought about Henry and that sweet, sweet kiss. I hoped for more. Much, much more.

Chapter Twenty-Five

SCAR

THE NEXT FEW DAYS WERE QUITE POSSIBLY THE HAPPIEST OF MY LIFE. Henry and I wiled away the hours studying and kissing, then studying and kissing some more. Rather than be outraged by it, the General seemed more than happy with our wanton behavior. If anything, I would have gone so far to say that he openly encouraged it. He smiled indulgently as our hands clasped under the table and didn't bat an eyelid when we secreted off to some dark corner to be on our own. My own dad would never have allowed it, but then, I wasn't the General's daughter, after all. What was the adage? *Daughters must be chaste, but sons may sow their oats.* Not that oats were being sown anywhere, but the thought went some way to explaining the General's attitude.

If Eleanor felt any jealousy at the contrast in our circumstances, she didn't show it. Indeed, she encouraged us at every opportunity, smiling knowingly at her older brother when he squeezed my waist and then again at me when I blushed for it. I felt blessed. I was one of the family. Accepted by all. Or so I thought.

The sun was unseasonably friendly today, and putting my book aside for a moment, I sat back on a bench outside the Abbey and basked in its warmth. I heard footsteps heading toward me, and when I opened my eyes, there was Henry, hovering over me, looking down. He was cupping something small in his hands, and I wondered what it might be.

"There's someone I would like you to meet," he said, as he sat down next to me.

Curious, I turned on my seat to see what it was. Henry opened his hands a little, leaving a small hole through which a tiny hamster popped his head out. His nose twitched as he sniffed the fresh air and took in his surroundings.

"This is Eddie Van Halen, my familiar."

I laughed out loud and then cooed as Henry offered me his tiny friend and lowered him gently onto my outstretched palm.

"He's very friendly. You won't scare him," Henry said.

Indeed, the little fellow just sat there, looking up at me with the quiet confidence of an alpha cat. "Isn't he small for a familiar?"

"You think so? To be honest, I don't use him much. He's more of a companion than anything."

"I can't believe you've deceived me all this time."

"What? How?"

"By not telling me about this wittle cutie pie."

"Oh, right, sorry." Henry petted the back of Eddie's head with the tip of his finger. "As you know, all magic has a cost, especially ley line magic. With your earth magic, the cost is born by the plant or the powder, or whatever it is you're using, but it's a little different with ley line magic."

"Yep, prolonged use drains your energy and wears you down." Henry cocked his head sideways at me. "I've been keeping up with my reading." I added.

"Just so. I've seen unshielded witches shrivel down to nothing and turn into little more than warty hags."

Put that way, ley line magic didn't sound quite so appealing.

"That's the point of a familiar," Henry explained. "Eddie here does a good job at siphoning the excess for me, so neither of us suffer too much. If, like me, you don't plan on using ley line magic much, you might not even need one, but if you do, you should certainly look into getting a familiar of your own."

"I see." Of course I wasn't completely ignorant on the purpose of a familiar, but I hadn't seriously considered one before now. "What do you think I should get?"

Ever so carefully, Henry lifted Eddie from my hands and slipped his friend into the safety of his shirt pocket. How many times had it been secreted in there without my knowledge? The thought made me smile.

"That's up to you, of course, but I wondered if I might introduce you to another little friend of mine."

Henry shifted sideways, and this time he put his hand into his jacket pocket and pulled out another small and fluffy bundle, all curled up and snoozing. At first, I thought he'd brought me a strange-colored kitten, because its coat was a mix of black and fire red, but when it lifted its sleepy head, I saw it was a baby fox.

"Oh my Gaia, give that to me!" I gasped, raising my hands eagerly to receive it. "He's so precious. What's his name?"

"*She* is Scarlet, though I just call her Scar," he said, depositing the adorable critter into my hands. "She's an orphan, and I just finished weaning her."

"Oh my, you're quite the Dr. Doolittle." I laughed. Scarlet was the most beautiful thing, though she smelled a little musky. "Is she house-trained?"

Henry smirked. "Getting there. What do you think? Do you want her?"

"Where on earth did you get her from?" I asked.

"Her mother lived in the cemetery for years. She passed after giving birth to this wee one. It was touch and go for a while, but I managed to save her."

I wasn't sure what to say. Scar looked up at me with a pair of sleepy brown yet intelligent eyes. Did I think I could click with her? Maybe. And it was the closest thing to a gift Henry had ever offered me. "What about Sylvia? She might not like me bringing an animal into the apartment."

"Already taken care of. She said she wouldn't mind at all. Oh, and I already put in the paper work for a familiar license, so you don't have to worry about that either."

That was presumptuous, I thought. Henry must have guessed what I was thinking because he added, "I thought Eleanor might want her, but she said no. Scar's such a darling and too rare to be ignored. If you don't want her, someone will snap her up quick enough."

I relaxed a little. "Ah. Can I think about it?"

Henry's eyes softened. "Of course. Choosing a familiar is a big thing. You'll want to be sure about each other."

"Thanks." I raised her up to give her back to him, but Henry shook his hand. "How about you two spend some time together? See how you get on. You'll know quickly if you bond. And as soon as you do, she'll start storing some of that magic you're spindling."

"Okay."

I set Scar down on my lap, where she immediately curled up into a tired little ball and fell asleep. Henry inched closer to me on the bench and idly played with my hair. He lowered his head to my neck, and I had just braced myself for a kiss when all Hades broke loose behind us.

"I told you, I don't want you bringing that filth in my home." Something had riled the General and riled him good. I glanced anxiously at Henry, who was sitting stiffly beside me, straining to hear what would come next.

"Don't call him that, Pop. It's offensive. His name is Victor." Eleanor said.

"I don't care what his name is. I will not have a werewolf in my house, and that's final. I forbid you to see him again."

"You can't forbid me. I'm old enough to see whoever I want."

"Yes, you are. But I don't have to support you if you don't listen to me. You'll be out on your ear, quick as a flash."

"Fine. Then I'm leaving."

We heard scraping chairs and a door slam, and a moment later, Eleanor ran from the Abbey, her eyes full of the tears she would soon shed. Henry jumped up and moved to comfort her, but she shooed him away. With a wave of her hand, a purple stream of magic circled the willow, which opened to receive her, and then she was gone. Henry turned back to me, and after securing Scar in my arms, I stood up, but he shook his head.

"You should probably wait here. Let me go inside and see what I can do."

I had no desire to confront the General, not in his current frame of mind, so I did as Henry asked and sat down. Scar slipped through my hands and stood to attention on the bench, her body alert as she looked back to the Abbey. She then fixed her gaze on me, as if trying to read my mind, communicate, or something. I shook my head. "Sorry, Scar, I don't know what to tell you. This one's out of my control."

I picked up my book and held it tight on my lap, as much for something to do as anything else. Shifting around in my seat, I stared at the ground—after all, I was only a guest here and didn't know quite how to behave in the midst of all this family drama. So I sat there, feeling like a complete lemon, not sure whether I should go inside, wait to be fetched, or what. I was thankful at least that it wasn't raining.

A few minutes passed, and though all was quiet inside the Abbey, I had a hunch it wasn't a good time to go in there. But I couldn't sit here all day. I needed to stretch my legs and get moving. Scar seemed to be having the same thought, for she jumped down off the bench and scampered over to the willow.

"Come back," I cried, trying to keep my voice down, not wanting to draw attention to either of us.

As I approached, Scar kept looking back, but as soon as I got close, she would run a little farther on, until at last, she disappeared under the hanging branches of the tree.

I had nothing better to do, so I followed behind her. There was no sign of Eleanor on the other side. I could only imagine she had gone to find comfort in the arms of Victor, as I would have done had I been in her place. The familiar outline of the New York skyscrapers loomed mysteriously before me, reminding me that we were literally feet from the bustle of the metropolis, but in all other regards, we might as well have been a million miles away. Perhaps I should have asked where Victor lived, and now regretted that I hadn't, since Eleanor could easily be anywhere in a city such as this. If she didn't want us to find her, we never would.

"Come on, Scar. Where are you?" I called. I'd have thought with her distinctive black-and-red markings, the little fox cub would be easy to spot, but since bounding through the willow, she'd completely disappeared. "Scar! Come on now, honey." My pace quickened as I grew more anxious. How would I explain losing her to Henry? Like he didn't have enough on his plate as it was. "Come on now, Scar. Don't make me spell you!"

Out of the corner of my eye, I saw a flash of something red over by a broken headstone. Relieved, I made for it, but there was no sign of Scar when I got there. I was about to give up when I saw the tip of a small but bushy tail disappear behind another stone.

"You little rascal."

I followed again. I found Scar at last, curled up in a ball on the grave of Eleanor Tilney. The naughty little tyke appeared perfectly content with herself, looking up at me as if to say, *what took you so long?"*

I shook my head and was about to pick her up when a familiar chill came over me. Transfixed, I instinctively reached for my ring, touching the inset stone and holding my breath as I tried to channel my sensations through it.

The usual thrill of the connection was there, but for the first time, I felt no fear. Whether this was foolish or not, I couldn't say, but I tried to relax as I waited for the spirit to rise from the dead and say what she had to say.

Gently, the sod over the grave seemed to pulse, and then an ethereal specter rose from it and hovered just inches from where I stood. I recognized her at once. Eleanor Tilney—the deceased mother, not the distraught daughter—looked just as I remembered her from her pictures. She appeared very young, much younger than she would've been when she died, and I wondered if spirits had the power to determine the image they presented to the physical world.

For a moment, Eleanor floated silently in the air, a little bewildered as she took in her surroundings. I could feel what she felt and sensed what she thought as her mind adjusted, and she began to focus on where she was. It was amazing, scary, and strangely fantastic.

"You must bring her back," Eleanor said. She spoke slowly and purposefully, but otherwise her voice was so like her daughter's, it took me by surprise.

"I would if I knew where she was," I responded.

"You must find her and bring her back. Otherwise she'll be lost to us forever."

There was no melodrama in her words, just a pining sadness, a mother fearing for her child. My heart ached, and I found myself ready to promise her anything.

"I'll do what I can," I said. "I promise."

"Bring her back. Bring her ba—"

Eleanor's voice trailed away, and her image began to fade along with it.

"What on earth are you doing?"

Startled, I jumped and saw the General standing directly behind me. His hands were set on his hips, and his face was red with fury. Stunned, I was at a total loss for words.

"I—I—"

"How dare you summon my wife? This is how you repay me, after I've shown you the hospitality of my home? How dare you!"

"I didn't summon..."

But the General's blood was up, and he cut me off. "Leave. I want you to leave at once. Go on! Get out now." He rudely pointed over to the gates. "Take your wicked practices and get out of my sight. I never want to see you here again."

I looked around him to the willow, knowing Henry was still in the Abbey and wishing he would come to me now.

"But my things," I argued. "I need my things."

"Never mind those." He reached into his pocket, pulled out a hundred-dollar bill, and flung it at me. It landed inches from where Scar still sat, and the poor thing scampered quickly away, seeking the safety of the willow. "There. Take a Magic Cab and go. I'll have your things sent on. Just leave now."

The General stood firm, barring my way between me and the willow tree. I knew he was still reeling from his fallout with Eleanor, but I didn't know what to do. Completely lost for words, I shook my head, and leaving the money on the ground where he'd tossed it, I walked to the cemetery gates. As I approached them, the locked gates swung silently open, and I could clearly see the bustle of the Magic Apple on the other side.

I wanted to scream. I wanted to cry. I wanted Henry by my side. But I did none of these things, and Henry didn't come to find me.

In my confused state, leaving seemed the only thing to do.

And so, I left.

Chapter Twenty-Six

A FRIEND IN NEED

THE GATES SWUNG SLOWLY BEHIND ME, AND ONCE THEY WERE CLOSED, I knew there was no going back. I heard a clunk as they locked. I felt like I was in a trance. *Please Gaia, let this be a dream,* I thought. *Please let me wake up.*

But it was no dream, and I was awake. All around me, the city buzzed, with business going on as usual. I felt strangely disorientated, but this time knew it was the power of the enchantments that protected the Abbey; those same enchantments that made sure no one was looking its way when the gates opened to let the Tilneys in or out.

I tried to focus, but it was hard to think straight. Henry was just a short distance away from me now but might as well have been on the other side of the moon. I lingered for a minute, but my head was spinning with anxiety and confusion. In the end, I had no choice. I had to move on.

I was vaguely aware of the direction I was going. I really didn't know New York that well, and since I had no money with me, I could hardly hail a cab to take me back to Sylvia's apartment. For a little while, it was all I could do to put one foot in front of another, let alone navigate to the Village. Thankfully, the farther I got away from the cemetery, the less foggy my mind became.

At the street corner, I stopped and waited for the Don't Walk sign to switch to Walk. Just as I was calculating how long it would take to get back to Greenwich on foot, a car horn honked, and a Magic Cab pulled up right in front of me. I recognized Wally at once—not by his face, but by the fact he was so huge, he blocked the view through the window so I couldn't see the other side of the street.

"Where to, pretty lady?"

I smiled sadly at his kind face. "Not today, Wally. I don't have any money with me. Thank you, though."

"Oh." In that moment, Wally looked sadder than I did. But then his face lit up like he'd been struck happy by a sunbeam. "Doesn't matter. Wally take pretty lady wherever she want to go. She pay another day."

Perhaps I should have said no, but I was so grateful I just slid into the back of the Magic Cab and breathed a sigh of relief.

"Where to?"

"Back to Greenwich village," I said.

"No boyfriend today?" Wally asked, as he steered slowly away from the curb, almost slamming into another car.

"Are you out of your mind or something?" the other driver shrieked. Wally's smile didn't falter, as if he hadn't heard the man yell at him at all, which was nigh impossible. The entire Upper East Side must have heard him.

This time there was no need to contradict him about Henry's boyfriend status, but my heart sank. I remembered how happy I was the last time I rode in this cab. "No," I replied. "No boyfriend today."

"Too bad. I like him."

Too bad, indeed. "Yes. So do I." I didn't want to talk about it. I wanted to think and get my head straight. I stared out of the window, my mind not registering a thing I saw through it.

Now that I was calmer, I thought about what the General must have said to Henry after so rudely tossing me from his home. I imagined Henry would be livid, and was probably already on his way downtown, and might even be at the apartment before me. I hoped he'd remember to bring me my phone and bag at least.

But then a darker thought seized me. *Would he come for me?* As rational as my first thoughts had seemed, a degree of doubt kept niggling at the back of my brain. What if Henry accepted the General's view of things and thought I'd deliberately summoned his mother's spirit from the dead? How would he feel about that, since I knew how he felt about letting spirits rest in peace? And this was his own mother. What if he shared the General's ire? *What if he hated me now?*

My gaze fell on the back of Wally's seat. There was a small screen there, rotating through a series of ads aimed at the paranormal market. Right now, it played an ad showing a young couple on top of the Empire State Building. Hand in hand, the two were visiting during the summer solstice. The young witch sighed and affectionately rested her head on her partner's shoulder. Together they looked out over the colorful streams of ley lines, which lit up New York's nightlife like the aurora borealis. Blissfully content, the girl glanced up, and the wizard looked down and he kissed her.

I burst into tears.

All at once, the Magic Cab came to an abrupt stop in the middle of the street. The traffic was reasonably light, but Wally had parked across two center lanes without a second thought. He squeezed out from behind the steering wheel and a moment later was sitting in the back of the Magic Cab with me. Sitting beside me like this, he was simply enormous, even for a dwarf troll. I could have been crushed to death, pressed up against the cab door as I was, but instead, he wrapped a pair of gigantic arms about me and pulled me tight into his chest.

"Someone need a hug," he cooed and began rocking me back and forth like an upset baby. He smelled of damp earth and mortar, but it wasn't unpleasant.

I didn't resist him because he was right—I could use the hug. All around us, drivers were leaning on their horns, but Wally didn't give a hoot about them. The big softy had a friend to comfort, and nothing was going to distract him from taking care of that.

"That it, pretty lady, you cry all you want," he said. "Get it out. I told Ethel about you and your nice man. She like you too. She like to meet you."

"Thank you," I said and pushed away, though only because he was squeezing the life out of me, and I needed to breathe. I wiped away my tears. "Tell her I like her too."

"Better now?" he asked.

"Yes, all better now, thank you."

Wally smiled, and I was glad he was my friend because that enormous mouth of his could probably swallow me whole.

Outside, the horns were becoming more and more irate. And then there was a tap on the window, and an angry banshee in a purple-and-green pizza uniform began shouting through the glass and banging her heavily ringed knuckles against the pane.

"What the heck are you playing at?" *Rap, rap, rap.* "Do you realize it's rush hour? People have jobs to do, you know." *Rap, rap, rap*. "Oh, come on! Are you some kind of moron?" Her voice was escalating to a critical point, and the more Wally remained oblivious, the higher her pitch became.

"Um, Wally, you better get a move on before she goes full-on wail, which could be any moment now."

"You sure you okay, friend?" he asked, taking the liberty of wiping a tear from my cheek. He had chubby fingers.

"Yes, I'll be fine. Come on. We'd better get going."

Wally shuffled awkwardly to the opposite door and slowly squeezed out of the Magic Cab. The irate banshee still hovered, no doubt to make sure Wally really meant to leave. She waved her arms in the air and pulled insanely on her tangle of hair, but she didn't go into a full wail, and thank Gaia, too, as that would have stopped traffic dead. And cracked more than a few windows too.

Back in the driver's seat, Wally glanced one more time into the rearview mirror to check on me, and then slowly—and thankfully—we were on our way again. The banshee was still crying behind us, her wretched screech carrying over the noise of city traffic for several blocks until, at last, I couldn't hear her anymore.

I sat back in the solitude of the passenger seat and longed to return home in Pennsylvania.

Chapter Twenty-Seven

ALL ALONE

HENRY WAS NOT WAITING FOR ME IN THE HALL TO THE APARTMENT. Disappointed, I silenced the voice of doubt that wouldn't go away and consoled myself with the thought it was still early, and that he would come find me when he could. For all I knew, he could still be arguing with his father, telling him in no uncertain terms what a stupid old fool he was, and how could he even *think* I'd do such a thing? Because I wouldn't.

Banana Peel, I thought angrily. The door banged open, and I stamped inside. It slammed shut behind me, bringing me to my senses. "Sorry," I said to no one in particular. No need to take my mood out on Sylvia's apartment fittings.

The apartment was eerily silent. I tapped politely on Sylvia's bedroom door, and when there was no answer, I opened it. She wasn't there. I tried knocking on my door, wondering if perhaps Isabella was asleep, but again, when I popped my head inside, no one was home.

The shop wouldn't be open today. Maybe they had gone out for lunch together?

More exhausted than I should feel, I slumped down on the sofa and stared at a window. If only Sylvia had put in a landline. I felt so lost without my cell phone. How had anyone survived before those things existed? I hoped Henry would be quick about bringing my things.

Maybe I could call to him telepathically? True, I didn't have any of the Egyptian pixie dust he'd used on me before, but then he'd said you only needed to use it the once, just to get things moving. I closed my eyes and concentrated. No matter how hard I tried, I couldn't sense him. I guessed it would help to have some idea about where he was, to have a point of reference. I kept thinking about the Abbey, but if he was there, I wasn't reaching him. Perhaps the enchantments blocked my reach?

When the girls got home, I'd be able to make some calls, but until then, there was nothing I could do. I thought about hunting for a public payphone. After all, there had to be one somewhere in New York, but I wasn't sure I could remember Henry's number, and I doubted his number would be listed anywhere.

Frustrated, I grabbed the remote and flipped on the television, but it was just noise that couldn't grab my attention. I got up and wandered over to the refrigerator. Bottles clinked as I opened the door, but there was hardly anything on the shelves. I guessed no one had done a shopping run. Perhaps that's where they were now?

Bored rather than hungry, I decided not to pop out for a bite of anything. What if Henry showed up while I was shopping and I missed him?

I poured myself some water, numbly watching as the cool liquid sloshed against the side of the glass. After taking a sip, I sat down at the kitchen counter. Normally it was covered in clutter, but someone had taken the time to tidy everything away. Sylvia, I guessed, rather than Isabella. I took a deep breath to clear my mind. If only I'd had my magic book with me. I was pretty sure I'd find something in there to help me.

Weariness turned to anger as I pondered my situation. The General was right to be upset at what he thought I had done, but he was totally out of line throwing me out like that without giving me the chance to explain. He had been wrong about me and had abused his position of authority, tossing me into the street without any of my things. Who did that? What kind of a monster was he? Poor Eleanor. No wonder she'd sought comfort elsewhere.

Thinking of Eleanor made me think about my promise to her mother. My spell book contained plenty to help me with the dead, but what about the living? I didn't recall seeing any detection spells, but then, I hadn't really been looking for one. In any case, my promise wasn't to find her so much as to bring her back to the Abbey. Even if I found her, reconciling her with the General would have been no easy task, even before he flung me out on my ear. But now? In hindsight, I realized I'd been stupid to make that promise, but I had, and now I'd have to figure out how to make good on it.

If only Henry were here. I didn't realize how much I'd come to depend on him until now. His was the voice of reason, the voice I trusted, my best friend. I tapped my foot impatiently on the bar of the stool. "Come on, Henry, where are you?"

The specter of doubt resurfaced. How long had it been since I left the Abbey? Surely Henry had had it out with the General by now. I mentally calculated how long it would take him to pack my things and then come downtown to find me. Traffic had been moderately light on the road with Wally, but it was later in the day now, so things might have changed. I stared at Sylvia's oversize magic clock on the wall. It rarely registered with me, since Mom had one just like it. In fact, most magic families did. Like most clocks, the face told the time of day, and like some, it depicted images of constellations and would pulse a beautiful shade of blue at the start of a new lunar cycle. The divination hands pointed to the optimum place for you to be, be it work, home, play, travel, dining, and so on. Right now, it was set at Sylvia's apartment, but as I stared at it, the divination hand began to pulse. The clock began to whir and chime, and then the hand began to spin. It turned almost a full clockwise circle and came to rest at the 3-D image of my house. *It thought I should go home?*

I shook my head, not caring for that particular forecast. I wanted to be here, needed to be here. This was where Henry would come for me, after all. But the hand remained obstinately still, no matter how much I hoped for a different reading.

Waving my hand dismissively, I took another sip of my water and slipped off the stool, carrying the glass back with me over to the window, where I looked out on the street below. It was just another day down there. No sign of any heartache anywhere. Like you could see it. I would have laughed at myself if I didn't feel so lost and alone.

I must have fallen asleep on the sofa. I woke to the imprint of the cushion on my face and peeled my cheek off it as I pushed myself up. My unfinished glass of water still rested on the windowsill where I'd left it.

It was almost dark outside, and the apartment felt quite empty, even with me inside it. I reached across and turned on the lamp. *What time is it?* The clock registered a little after eight. I'd been sleeping for hours.

Could I have missed Henry? Anxious, I ran over to the door, looking for any signs he might have been here, like a note under the door or pinned outside, anything. But there was no note, even though I flipped over the welcome mat to be sure. Nothing.

Discouraged, I turned on some more lights and returned to the refrigerator. I was a little hungrier now, though not much. The only thing that looked half appealing was a block of cheddar cheese. I pulled it out, and taking a knife from the drawer, I cut off a small chunk. It was an effort to chew, and the heavy cheese was hard to swallow.

Where is everyone?

Something was wrong, I knew it. Too much time had passed for Henry to be held up by traffic. I had to face the fact that he wasn't here because he chose not to come. What other reason could there be? He must have known this was where I'd run to, and he must know I'd be anxiously waiting for him to arrive. Could it be he was more like his father than I'd supposed him to be? Like Mom always said, *The apple never fell far from the tree.*

Anger stirred in me again at my banishment and neglect. The General had no right to hold my belongings hostage like this. Sylvia would go ballistic when she found out. I smiled a little, imagining her going off at him when he showed up for work. If he showed up. My smile faded.

I thought about taking a taxi back to the Abbey, but what was the point? I could stand on the sidewalk and rattle those gates for hours, but they might not answer me, might not even hear me. And those enchantments might make me forget why I'd gone back there in the first place. No. At this time, there was little I could do but wait and see. I hated feeling this helpless. I was a doer, not a waiter.

After swallowing the last of my cheese, I slipped into my bedroom, sat down on the end of the bed, and opened the drawer in the bedside table.

I'd been careful not to spend all the money Sylvia had given me, and I flicked through the envelope now, counting how much I had left.

Where on earth have they got to?

There was just enough for a bus journey home and perhaps something to eat. That calculation had come unbidden, and I shook my head, not quite ready to concede defeat yet. But what choice did I have? That darned clock was ticking, and for all I knew, Sylvia and Isabella might be gone for days. And I couldn't blame them if they had—after all, I couldn't expect them to sit around and twiddle their thumbs, waiting for me to return from the Abbey. I supposed they'd have to come back at some point for the magic shop, but it wasn't as if Sylvia kept regular hours.

Defiant, I returned the money to the drawer and closed it. But I had to be practical too. The first rule of magic was you couldn't conjure something from nothing, and a witch couldn't live on cheese alone. And Gaia help me, the fact of it was, I needed my family right now. Maybe they couldn't help me, but they could love me, and I needed to feel some love. More than anything else in the world. I reached up and touched the silver necklace Dad had given me on my coming-of-age birthday. I thought about his wisdom and what he would have wanted me to do, if he were in my shoes.

I made a decision: I would sleep on it. And if when I woke, if I was still alone, I would trust the magic of the clock and buy a ticket and leave New York. Fully dressed, I fell back on my bed and curled up around a pillow. I closed my eyes and dreamed of Henry. The *swine.* Where in Hades *was* he?

Chapter Twenty-Eight

HOME AT LAST

It was like the magic within me had died. Before today, I had never realized how my mood impacted my energy, but now I felt its absence keenly. I'd woken this morning to an empty apartment and had moved forward on sluggish autopilot ever since. I'd got up, showered, dressed, chewed on another piece of cheese, and wrote a note to Sylvia to thank her for her hospitality and to tell her where I was going. But not why. Then I left.

I felt lost and abandoned by everyone, like someone had blown out my pilot light, leaving me cold and alone.

As I sat on the bus, leaving the city behind me, and watching the foothills of the Pocono mountains rise up before me, I thought about little else other than Henry. Just yesterday, we'd been kissing, oblivious to everything and everyone around us. Perhaps if we'd been less wrapped up in ourselves, we might have seen this blowup between the General and Eleanor coming, but sadly, we had not. I racked my brain, searching for clues and signals that might have resulted in a different outcome—I really hadn't predicted Eleanor telling her father about Victor, after everything she'd said to me—but all I could remember was how blissfully happy I'd been, and could think of nothing but Henry's love and all the things we'd promised to each other. So much for that. At the first test, he'd abandoned me and disappeared off the face of the earth. Three cheers for true love.

I'd kept to myself on the bus. The seat beside me remained vacant, and right now, my bag was sprawled across it. I reached inside and nibbled on the tuna sandwich I'd bought at the station. I didn't have much of an appetite, and the bread tasted stale. I checked the sell-by date. Go figure. The sandwich only had minutes left to live. After a couple of nibbles, I put the half-eaten cardboard back in its plastic wrapper and stowed it away. If I met a hungry cat on my travels, I'd offer it a treat.

Outside, the day was miserable. The dull, overcast sky couldn't have mirrored my mood more completely if it had tried. I was grateful when at long last the bus pulled into town, and I grabbed my things and got off. Home was a fair walk or a taxi ride away. I couldn't wait to be there and only hoped I could make it before the heavens opened up and the rain came down, because it looked like it was planning to do just that.

I was getting my bearings when a familiar voice called out to me. "Cat! Oh, thank Gaia I caught you!"

The familiar face of my dad couldn't have been more welcome. He stood a few feet away from the bus wearing jeans and a raincoat. His posture was slightly bent over, as if already anticipating the rain.

"Dad! What are you doing here? How did you know I'd be here?"

"Your mom said you would be arriving on a bus. I just hoped it was this one and I hadn't missed you!" Dad smiled as he bent down to kiss me on the cheek. "You don't think you got those clever genes from your mom, now, do you?"

I almost laughed.

"Come on," Dad said as he grabbed my bag. "It's going to pour down any moment. Let's go jump in the car and we can talk properly there."

I followed without question and a few seconds later was strapping myself into his Highlander. Dad had put my bag in the back, and climbed in beside me, buckling up.

"Wow, this feels weird."

"Being home?"

"No, sitting up front with you, usually I'm squeezed into the back with the screaming multitude."

"You hungry?" Dad asked.

I thought about the less-than-appetizing sandwich in my bag. "I had a nibble of something on the bus, thanks."

He looked at me critically, like a doctor examining a patient. "Are you sure? Because you look like you need fattening up. Have you lost a little weight since you left?"

I couldn't say I'd noticed and shrugged. "So how did you know I was coming?"

"We got a call from Sylvia earlier this morning. You left her a note," Dad replied.

"Ah."

Well, I was glad she was back at the apartment, but now wondered if I'd done the right thing after all in coming home to Pennsylvania so soon. I stared out of the window. So much for the wisdom of the magic clock.

"She sounded pretty worried. I promised you'd call her when you got home."

"I will," I said. "Did anyone else call?"

"Don't think so. Were you expecting someone?"

"No, I was just wondering. Never mind. Thanks for collecting me." At that moment, he had to turn left, and I was able to hide my disappointment by shifting to look out of my own window.

I remained quiet for the rest of the journey. Every now and then, Dad would glance my way, his handsome brow a little furrowed as he worried about me. I wasn't in the mood to talk. Not really. I yawned, pretending I was tired to explain my silence. I wasn't sure what to say. How would he react if he heard the General had flung me out? I suspect he'd challenge him to a wizard duel, and though Dad was skilled with a scalpel, I doubted his powders and potions would stand up too well to a man skilled in wand craft. Enchantments or no enchantments, the General couldn't stay locked in the Abbey forever, and when he came out, I knew Dad would be waiting. But without telling the General's part in this fiasco, I wasn't sure how to frame the rest.

After a short drive, Dad pulled up to the house and put us in park. He turned off the engine. "Are you sure everything's okay? You're awfully quiet. You know you can tell me anything. Anything at all."

I didn't want to lie to him. "No, it's not, Dad. But it will be. I just need a little time. And thanks." I leaned across the seat and kissed him and then dashed out of the car.

Mom was waiting for us at the door. It was unusually quiet, and I realized the kids must be at school. That was something. I wasn't sure I was up to seeing them all right now. As soon as I reached the step, Mom wrapped her arms around my shoulders and almost squeezed the life out of me in a great hug.

"We missed you," she said, planting hundreds of mom kisses on my cheeks.

I didn't resist or push her away. Instead, I hugged her back. "I missed you too."

"Have you lost weight?"

"Not you too. I don't think so? I've been eating, honest."

The rain was beginning to spit hard, promising lots more to follow. "Come on, ladies. Let's get inside." Dad ushered us forward from behind, and I was instantly greeted by the familiar smells of home-baked cookies and coffee. Mom had rustled up my favorites.

I hung up my poncho, and Dad slipped my bag on the hook next to it. It was comforting seeing all those rows of hooks, currently empty while the kids were out. I looked down at the discarded shoes and around at the scattered toys and abandoned clothes and blankets. Sylvia's place had been so organized by comparison. It was good to be home.

I meandered over to the kitchen table, and a minute later, Mom deposited a hot and frothy latte in front of me. "Thanks," I said.

She sat down across from me, and I saw them both exchange worried glances.

"Why didn't you call and tell us you were coming?" Mom asked.

"I don't have a phone right now," I said.

"You lose it?" Dad asked. "Those things are expensive to replace."

"Misplaced it. It'll show up sooner or later."

Dad bit his lip. Any other time he would have laid into me, but not today. He was far too sensitive for that.

Mom's coffee was rich and refreshing, and I reached across for one of my favorite chocolate covered shortbreads. I ought to call Sylvia, but I needed to use one of their phones and didn't want to make the call in front of them.

"How is everyone?" I asked.

"Good." Mom smiled, and reassured that at least I was in full possession of my life and limbs, she got up and began pounding something in her mortar.

Dad slipped his phone out of his pocket and handed it to me. "I have to get back to work shortly, but make whatever calls you need. Just be quick."

I took it from him gladly and, standing up, grabbed hold of my coffee. "Do you mind if I take this up to my room?"

Dad nodded. And off I went.

With my door closed behind me, I sat in my wicker chair with my right leg hooked under me. I couldn't wait to speak to Sylvia. She was my direct link to Henry, and angry as I was, I was still desperate for news of him. Plus, whatever he thought about this business with his mom, he owed me an explanation for abandoning me. I deserved that at least.

I deposited my coffee on the little table beside the chair and pulled up her number from caller ID.

Her phone barely rang before she answered. "Oh, by Gaia, Cat! What in Hades made you run away like that? I saw your note as soon as I got home. I was worried sick! Wait a minute. I want to be there."

The face of Dad's phone inflated like a hot bubble, but instead of popping, the plastic grew and grew into the robust shape of Sylvia. Her image kept growing until it was the size of a Maine Coon cat, and then the bubble popped off the phone and drifted to a few feet away from my face.

Wow, I thought. That was one I hadn't seen before. I would have to learn that one.

"There, that's better. I can see you properly now. So tell me everything. Don't leave out a single thing."

I kept my voice low and told her everything that had happened at the Abbey. She listened intently, interrupting with only the occasional, "What?" and "No?", "He did what?" and "No way!" Then she said, "He didn't even let you go back inside to get your phone? What a monster. No wonder you headed for home. You couldn't contact me, and you couldn't contact Henry. It's unforgivable."

I couldn't have agreed more, but that went without saying. "And when I got back to the apartment, you were gone, so I decided I ought to come on home," I finished.

"Yes, sorry about that. Funnily enough, I went back to Pennsylvania myself. My darling Matt was pining for me and needed a little love. I must have just missed you when you left. Bad timing."

"What about Isabella? Where is she?"

Sylvia was silent for a moment, and her natural smile left her face. "Let's just say that little fae experiment didn't quite work out. Her brother came and collected her yesterday. I don't think we'll be hearing from her again."

"Oh, sorry to hear that." And it was true. Isabella was a wild one, to be sure, and she sometimes got in the way when I wanted to be alone with Henry, but she had been a lot of fun and had never been mean to me. I thought about Jimmy. Perhaps it was for the best she was gone, if only for his sake. As for her brother, well, it wouldn't bother me if I never saw him again. "What did she do?" I asked.

"Nothing. Not a thing. That's the problem. All partying and no work. I'm sorry and all that, but I can't afford to have someone around who isn't pulling their weight. That's what Henry said, and from what little I saw of her, I had to agree with him. Talking of Henry."

My heart skipped a beat when she mentioned his name. "What of him?"

"I could tell you myself, but I suspect you would rather hear what he has to say directly from him."

"What?"

Her smile widened like a Cheshire Cat. "Toodle-oo. Talk later!" The Sylvia bubble floated back toward my phone, colliding with an audible *pop,* and just like that, Sylvia was gone.

At that moment, two things happened at once. First, I heard a strange rumble outside, like low thunder, and the braying of several horses, unless I was very much mistaken. Riders weren't unknown in this neck of the woods, but this didn't sound like a single rider. And who would go riding in this downpour?

I pulled out my leg from under me and was about to go look out of the window when there was also a knock at my bedroom door. I turned instead to answer that.

It was my dad. One eyebrow was cocked higher than the other, like he didn't know whether to be puzzled or amused.

"I think you'd better go take a look outside."

Confused myself, I handed him back his phone and ran past him and down the stairs. I didn't know who would be waiting for me down there, but I prayed my heart was correct and that I wouldn't be disappointed. My mom stood by the kitchen table, looking equally as amused as Dad had been. I didn't stop to speak but flung open the front door and ran out into the rain.

I stopped in my tracks when I got to the front step. A spectral coach-and-four was parked on our front lawn. The horses, which were almost transparent, snorted and stomped on my dad's weedy turf, pulling at the dandelions and shaking their manes in confusion when their ghostly teeth failed to make purchase with the crop.

Their frosty breath was labored, like they'd been driven long and hard over some distance. To me, it was like a scene straight out of a Jane Austen novel—only the horses were long dead, and I was no Elizabeth Bennet.

And there, sitting in the driver's seat, soaked to the skin and with a riding whip in hand, sat Henry, looking like a drowned rat in a wet white shirt and leather jacket. And he was smiling.

Chapter Twenty-Nine

A HOUSE GUEST

"I DON'T SUPPOSE YOU THOUGHT TO TAKE THE CAR?" I SHOUTED.

Henry raised his hands as if to say, *as you see*, his smile still fixed to his face. "I couldn't. Eleanor has it. This was the best I could do at short notice."

I ran out into the rain and over to the carriage. Henry jumped down and pulled out a bag from inside it. "Your things, I believe." He handed the heavy bag to me—*good, he remembered my book*—then, with a swish of his hand, he said, "*Tâwian ungesýne,*" and the coach-and-four disappeared.

"Where have you been?" I said, raising my voice so he could hear me over the rain.

Henry reached down for my hand and then moved to kiss me, but I was in no mood for that and held him at arm's length. "Hold your horses," I said, and then chuckled. Henry grinned with me. When I recovered, I gritted my teeth to adopt a sterner expression. "You know your dad threw me out, right? Why didn't you come to me at the apartment? I thought you'd abandoned me."

The rain literally dripped off the end of Henry's nose, and he pointlessly wiped it away. "I didn't know. When Dad came in, he didn't say a thing about you or what happened with Mom's spirit. He only told me later. We had a fight about Eleanor, and since he wouldn't listen to reason, I took the car and went out to find my sister."

"Is she okay?" I asked.

"So-so. She'll be all right soon enough. Anyway, I didn't get back until later that night and thought you were in bed. This morning when I found out you were missing, I called Sylvia, who told me where you'd gone. The rest I learned from Dad."

"What did he say?" I asked, bracing for battle.

"He told me he sent you off, and when I asked why, he said because he caught you summoning my mother's spirit."

"That's not true!" I said, heating up inside. "I didn't summon her at all. Scarlet ran off, and I found her on your mother's grave. Your mother rose for a reason, to give me a message concerning Eleanor. I had nothing to do with it, nor would I have, even if I wanted to."

"I know that," Henry said. "I'm not an idiot. And I told him as much. He said I was a lovestruck fool and could run off like my sister. As far as he's concerned, we could both go to Hades."

I softened a little, sorry that he'd fallen out with his father over me. "I wanted to call you, to tell you, but I had no phone and no spell book. Then when you didn't come for me at the apartment, well, I just assumed—"

Henry smiled and shook his head. "You didn't think I would come for you? For a smart little witch, you can be thick as mud some days. You know I love you, don't you?"

How many times had I yearned to hear these words? Now he'd said them, they had a magic all their own. My heart was bursting, and I forgave him everything. Not that I was going to make this easy for him.

"So you used your power as a necromancer to wake these horses from the dead and came rushing to see me in Misty Cedars?"

"Something like that." Henry's eyes widened in amusement.

"You didn't think to take a bus like I did, or like any reasonable person would have done?"

He shrugged. "It seemed like a good idea at the time. I was in a hurry, and like I said, Eleanor wanted to hold on to the car. Plus, I didn't think they would allow this little lady on the bus."

Henry slipped his hand inside his jacket pocket and pulled out something red, black, and furry.

"Scar!" I cried.

I scooped her in my arms, and then after squeezing her as tight as I dared, I flung my arms around Henry and kissed him for all I was worth. I knew how he hated disturbing the dead, but when I needed his help, he'd put his scruples to one side and had done it without hesitation to save me. That was love. That was all I needed to know. As for the rain and the cold, well, what did I care about that? Henry loved me. I loved Henry. Everything else was dressing. If I'd wanted to, I could have conjured a heat spell, but why kill the moment?

Poor little Scar was all forgotten, but a tiny yelp reminded me she was trapped between us. I laughed and pulled away. "Sorry, sweetie," I apologized and then pet her small head. She looked up at me with affection, and I felt a warm buzz all over. She had bonded as a familiar, and I couldn't have asked for a better one. I smiled at Henry, and this time it was his turn to wipe the rain from my face. Eddie's head popped out of his shirt pocket. I guessed the hamster was wondering what on earth was going on.

"I suppose we'd better go in," I said. "My parents must think we're insane."

Henry glanced warily over to the window, evidently less assured of his welcome than I was, even though I could see he was shivering. "You sure your dad won't mind me coming in?"

"I'm sure. In any case, he's off to work in a bit, and you're in luck—Mom made cookies."

"If you say so."

Beaming, I took Henry by the hand and pulled him toward the house.

Once inside, I impressed him with a new spell I'd learned shortly before my stay at the Abbey had ended. "*Drýgan wiðûtan.*" A stream of yellow magic, rather like a sunbeam, caressed us, and a moment later we were both completely dry. Mom looked across at me, frowning, but if she objected to me using ley line magic at home, she didn't say. I could almost imagine her thinking, *maybe just this once.*

"You remember Henry, don't you, Mom?"

She nodded. "Of course. How are you?"

"Very well, thank you," he answered, smiling.

Mom's gaze fell on Scar. I didn't think she'd mind. After all, we had more than a few pets of our own, but I wasn't expecting her to gush as she did.

"Oh sweet Gaia, what a beauty! Where did you find her? I've never seen anything so cute in my life."

"Her name is Scar," I said. "Well, Scarlet. She's my new familiar. Henry brought her back for me. Do you like her?"

"Like her? What's not to like? She's adorable." Mom scooped her from my arms and spun her around like a small child. Thankfully Scar didn't seem to mind. The little cub seemed perfectly happy being in my mom's arms. Mom raised her up and sniffed her. "Is she house-trained?"

"She's clever enough to ask to go outside if she needs to commune with nature," I said.

I pulled a chair out at the table and sat down, ushering Henry into the chair next to me. He glanced at my mother, who was busy putting dog food into a bowl. When Mom saw Henry was waiting for her, she nodded her approval, and Henry sat down. Mom set the food down in the corner of the kitchen where Scar began chomping away. Content, Mom turned her attention back to us.

"What would you like to drink?" Mom asked. Her gaze went from me to Henry, and I could almost hear the gazillion questions she had for us but was too polite to ask. "I have coffee, tea, chocolate? Anything you like."

"I would love a mug of chocolate." I blushed, thinking of the last time we'd had chocolate together.

"Chocolate it is," Mom said. While she fussed about making some, I offered Henry some of Mom's cookies. I smiled inwardly when he reached for the shortbread, just as I had done.

"What happened with Eleanor?" I asked. "When you saw her? How did you find her?"

"After she ran away, I looked everywhere, all the usual places. I was beginning to give up, but then she sent me a text and told me she was staying at Victor's place."

"You said she was okay?" I asked.

Henry pursed his lips. "She's fine. But she doesn't want to see Dad again. Frankly after what he did to you and to her, I'm not sure I want to either."

Mom, who couldn't help but overhear us, turned around to read our expressions, but she didn't interrupt. I suspected she was bursting to know what the General had done and what was going on, but she kept her thoughts to herself.

"So what are you gonna do?" I asked. "Where will you stay? Are you going back to New York? What about the shop?"

Henry shook his head and then raised his hands to take the steaming mug of hot chocolate Mom had just poured. It was too hot to drink yet, so he placed it carefully on a cork coaster and helped himself to another cookie. He winked at Mom, who looked very pleased with herself.

At that moment, Dad came downstairs. He had changed for work and headed straight for the sink without acknowledging Henry at all. He paused when he saw Scar, who right now was curled up in a doggy bed and was snoring softly. Mom shrugged when he looked at her for explanations. Then he turned around and faced us. I held my breath, wondering if he objected to Henry being here.

"If you need a place you stay, you can stay here," Dad said. Mom stared at him in surprise. In fact, we all did. "On the couch, mind you." His gaze shifted from Henry to me and then back again. "Until you figure out what you intend to do and sort yourself out."

"Thank you," Henry replied. "I don't know what to say. I don't know what I'm doing. I was going to talk to Sylvia to fix something short term until I found a place to camp down."

"Well, you're welcome to stay here 'til you do. Just don't eat all those shortbread cookies," Dad said. "They're my favorite too."

I grinned, and jumping from my seat, I ran over to the kitchen to give Dad a big hug.

"Okay, okay. Don't crease the shirt," he protested. "I have to get to work."

I kissed him anyway. "You're the best dad ever, you know?" I said.

"Naturally," Dad replied. Then he kissed Mom on the cheek and headed out of the house.

I don't think Henry had ever been surrounded by so many children before. It had been a long day for us both, and we needed to relax, but there was no relaxing with the tiny terrors running rings around our feet and crashing into legs and chairs and pretty much anything that got in their way. The fact that we were there at all didn't help, since it made them more than usually excited to see us. Henry took it with good grace, but before long, I could see he'd had enough and needed to escape.

"Come on," I said, jumping up off the sofa where we'd been sitting hip to hip. "It's not raining any more. Shouldn't we see to your horses?"

Henry didn't need to be asked twice. "Good idea," he said, standing up with me. I knew they didn't need a lot of seeing to. After all, they were already dead, but it seemed as good an excuse to get out as any.

"Take your shoes off when you come home," Mom said. "It's muddy out there. And don't be *late*." She said the latter with more emphasis. I didn't respond. It was strange, being back under her scrutiny after having had so much personal freedom in New York. I wasn't sure I was comfortable with it anymore. I liked that she cared, yet I felt constricted.

"We won't," Henry replied for both of us.

I slipped into my poncho and, as a precaution, pulled on a set of rubber boots.

"What size are you?" I asked.

"Eleven," Henry said.

"Dad takes an eleven and a half, but these should fit you." I picked Dad's boots out of the lineup and handed them to Henry.

Henry squared them to the sole of his foot, then kicked off his own shoes, and tried them on.

"They're a little on the big side, but I can walk in them. You sure your dad won't mind?"

"Not a bit."

Once we were both coated and booted, we went outside. The rain had certainly ceased, but the moon was bright, and I could see puddles everywhere; Mom had been right to warn us against the mud.

Henry stepped carefully over to where he left the horses and once again, waved his hand through the air. "*Sîe forðgesýne*." The horses reappeared. I could hardly see them, it was so dark, but I saw their glowing breath misting in the air. "Thank you for waiting," he said, affectionately patting the neck of the horse closest to him.

"You can feel them?" I asked.

"And ride them. It is part of our gift. Would you like to try?"

Excited and curious, I nodded.

Henry slipped his hand through the horse's bridle and slowly turned the set back in the direction they had come from. Once they were in position, he took me by the waist and hoisted me up in the passenger seat. I was a big girl and could have done it myself, but I liked him helping me. It was the weirdest thing. If I closed my eyes, I felt like I was sitting on a carriage, which I knew I was. But if I opened them, it was like I was floating midair in a seated position, and I could barely see the coach below me or the horses ahead.

"This is weird," I said.

"Perks of the job."

"My neighbors are going to flip out if they see us." I said.

"I didn't think you had any, other than the Allens. Anyway, no one will see you. Once you touch the dead, you disappear yourself."

"My parents saw you."

"Because I wanted them to."

I still had a lot to learn.

Henry handed me the reins. A moment later, we were rolling on.

"Where are we going?" I asked.

"Just to the cemetery. It's time these beauties were sent home to their rest."

"But this isn't their cemetery," I reasoned.

"It doesn't matter. They will find their way home. The dead can always connect with the ones they loved, both above and below ground. You'll see, one day."

I wasn't quite sure what that meant, and I didn't want to ask him.

It was pleasant, rolling along with Henry at my side. He was so close his body warmed me, and I leaned in closer, glad to have him back in my life and choosing not to cast a warming spell, since I liked snuggling up. Above us, the stars shone a little more brightly than I ever remembered before. I thought about the morning and how so much had changed in these last few hours. I didn't care two hoots what the General thought of me, as long as I had his son and his love.

"Tell me more about my mother," Henry said. His voice was wistful, and I felt sad I'd had the chance to see her when he had not.

I thought for a moment as the cart rolled on. “I thought she was very beautiful. She reminded me of Eleanor in some ways.”

Henry nodded. “Yes. They were very much alike, physically and in personality.”

“She wanted me to help reunite Eleanor with the General. She made me promise.”

Even in this pale moonlight, I could see Henry shake his head. “That’s never going to happen. She made it very clear to me she wanted nothing to do with him ever again. If you gave my mother your word, I’m afraid you’re going to have to break it. Nothing will reunite those two. My father has done his worst. I’ve never seen my sister so angry. Or him, as it goes.”

“Didn’t you have a clue about Victor?”

Henry took a deep breath. “She swore me to secrecy, but I suppose the cat’s out of the bag now, as they say. Yes, I knew. To be honest, I wasn’t that thrilled about it, either. You know how violent they can be when they turn. I was worried about her. But then I met him, and well, he’s not a bad sort.”

“How did you meet him?”

“At the shop, as it happens. He wanted a silver wristband to stop him from turning into a werewolf when the full moon rises. Plus, he also wanted to check me out. Eleanor had mentioned I worked there.” He snorted. “He just came right out with it. ‘I’m Victor, I’m a werewolf, and I’m dating your sister.’ I had to check the calendar to make sure it wasn’t April first. Judging by the Porsche parked out front, the guy’s friggin’ *loaded.*”

I nodded. I’d heard that silver bullets, or any kind of silver weapon, could kill a werewolf. But I didn’t know that deliberate contact with silver could inhibit lycanthrope transformation. I wondered what the effects were—and how painful it might be to the wearer.

“That must have been an interesting conversation.”

“Yeah, well, I know he cares about her deeply. I still think she’s mad, but I’ve met worse.” He squeezed my hand softly. “I’m sorry. It’s not fair that you got caught up in any of this business. None of this is your fault. I know that, don’t worry.”

I leaned my head onto his shoulder, thankful that he trusted me and took me at my word.

The cemetery wasn't too far from the house, but I had moved forward slowly, wanting to prolong my time alone with Henry. Still, short of putting the animals in reverse, we were soon at our destination. After a stolen kiss and cuddle, I jumped down.

Once safely on the ground, Henry patted the horses one last time. "Well, my friends, it's time for you to return to your slumber. Thank you for all your help." Then he raised his hands in the air and cried, "*Oncirran ætniman dôð lîflêas.*"

I remembered that one from my spell book, although it was always a challenge to get all those dratted inflections right. Just one mispronunciation and the entire spell would collapse like a Jenga tower—but Henry made no such mistakes. I recalled the words meant, *return to the dead.* At once, the horses broke into a gallop, riding through the cemetery wall as if it wasn't there. Then, the front horses took a great leap, and with a final cry, the coach-and-four dived headfirst into the ground.

The wheels rumbled as if on gravel, and then they were gone.

I thought I heard one last whinny, but it was probably my imagination.

"Wow, that was awesome," I said.

Henry linked his fingers through mine, and together we turned to head back to the house.

Chapter Thirty

THE TEARS OF MISS MORLAND

I WOKE WITH A START. I HAD BEEN DREAMING ABOUT THE DEAD. AT least, I thought I had been. Like most dreams, the details began slipping away the moment my eyes had opened. I closed them again, trying hard to get back to it. I sensed someone had been telling me something, something important, but no matter how much I willed it, however much I tried, I simply couldn't quite make the connection. Though I *felt* the importance of the dream, I couldn't remember its substance.

Frustrated, I sank into my pillow and tried to fall back to sleep. The dream was gone, but its echo was still in my head, taunting me. After half an hour of pillow crunching and tossing about, I gave up. I slipped out of bed, and because Henry was sleeping downstairs on the couch, I chose not to be seen in my jimjams and got fully dressed.

The house was almost silent. I could hear Henry sleeping soundly downstairs. He wasn't snoring, but I supposed we'd all worn him out, and his breathing was heavy and deep. I tiptoed over to where he lay and stared down at his face. I could just see him in the dark. He looked so peaceful and handsome, and I didn't want to disturb him.

"Catherine." The female voice in my head was loud and clear, and startled, I took a step back. I thought perhaps it was Mom, wondering what I was up to down here, but there was no one downstairs, and no movement up above.

"Catherine," the voice said again. This time, I was sure it wasn't Mom. Looking down, I noticed Henry slept on soundly. His breathing was as rhythmic as ever, and then he sighed and rolled over on his side.

Without knowing how or why, I knew what I had to do. I tiptoed over to the door, pulled on my poncho and boots, and carefully tugged on the door latch, careful not to disturb Henry. I heard a whimper. Scar was a footstep behind me, her eyes wide and hopeful. I was afraid she might bark and wake him up. "Shush, baby. Not tonight. Go back inside." I leaned down and gently nudged her inward as I closed the door as quietly as I could.

The night was cool but bearable. I retraced my own footsteps, set on returning to the cemetery, sensing the eyes of the owls that I knew were all around me, watching from the shadows.

The closer I got to my ancestor's grave, the more I sensed her. I pictured her as she was that first time I saw her, all those years ago when she appeared before me dressed in white. Would she look as I remembered her? Or had time played tricks with my memory? I knew I would shortly find out.

The spirit of Catherine Morland was waiting for me by the grave. I was not disappointed. She looked just as I recalled, her skin deathly white, her silver hair floating unnaturally about her, swimming slowly in the ley line energy that brought her to me from the beyond.

This time, I was not afraid. I could feel her need to communicate with me. This time, I had come as a grown woman, not a helpless, ignorant child, afraid of the force growing inside her. I knew I had the power to make her go or let her stay, and knowing this gave me courage. I noticed she had the same cheekbones as I had, just like my mother's, but that was where the familial resemblance ended. Her eyes were large and black, her lips thinner, her figure gaunt. I didn't remember seeing the marks of the noose on her neck before, but they were clearly visible now. She reached her spectral hands across to me, beckoning me to her. I approached.

"Little Catherine, my, my, how you have grown," she said. "Come closer, so I may see you properly." Her voice was hollow but calm, slow, and purposeful. She had crossed over from the beyond to communicate with me, and each word was pronounced carefully, leaving no room for misunderstanding. I felt only kindness in her, no evil, and I stepped forward just as she asked.

"You wanted to speak to me?" I said.

"I have oft wanted to speak to you, my child. But today, I come on behalf of another. Listen close, for I cannot tarry long..."

She closed her eyes, and her image became faint. I could tell she was slipping away. She had crossed without assistance, and the strain must have been enormous for her. I held my hands out before me, my palms facing down toward the earth. If I didn't help her, I feared she might fade away at any moment. I focused on my azurite ring, invoking a connection with it through which I could harness my magic. Then, when I sensed some harmony, I tapped into the power of the ley lines surrounding me and spindled as much magic as I could amass. That same feeling of delight washed through me, and when it became almost too much to bear, I let it go, sharing as much as I could with Catherine. Her spectral image froze and then jumped back, surprised by the force of the energy I'd spindled. But her form became more stable, and she moved a little closer to me and away from the grave.

"I see you have grown in other ways, also," the old woman smiled. "And I have a song for you. You must promise to remember it."

Odd, I thought. I wasn't expecting that. The last thing I thought she wanted was to sing to me. "I'll try," I said, thinking I'd made enough promises to the dead of late. That and my memory wasn't always perfect. I hoped I wouldn't let her down.

Catherine closed her black eyes and nodded once or twice, as if rehearsing the words in her head. And then she began to sing.

Dancing with my sweetheart and my children, one to three,
With the Goddess there beside us under shade of willow tree,
Turn the circle once then twice,
And sing out all our praises
As we thank you for our blessings on this gentle bed of daisies.

Merry meet and blessings be, we spin under the light,
We dance together, hands entwined, 'til day turns into night,
Circle in, and circle out,
We sing with all our heart,
Receive our thanks, O blessed one, and pray we never part.

Her voice was eerily beautiful, a strange blend of hope, love, lamentation, and despair. It was not a sound I had heard from the living, nor thought I would ever hear again. It had a power of its own, and I listened to the words, completely entranced.

The song ended, and Catherine opened her eyes. Strange, though they were black and lifeless, they were now filled with tears.

"Why are you crying?" I asked.

"These are not my words, but the words of another. I can feel her pain as she recalls them. They come from a place of love and a place of regret."

I nodded, believing I understood.

"Remember your promise," Catherine said. "You must recite the words, exactly as I sang them. Change nothing, for the words are magic."

It was my turn to close my eyes. I repeated the song in my head until I thought I had it. Somewhere in the cemetery an owl hooted, breaking my concentration. Irritated, I opened my eyes and found myself standing in utter darkness.

"Wait, what?" *Shoot, was it merry meet and dance together, or merry dance and meet together?* How was I supposed to remember that after just one hearing? I prayed I'd be able to recall it perfectly when I had to.

Chapter Thirty-One

BETRAYAL

THE NEXT TIME WHEN I WOKE UP, I FOUND SCAR CURLED UP AT THE bottom of my bed. It was the strangest feeling. I'd not used all the magic I'd spindled in the cemetery last night. and as she lay there sleeping, I could feel her siphoning off the excess. It felt like cool water running through my veins. Weird, but interesting. Oh well, that was what familiars were supposed to do, wasn't it, to balance energy levels? Who was I to complain?

Everyone else had risen long before me, and I descended the stairs to find madness and mayhem in the kitchen. And Jimmy. He still wore his coat, and I got the impression he'd just arrived. Right now he was chatting to Henry, as he chowed down on a generous plate of Mom's bacon and eggs.

Jimmy smiled as I approached, but the sparkle was missing, and I sensed all still wasn't well with him.

"Hey, Jimmy, when did you get home?" I asked. I gave him a sisterly kiss on the cheek and a quick hug.

"Just," he said.

I glanced over to where Mom was fussing about putting the finishing touches on another impressive breakfast plate. I suspected those eggs were not for me. *Mothers and sons.*

"I didn't think you'd be home for a few more days. How were the exams?"

He shrugged and sat back in his seat as Mom deposited a pile of food in front of him. "I don't know what they feed you in New York, but you're all thin as rakes." She shook her head. "I've a good mind to go back with you when you return."

A loud bang had Mom running into the rarely used dining room. I shifted slightly just in time to see our youngest brother, Joe, playing with Mom's mortar and pestle. He was covered head to toe in a green vapor, and the place stank of rotten vegetation. Joe was grinning, like he'd made the discovery of a lifetime.

"Why, you little—"

We never heard the end of that sentence. Joe had seen her coming, and she was forced to chase him out into the yard. A moment later, I could hear laughter as Mom joined in their games outside.

Jimmy nibbled on a little bacon and then pushed his plate away.

"Are you not going to eat that?" I asked.

Jimmy shook his head. My own appetite was back with a vengeance, so I set into the food at once, laughing with my mouth full when Henry looked at me sideways.

I swallowed hard. "What, a girl can't eat?" I was already piling the next lot on my fork.

"Your appetite is a beautiful thing to behold," Henry said, mesmerized. I blew him a kiss.

There was so much I wanted to ask Jimmy, and I hoped we'd find some time alone together. Henry must have sensed something of the sort because he sat back and stretched. "You know, while I'm here, I might pop over to see how Matt's getting along. You don't mind, do you, Cat?"

I shook my head. "Not at all."

"Good. I don't suppose I'll be long. Once you've finished that mountain of food, come over and join us, if you feel like it. Otherwise, I'll be back in a bit."

Henry stood up and took his plate over to the sink where he rinsed it off. Jimmy glanced at me and raised his eyebrows as if to say, *I bet Mom loves him.* I suspected she already did.

"Won't be long." Henry planted a fat kiss on my cheek, and a moment later he left.

"Well," I said, wasting no time now that we were alone. "What's going on?"

Jimmy thought for a minute, and I got the feeling he was struggling to put his thoughts into words. Then he shook his head, and after looking past me and reassuring himself Mom was busy outside, he pulled a little red pouch out of his pocket. He placed a small amount of white powder into the palm of his hand and blew all of it into the space over the kitchen table.

"Dude!" Just in time I scrambled to move my plate out of harm's way.

A dull mist began to form, which separated into two wisps of smoke. Each began to twist and turn, rolling into themselves like angry, tempestuous clouds.

At last, I could make out two cloud-shaped people. The first was Isabella, the second her brother, John. I winced when I saw him. I'd really hoped I'd seen the last of him.

"You'd better go in a minute. He'll be here any moment," the Isabella-shaped cloud said.

"Don't worry, I'll be gone before he gets here. I still can't believe he's giving you a second chance, not after that dirty picture you sent him. He must be desperate." John sneered sarcastically, and I suddenly wanted to punch him.

"Well, he begged," Isabelle replied. "You know I can't resist a man who'll do anything I tell him."

"Unlike Freddy."

Isabella sighed. "Ah, yes, well, Freddy's a *real* man. Jimmy doesn't even come close. But you know, I'm flat broke, and there's no way I can stay in New York unless someone helps me out. I need to keep his grubby little hands on me for a while longer, at least."

John snorted. "Well, good luck with that. I didn't even get to first base with that stuck-up sister of his. Not that it matters since the family isn't half as well-off as we thought. Earth magic! Frankly, if I were you, I'd ditch the brother as soon as you can. Sounds like he's going to be as big a loser as their plodding father."

"Of course I will. Once I find myself some rich stud with a trust fund and a big..." She wiggled her eyebrows and smiled suggestively. John laughed like a braying donkey. "Now get a move on. Lover boy could be here any moment."

Jimmy angrily swiped his arm through the image, causing the clouds to disperse and disappear. His jaw was clenched, and I could tell the scene still hurt him. "Sadly, for Isabella, I got there a little early and overheard them both."

"Oh, Jimmy, I'm so sorry," I said.

He shook his head. "I'm a fool, but I'll get over it. I can't believe I let her talk me into seeing her again. You must think I'm a total idiot."

"Not at all. We're all a bit stupid when we think we're in love."

"Well, for the record, I didn't beg. It was the other way round. She called me."

I didn't care one way or the other. Isabella was in the wrong, and Jimmy was better off without her. That was all that mattered in the end. "Look at it this way—it might hurt like crazy now, but at least you got to see her true colors before you got in any deeper."

"I guess."

I got up and kissed the top of his head. "You want me to hex her panties? They'll always feel annoyingly bunched, and she'll never know why."

He laughed, and I was relieved to hear it.

"What are you going to do now?" I asked.

"I dunno. I think the exams went well. Rather than wait for the results, I might head off to Florida with some friends and have a little dude time."

"The beach is an excellent idea. I wish I could come with you."

"Yeah, right. I have a feeling you're happy staying right where you are." He jerked his chin in the direction of Matt Allen's house.

"You have a point. Talking of, if you don't mind, I might mosey over there for a bit. There's something I need to discuss with Henry."

Jimmy chuckled. "Discuss. Right. That's what they're calling it these days."

I slapped him playfully on the shoulder. "Don't be cheeky."

As Jimmy went off in search of the others, I stuffed the last piece of bacon into my mouth, and after rinsing off my own plate in the sink, I set about cleaning up the rest of the breakfast things. I knew Jimmy was going to be okay. Maybe not for a bit, but he'd get over it. He just needed some time. And now I was glad Sylvia had let Isabella go. It would have been awkward to share a room with her after this. I would have done more than shrink her panties, that was for sure. And then my thoughts turned to Henry and the song Catherine had asked me to memorize. I began to scrub a little faster, intending to go find Henry as soon as I was done.

When I'd got in last night, I'd written down Catherine's song while it was still fresh in my mind. I opened my notebook now and studied the song lyrics. I prayed I had it right. Gaia alone knew my memory wasn't that fabulous, especially having heard it just the once.

Now, with the page folded neatly in my pocket and the cooking things all dried and put away, I wandered over to Matt's house. As I passed Catherine's grave, I whispered, "I suppose it would have been too much to ask you to write it all down for me." There was no response, and I carried on walking.

I found Matt and Henry outside. Matt was hammering nails into his chicken coop, doing his best to repair some warped wood that had pulled away from the structure. Henry was helping him by pushing onto the dampened wood and making it as flat as possible. Neither heard my hellos over the noise of Matt's hammer. I had to admire his determination to fix everything himself and not rely on magic. Fitter than anyone I knew, I had no doubt the wiry man would outlive us all.

Matt looked up and saw me coming before Henry did. "Have you come to give me a hand?" he asked, an easy smile on his lips.

"Sure, I can help," I said. "What do you need me to do?"

"We're almost done here. Would you feed the chickens?" Matt suggested.

There wasn't a chicken in sight. I supposed the hammering had driven them off. Matt nodded toward a large food container by the side of the coop. I picked it up, and almost at once, what seemed like a million birds came out of nowhere and began to cluck and peck excitedly around my feet. Matt and Henry grinned.

As Matt finished hammering, I tossed the seed and watched as the birds fought for pole position. They looked well-fed, but anyone would think they hadn't eaten in days. They were that aggressive, fluttering their wings and trampling over each other. I spread the feed out evenly, and by the time Matt was sliding his hammer back inside his belt, I was done. Although trying to convince the chickens that there was nothing left in the bucket was another matter entirely.

Matt took a step back to admire his handiwork. "There, that should hold through the winter."

"Looks good as new," I said.

"Well, that's my repairs done," Matt said. "I like to get everything in shape around here before the frost sets in. Now I could use a cup of tea. Come on inside, and I'll make us all something warm to drink."

Matt led the way, and Henry waited for me to go before him. It was dark inside, Matt turning on no more lights than was necessary while Sylvia was away. We followed him into the kitchen and sat at his table while he set about boiling some water. I was still full after breakfast, but I always had room for another cup of tea.

Matt removed his tool belt and deposited it on the large kitchen table. I thought about Mom, who would have had a fit if Dad did the same in our house.

"So where did you disappear to last night?" Henry asked.

"I thought you were asleep," I replied.

"I was. But I heard you come back in. And Scar was running around like an idiot. She wouldn't settle down."

"Who's Scar?" Matt asked, washing his hands at the sink.

"Henry brought me a familiar," I told him. "She's a lovely fox cub. You should see her colors. Her name is Scarlet—Scar for short. I should have brought her along with me."

"I'm glad you didn't." Matt smiled. "Chickens."

I laughed at my stupidity. "Sorry."

"That's okay. You made a *faux* pas."

We all chuckled at that. Then I said to Henry, "Sorry, I didn't mean to wake you."

"Only barely. I rolled over and went straight back as soon as you disappeared upstairs. So where did you go?"

Matt joined us at the table and looked just as curious as Henry did.

"If you must know, I was summoned to Catherine's grave last night. She woke me from my sleep, and I went out there to find out what she wanted. She sang a song to me."

"A spirit sang you a song?" Matt asked, leaning forward, intrigued. "What kind of song?"

"Just a silly song, but she said there was magic in the words. It didn't sound too magical to me."

"How did it go?" Henry asked.

"Hold on. I wrote it down." I reached into my pocket and pulled out the folded slip of paper.

Henry leaned across the table to take it, but I pulled it away. "Don't be so grabby!"

"Sorry."

"She asked me to sing it," I said.

The two men exchanged glances and then sat back in their chairs.

"Well then, let's hear it," Matt said.

"I, umm, well, I don't have the best singing voice." I felt my face reddening with embarrassment. "Anyway, here goes." I cleared my throat.

I thought about the melody, and after taking a deep breath, I began to sing. The two men listened in silence. Matt, his brow furrowed as he focused on the words, and Henry, biting his lip as he recognized the song. I could only imagine the emotions unleashed inside him and hoped the memory wouldn't cause him too much distress.

When I was finished, I could see he was choked, but he hadn't completely lost it as I half feared he might.

"That was beautiful, thank you," Henry said.

My cheeks grew hot.

"If that's not your best singing voice, I can only wonder what it must sound like," Matt added.

Henry stared down at the table, his thoughts temporarily elsewhere. Then he sighed and said, "I think the words are 'we spin under the light' not 'shine,' and there's a little pause after 'once' in 'Turn the circle once, then twice.'" He reached across for the note again, and this time I let him take it.

I watched as Henry read what was written there. His knitted brow deepened as he read. When he was done, he said, "I don't understand. Why would *your* ancestor sing this to *you*?"

"Your mother wanted me to reunite your sister and your dad. Somehow this is supposed to help us, and Catherine acted as messenger, I suppose. You said yourself they find a way to communicate."

Henry studied the words again. "It's funny. I'd forgotten this for so long, and now..." The words caught in his throat, and I think Matt sensed something of what he was feeling, because he chose that moment to stand up and finish making the tea.

I reached for Henry's hand and squeezed his clenched fingers, a gesture he acknowledged with a slight nod. "Sorry," he said. "It just feels so strange. I remember it now. I remember the day she sang this. It was such a happy evening, and Dad, well, it was like he was a different person. I remember the joy and the delight we all felt just being together." He paused again and shook his head. "Funny how I forgot it so completely. I wish you could have known us back then. We were such a different family. We lost so much when she died."

Matt slipped a hot drink in front of Henry.

"Thanks," Henry said.

"I wish I knew what we were supposed to do with it," I said.

Matt chuckled. "Seems pretty obvious to me."

"Oh?" I asked.

"Well, it's a song, isn't it? You're just supposed to sing it."

"I just did. Where's the magic?"

Matt scratched his head. "*Young people*," he half whispered under his breath. "Like the spirit said," he continued, "the magic is in the words. Sing it to those who need to hear it and let the words do their thing. Simple. That's old magic, that is. The deep stuff."

"So I just sing this to Eleanor and the General, and all will be well?"

"Exactly so," Matt said. "I suppose the tricky part is getting them together and making them stay long enough to hear it." He chuckled. "*That* is going to be the hard part, I reckon."

I nodded. He wasn't wrong about that.

While Henry sipped his tea, I wondered how I was going to go about this. With Henry's help, I was confident I could get to Eleanor easily enough, but the General...he was another matter entirely. Would he even let me in the Abbey after our last encounter, let alone give me a chance to sing a little tune for him?

I accepted the mug of piping-hot tea Matt gave me and tried to come up with a plan. I shook my head. Singing! Why couldn't she ask me to raise the dead or something a lot less painful? Just fabulous.

Chapter Thirty-Two

RETURN TO THE ABBEY

The journey back to New York was nothing at all like the miserable one I'd had leaving it. For one, I had Henry by my side. The stark ache of disappointed love was gone, replaced by the feelings of hope and anticipation for all the good things to come. I sat in the window seat of the bus, more appreciative of the view beside me than the rolling hills outside. There was something else though, and that something prevented me from having all the wonderful sensations associated with young love reunited—and that feeling was dread. I had a difficult task before me, and since more than my own happiness was at stake, it made it seem all the harder.

When I got especially nervous, I would squeeze Henry's hand, and guessing something of what I was feeling inside, he would take up my hand and kiss it, wanting me to believe everything was going to be all right, and not to worry. As ever, he had more confidence in my abilities than I had.

Scar shifted uncomfortably between us under her blanket. Technically, no pets were allowed on the bus, but I'd smuggled her on with no difficulty, having whispered to her not to make a sound. She blinked her understanding, but we were close to our destination now, and I could tell she was growing restless.

"You'll be able to stretch your legs soon," I whispered.

Henry put his hand where the outline of her head was evident through the blanket and gave her a discreet stroke. None of the other passengers on board paid any attention to her. Nothing to do with the tiny concealment charm I'd invoked, I was sure.

Our plan was simple. Having discussed the options at length with Henry, we'd decided to just march into the Abbey where Henry would confront the General, leaving me free to sing his mother's song. If he gave me any trouble, Henry would be there to calm his father down. We hoped Eleanor would be no problem at all, since we knew she would be more than happy to see us and could hardly object to hearing a simple ditty from her youth. Whether she would agree to seeing her father again was another thing entirely.

At long last, the bus neared the station, the driver made a few laborious twists and turns, and the engine noise grew louder while it maneuvered in low gear. All around us, the passengers gathered their belongings in anticipation of disembarking. I carefully lifted the blanket laid across the pair of us and lowered it gently into a large wicker basket Mom had given me for the trip. Anyone else peering inside would only see a basket of apples. Indeed, even I caught the sweet aroma of prize-winning Red Delicious, invoked by the enchantment. I handed the basket to Henry while I pulled on my poncho.

"Ooh, those look good," said the woman standing by the seat next to ours, blatantly ignoring the *Do Not Stand While Vehicle Is In Motion* signs dotted strategically around the bus. Unfortunately, Henry's enchantment was too good, and those apples just a little too tempting. She stretched her hand across, and for a dreaded second, I thought she was going to help herself to Scar. There was nothing I could do to stop her, but Henry saw the danger, and quick as a flash, he mumbled a confusion spell under his breath.

"*Scamu*!" As soon as the spell left his lips, the bus wobbled, and the woman's focus veered away toward the back of his chair as she struggled to keep her balance. A vagueness clouded her expression. She shook her head, and forgetting all about the apples, she continued to collect her things.

"Well done," I whispered to Henry as the bus came to a jerking halt. I also had to steady myself and then waited in my seat as the inevitable scramble to get off began. For Scar's sake, I decided it would be wiser to sit down again and wait for the bus to empty before joining the mass exodus. One look at Henry confirmed he agreed.

When we did finally get off, I thanked the driver and then stretched my back, glad to be out of that confined space.

After lifting the concealment enchantment, we let Scar down on a grassy verge to relieve herself, but she scampered behind a tree. About twenty seconds later, she trotted back, much lighter on her paws and looking a lot happier. After scooping her up again and putting her back into her basket, Henry hailed a Magic Cab to take us up to the Abbey. I was a little disappointed not to see Wally in the driver's seat; it would have been unrealistic to expect him, I supposed, but I instinctively looked for him just the same. This time our driver was a badly balding goblin with a greasy comb-over. As soon as we gave him our destination, he forgot all about us and focused on his driving. He zoomed along quickly, and I found myself wishing he would slow down, being not especially keen to reach our destination. All too soon he got to the Upper East Side, and I saw the familiar gates of the cemetery looming just ahead.

Since Henry still had hold of Scar's basket, I pulled out my purse and paid the driver. I was midway through saying thank you when he drove off.

"Well, really," I said, watching his rude butt zoom away.

The familiar unease hit me almost as soon as I stood on the sidewalk. I shuddered, wanting to get as far away from this place as possible. However, this time I was mentally prepared for it, since I knew it was just the enchantment working its magic, but what I didn't expect was to see Henry turn deathly white. Then he staggered to the point I feared he might faint.

"What's wrong?" I asked, taking the basket from him just in case.

"I'm not sure," he said, trying to catch his breath. "I don't feel too well at all."

I took his hand and noticed his flesh was icy cold. "So I see. Quick, unlock the gates so we can go inside."

Henry turned toward the gate, but though he raised a hand, he quickly lowered it. "I, um, I don't remember the spell. I can't do it."

Something definitely wasn't right, but there was nothing I could do, and Henry wasn't looking good at all.

"Come on," I said, looping my arm through his to give him some support. "You didn't eat anything on the bus. Maybe you just need a drink or something."

"Yeah, maybe."

I led him along the sidewalk, but as soon as we passed the cemetery, he stopped in his tracks and his color returned.

"I can't believe he did that," Henry said.

"What?"

"Dad. He's altered the enchantment. Now I can't get back inside."

"Altered it? Can you fix it?"

Henry shook his head. "Not easily. Dad found this specific enchantment during his research into the Elder Wars, or maybe the Fantastic Wars. I can't remember which. We'd need the Necromancer Scrolls to lift or change it. There's no other possible way."

"So we find another copy of the Necromancer Scrolls," I said optimistically. "Then we fix the enchantment, and we're good."

"There are no copies. We own the original, and as far as I'm aware, no copies were ever made."

"You're kidding me." I said. "So our one and only hope is on the other side of that enchantment. Well, great. Now what are we going to do?"

"We could have Eleanor try, I suppose, but I doubt she'll have any more luck than I did. If I could convince her to come over, that is. Song or no song, I don't think she'll be too eager to see him."

So much for the easy solution. Still, if I was totally honest with myself, a part of me was a little relieved. I really didn't want to see the General, and I certainly didn't want to hum him a tune. But I also didn't want to break my promise to Henry's mother and wasn't quite sure what Henry would think of me if I did.

"We'll just have to switch to Plan B," I said.

"What's that?" Henry asked.

"I don't know. I'll have to think of it. But two heads are better than one, and three and four even better than that. I vote we go to Sylvia's now and ask for her advice. Maybe invite Eleanor over, if she'll come. Between us all, we should be able to come up with something. What do you think?"

"Sure. It's not like we have a lot of choices, do we?"

My head was throbbing with possible options, all of which I knew were useless. I needed to think and would do so much better with some homemade brew inside me. And Sylvia was wise. If anyone could help us, I believed she could. I stepped over to the edge of the curb, and with Scar held securely away from the traffic, I hailed another Magic Cab.

Chapter Thirty-Three

FIRST IMPRESSIONS

HENRY TOLD ME SYLVIA WAS HOSTING SOME KIND OF MAGICAL networking gathering at her shop. Delighted to hear we were back in the Magic Apple, she would join us as soon as she could break free, though probably not until later that afternoon. After speaking to Sylvia, Henry called Eleanor. At first, it sounded as if she wouldn't even discuss her dad, and Henry kept throwing frustrated glances at me and walked around the apartment in agitation. He kept reasoning with her, and from his own tone, I gathered she softened a little. But when the call ended, he shook his head. "The best I could get were a few *maybes* and *we'll sees*. I can't be sure she'll come."

All we could do now was hope that she would.

Henry gave Eddie Van Halen a piece of carrot to nibble on and then collapsed on the sofa. He didn't look well at all.

"Are you okay?" I asked, perching my thigh on the arm and ruffling his hair. He felt awfully hot.

"I've got a bit of a headache, that's all," he said, shifting out of my reach. "I think I just need a little air. Did you say we needed some groceries? Give me a list, and I'll go get some."

"Sure."

He'd never veered away from me like that, but I put it down to his headache. I jotted a few items down on a note and gave it to him.

"Thanks." Henry left the apartment without so much as a backward glance. I really hoped he wasn't coming down with something nasty.

After fixing Scar's lunch, consisting of a little cold chicken Mom had packed for us before we left, I pulled out my magic book and flicked through the pages, searching for something, anything, that could help us with the General. Being tailored to my own magical needs, the book yielded page after page on communing with the dead or how to interpret ghosts who spoke a different language, even some weird stuff I could never imagine having a need for, like handling unrequited love for the dead, or spectral toothache, magic, or myth, and what to do about it. But there was very little in the book on creating enchantments, and absolutely nothing at all about how to break them.

After eating her lunch, Scar had taken a short nap on the sofa, but now she hopped up on my knee, and with another push, she pounced on top of the table and began sniffing the pages of the book. She then started to paw at them. Thinking she might tear it, I closed it up and pulled the book to one side. "Sorry, Scar, you can't play with this." I looked around the apartment, wondering if there was anything I could throw for her. Scar wiggled under my arm and positioned herself between me and the book. She began gently pawing again, this time at the jacket.

I was about to pick her up to put her down on the floor when she turned to look at me. Her intelligent eyes pierced mine; I felt some meaning in her gaze and wished I knew what she was trying to say.

"What is it, baby?" I asked. "Are you still hungry?"

She shook her head. Surprised by her response, I sat back in my seat and gave her some room. She turned, and her paw rested on the book again. She was careful though, her touch too gentle to do any damage to the cover.

"Okay," I said, reaching around her to pull the book closer. "You want me to open this?"

This time Scar remained perfectly still, which I assumed meant yes. There were hundreds of pages, so rather than turn one at a time, I leafed slowly through it again and waited to see what she would do. I was about two-thirds through the volume when her paw shot out, stopping me at a particular page. She then hopped over my arm and waited patiently by the edge of the table. I spread the pages open and read.

I found myself hoping the page would reveal something about breaking enchantments, but it contained nothing about enchantments at all. The heading read, *How To Choose Your Familiar*. I sighed and scratched Scar's ears. "Thank you, Scar. I'll read this soon, I promise." Defeated for now, I was about to close the book when Scar shot out a paw to stop me from closing that page. Her determined gaze never left my face, and knowing I was beaten, I resigned myself to giving it a proper look. "All right, all right, I'll read it now, I promise."

I took another deep breath and focused on the words written there. I skimmed over the section on choosing familiars, the traits that work versus those that don't, and the kind of disaster to expect when you get it wrong, which read something like a bad dating guide with curses hailing down on the witch or wizard through generations to come. It said choosing the right one required patience, love, and a little magic. *Or a new boyfriend,* I thought. My attention fell on a pretty rhyme, which I read to Scar, if only to show her I was taking this seriously.

Like falling in love, there's a mutual trust,
Respect and compassion is also a must,
As your lives intermingle, your knowledge will grow,
Till the two become one, sharing all that they know.

Suddenly Scar spun around, chasing her tail. After two quick spins, she stopped and glared at me, panting. Something had tickled her, and I read the passage again, wondering what excited her in particular, though I looked up none the wiser.

There was a funny knock at the door, almost as if someone was tapping it with their shoe. Still pondering the meaning of the rhyme, I left the book open and went to answer it. At first, I couldn't see who was on the other side, because they carried a pile of purple boxes stacked so high it hid their face.

"Oh, thank you, thank you for getting the door," Sylvia said. "Would you take a couple of the boxes? Thank you! I'm not sure how I'd have managed if you hadn't been here. Thank you so much."

The boxes were so light I thought they might be empty, and I carried the ones I'd taken from her and deposited them on the kitchen counter. "You're back early," I said. "Henry said you wouldn't be done until later today."

"I know," Sylvia said as she placed her boxes next to mine. "But I was so excited to know my young people were back, so I wrapped up the business early and came home as soon as I could." She looked around. "Where is Henry? Isn't he with you?"

"Shopping for groceries."

"Good, good. I must admit, now you're both back, I'm so looking forward to spending more time with Matt. I've been so busy with work and everything. He understands, dear man that he is, but it has been hard for him, I know. I think I'll take him on a little vacation in the north, Alaska or something. I think he'll like seeing the glaciers."

"I'm sure he will." I loved Sylvia's carefree attitude, how she could just zoom off to Alaska or anywhere else whenever she wanted to.

Sylvia handed one of the boxes to me. "I was giving these away at the thing, but I had a few left over, so thought I'd bring you some."

I slipped off the lid and pulled a long purple witch's cloak from the inside. It was much heavier than I imagined, yet the box containing it had weighed almost nothing at all. I was familiar with this kind of magic, which was easily invoked using a special powder called trammeling, made from the crushed shafts of bird feathers. Mom often used it at home to help her move furniture if Dad wasn't around. "Wow, this is beautiful," I said, wrapping the cloak around my shoulders and admiring myself.

"Take as many as you like," Sylvia said. "I always give out some little magical thing at these events. It's good for business."

"But what does it do?" I asked, hoping against hope they might help me slip past enchanted gates or make me invisible or something.

"Oh, they just have a temporary spell on them," Sylvia said as she sat at the table and reached down to pet Scar. "But my customers expect a little swag. They guarantee the wearer excellent first impressions when they meet someone new, but it's only good for a first encounter, and after that, the magic wears off. My customers love them. They're excellent for conventions and such."

"Thank you, it's lovely." The material was heavy and looked warm. It even had a hood, which I pulled over my head. Unfortunately, the hood was cut a little too big for me and flopped over my face. I held my hands out before me, half expecting to be blind, but then I noticed the strangest thing. I could see.

I reached up, wondering if the material on the hood was different from the rest of the coat, but it was thick as ever.

The only problem was, though I could see, I wasn't seeing what I was supposed to see. Instead of the kitchen walls, my point of view had shifted, and I was staring at the skirting board around the floor. And shoes. Stranger still, they were my own. "What the—!"

"What's the matter?" Sylvia asked.

"Something's weird. I'm looking at my own ankles." Feeling a little giddy and off-balance, I reached up and pulled the hood off my face. To my relief, my vision returned to normal.

Sylvia scratched her forehead, and then she laughed. "Oh yes, I forgot about that. Most enchanted things don't work on animals. Not that Scar would ever need one," she cooed. "Scar always gives a good first impression, don't you, diddums?" She scratched Scar under her chin. "So while you were blinded, she became your eyes and ears. It's one of the benefits of keeping a familiar. They compensate for your shortcomings."

I slid the cloak off my shoulders, folded it, and put it back inside its box. "I'll keep one for a special occasion." I wished the spell could include calming down cranky old farts and making them more reasonable, but alas.

"Keep as many as you like. You never know when they're going to come in handy."

Scar trotted happily to her bed, and after turning a couple of times, she settled in, ready for another nap. Sylvia straightened up, and her gaze fell on my book, which was still open at the table.

"I'm glad to see you still at your studies, in spite of this other business with Henry's family," she said. "Very proper, very good."

I sat down adjacent to her. "Um, I wasn't studying exactly. Henry and I went to the Abbey, but the General has changed the enchantments protecting it, and now even Henry can't get in. I was looking for a spell to help us get around it."

"I'm sorry, my dear, you can't break one of these. You know that, right? Not unless you know the particular spell he cast so you can reverse the incantation."

"I know," I said gloomily. "The problem is the spell came from a scroll the General keeps *inside* the Abbey. There must be a way we can get to it, there must be."

"I wish it were so, I really do." Sylvia shook her head sadly and peered over the open page before her. She tilted her head, puzzled. "So you thought you'd find what you were seeking on the familiar page?"

I laughed. "No, not at all. I was just scanning through the book in general when Scar got all excited and picked out that spot."

"Hmm." Sylvia studied a little harder and put her forefinger to her lips. "You know, foxes didn't get their wily reputations by being stupid."

"What do you mean?" I asked.

"Confusion enchantments are powerful things. I've never known a *witch or wizard* who was able to break one..."

My mind raced ahead, understanding where she was going with this. "But most enchantments have no effect on animals," I finished for her. "Scar can become my eyes and ears, and can break into the Abbey and maybe steal the scroll us." Even as the words gushed out and my enthusiasm got the better of me, I realized how farfetched the idea sounded, but then again, Scar was an exceptionally intelligent familiar. Maybe it could work. Just maybe.

I flushed with excitement and turned the volume so I could read the rhyme again.

As your lives intermingle, your knowledge will grow,
Till the two become one, sharing all that they know.

"It seems your fox is smarter than we are."

I glanced down at Scar, who was now snoring soundly.

"Smart girl," I said. Her ear twitched, but otherwise she slept on.

"There is a problem, though," Sylvia mused. "She's still a baby, and if it's a heavy book, she might not be able to carry it out of the Abbey."

My focus shifted to the kitchen counter and the pile of boxes still stacked there. I smiled. "I think I know how we can get around that too."

At that moment, the door opened. Henry came in, carrying a large brown bag full of groceries, with a French bread stick poking out. We must have looked very pleased with ourselves because he stood in the doorway and stared at us both.

"What's happened?" he asked, his brow furrowed as his gaze shifted from me to Sylvia and then back again.

I exchanged a wicked twinkle with Sylvia, and then I smiled. "Good news! I think I've just found our Plan B."

Henry put down the groceries and joined us at the table. Excited myself, I couldn't wait to tell him what it was.

Chapter Thirty-Four

A DAMAGED AURA

WHILE SYLVIA PUT AWAY THE GROCERIES, HENRY LISTENED AS I TOLD him about our plan, but his smiles were faint, and I could tell he still wasn't quite himself. "No better?" I asked.

He shrugged. "I guess Eleanor didn't show up?"

I shook my head. It bothered me to see him so dejected. Come to think of it, he'd been down since we'd arrived in New York and the easy smile I loved so much to see was gone.

"It's still early. She might still come."

He didn't look too convinced. I went to grasp his hand, but he pulled his away, keeping it under the table and out of my reach. I bristled. He'd never shied away from me like that before.

"You know, I think I might have a lie down after all," he said. "My head isn't feeling much better. Wake me in an hour or so if I don't get up."

Have I done something wrong? He'd never been this cold with me in the past. And he looked funny. I couldn't put my finger on quite what it was, but something about his appearance was off.

As soon as the bedroom door closed, Sylvia slid into his vacant seat. "Has he been like that for long?" she asked.

I sat up straight, still hurt by his altered behavior. "You noticed?"

"It's not like I could miss it."

I leaned over the table and cupped my chin in my hands as I thought about it. "He's been funny since we got back in town. He was fine on the bus, but then he complained of a headache, and he's acted weird ever since."

"Do you remember when he first started to complain?" Sylvia asked.

"He mentioned the headache just a bit ago. But he's been acting odd since we went to the Abbey. He almost fainted when we got to the gates. I would say it started around then."

Sylvia bit her lip as she thought. "Well, I didn't want to alarm anyone, but I've known Henry a long time, and I thought there was something weird about his aura when he came in."

"His aura?" I asked. "Weird? What do you mean, weird? Like broken?"

"Damaged might be a better word. I've seen it before with some of my customers at the shop. You said he acted all funny at the Abbey, so tell me, what other enchantments has he been exposed to lately?"

I thought for a minute. "I can't say for sure. Henry only joined us recently. I sang Catherine's song to him yesterday. Could that be it?"

Sylvia nodded slowly and sagely. "Quite possibly. The song would have touched his emotions, affecting a similar part of the brain to his father's spell."

I gasped. "Oh Gaia, really? It's damaged his mind?"

Sylvia reached across the table and gave my hand a reassuring squeeze. "Don't worry, it's nothing so terrible. It happens all the time. His recent emotional-based memories are affected, that's all. It'll pass in time."

I wasn't sure whether I should be upset by this. I swallowed a lump in my throat. "His memories? Like he's forgotten who I am?"

"No," she said. "He clearly hasn't forgotten who you are. Or any of us from what I can see. We'd have noticed that sooner. But he's struggling with something, and from what little I saw, it concerns how he feels about you." She squeezed my hand tighter as she said this. "He may have forgotten that he loves you," she said sadly.

"He *WHAT?!*" I almost flipped the table. Sylvia flinched and made calming gestures, but this was no time for calm. I got up and stamped around the room, enraged by what had happened. First that darn song and then the General's little surprise at the gates had scrambled my love's mind. I wanted to scream. I wanted to break things. I wanted to cry.

"Only temporarily. Things will be back to normal soon, I'm sure."

I wasn't reassured, and part of me wanted to run in to see Henry, but if he needed to sleep, probably the last thing I ought to do was to wake him. But I needed him so badly.

"There must be something I can do?" I said. "You can't just forget you love someone."

Sylvia stood up and walked over to her small computer desk and powered on her laptop. "Let's see what MagicNet suggests. I use this all the time for stuff, saves having to dig up a ton of old magic books. Hold on, lemme see..."

As I peered over her shoulder, she scrolled through the index of spells and waved her hand dismissively over the ones she considered useless. Then she sat a little straighter and pointed to the screen. "Ah, this might do it. Okay, health warning, a spell of repulsion may have a lasting effect on the unprepared. They might develop a strong belief that Milli Vanilli were the best dance pop duo ever, that airplanes cannot fly because their wings don't flap, or develop a sudden craving for pickled gherkins. *Hmmm.*" She pressed a finger to her lip. "That would certainly explain why there are now three jars of pickled gherkins in the fridge. Howling at the moon—no, wait, that's lycanthropes only. Yada, yada...here it is! Short-term memory loss and jumbled perceptions. Oh dear. Emotional discombobulation may be experienced."

"What's that mean?" I asked.

"Turmoil, confusion. It's not that Henry doesn't still love you. It's just that he isn't sure why, and that's vexing him. But it does say if the spell is reversed within a couple of days, before they become fossilized, the effects will probably fade quickly."

"Probably?" I didn't like how she sounded less sure of herself now. My gaze fixed on the door of the bedroom, and I imagined Henry lying in there. How I ached to wrap my arms around him and hear him whisper everything would be okay and that he still loved me. Perhaps Sylvia was wrong. But I couldn't argue with how I felt, and in my soul, I knew that she was right.

Sylvia gave me her warmest smile and pushed up from the table. "Look, let him sleep for a bit, and think about Scar. Remember the red squirrel?"

I nodded, recalling that first time I'd visited Sylvia in her house and the squirrel I had summoned with the cookie. "Sure."

"I have some kitten kibble somewhere in the place. Hold on." She opened a few cupboard doors and pulled out a box of cat food. She shook it, and as if by magic, Scar woke up and stretched out her paws in a downward-facing fox pose. "Hmm, almost empty, but there should be enough." She handed me the box. "Why don't you practice sending Scar on little missions around the apartment and reward her with the kibble? That'll keep you busy and your mind off...other things. I'm going to make dinner for us all, and then we can plan your attack on the Abbey. Nothing focuses the mind so much as keeping busy—at least, I've always thought so. Now what would you like for dinner? I can fix us a French-bread pizza if you're in the mood for something different. Or how about a nice stew? I'm sure we have enough in for that."

"Whatever you like," I said flatly. The last thing I wanted to think about was dinner. Now that Sylvia had mentioned it, I had noticed a wilted grayness about Henry's aura when he'd returned from the shops, but I'd chalked it up to his headache. "You know, the pizza thing sounds nice. It's Henry's favorite, and the taste sensation might jog something. I dunno."

"Good idea," Sylvia said. "Now you're thinking."

My heart sat in my chest like a lead balloon, but Sylvia was right. Feeling sorry for myself would do nothing. I needed to get Henry out of my mind, and to focus. If reversing the enchantment would bring his love back, then the sooner I fulfilled my promise to his mother's spirit, the better.

I shook the box of kibble, and Scar hopped up on my lap and onto the table. I popped the first treat into her mouth. *Run into the bathroom and grab me some toilet paper*, I said in my head, and off she went. While she was gone, I retrieved the cloak Sylvia had given me, and after placing it around my shoulders, I pulled the hood over my eyes. As before, my point of view shifted, and now I watched as Scar used both paws to spin the toilet roll. After tearing the sheets off with her teeth, she scampered back to me, trailing a long sheet of paper behind her, like a scroll.

Sylvia's eyes practically popped out of her head in surprise. "I must say, I've known dozens of familiars, but I've never seen one as clever as this little minx. You know, this might actually work."

I pushed the hood off my face and smiled. "Let's hope so."

Chapter Thirty-Five

THE PLAN

If nothing else, the smell of sizzling tomato sauce and beef had drawn Henry from my room. Throughout dinner, his focus had been on the front door and, more notably, not on me. I knew he was hoping Eleanor would show up and must be disappointed that she hadn't. Not even my text promising both her and Victor a sumptuous feast had done the trick. My phone remained resolutely silent. Which was strange in itself. After all, I hadn't done anything to offend her. Why wouldn't she answer my calls or texts?

As we ate, I kept glancing at Henry, hoping for any outward sign that he was getting better. But though he acknowledged me as another person in the room—"*Would you pass the garlic bread please, Cat?*"—he showed no signs of particular affection and kept himself well out of my reach. I might as well have been anyone. It was all I could do to not cry.

"So I think we all know what we've got to do," Sylvia said.

"Yes, I think so," I said, hoping to sound more upbeat than I felt. "But maybe we should talk it through, step by step, just in case."

"Good idea." Sylvia gave me an encouraging nod, which I mirrored immediately to reassure her I was okay. I wasn't, but I hoped I soon would be. We both glanced at Henry, who was still chewing his food and staring into space. He still looked a teeny bit distant and unconnected.

"According to Henry, the General is always in bed by one o'clock, so we should all leave here a little before two, by which time he should be sound asleep. Is that right, Henry?"

He hesitated for a second and then nodded, but did not make eye contact. I soldiered on.

"Sylvia will secure us a Magic Cab for then." She nodded. "My job is to steal the scroll. Before we leave the apartment, I'll scoop some of the trammeling powder from the cloak boxes and put it into a small pouch I'll tie around Scar's neck."

Scar, who was listening intently, straightened up like a little soldier when she heard her name. I reached down and affectionately stroked her ears. "It won't hurt her if she swallows any of it, will it?" I asked.

"No, she'll be fine," Sylvia said. "It'll be no worse than if she swallowed a spoonful of sugar. It's not enough to make her float up and away."

"Good. Right, then I guide her to the willow and into the Abbey. Though she probably knows the place better than I do," I said as an afterthought. "Once inside, I'll steer her into the General's study where the book should be on the desk. Umm, Henry?"

At last, his attention shifted to me, but his expression was neutral, like he was being addressed by a stranger. I hoped I hid my hurt. "Um, how do I find his study? I couldn't find my own toilet when I was there before. I have a horrible feeling Scar's going to get totally lost if we're not careful."

"It should be easy enough. It's on the ground level, no stairs involved, and as long as Scar clings to the wall on her left, she will find it. His study is the last room before the hall ends before you have to turn right to go down another corridor. You should have no trouble at all finding it. Look for the portrait of the famous elf general Gavenold opposite the study door. You can't miss it, purple uniform, gold braid, nasty purple cap."

"Okay!" I said, sounding way more confident than I felt. "And the scroll will definitely be on the desk?"

"Always is," he said.

"Once she gets there, she opens the door—err—how will she open it?"

"You can open it for her," Sylvia said. "Cast a silent spell like you do here at the apartment, only don't use *Banana Peel,* which only opens my door. Use a generic one."

"*Torhtlic duguð*?" I asked.

"Yup," Sylvia said. "That'll work. That command will open anything, as long as the door's not locked."

"And will it be?" I asked Henry.

He shook his head. "No, Dad never locks any of the Abbey doors. He trusts in his enchantments."

"Sounds a bit tricky. I've never projected a spell before."

"Practice here," Henry suggested, cocking his head in the direction of the front door. "It's not locked right now. You should be able to open it."

That was a good idea. I put on the cloak again and wandered into my bedroom to put some distance between me and the front door. "Back in a minute." Once the door was closed, I pulled the hood over my face, and thanks to the magic of the cloak, I was immediately seeing the world through Scar's eyes.

"We need to open the front door," I thought.

The room spun quickly as Scar jerked to turn around. She meandered through the legs of the kitchen table and chairs, and then I saw her paws as she leaned on the base of the door, trying to open it though it wouldn't give way.

"*Torhtlic duguð*." As soon as I spoke the words, the latch turned, and the door opened. Excited, Scar did her little spin thing and ran back to join the others. I pulled the hood off my face and returned to the main room.

"That worked well," I said, wandering over to the door and closing it again.

"Yup, looked good to me," Sylvia agreed.

Henry smiled wanly.

"Okay. So then once she's inside, Scar sits on the scroll or book, or whatever it is, which the powder will make as light as a feather, and once she has it, she should bring it back to us by the gate. Once she does, Henry should be able to reverse the enchantment, letting us all get inside. Then Henry and I will sneak into the General's bedroom, where I'll sing my song to him while he's asleep so he can't object. And that's the plan! Anyone have any questions?"

Henry frowned. "I guess not. Though if it wasn't for my mother, wild horses wouldn't drag me back there."

I knew the feeling. And I wished we had more time to practice, but if MagicNet was right, we only had a couple of days before Henry's memory loss became permanent, and one of those days was already gone. Time was running out—fast.

Henry stared at his phone. I knew he was checking to see if Eleanor had left a text. No magic required to figure that one out. His disappointed expression told me all I needed to know.

"What time is it now?" I asked.

"A little before midnight," Sylvia said. "I'll book us a Magic Cab now. We shouldn't have any trouble around two, but you know what New York is like. Better to book it now. I suggest you two keep going over the plan and practicing. The time will be gone before you know it."

I nodded. Never a truer word.

While she was busy making the call, I instinctively reached for Henry's hand without thinking. This time, I noticed a kind of mistiness swept over his eyes before he snatched his hand away. "Why do you keep doing that?" he asked.

"You really don't remember, do you?"

He stared at me intently, like he was trying to. "Remember what, exactly?"

"Henry, listen. Before we went to the Abbey and you got hit by that revolting spell your father put on the gates, which gave you a serious case of the wobblies, you and I had gotten close, I mean *really* close. You've forgotten all that, and it's breaking my heart."

"Close?"

"Yes, close. We're not just going back because your mother wanted us to. We're going there for us. That's why we're planning to get the scrolls from the General's study, so we can reverse the spell and, I hope and pray, have you remembered everything, most especially me, since frankly, and I'm not wanting to frighten you here, I want to spend the rest of my life with you. Now I realize you're not quite yourself at the moment, because I'm seeing horror growing in your eyes the longer you listen to me. Maybe you think I'm some kind of ranting madwoman, sometimes I wonder about that myself, but that's how things were before the spell affected you, and I'm going to do everything I possibly can to get my Henry back, and if that means raising an army of the dead and burning down the Abbey and that scroll along with it, then so be it, that is what I'll do!"

I could see him stare and try to remember, but then he shook his head sadly. "I'm sorry. I can't—I mean, I just don't remember. Excuse me." He pushed his unfinished pizza away, barely touched, and once he was up, he disappeared inside the bathroom.

I wanted to scoop him into my arms and kiss him insanely like they did at the end of a romantic movie or on a succubus prom date, but I didn't. I knew he'd resist me, and the thought of him finding me repellant broke my heart. I missed our intimacy greatly, but I steeled myself by remembering that in a few hours all could be well, and that in a short while he'd be my old Henry again, just as he was before. That time couldn't come soon enough for me. If only the General went to bed a little earlier. I wasn't sure if I could survive the wait.

Chapter Thirty-Six

SCAR BY NIGHT

The Magic Apple never slept. It was two in the morning, yet all around us vehicles were zipping along the Upper East Side. Magic Cabs were dropping their fares, and someone, somewhere, was always expecting a pizza. Perhaps the travelers were a little more considerate than their daytime comrades; horns weren't leaned on quite so readily, and police cars zapped their sirens just the once, but in all other regards, the city buzzed on, caring not a jot about the lateness of the hour.

Our driver had dropped us at the end of the street, about a block and a half away from the gates of the cemetery. This had been my idea. Henry's brain had been fried enough, and I dreaded to think what further exposure would do to him. We all agreed it wasn't worth the risk. I would text him when I had the scroll, but not a moment before.

We now stood on the sidewalk outside the *All Shook Up* elven cocktail parlor, a small bistro-like place that remained open twenty-four hours a day. A cardboard cutout of an older Elvis with pointy ears was by the door, his midriff listing the drink specials of the day. An emerald-green elven ring on his chubby finger pointed the way inside.

Sylvia hovered by the door, reluctant to go in. "Are you sure you don't want to go over the plan one more time? There are so many things that could go wrong. You've had so little time to practice." She reminded me of

Mom. She wasn't nagging. She was just concerned for me, and Scar too. I got it.

"Don't worry," I said. "We've been over it a thousand times already. It'll be all right, I promise."

"But do you have everything you need? The cloak? The powder? Salt? Your spell book in case of an emergency? And you're wearing your ring, right?" she continued.

I raised my hand and showed her the ring to reassure her. Then I pointed to Scar, who wore a little pouch tied around her neck by a small piece of decorating ribbon. "All that, and I have my phone, don't worry. I've checked everything several times."

I turned to Henry for moral support. He looked like he wanted to say something, but no words left his lips. I guessed in the end he just didn't know how to respond to me.

"I'll text you as soon as I have the scroll," I said, touching his arm. This time he didn't pull away, but I would have liked a kiss. Maybe that was expecting a little too much. However, to my surprise, he took my hand and squeezed it.

"I wish..." Whatever he was thinking died on his lips. "Good luck," he said and kissed me awkwardly on the cheek. Like he thought he ought to. It was something.

"Thank you." *I'm going to need it.* "And don't have too many of their witch's brews." I nervously laughed, cocking my head toward the cocktail parlor. "I need you sober." Not that I was worried. It was just me putting on a brave face.

"We won't," Henry said. "And I'll try Eleanor again. She's usually up this time of day. You never know."

"Good idea," I said.

He opened the door, ushering Sylvia inside ahead of him. I waited until the door closed behind them both. Then suddenly Scar and I were alone. I felt a little choked.

"Come on," I said, realizing that a young witch in a cloak out all alone with a black-and-red fox cub might look ominous. "We'd better scoot."

We hurried along the sidewalk, Scar keeping pace and close to me. There was a ton of stuff in my backpack, but Sylvia had had the sense to sprinkle some of the trammeling powder on it, so I barely felt it at all.

As we neared the gates, I paused. When we'd gone over this at the apartment, everything sounded simple enough, but now I was here, I realized how odd I would look, just standing there by the gates, a hood covering my face as I channeled my thoughts into Scar. What if someone saw me? With my focus on Scar and the scroll, I might miss someone creeping up on me from behind, ready to mug me. Or maybe I'd look like I was casing the joint. Either way, it didn't seem like a smart idea.

Not for the first time I found myself wishing this cloak made me invisible. But it did not. Quite the opposite. It was bright purple. I would have to do something about that.

Just beyond the gate was a large maple tree. Its leaves were long shed, and its bare branches did nothing to obscure the streetlamps or the light of the moon that shone brightly through it and onto the gates.

Luckily, I didn't need a spell book for this. Just a little good old-fashioned earth magic. I walked slowly to the railings, ignoring the inevitable sense of unease and doom, and reaching through, I snapped a bloom from one of the witch hazel plants growing inside the gates. I rubbed the spikey flower in my hand, forcing the petals to break.

Once the petals were as fine as I could make them, I knelt before the trunk of the maple tree and, using my hands, clawed at the earth around the base. The dirt was cold and unyielding, turned hard by the season. I did not give up and kept clawing, until at last, I made the smallest of holes. It wasn't deep, but I hoped it would be enough. I gathered my flowers, put them inside the hole, and covered it all with the dirt.

Earth Mother, receive this gift I bring,
And wake this tree from sleep to Spring.

I stood up and waited for the magic to happen.

It was hard to see at first, the effect was so small, but the maple began to bud, and then one by one, the leaves uncurled to open. In less than a minute, the entire maple was adorned by new leaves, and most importantly, it blocked the light, which just moments ago had streamed through its limbs.

I knelt, partially hidden by the low branches and huddling low. A young couple walked by. They were laughing and giggling, very much into each other, taking every opportunity to touch and caress. I got the feeling they had only just met. I waited for them to pass, praying the enchantments around the cemetery stopped people noticing anything in particular—and thankfully they showed no interest in me at all.

They were soon gone. If anyone else passed by, I hoped they would take me for a vagrant, using the trunk of the tree as a shield from the cold.

"Are you ready, Scar?" I whispered.

Scar's large brown eyes fixed on mine.

"Okay, here goes."

I pulled the hood over my head.

The world became a contrast of brightness and shadows. I squinted, adjusting to Scar's night vision, which was clearly better than mine. A series of lights blinked all around me, and staring hard, I realized they were the eyes of other night predators, sitting in the trees or observing things from the shadows. I pulled the cloak a little closer, suddenly feeling very exposed.

Go inside big house. Find toilet paper. Mama watch. Okay?

Scar scurried over to the railings and quickly wiggled through the narrow fencing. I followed her, mesmerized, as she trampled the twigs beneath her feet and listened intently to the crunch of dead leaves as she twisted and turned through the graves of the cemetery. And the smell. Scents attacked me from every direction, some familiar, some not so much. The aroma of sweet, musty earth invaded my nostrils, but it was more than that—it was like I could smell every living *and dead* thing around me. Overwhelmed, I sat back against the tree, struggling to process the speed of Scar's thoughts and the manic world of night now racing through my head. I felt dizzy and a little sick.

Come on, Cat. Deep breaths. You got this.

In no time at all, Scar reached the willow tree, and a moment after that, I could see the silhouette of the Abbey with the moon behind it, casting ominous shadows.

I caught my breath. It was so strange how the building I had come to love now filled me with dread. So much of my happiness rested on the outcome of tonight's caper, and although the General was hardly the evil wizard of fairy tales, I had come to think of him in something of that light. His obstinacy and pigheadedness stood between me and the man I loved. Like the heroine in the fairy tales, I hoped I would prevail.

Keeping low to the ground, Scar hurried over the grounds and up to the doors of the Abbey. She leaned against them, but they were closed and would not yield.

Torhtlic duguð, I thought.

The doors did not open.

Torhtlic duguð, I repeated. Still, they would not budge.

Darn it, Henry had been wrong, and the General had locked the front doors after all. I could have kicked myself. This was always going to be a possibility, and I should have prepared a contingency for it. How dumb could I be?

Think, Cat, think.

I could sense Scar was waiting for my instructions by the door. I had to come up with something, and fast.

Scar, run that way. Good girl. Look up, look at window. Scar, get inside? I felt sick from the continually jerky Steadicam movements, but I wasn't going to quit now.

Scar didn't need to be told twice. Quick as a flash, she darted off into the night, clinging close to the walls of the Abbey. She leaped up and checked each window in turn, pushing against them to see if any were open. Even with my opening spell, they all remained annoyingly shut.

Scar had almost gone completely around the Abbey, and I had just about lost all hope when her keen eyes landed on a little movement a few feet away. Two white lights darted, then stopped, darted and stopped again, and then scurried off into the shadows.

Instinctively, Scar gave chase. I could feel her heart beat a little faster as she went after her prey.

No, Scar, no! I cried mentally. *Stop it!*

But Scar didn't listen. Her undisciplined cub mind was on autopilot, and nothing was going to stop her fun. I realized that what she was chasing was a small field mouse. I held my breath, figuring she would soon either give up the chase or win her prize and be done with it. What if she caught it? Oh Gaia, I really wasn't sure if I could bear listening to, and worse, *feeling* Scar crunching on her warm, tasty snack. I hadn't prepared for this!

The mouse ran to the safety of the Abbey wall, no doubt following a well-trodden trail to make its escape, and I watched as just inches away, it scurried and bounded and leapt. And then disappeared.

Scar pawed at the large clump of grass through which the mouse had vanished. It parted to reveal a small window with a rusty iron grill over it. The window was low down at ground level and was partly open, allowing a little light and air into the Abbey cellars. It was so small it had probably passed the General's notice. I imagined he thought none of us would be able to squeeze through it, and he'd have been right.

But for Scar, it presented no challenge at all. She stuck her nose through the grill, and with a few twists and turns, she was able to pass through the narrow opening.

Scar hopped down from the narrow sill and onto a wooden table below. I breathed a sigh of relief.

She was inside.

Chapter Thirty-Seven

THE SCROLL

SCAR JUMPED DOWN TO THE FLOOR, AND FOR A MOMENT, I LET HER follow her own nose. While she sniffed and examined every corner and shadow in search of her mouse, I took the time to collect my thoughts. We were supposed to have gotten in through the front door. Now I had to recalibrate for another part of the Abbey. In all honesty, this wouldn't have been easy for me in any building, since my sense of direction was lousy, but in the Abbey, with its black walls and secret entrances, it was especially hard. I wished Henry were here to guide me. I thought about texting him for a moment and asking him to come, but what if I lost the connection with Scar? We'd broken through the enchantments together, but if I severed the link to her now, was I sure I'd be able to make contact again? I decided I would only take the risk if I had no other choice. Right now, there was no need to alter the plan. I had to try on my own.

Scar. Find door for Mommy.

Scar had been sniffing around a few barrels and boxes. This room was used as a cellar. The pungent aroma of old brandy filled my nose, temporarily blocking out all other scents, and I wondered just how much alcohol the family kept down there and how old this stuff was. I was willing to bet it was the good quality brandy rich families had. Lucky for the General. Lucky for the mouse.

Scar sneaked out from behind one of the larger barrels and crept along the wall until she found a door. This time, it was cracked open just a fraction. She pushed her nose through the opening and squeezed outside.

Scar, find stairs.

Ever so deftly, Scar raced along the dark corridor, keeping instinctively low to the ground. She soon reached a short flight of stairs that led up to a higher floor. I still had no idea where she was, since one corridor looked pretty much like another.

Scar sniffed the air. Hmm. Apparently, the General had eaten chicken for dinner. I could smell the roasted skin as if I was right there. And then a lightbulb went off over my head. During my stay at the Abbey, I'd been limited by my own senses and had stumbled about in the dark, unable to get my bearings or find my way from one room to the next. Scar had a natural advantage I'd never had: her sense of smell. The dining room and kitchen were on the same floor as the study. If Scar could find her way there, finding the study would become infinitely easier. At least that's what I hoped.

Scar, find chicken.

Her sudden joy told me this was a command after her own heart. She raced along, stopping every so often to sniff the air, making sure she was still on the scent. Some of the doors she passed were open. I wondered if I would recognize any.

Scar, look inside.

Every time I asked her to, Scar would stop to stick her head inside, but her growing frustration made me realize I was slowing her down. This was her area of expertise. I needed to stop being a backseat driver and trust in her abilities. I stopped second-guessing what she was about and let her go off on her own.

Onward she went, joyfully sniffing the air as she detected the invisible trail of deliciousness unwittingly left by the chicken. As she turned into the next corridor, the chicken odor intensified. Dead ahead, I spotted a room with double doors, and I instinctively knew she'd found the correct place. Scar did too, and she was about to run triumphantly inside when she stopped in her tracks, her right paw suspended in midair. There was a new scent on the air, one of redwood and wild sage. She didn't like it one bit. Neither did I.

What is it? I whispered, as if I could be heard outside Scar's head, though I knew that was silly.

Scar inched forward and peered through the tiny crack in the double doors. At first, I couldn't see a thing, but then a pair of soft velvet slippers walked around the kitchen island. I heard a slight scraping on the stone floor as a stool was dragged from the counter, and then I watched as the slippered feet planted themselves on the stool. My heart sank. What was the General doing up at this hour?

Come away, Scar. Don't be seen.

She slipped back into the shadows and trotted silently down the hall.

My heart was racing. I reasoned the General had probably woken up for a nighttime snack or something. Stuff like that happened all the time. I hoped and prayed he would soon go back to bed. In any case, if we were silent, it shouldn't matter. If all went well, Scar would be in and out without him ever knowing she was there at all.

In the meantime, we still had a study to find. I thought I recognized a few of the family portraits and sighed with relief when, after turning the next corner, Scar found the Abbey front door.

Good girl, Scar. Mommy's so proud of you. Sorry about the chicken. Mommy has treats.

I sensed her tail twitch in pleasure, but then she soldiered on.

Keep going, last door.

When Scar reached the end of the corridor, she looked up. There, just as Henry had told us, was the portrait of the general elf, dressed in his purple-and-gold uniform. His disapproving eye glared down at us, or so it seemed to me. I'd heard some pictures were haunted and prayed that wasn't the case here. Henry would have mentioned if they were, or at least I hoped he would.

The door to the study was closed.

Torhtlic duguð.

This time, the spell worked, and the door swung open. Scar looked over her shoulder, checking the coast was clear. All was silent, and she slipped inside.

I was a little taken aback when Scar began to look around. With a name like the General, I half expected the study to be an exercise in discipline, with highly polished surfaces, clean lines, closed drawers, and everything in its proper place, all tidy and neat. I was not prepared for the Aladdin's cave that confronted me. Volumes of books were scattered on every surface. There were jars of herbs and pickled-like somethings I had no desire to examine more closely. I even recognized a small vial of confusion oil from our shop, sitting on a shelf. That explained a lot. Papers and journals were strewn on the floor, like someone was searching for something, and if it weren't for the layer of dust on some of the books, I'd have thought he'd just been burgled.

The General's housekeeping shortfalls were not my concern.

In the corner to the left of an open fireplace was an armchair. It was the only clean spot in the room, and the only thing besides it was a picture of his wife, only she looked much older than I was used to, so I guessed it had been taken just before she died. I would have liked to examine it properly, but now wasn't the time.

Desk. Toilet paper. Hurry.

Scar leapt across the room, landing on the General's desk in a single bound. The scroll was here all right. There was just one problem. Which one? There were several scroll-like documents, some covered in text, others depicting hieroglyphic-like drawings, which meant nothing to me at all. At my command, Scar quickly examined each one. They all looked so similar, with archaic curly scripts that made them difficult to read. I noticed one of them was illustrated with tiny warriors, armed with bows and arrows and spears, reminding me of the stylized wall paintings I'd once seen in a book about Egyptian tombs. But that wasn't all. Midway down the parchment, a figure stood alone with his arms raised above his head and hundreds of small figures around him were running away, leaving their weapons abandoned on the ground. This *had* to be it! What else could have made the warriors drop their weapons and flee in confusion if not a spell of repulsion?

Scar. Scratch bag. Powder.

Scar sat back on her bottom and cocked a rear leg up to her neck, like she was about to scratch her ear. Two tugs later and the loosely tied ribbon came undone, landing near the edge of the General's desk. Then she started scratching and tearing at the opening to the pouch.

Open bag. Use claws. No eat, taste bad.

Her cub nails were small and clumsy, not only marking the surface of the desk but making tiny scratches in the wood stain. I hardly dared breathe, afraid she might be overheard.

In no time at all, the pouch was open just enough to free some of the powder inside. Gently, she picked it up between her teeth and dropped the pouch on the scroll. A little fell out, and she nudged the scroll with her nose. Deeming it light enough to carry, she caught the edge of her scroll in her teeth.

Carry. No tear. Good girl. Bring to Mommy.

Her tail wagged with pride, and she was about to jump down to the floor when I heard footsteps just outside.

Scar! Hide!

I sensed a flash of panic, and then Scar jumped back across the table and turned this way and that, unsure of what to do. The scroll was still in her mouth, and I felt her confusion.

Under the chair, now!

With clearer instructions, Scar leapt off the desk and landed under the chair, just as the General turned on the light. He carried a mug of something in his hand and was rubbing his eyes with the other. I prayed it wouldn't be long before he left to go back to bed.

I watched as he slid behind the desk, putting down his mug and turning on his table lamp. And then he froze. Horrified, I realized he was staring right at the pouch Scar had left on the table.

Quick as a flash, the General opened one of the drawers in the desk, pulling out his wand. In his hurry, he accidentally knocked his drink over his precious scrolls.

"Confound it," he cried, momentarily distracted.

This was our chance.

Run, Scar, run!

With the scroll still caught in her teeth, Scar bolted for the door. Though it was weighed nothing, it was still big and bulky, and the poor cub almost tripped over her tiny feet, but bless her brave soul, she refused to let it go.

Zap! Zap!

Angry red blasts of magic came thick and fast, barely missing Scar each time.

Once at the door, Scar looked back over her shoulder. Furious, the

General jumped out from behind the desk, knocking over his chair in the process and losing his balance. It was just as well because another blast of magic barely missed her head. Scar yelped in anger and then ran off as fast as she could, the General now inches behind her.

Zap! Crash!

With no light to guide him, the General shot blast after blast into the dark, smashing picture frames and blasting chunks of marble from the wall. The General might have been old and slower, but his anger seemed to spur him on, and he remained just feet behind. Scar did as best she could, but the large scroll kept tripping her up and slowing her escape. She just couldn't shake him off.

When another bolt of red magic barely missed her head, my heart stopped, terrified. If she died, I would never forgive myself.

Come on, baby! Find Mommy!

Down the stairs Scar ran, along the corridor and into the cellar. With a giant leap, she soared from the door to the table, and pushing off her hind legs, she jumped onto the open sill of the basement, reaching it just as the General burst into the room.

She tried to wriggle through the window, but the scroll got wedged in the grill.

Scar struggled, tugging as best she could to release the tangled parchment.

The General aimed more carefully this time, as if he were sighting down the long barrel of an elephant gun.

"Now I've got you, you little monster."

Scar leapt into the air. I saw a dazzling flash of red light. And then everything turned black.

Chapter Thirty-Eight

AT THE GATES

My heart literally stopped. I could see nothing. I strained my ears, hoping against hope for a sound, a whimper, anything that would tell me Scar wasn't dead.

Had I killed her?

She was just a cub after all. Had this all been too much for her? *Had I taken her out too soon? Before she was ready? What in Hades had I been thinking?*

The enormity of what had just happened was sinking in when the faint smell of root beer teased my nose. I sat up straight and was about to remove my hood to figure out where the smell was coming from, when I saw a pair of bright eyes. And then I heard a trill-like chirp.

It was Scar, and she was alive!

It was odd though. A pair of eyes loomed above her, looking down. Scar twisted and turned, and I realized she was tangled in a witch hazel shrub, a few feet away from the Abbey window. That's why I could smell root beer. She must have landed in it when she leapt to her freedom. The lights above her were the startled eyes of a barn owl, looking down at her from its perch somewhere high up on the Abbey.

My baby was alive, and right now, that was all that mattered. I clapped my hands with joy and relief.

Scar. Scroll to Mommy.

Scar turned herself right side up and backed carefully out of the shrub, wriggling until she was free.

The scroll was still caught up inside the lower branches. She nipped the end of it in her teeth, and after a few gentle tugs, she managed to pull it out. We both froze again when we heard a great lock being unbolted somewhere inside. Any moment now, the General would appear from the other side of the Abbey, looking for his scroll and angry as hell.

Run, Scar. Run now!

Scar bolted so fast she threw me off-balance, and I leaned against the maple tree for support.

Don't look back, Scar. Just run.

I didn't need to see him to know the General was somewhere behind her. Flashes of light illuminated the grounds, but lucky for us, his focus remained in the area by the small window she'd escaped from. My cunning friend played to her instincts, moving at great speed but clinging to the shadows that hid her. While the General's back was to her, she ran straight to the willow and then out into the cemetery.

I'd been holding my breath the whole time. I hadn't moved from my spot under the tree, yet I was sweating, partly because of the adrenaline pumping through me, and because any exertion Scar felt, I felt.

Till the two become one, sharing all that they know.

Scar was just a few feet from the gates now, and her focus latched onto me. I saw myself hidden under the tree, a misplaced dark shadow in her eyes. I sensed her relief and joy.

She had done it! Now that she was close, I threw the hood off my face and gasped, drinking in some much-needed fresh air and delighted to see her safely returned. Scar twisted through the iron fencing, the scroll secure in her mouth, her ears high and her eyes bright as she exalted in her own achievement. Best fox ever!

I pulled her close, rubbing her hard and giving her a once-over, searching for any sign she might be injured. For the most part she looked fine, but there was a nasty scorch mark on the brush of her tail, and I closed my eyes to thank Gaia. I suspected if it had touched her skin, she'd have been done for. But she hadn't, and she was a rock star.

Relieved, I squeezed her tight.

"Good Scar! Treats for you all week!"

I stopped petting her long enough to grab some of the promised kibble from my pocket. She dropped her scroll, and I let her nibble on a few pieces. While she ate, I remained on alert, not taking my eyes off those gates.

"Come on, more later. we'd better run before the bad man comes after us." I said this more to myself than to her. I pushed off the ground, and together we headed off as fast as we could, putting as much distance between me and the Abbey as possible.

The more I thought about the General, the angrier I became. If he tried to harm Scar again, I'd punch the old fool in the nose, never mind the consequences. His behavior was unacceptable. The entire idea of him somehow reconciling with his family had lost its appeal for me. If not for Henry's feelings, and Eleanor's too, I would gladly have walked away from the Abbey and never looked back.

Every now and then, I peered over my shoulder, expecting to see the General in hot pursuit, but we were not followed. The farther we got, the more my horrible sense of unease faded. Exhilaration took its place.

We had done it! Scar and I had the scroll. Now all we had to do was find the others, and if Henry could reverse the enchantments, all would be well.

I began to slow down as I approached the *All Shook Up* elven cocktail parlor.

I pulled the pack off my back. "Come on, Scar, up," I said, holding out my hands to her and clapping once. Scar leapt into my arms, and I put her and the purple cloak in the bag. She soon settled in, safely out of sight. I fed her another piece of kibble from my pocket and then slid back under the straps.

It wasn't hard to find the others. Sylvia and Henry were huddled at the end of the bar, closest to the door, and they both stood up the second I walked in.

Henry's attention went straight to the scroll in my hand. He smiled, relieved. "You got it then."

"*We* did," I corrected him as I handed it to him. "I hope that's the right one. And Scar was brilliant."

Henry pulled the scroll open and looked over the words. Sylvia stared over his shoulder, her attention darting from the scroll to Henry as she anxiously awaited the verdict. I knew how she felt. I would die if we'd stolen the wrong scroll.

"Yes, this is the one," Henry said at last. "Well done."

We all breathed a sigh of relief.

"Look, we'd better hurry," I said. "Your dad caught us stealing, and he might be raising new enchantments as we speak."

"He saw you?" Sylvia asked, her eyes popping out with surprise.

"He saw Scar. And he was mad as hell. He almost killed her when she ran off with the scroll."

They both nodded grimly.

"You're right," Henry said. "And he knows Scar, so he'll know it was us. He's probably already planning his next move to block us. We've got to get back there now and finish this thing."

We all agreed. Sylvia dropped some cash on the bar, and in less than a minute, we were back on the street, walking at a brisk pace.

The closer we got to the Abbey, the greater my anxiety for Henry became.

"Are you sure you want to be the one to do the counter spell? I can do it if you like. I don't mind."

Henry didn't drop his pace but continued full steam ahead, his focus unwavering.

"No. I want to do it. He's my father after all. I think it should be me."

"I know, I know," I argued. "I understand completely. But what happens if something goes wrong? I mean, what if it's worse this time? What if more than your memory is affected? I don't know what I'd do if anything happened to you. I don't like you taking that risk."

"She's right, you know," Sylvia added. "You can't be sure what will happen if you're exposed to a confusion spell again. Maybe I should do it—no offense, Cat, but you might not be ready yet. Do you want to give me the scroll?"

She reached out to take it, but Henry refused to slow down and held resolutely onto the parchment.

"No, sorry, I know what you're trying to say, but it has to be me."

"Why?" I said, my worry turning to frustration.

He stopped in his tracks at last and pulled me to one side.

"It's hard to explain. But I must try. You have to let me try. Everything you said to me...I want that back. If I don't do the counter curse, I might not change and..." He lowered his voice and brought his lips close so only I could hear. "I might not remember. Please. I really want to do this."

His gaze penetrated mine, imploring, like he wanted me to understand what he was feeling. I couldn't lie—I was worried, but I respected his need to do something, to not feel completely helpless.

"Okay, we'll do it your way. There's some salt in my pack. If nothing else, we can put you inside a circle. That should give you a bit of protection, at least."

Henry's face muscles relaxed. He squeezed my arm gently. "Thank you."

Gaia help us all, I thought. "There's a maple tree a little distance from the gate. I hid there while Scar was in the Abbey. It was a good spot; I didn't feel quite so weirded out while I stayed close to it. I think that's where you should do it. It might be safer than right in front of the gates."

"Yes, I know it." He looked down the street and pointed to the exact tree.

I nodded, and we carried on.

The streets had cleared, and the cemetery was unusually quiet. Perhaps it was the lateness of the hour, but I was afraid the General had beaten us to it and had already cast new spells to repel us.

Henry evidently had the same concern because he didn't waste any time. He stood under the tree exactly where I had and opened the scroll vertically, reminding me of a town crier reading an old-time public announcement. Sylvia pulled the tub of salt from my backpack, and I heard Scar sniffle curiously on the inside.

"There, there, sweetheart," Sylvia whispered, petting her. "You just settle down. Your work is done for tonight." Scar licked her hand. "Good girl. Go to sleep."

Sylvia joined Henry and poured a generous circle of salt all around him.

Once she was done, she slipped the pot back in my pack and secured the straps. We were all set.

Sylvia clasped my hand and locked my fingers with hers. We exchanged fearful looks, and she tightened her hand to reassure me. I inhaled deeply, and after taking a breath of this own, Henry began to speak.

O'er land and down to sea,
Evil begone, away with thee,
For doute ye not, I cast this spelle,
And bid ye demons return to hell.

The night became so cold Sylvia and I instinctively held on to each other. The hidden beasts of New York, the foxes, squirrels, and rats all cried out at once, and anything with wings took to the skies, screeching in perfect unison. I heard a little whimper in my pack and knew that whatever it was, Scar had felt it too.

Overhead, the dark clouds drifted faster across the night sky. The silvery winter moon shone eerily over the cemetery, highlighting the stone graves, which cast long, sinister shadows across the gloomy earth.

The wind stopped blowing, and the clouds hid the moon and stars until there was just black above. No one moved. And then the moon slipped slowly from behind a cloud, casting its light on the world once more.

"Henry, oh sweet Gaia, are you okay?"

I could barely see him in the shadow of the tree, but he was standing perfectly still, and the scroll had fallen to the ground, landing inches from his body. His arms were still extended, and he was staring down at himself, like someone had surprised him by throwing a cold bucket of water all over him.

"Henry?" Sylvia repeated.

Fearing the worst, I dashed to his side, terrified of what I might find.

"Henry. Henry!"

In a flash, he grabbed my hands and pulled me to him so quickly he knocked the wind out of me. Then he kissed me, harder than he'd ever kissed me before, and I found myself not caring if I could get back into the Abbey. All I knew was Henry was kissing me now and doing one hell of a job of it.

In the end, I had to pull away, if only to come up for air.

"Sorry, who are you again?" he said.

Twit. I punched him hard on the arm.

"The enchantment is broken." He grinned. I could see the old Henry reflected in his eyes. *Thank Gaia!*

"You think?" I said, as a wave of relief washed through me, warming my soul even though it was cold.

"And we have some serious catching up to do." He pulled me close and began kissing me again.

"Ahem!" Sylvia coughed into her balled fist. "I'm sure you two have plenty to discuss, but we're not done yet. If we don't act fast, your dad might lock you out again."

She was right, of course, but it was hard letting Henry go, having only just got him back.

Henry cupped my hands in his and kissed them. "We can discuss this later," he said. "Come on. Let's get this business over and done with."

My relief evaporated as I steeled myself for the unpleasant task to come.

Henry reached for the gate. He hesitated, perhaps not fully trusting all enchantments were cleared even now.

"Allow me," I said and turned the handle for him. The gates opened with a mild *creak,* and I stepped inside. I felt fine. If the General had cast something new, I wasn't detecting it.

Once inside the cemetery, Sylvia closed the gates behind us. The faint sound of the city was lost with it, leaving only the silence of the night. It was time to face the General. Henry took my hand. We all took in a deep breath and marched resolutely toward the willow tree. It was time to do what I'd been tasked to do—to sing to him. Given all the General had just tried to do, I would much rather have punched him in the nose.

Chapter Thirty-Nine

THE STUDY

A FAINT LIGHT LIT A CORNER WINDOW OF THE ABBEY. THE GENERAL was still awake. I hesitated at the Abbey door. Whatever Henry's mother wanted of me, I still couldn't just barge inside and demand the General hear me out. This wasn't my home. For the first time, I felt like an intruder. An angry one at that.

Henry had no such scruples. He marched straight up to the Abbey door and waved his arm over the entry. Reassured there were no new booby traps, he pushed it open. At least the General hadn't locked it this time. Henry looked back to where we trailed behind him, his expression grim. "I guess he's expecting us."

Henry stood to one side, allowing us to pass, and Sylvia closed the door quietly once we were all inside. I stiffened, wondering if the General knew we'd arrived. Maybe he'd been watching for us from the window. I know I would have been. I twisted the ring on my finger. Henry might be his son, but I'd seen what the General could do when his blood was up, and there was no way I was going back there defenseless. I summoned all the magic I could hold.

Scar peeked out of the pack, quivering in fright.

"Be calm, baby. Nothing's going to happen to you, I promise. Mommy's just being careful."

Scar slithered back inside.

Sylvia must have seen me because I saw her hand go down to the pocket where I knew she kept her wand. She was a smart cookie. I was glad she'd decided to come along.

Henry slowed as he neared the study. The door was ajar, and he pushed it open wide.

"So you've come then," the General said. It was a statement, not a question.

At that precise moment, Sylvia and I reached the study. We found the General sitting behind his desk; the scrolls Scar had recently scattered in all directions were now neatly piled in front of him. He held on to the red pouch of trammeling powder and was fingering the ribbon that tied it.

His thoughtful expression died when he saw Sylvia and I were with Henry. His cheeks became red and flushed, and he slammed his fists onto the table before jumping to his feet. He must have seen Sylvia's wand because he instantly withdrew his own.

"What on earth are they doing here?" the General exclaimed. "I thought you were coming to apologize."

"Shut up and listen for a change," Henry said. "And I have not come to apologize. If anyone ought to be apologizing, it's you! You and your foolish, dangerous spell casting. You scrambled my memories, and you nearly cost me everything!"

"Get out," the General said. "If you've not come to say you're sorry, then you have nothing more to say."

"Not until you hear us," Henry continued.

"No, I will not. Get her out of here, or I'll..."

The General waved his wand in my direction, and Henry dived over the desk to grab his arm. They tussled for a moment, and I thought Henry had the better of him, but his father brushed him off and backed into a corner, sending a few jars and books crashing to the ground. The smell of vinegar and ammonia invaded the room.

"I curse the day you ever set foot in my home," the General screamed at me. "Get her out and don't ever bring her back."

"I'll go, and gladly," I said. "But I made a promise to someone, and I intend to see it through. Your wife gave me a message for you."

This time, the General snatched a bowl from his shelves and angrily smashed it to the floor. "She gave *you* a message? I've read every necromancy text ever written, spent hours on my knees before her grave begging her to come back. Why would she give a message to a stupid little witch when I, the man who loved her heart and soul and has ached for her every day since she left me, has heard nothing? *Why?*"

He was shaking with anger, and I could see tears of frustration in his eyes. He raised his wand again and pointed it at me once more. At this moment, he was capable of anything. I hoped the blast of energy I had spindled inside my ring would be enough to cast a defensive shield if I needed it to. I raised my hands, ready to defend myself. Henry and Sylvia stood aside, their own wands drawn, ready to help me if it came to it.

A gentle voice behind me stopped everyone cold. "Put your wand down, Father. Enough is enough."

I turned. Eleanor stood in the study door, and Victor was just behind her. They were dressed in matching leather coats, very Goth, their expressions unreadable. I guessed she'd received Henry's texts after all.

The General's wand remained high, but he tilted his head and narrowed his eyes in confusion.

"Put the wand down," she repeated, "and we can talk."

The fire went out of him, and the General stumbled forward, collapsing into his own seat. Henry took the opportunity to step forward and gently slipped the wand from his father's hand.

"You decided to come after all?" Henry said to Eleanor.

She nodded. "I didn't come for you. Or anyone else for that matter," she said, glancing at me. There was something in her eyes that surprised me. It felt like—disappointment? Anger? I wasn't totally sure. "None of you have anything to say that either Victor or I want to hear."

"Then why did you come?" the General asked. His voice was empty, defeated.

Eleanor took a sharp intake of breath and stood up straight. "I came for our mother because it seems she wanted me to. That's the only reason I'm here. So whatever message you say she has for us, Cat, say it quickly and be done, so we can all get on with our lives."

"It wasn't a message—it was a song. My ancestor, Catherine Morland, sang it to me in my family's cemetery."

"Then how do you know it was intended for us?" Eleanor asked, bewildered.

"Trust her," Henry said softly. "Cat already sang it to me. It's the song we could never remember. You'll know it when you hear it."

"Don't!" the General cried. "Don't say another word. I can't bear it. Why do you think I cast those spells of forgetfulness on you in the first place? It breaks my heart to hear what we once had and have lost forever. I knew if you remembered it, you would sing it, and I'd suffer the pain of losing my darling Eleanor all over again. So don't. Please, don't."

The General covered his face with his hands. He didn't cry, but his agony and loneliness filled the room, touching us all.

Eleanor and Henry exchanged glances, and I guessed a little of what they were feeling. I understood the General's motives, but it had been cruel to remove such a precious memory of their mother. I wasn't sure if this revelation would unite them or drive them all further apart.

While they all battled with their feelings, I slipped around the desk. Sylvia smiled gently, encouraging me. I put my arm around the General's shoulders and tried to help him sit up. At first, he brushed me away, his anger not quite abated and still boiling close to the surface. Anything might rekindle it. But I understood him better now, so I was less intimidated by it. I stood by patiently and waited for his gaze to lock on mine.

"You loved her very much," I said. "And I can feel the weight of that loss even now. The thing is, I don't know why I have this gift, when others may deserve it or need it more than I do. But that decision was never mine. It was another's. All I know is your wife loved you all and loves you still. So much so she rose unbidden from her grave when she thought you all in danger of breaking up. Please let me give you her message. Please let me sing you her song."

The General's brow furrowed in confusion. *"Unbidden,* you say?"

I nodded. "Whatever you think, I didn't summon her. I wasn't even thinking about her at the time. I was searching for my familiar, who was curled up on her grave. Your wife revealed herself to me."

The General sought Henry's attention. "Is that true?"

Henry nodded. "Let her sing her song. She sounds just like Mom did when she sang it, and I've missed her so much."

The General's gaze went from Henry, to Eleanor, and then to me. At last, the fight went out of his eyes, and he nodded.

It was now or never. After an encouraging nod from Sylvia, I filled my lungs with air and began to sing:

Dancing with my sweetheart and my children, one to three,
With the Goddess there beside us under shade of willow tree,
Turn the circle once, then twice,
And sing out all our praises
As we thank you for our blessings on this gentle bed of daisies.

Merry meet and blessings be, we spin under the light,
We dance together, hands entwined, 'til day turns into night,
Circle in, and circle out,
We sing with all our heart,
Receive our thanks, O blessed one, and pray we never part.

As I sang the words, a dreaminess fell on the General and his children. Henry, who had heard the song before, smiled affectionately, as if remembering an old favorite. Eleanor gasped, and her eyes filled with tears. She was so overcome, we all thought she might faint, but luckily Victor stepped forward and led her over to the General's armchair where she sat down. The General himself stared dead ahead, but though he didn't make a sound, the familiar hardness of his expression began to wither, making him look more like his son Henry than ever, and the years seemed to fade from his face.

When I was done, he nodded thoughtfully. After a moment, he took my hand in his and kissed the back of it.

"Thank you," he said. And then he raised his head and addressed his children. "I'm sorry. It all just hurt too much, you see. I loved her ever so dearly."

Henry rested his hand on the General's shoulder. "So did we, Dad. So did we."

"I know," the General said. "Will you ever forgive me?"

Eleanor's lips were set. She took hold of Victor's hand and squeezed it. "I can forgive you for the past, Dad, but it's my future that concerns me. I love Victor. I am going to be with Victor. I love him, like you loved Mom. Until you can accept him as part of the family, it can never be as it was before. Don't you see that?"

Slowly, the General got out from behind his desk and joined them both by the armchair. He stood in front of Victor, standing just an inch or two taller than the werewolf.

"It looks like my daughter can't be happy without you," he said. He fell silent, and we all waited anxiously to hear what either of them had to say. "I don't care how much money you have or who your people are. You hurt one hair on my daughter's head when you turn, and I will hex your fangs off. Are we clear?"

"Yes, sir," Victor replied. "But believe me, your daughter's life is worth more than my own to me." Victor pulled a small glass vial from inside his leather coat. "This contains a deadly mixture of silver buckshot and wolfsbane oil. I engaged a wizard to weave a spell that will break the vial if I ever try to harm *anyone* while in my werewolf form."

The General nodded and took Victor's hand and pumped it. "Very well, then. That's good enough for now. Welcome to the family."

Victor smiled and breathed a sigh of relief. We all did.

Eleanor kissed her father on his cheek, and Sylvia began clapping happily. It seemed everyone was friends again. Henry's mother's wish had been fulfilled.

Henry took hold of my hand and smiled at me. "Well done," he whispered.

I beamed. *Well, thank Gaia this is all fixed at last,* I thought.

I still hadn't forgiven the General for attacking Scar or for calling me a stupid little witch, but at least it was a start. Perhaps I should let her out so she could pee against his leg or something. Maybe not right now. But oh, the temptation.

Chapter Forty

A REUNION

At Henry's suggestion, we all vacated the General's small study and convened in the kitchen, where Henry and Eleanor set about making everyone a hot drink.

As I slipped the pack off my shoulders, I heard a tiny whimper. Poor Scar. She'd had quite a night. I approached the General.

"Sorry to bother you, but I don't suppose you have any leftover food in the fridge, like chicken? For my familiar. She's hungry."

He stared at me for a long second, and I didn't know how he was going to respond, but then a hint of a smile touched his lips. "I'm sure we can find something for such an *industrious* familiar."

He found a metal bowl in a cupboard and opened the fridge door. He reached inside and picked at something, and when he turned to me, there were indeed scraps of chicken in the bowl. But when he put the bowl down, Scar backed away from him, the memory of his attack still fresh in her mind. And in mine too. But at the first sniff of chicken, all sins were forgotten, and now she wolfed her reward down. Satisfied that he was forgiven, the General held his hands sheepishly to his torso, then decided to be brave, and bent down to pet her. Scar growled through her teeth, though she didn't stop eating. Once zapped, twice shy. The General wisely withdrew his hand and backed away to a safe distance. I smothered the impulse to whisper, "Good girl."

Sylvia gave me a warm hug and kissed both my cheeks in her usual style. "Forgive me," she said. "Now that everything's settled, I need to get these old bones off to bed. I haven't got the energy I used to have you know. You don't mind, do you, Cat?"

"Not in the least," I said, but since she had more energy than any other witch I knew, I suspected she had other reasons for making good her escape.

"I'll see you back at the apartment." Sylvia glanced over at Henry and then smiled at me meaningfully. "Don't you be late, now."

I grinned. "I promise, I won't. And thank you."

After hugging Henry, she bid a cordial good-bye to everyone else.

"Let me help you get a Magic Cab," the General said.

Sylvia shook her head. "Thank you, but no." She looked around to where Eleanor poured hot water into several mugs. "You belong here with your children. I'll be fine."

"Well, if you're quite sure?"

"I'm a big girl." She laughed. "And I know my way around."

Nevertheless, the General gallantly escorted her out of the kitchen and to the Abbey entrance.

Henry slid a mug of warm cocoa my way.

"Thanks." I smiled at him and pulled the drink toward me, but I didn't have the strength to bring it to my lips. The night's excitement had left me fit for nothing but my bed and a long lie-in in the morning. Actually, it was already morning. *Oh well.*

While the General, Henry, and Victor indulged in genial man-talk, Eleanor sat on the corner of the island and sipped at her drink. I was glad of the opportunity to speak with her alone. At first, she refused to look at me, and I began to wonder if I'd get the chance to say anything. In the end, I decided to just go for it.

"I'm really glad you came, if only so I didn't have to sing that blessed song again."

Eleanor stared at me over the rim of her mug, and I could see the thoughts churning away behind her eyes. There was a brief pause, and I began to think she wasn't going to say anything, but then she put her drink down, and with her usual directness, she came straight to the point.

"I'll be honest with you, Cat. I thought you were someone I could trust. I don't mind admitting it hurt to find out I was wrong."

"I don't understand?"

She looked around, and apparently satisfied the others weren't listening, she lowered her voice. "I told you about Victor in confidence. I never expected you to go blabbing about him to Pops."

The penny dropped. No wonder she'd refused to answer my texts. She thought I'd broken my promise and told the General about Victor. "But I didn't," I said. "The first thing I knew about anything was when you and your dad were shouting at each other, and then you ran out of the house and left us. I didn't tell your dad anything. I have no idea how he heard about Victor, but I swear before Gaia, he never heard it from me."

Eleanor sat back, dubious, shaking her head.

"It's the truth," the General said. It appeared he'd been listening to us after all. "Cat didn't tell me anything."

"Then who did?"

"Nobody *told* me. But it wasn't hard to figure out. I could smell werewolf in the Abbey. You think a few breath mints and a spray of perfume would fool me? The whole place reeked of him. No offense," he said to Victor, who had just joined us at the table.

"None taken," Victor said good-naturedly.

Thank Gaia for that.

"I knew the second I came home he'd been here. I might be old, but that doesn't make me an idiot."

Eleanor examined her hands while she thought. After a moment, she nodded and looked up at me. "I'm sorry," she said. "It seemed the most plausible reason. Forgive me."

"There's nothing to forgive," I said, as a wave of relief gushed through me. "At least now I know what you were thinking. I thought I'd gone mad. Well, mad-er."

She laughed. "Well then, friends again?"

"Friends," I echoed. "Is this when we're supposed to hug?" I didn't wait for an answer, but leaving my chocolate untouched, I jumped up and squeezed her tight. Eleanor laughed again and hugged me back. I caught a faint whiff of werewolf in her hair. I decided now wasn't the best time to mention it.

When I sat down again, I stared at my drink. Beyond exhausted, not even the delicious aroma of chocolate could tempt me now. Henry must have noticed my head drooping or something because he crossed the kitchen and picked Scar up off the floor.

"Come on, sleepyhead," he said to me. "Let's get you home."

I rose, grateful, and slipped my pack over my shoulders. Henry planted Scar safely inside, and once she was settled, it was time to say good-bye.

I hugged Eleanor again, and Victor also, though I wasn't quite ready to be so friendly with the General, not yet. I cordially shook his hand instead. Going by his expression, he preferred this.

"Let me walk you out, son," the General said to Henry. He raised his palm, ushering Henry and I out ahead of him.

As we reached outside, the cold wind pinched my cheeks, and I pulled my poncho close about me. The sudden gush of air made me feel even more tired than I'd felt before. I longed for my bed.

The General didn't turn back at the door, but instead he walked out with us as passed the willow and into the cemetery. I didn't have to be told where we were going. I knew it in my heart.

There was no moon in the sky, but somewhere in the east, a new sun was rising, casting a dull monochrome light around the stone graves. It illuminated the frost on the ground and the delicate spider webs that decorated the graveyard. Everywhere was strangely peaceful.

We stopped at Eleanor Tilney's grave, and after staring at it thoughtfully for a moment, the General waved a hand over the sod, and the wilting lilies in the pot curled up and bloomed again.

"If only it were so easy to rouse your mother," the General said to Henry.

My heart was breaking to see him so forlorn. I thought about myself, Eleanor, and Matt. We had each found a love, and in that moment, it seemed so unfair only the General remained alone. Whatever his misgivings, I prayed with all my heart he could find peace.

A light mist swirled around the grave, and then a silvery form rose up from the earth and took shape. Eleanor drifted to her late husband, hovering mere inches from his face. I glanced at Henry, wondering if perhaps he'd broken his own rule just this once and summoned his mother, but he shook his head. I thought about the prayer I'd just uttered. Had I summoned her without realizing it? It was possible. If I had, I hoped the General would forgive me.

"Nell," the General said. I caught the sob in his voice as years of unshed tears filled his eyes.

Eleanor lifted her spectral finger to his lips, quieting him. She drew close, her eyes dilating. "I love you," she whispered to the General. Then she floated alongside him, and taking her husband by the hand, the two meandered silently among the quiet graves. Neither gave us a backward glance, but I didn't expect one. This was their time; they needed no other company. Both seemed at peace.

They disappeared behind the willow, and I turned back to her grave and reread the inscription on the headstone.

"What does it mean, Gaia will atone?" I asked.

At first, Henry didn't answer, and I didn't press while he conquered his own emotions. Then he straightened and let out a big sigh, his breath fogging in the chill air. He took my hand. "I never asked him, but I think it means Gaia will atone for taking her from him so soon. At least, that's what I like to think it means. He's not as bad as you think. You'll like him more as you get to know him better."

Maybe. I didn't dare answer. Not yet anyway. And then another thought occurred to me. "I wonder why your mother chose me and not you to deliver her song?"

Henry thought for a moment and shrugged. "Who knows? Maybe Dad's first charm would have prevented me sharing it with the others." He smiled and pulled me close. "Or maybe she just wanted you in my life. Mothers have their own kind of magic, don't they? She must have had her reasons."

"I guess." I stared across to the willow tree and thought about everything the two had done in the name of love. "I never realized he loved her so much," I said. "To be honest, I didn't think he had it in him."

As Henry gazed down into my face, he brushed the backs of his fingers over my cheek and spoke to me softly. His forehead connected with mine, and our lips were so close I could almost taste him. "He's a Tilney. When we love a woman, we love them forever. No half measures. It's 'til death us do part. Always."

"I bet you say that to all the witches," I said.

"No, just this one."

He leaned down and kissed me, and my heart swelled with joy, thankful to Gaia that my Henry had come back to me. I had never felt so alive among the living or the dead. I was blessed.

***

Thank you for reading! Did you enjoy? Please add your review because nothing helps an author more and encourages readers to take a chance on a book than a review.

And don't miss more in the Soul and Shadows series coming soon!

Until then read more paranormal romance like SMOKE AND RITUAL by City Owl author, Melissa Sercia! Turn the page for a sneak peek!

You can also sign up for the City Owl Press newsletter to receive notice of all book releases!

SNEAK PEEK OF SMOKE AND RITUAL

By Melissa Sercia

Something was wrong. The liquid burned, hot like fire as it trickled down my throat, swirling around my stomach. *Why couldn't I get this right?* I mixed it just the way Jane had told me to—two sage leaves, a vial of honey water, three oyster pearls, and a pinch of mountain ash. Now she was staring at me, arms crossed, looking like I just killed her favorite pet.

She furrowed her brow. "Arya, you forgot the willow bark. *Again.*"

Of course I did. I'd been training at Sanctum for ten years and I was the only witch who couldn't master this. I could read spells in three different languages, fight off shadow demons in simulation without even breaking a sweat, and conjure all of the Four Winds, but I couldn't remember a simple potion recipe.

I rubbed at my eyes, my vision blurring from the potion fumes. "Sorry, Miss Jane. I'll remember next time."

Her antique spectacles slid down her nose as she walked. "That's what you said the last time. And the time before that. I'm concerned you aren't taking any of this serious, Arya. Your mother was a great potion master. I find it hard to believe that you didn't inherit any of her abilities."

Ouch. I barely knew my mother, or my father for that matter. They had both died, fighting in the Blood War, a war that Jane's own daughter, Gray, had started, and won. But so many, like my parents, didn't survive it. I was only eleven years old when I was brought here to Sanctum—a safe haven for creatures like me. Nestled on a jagged cliff in the North Sea of Scotland, Sanctum was a place where all creatures were welcome—witches, dhampirs, werewolves—even harpies, though not one single harpy had ever come. The harpies didn't mingle with anyone but themselves. The rest of us were happy to be here. We could live and train under a blanket of safety and protection.

But it wasn't my home. My family wasn't here.

With each passing year, it got harder and harder to remember what my parents even looked like. All I had left was a faint memory of my mother, the harsh tone of her voice as she warned me to stay away from our birth coven, the Sylphs. As a branch of the four Elemental covens, we could control the winds, and I had mastered them. But just days after my twenty-first birthday, I still had no answers for why she had kept me from them. Every witch had a coven. Except for me. I was alone.

My palms itched from the faulty potion. "May I be excused, Miss Jane?"

Without looking up from her spell book, a thick dusty text with torn edges and burnt corners, she waved me off. "Don't forget next time," she murmured.

Without hesitating, I sprinted out of the room. I wanted to get as far away from those potions as possible. Traces of the spoiled liquid still lingered, leaving the back of my throat raw and scratchy like wet sandpaper.

Slowing my sprint to a brisk speed-walk through the corridors of Sanctum, I did my best to ignore the snickers and whispers from the other students, who most likely heard my latest scolding. It was something I had gotten good at—shutting out the world that I never felt like I belonged in. It seemed no matter what I did, there was always someone there to remind me that I wasn't good enough. Today was no different as I did my best to deflect their icy glares.

Passing the meditation room, the familiar scents of jasmine, myrrh, and sandalwood teased my senses. It was comforting. I should have spent more time in there but having it all to myself proved to be a challenge. One night, a few years ago, I remembered to set an alarm to wake me up right before dusk. The halls were dark and empty as I crept down there, barefoot and drowsy from sleep. And just as I'd hoped, the whole room was mine alone. But I was too relaxed. At some point, I must have dozed off, the sound of cackling jolted me awake. A group of Crescent witches laughed and pointed while I ran out, wiping the drool from my face.

I hadn't been back to the meditation room since.

Picking up my pace, I whipped past a row of ornate wood-carved doors just as colorful puffs of smoke seeped out from underneath—a sobering reminder that there were witches in there who had no trouble brewing a simple potion.

The clanking of swords echoed out from one of the combat training rooms as I turned down another corridor. Filled mostly with dhampirs and Lupi wolves, they couldn't have cared less about my status, but the stone walls of Sanctum were thin if you were a witch. There were very few secrets here. It was irritating. *At least I still had one secret that was mine alone.*

I pulled up the hood of my cloak and focused on the path ahead, wishing I were invisible. It would have been nice to get to the Three Blind Mice without confrontation for once. Sanctum's in-house pub was an exact replica of the one in New Orleans—built here as a tribute to the man who owned it. Apparently he was Gray's lover and died protecting her from Cerberus. I was just grateful that I could get a drink without veering too far from my room.

Eyeing the entrance, I could already feel the warm presence of my friends on the other side. My muscles relaxed as I pushed open the thick cherrywood door and sauntered over to their table. Letting out a sigh, I sank into the deep leather booth and signaled to the server at the bar.

Sapphire leaned forward, expectant, while Diego stifled a giggle by pretending to cough. He loved to tease me and often told me I had an unhealthy flair for the dramatic. Sapphire, on the other hand, was good at deflecting. She could always tell when I was in one of my moods but often refused to acknowledge it.

I pushed a strand of dark black hair behind my ear, catching a quick glimpse of the newly dyed blue streak that ran through it. "I need a drink, stat. Preferably one that doesn't burn my throat."

Diego chuckled, his brown eyes lighting up. "Failed your test again?"

I sank farther back into the booth, folding my arms to my chest. "Cute. This coming from the wolf who couldn't shape-shift without crying himself to sleep at night."

"She does have a point there," Sapphire quipped. Her dark eyes mirrored her mother's when she smiled. As the daughter of Zari—coven leader of the Rain Makers, Sapphire didn't smile in public often. The pressure to live up to her mother's expectations was a heavy burden. It also drove her to excel at everything.

"Hey, I was only a fledgling." Diego's deep melodic voice grew two octaves higher, sending all three of us into a fit of laughter.

As the server brought over my usual snifter of absinthe, or *green fire* as Diego liked to call it, Sapphire's smile vanished, her gaze fixated on her own drink.

"Penny for your thoughts?" I asked.

After a quick glance around the room, she lowered her voice. "There's talk that the Imperator hasn't checked in for a while. No one's heard from her partner either."

"Gray and Dragos? That's a little strange...but not shocking. Those two are always on the move. They're probably just taking a well-deserved vacation." I had met Gray once when I was first brought here, after the war. She was fierce and beautiful, and I wanted to be just like her. Though I'd never admit that to anyone. My skills were nowhere close to being as good as hers.

Sapphire shrugged as she sipped her martini, dangling the glass between her slender fingers with the poise of a socialite—unconcerned that up close, her palms were covered in callouses and knife scars. "No one has had any contact with her in the last six months. At least that's what my cousin told me."

Diego ran a hand through his wavy brown hair. He always had to make sure every strand of hair was in its perfect place. "If the imperator was missing, I think we'd know about it, *mi amica*." His Italian accent had faded from centuries of being away from his homeland, but came out when he used his native tongue.

There weren't many secrets at Sanctum, but those that existed were held close and locked away from those of us who weren't in the inner circle. There was a time when great atrocities had been committed here. Back before the war, when this sacred place had been a battleground between Gray and her enemies. The blood had been washed away, but sometimes I thought I could hear the hushed breathings of ancient ghosts between the cracks of its stone walls.

I hoped Diego was right, but Sapphire didn't look convinced. Knowing she wasn't one to partake in petty gossip, a tiny shiver ran up my spine. *What if it were true?* If Gray was in danger, then all of us would be too.

I had to force those thoughts away. Between the failed potion test and the questions I had about my own history, I had enough weighing on my mind.

"Well, I'm turning in, guys and girls. Try not to worry about Gray. She's survived this long. I'm sure she's fine." With that, I gave them each a hug and made my way back to my room.

The halls of Sanctum were like a maze. It had taken me years to get my bearings. Plus with all the witches crafting spells around every corner, some of the corridors would dead end without warning. Those were supposed to be childish pranks, but they made me feel even more foolish and alone back then. I could still hear their hysterical laughter like it was yesterday, patting each other on the back for succeeding in freaking me out.

Still, that was then. Now the others left me mostly alone. I did my best to blend into the shadows and not draw attention to myself. It was easier to manage the older we grew. The female witches became more interested in how they looked and the male witches became more interested in them. They forgot about me and I liked it that way.

The heavy steel door creaked as I opened it, but gave way easily, and I moved inside my room, flopping onto the bed. Using magic was exhausting, especially when you screwed it up. At least I had a firm grasp on my spellcasting. Satisfied that my locking spell was secure, I stretched out my arms and allowed my wings to unfold. The black feathers felt soft and comforting against my pale white skin. I flapped them against my shoulders, wrapping them around me like a soft blanket.

I'd been hiding this part of myself for so long it had become second nature. I was an Elemental Sylph witch with black wings—a rarity even within my own coven. At least that's what Jane told me. It was one of the few things I knew about my family's coven.

If the others found out what I was, I wouldn't be welcome here. They already thought I was weird enough. Jane and the council kept my secret in hopes that I would fit in better, but the Elementals didn't help Gray during the Blood War, and according to everyone at Sanctum, they couldn't be trusted. I couldn't risk them thinking that of me too. Not even Sapphire and Diego knew that I was an Elemental. The guilt that came along with it sometimes kept me up at night, but it was my cross to bear, and I didn't want to burden them with it.

Flipping through my copy of the *Sang Magi* spell book, I turned to the potion section again, desperate to understand what I was doing wrong... but all the ingredient names seemed to blur together. Not even the most sacred book of magic could help me. It was useless. I tossed it on the floor and buried my head in my hands.

A sharp pain seared between my temples and I rifled through my desk for a calming elixir. My ears tingled. Just when I thought I could finally relax, the silent comfort of my room was interrupted by a burst of frantic voices, echoing throughout the halls. This time of night was always so quiet, you could hear a pin drop. *What the hell was going on out there?*

Folding my wings back into my shoulders, I crept to the door and pressed my cheek against it. The brisk shuffling of feet was paired with gasps and whispers. With my ear still on the door, I reached for my hoodie and pulled it on, always careful to keep my back covered. Even with my wings hidden, two distinct black lines were etched into my shoulder blades, thick and somewhat raised like a freshly inked tattoo. The footsteps in the hall intensified, a mixture of heavy boots and pointy heels thudding against the floor with urgency. I threw open the door just as Sapphire came bumbling toward me, breathless.

"Arya! Something's happening. Everyone's heading toward the library. C'mon, let's go." She tugged at my wrist.

I let her drag me down the hall. "Hold on. Slow down. Why is everyone freaking out?" Faces full of shock and awe whipped past us.

She spun around, full stop, and faced me, almost knocking me back. "Chaos is here."

"*The god?*" I couldn't have heard her right. Maybe I drank too much of that calming elixir.

"No, the rock star. *Yes, the god.* We need to hurry and get in there." Her grip tightened around my wrist as we followed the frenzied crowd toward the Library of Covens.

My heart pounded. The gods didn't leave Elysium unless the fate of humanity depended on it. At least that was what happened the last time. The *only* time actually. Gray had convinced Chaos to help her fight in the Blood War against Cerberus, the guardian of the Underworld. But we were in an age of peace now. *Why was he here?*

As I scurried to keep up with Sapphire, my imagination went into overdrive, thinking of all the possible end-of-world scenarios. A sinking sensation formed in the pit of my stomach as we reached the entrance.

The library walls were covered in books that shot up to the ceiling, three-stories high. Polished oak ladders were strategically placed every few feet. They slid from right to left with ease. As I stepped inside, my feet gave way slightly into the plush red carpet. Traces of dust and the faint scent of parchment tickled my nose.

The energy reverberated through the room like sound waves. A soft wind began to hum in my ears, trickling all the way down to my fingertips. It tingled in my spine. My Sylph magic moved through me on its own. *What the hell is happening to me?*

We spotted Diego through the crowd and made our way over to him. As the blood rushed to my feet, I leaned back against the wall to steady myself. A cold wind filled my ears, thundering as if I had just stuck my head out the window of a moving car. The room seemed to spin as my equilibrium shifted and bile climbed up my throat.

"Arya, are you okay?" Diego placed a warm hand on my shoulder.

"Um, I think I'm going to be sick," I mumbled.

"Please don't. You know how queasy I get." A fresh sheen covered his face as he pleaded with me.

Breathe, Arya. Just breathe. "Sorry. Must have been something I ate." Deep down I knew that wasn't true. There was a force much stronger than spoiled food swirling around in my belly. I leaned further back against the stacks, wondering which sacred text I was soiling with my sweat.

Sapphire placed her hands on my temples. "Take a deep breath and focus on me." She hummed softly, rubbing my forehead.

I did as she said, breathing in slow while I gazed at her smooth face, her almond-shaped eyes, her black-as-night hair, getting lost in each intricate braid wrapped tight to her head, twisting in and out like branches. Within seconds my skin tingled and the wind in my ears began to settle. It rumbled low like distant drums, and then left my ears with the force of a vacuum. I released another deep breath and wiped a handful of sweat off my brow.

"Thanks. How did you do that?" My throat was dry, but I no longer wanted to throw up.

She shoved her hands into the pockets of her blue velvet coat, protecting them as if they were now vulnerable from the magic that had just been released from them. "I'm a Rain Maker, remember? Healing people...it's what we do."

I nodded, realizing that we never talked about magic. "I gotta stop eating in the Brew Market."

The Brew Market sprang up on Sanctum's Scottish shores not long after we first arrived here. It was full of black-market traders and thieves, trying to cash in on the new supernatural element that had landed. It was dangerous, but a welcome relief from the restlessness I felt inside these walls.

She squinted at me with that familiar look of ire on her face that she got whenever I broke the rules. "The Brew Market? You know we're not supposed to go near there."

Before I could respond, her attention turned to the commotion that was happening around us. Thank the gods. I didn't want to get into another argument about my extracurricular activities. Everyone was here—witches, dhampirs, Lupi, and everyone in between. Sanctum housed an interesting mix of species. The Lupi were born with wolf magic, but the Rougarou wolves were once human but had been bitten and then transformed by wolf magic. Their magic was much weaker and they were often treated as the lesser species.

Most of the dhampirs here were hybrids—blood suckers who could also do magic. They were immortal descendants of the sun god, Apollo, and belonged to an order called the Consilium. Ten years ago, Jane's daughter,

Gray, came along and took it over, inviting the Crescent witches and the Lupi wolves into the fold. After they had beat Cerberus, Gray created Sanctum for all of us. But I wasn't like the rest of them. And they all knew it.

Jane had positioned herself at the head of the room, and standing next to her was the most beautiful man I'd ever seen. Except he wasn't a man at all. He was a god. Chaos remained quiet, his face lighting up with amusement as most of the female beings, and some male, salivated at the sight of him. His dark hair hung just below his ears, shiny like obsidian and with a slight wave to it. It cast a faint shadow over his bronzed skin.

His eyes were dark like his hair, almost black. He scanned the room, allowing his gaze to linger over every face like he was searching for someone, or something. My breath caught in my throat when his gaze met mine. A fluttering stirred in my belly, a longing that I had buried deep. He flashed me a grin, and I stumbled back into the bookstacks. *Real graceful, Arya.*

Before I could recover, his gaze had already moved on. I cursed under my breath and hoped he didn't see. *Prayed* I wasn't blushing. Such a cruel betrayal of the body when blood and flesh revealed our innermost desires with bright red cheeks and sweaty palms.

Jane held up her hands to silence the whispers. "Attention, please. We have a very special guest with us this evening. He has traveled all the way here from Elysium to pay us a visit. Please join me in welcoming Chaos into our humble home. Come, let us feast."

The crowd erupted into cheers and applause. I, on the other hand, had a knot in the pit of my stomach. Chaos' energy was uncontrolled, but guarded. I couldn't get a complete read off of him...and I could read anybody.

Diego threw me a sideways glance. "How nice of him to grace us with his sexy presence. A little unusual though, don't you think?"

"It's beyond strange," I whispered, more to myself than to anyone else. "I wonder what he wants."

"Jane doesn't look alarmed." Sapphire shrugged her shoulders but her eyes narrowed as she watched Chaos follow Jane out the side entrance of the library.

Jane didn't look relaxed either. Apart from the gorgeous specimen accompanying her, I couldn't help but notice a slight twitch in her right eye and her lips more pursed than usual. From her tight bun, with not a single hair out of place, all the way down to her polished leather boots—our head mistress was always perfectly put together. So the presence of a tiny thread hanging from the sleeve of her tweed jacket bothered me immensely.

I shuffled behind my friends as the room began to empty out toward the dining hall. Despite all of the excitement, it was getting late and I was still exhausted from my training.

"I'm really going to bed this time. See you at lunch tomorrow?" I tried to stifle a yawn without success.

"I don't think sleep is going to help you pass that potion test tomorrow," Diego teased, a sloppy grin on his face. I feigned shock and punched a playful jab into his shoulder.

Sapphire shook her head as he stumbled off, chuckling to himself. "One of these days that wolf is going to piss off the wrong witch." A flicker of amusement, mixed with adoration, passed through her eyes.

"I think that's the only reason why he hangs out with us. We're his witch bodyguards," I joked.

Walking back to our rooms, we avoided the subject of tonight's festivities, opting instead to talk about mundane stuff—who had a crush on who, what we were going to wear to the Imperator's Ball, and how delicious the new honeycomb sugar cookies were in the dining hall. As we moved down the last corridor, a group of three blond-haired witches—Crescent witches from London—dawdled past, snickering as they turned their noses up at us. I did my best to ignore them, but it was just another reminder that I was without a coven. Sapphire was the only witch who would give me the time of day. Our mothers fought on the battlefield together. Sapphire said that bonded us for life. She had been my best friend ever since.

"Goodnight. Sweet dreams," I called to her as I shoved open the door to my room. She mumbled something similar back before disappearing down the dimly lit corridor.

I locked the door behind me and sagged back against it. Finally alone with my own thoughts, the image of Chaos resurfaced from where it had been lingering in the back of my mind. As tired as I was, I doubted I'd get any sleep tonight. They could have all the celebration feasts they wanted, but it didn't change the fact that the gods didn't leave Elysium unless something was wrong.

Don't stop now. Keep reading with your copy of SMOKE AND RITUAL by City Owl author, Melissa Sercia.

And find more from Adrienne Blake at authoradrienneblake.com

Don't miss book four of the *Soul and Shadows* series coming soon, and find more from Adrienne Blake at authoradrienneblake.com

Until then, discover more paranormal romance with SMOKE AND RITUAL by Melissa Sercia!

The voices haunt her... Their whispers taunt her with a war she never wanted... But Arya Frost has more to contend with than the cryptic voices disturbing her sleep.

Protected inside the haven of Sanctum after losing both her parents in the Blood War a decade ago, Arya is different from other witches. She's the only witch without a coven.
Or so she thinks.

As her powers accelerate, so do the revelations about her true lineage. Destined to become the Aether—a witch who can control all four elements—the Elemental covens want her magic, power she didn't even know she had.

And when the sexy and mysterious god, Chaos shows up, Arya's place in the world is put even more at risk. But learning who and what she is, and how to wield her power only tips the surface of the battle raging inside her.

She'll have to find a way to awaken her magic, deal with her growing attraction to Chaos, all while being thrust into the middle of a magical feud that has been building for centuries.

The Blood War might be over, but the war between witches is just beginning.

Please sign up for the City Owl Press newsletter for chances to win special subscriber-only contests and giveaways as well as receiving information on upcoming releases and special excerpts.

All reviews are **welcome** and **appreciated**. Please consider leaving one on your favorite social media and book buying sites.

Escape Your World. Get Lost in Ours! City Owl Press at www.cityowlpress.com.

ACKNOWLEDGMENTS

It takes a village to write a novel. I'd like to give special thanks to Tee, my editor, for her patience and constant support. Also to City Owl, for loving my words and getting them out there to you awesome readers. Lastly, a special shout-out to MacGuffin, my darling tuxedo cat, who drapes his paws over my keyboard and corrects my typos (or makes a few.) I'd be lost without him.

ABOUT THE AUTHOR

ADRIENNE BLAKE is a *USA Today* bestselling author of paranormal mystery and urban fantasy. She is also an Amazon Top 100 bestselling author. Her stories blend plot, humor, and darkness, all in one sizzling cauldron. Born in the UK and writing in the US, she and her partner are managed by three ruthless cats.

authoradrienneblake.com

ABOUT THE PUBLISHER

City Owl Press is a cutting edge indie publishing company, bringing the world of romance and speculative fiction to discerning readers.

Escape Your World. Get Lost in Ours!

www.cityowlpress.com

facebook.com/YourCityOwlPress

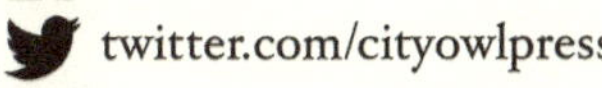
twitter.com/cityowlpress

instagram.com/cityowlbooks

pinterest.com/cityowlpress

www.ingramcontent.com/pod-product-compliance
Lightning Source LLC
Chambersburg PA
CBHW020646030726
47498CB00002B/397

* 9 7 8 1 6 4 8 9 8 1 0 9 8 *